THE
GREY DAWN

STEWART EDWARD WHITE

1ST WORLD
LIBRARY
Literary Society

The Gray Dawn

Stewart Edward White

© 1st World Library, 2006
PO Box 2211
Fairfield, IA 52556
www.1stworldlibrary.com
First Edition

LCCN: 2006938105

Softcover ISBN: 978-1-4218-3407-8
Hardcover ISBN: 978-1-4218-3307-1
eBook ISBN: 978-1-4218-3507-5

Purchase *"The Gray Dawn"*
as a traditional bound book at:
www.1stWorldLibrary.com/purchase.asp?ISBN=978-1-4218-3407-8

1st World Library is a literary, educational organization
dedicated to:

- Creating a free internet library of downloadable ebooks

- Hosting writing competitions and offering book
publishing scholarships.

Interested in more 1st World Library books?
contact: literacy@1stworldlibrary.com
Check us out at: www.1stworldlibrary.com

1ˢᵗ World Library Literary Society

Giving Back to the World

"If you want to work on the core problem, it's early school literacy."

- James Barksdale, former CEO of Netscape

"No skill is more crucial to the future of a child, or to a democratic and prosperous society, than literacy."

- Los Angeles Times

Literacy... means far more than learning how to read and write... The aim is to transmit... knowledge and promote social participation."

- UNESCO

"Literacy is not a luxury, it is a right and a responsibility. If our world is to meet the challenges of the twenty-first century we must harness the energy and creativity of all our citizens."

- President Bill Clinton

"Parents should be encouraged to read to their children, and teachers should be equipped with all available techniques for teaching literacy, so the varying needs and capacities of individual kids can be taken into account."

- Hugh Mackay

PRINCIPAL CHARACTERS IN TALE

MILTON KEITH: a young lawyer from Baltimore.

NAN KEITH: his wife.

JOHN SHERWOOD: a gambler.

PATSY SHERWOOD: his wife.

ARTHUR MORRELL: an English adventurer.

MIMI MORRELL: his wife or mistress.

BEN SANSOME: a lady-killer, destined to become an "old beau."

W. T. COLEMAN, or "old Vigilante," a leader.

DAVID TERRY: a leader on the other side.

JAMES KING OF WILLIAM: a modern Crusader.

THE SPIRIT OF SAN FRANCISCO AND OTHERS

I

On the veranda of the Bella Union Hotel, San Francisco, a man sat enjoying his morning pipe. The Bella Union overlooked the Plaza of that day, a dusty, unkempt, open space, later to be swept and graded and dignified into Portsmouth Square. The man was at the younger fringe of middle life. He was dressed neatly and carefully in the fashionable costume of the time, which was the year of grace 1852. As to countenance, he was square and solid; as to physique, he was the same; as to expression, he inclined toward the quietly humorous; in general he would strike the observer as deliberately, philosophically competent. A large pair of steel bound spectacles sat halfway down his nose. Sometimes he read his paper through their lenses; and sometimes, forgetting, he read over the tops of their bows. The newspaper he held was an extraordinary document. It consisted of four large pages. The outside page was filled solidly with short eight or ten line advertisements; the second page grudgingly vouchsafed a single column of news items; the third page warmed to a column of editorial and another of news; all the rest of the space on these and the entire fourth page was again crowded close with the short advertisements. They told of the arrival of ships, the consignment of goods, the movements of real estate, the sales of stock, but mainly of auctions. The man paid little attention to the scanty news, and none at all to the editorials. His name was John Sherwood, and he was a powerful and respected public gambler.

The approach across the Plaza of a group of men caused him

to lay aside his paper, and with it his spectacles. The doffing of the latter strangely changed his whole expression. The philosophical middle-aged quietude fell from him. He became younger, keener, more alert. It was as though he had removed a disguise.

The group approaching were all young men, and all dressed in the height of fashion. At that rather picturesque time this implied the flat-brimmed beaver hat; the long swallowtail, or skirted coat; the tight "pantaloons"; varicoloured, splendid, low-cut waistcoats of satin, of velvet, or of brocade; high wing collars; varnished boots; many sparkling, studs and cravat pins; rather longish hair; and whiskers cut close to the cheek or curling luxuriantly under the chin. They were prosperous, well-fed, arrogant-looking youths, carrying their crests high, the light of questing recklessness in their eyes, ready to laugh, drink, or fight with anybody. At sight of Sherwood they waved friendly hands, and canes, and veered in his direction.

"Yo're just the man we are looking for!" cried a tall, dark, graceful young fellow, "We are all 'specially needful of wisdom. The drinks are on some one, and we cain't decide who."

John Sherwood, his keen eyes twinkling, set his chair down on four legs.

"State your case, Cal," he said.

Cal waved a graceful hand at a stout, burly, red-faced man whose thick blunt fingers, square blue jowl, and tilted cigar gave the flavour of the professional politician. "John Webb, here-excuse *me*, Sheriff John Webb-presumin' on the fact that he has been to the mines, and that he came here in '49, arrogates to himself the exclusive lyin' privileges, of this assemblage."

"Pretty large order," commented Sherwood.

"*Pre*cisely," agreed Cal, "and that's why the drinks are on him!"

But Sheriff Webb, who had been chuckling cavernously inside his bulky frame, spoke up in a harsh and husky voice: "I told them an innocent experience of mine, and they try to hold me up for drinks. I don't object to giving them a reasonable amount of drinks—what *I* call reasonable," he added hastily, "but I object to being held up."

"He says he used to cook," put in a small, alert, nervous, rather flashily dressed individual named Rowlee, editor of the *Bugle*.

"I did!" stoutly asseverated Webb.

"And that he baked a loaf of bread so hard nobody could eat it."

"Sounds perfectly reasonable," said Sherwood.

"And that nobody could *break* it," Rowlee went on.

"I have no difficulty in believing that," said Sherwood judicially. "Your case is mighty weak yet, Cal."

"But he claims it was so hard that they used it for a grind-stone."

"I did not!" disclaimed Webb indignantly.

An accusing groan met this statement.

"I tell you I didn't say anything of the kind," roared Webb, his bull voice overtopping them all.

"Well, what did you say, then?" challenged Calhoun Bennett.

"I said we tried to use her as a grindstone," said Webb, "but it didn't work."

"Weak case, boys; weak case," said Sherwood.

The little group, their eyes wide, their nostrils distended, waited accusingly for Webb to proceed. After an interval, the sheriff, staring critically at the lighted end of his cigar, went on in a drawling voice:

"Yes, we, couldn't get a hole through her to hang her axle on. We blunted all our drills. Every Sunday we'd try a new scheme. Finally we laid her flat under a tree and rigged a lightnin' rod down to the centre of her. No use. She tore that lightning all to pieces."

He looked up at them with a limpid, innocent eye, to catch John Sherwood gazing at him accusingly.

"John Webb," said he "you forget that I came out here in, '48. On your honour, do you expect *me* to believe that yarn?"

"Well," said Webb, gazing again at his cigar end, "no—really I don't. The fact is," he went on with a perfectly solemn air of confidence, "the fact is, I've lived out here so long and told so many damn lies that now without some help I don't know when to believe myself."

"Do we get that drink?" insisted Calhoun Bennett.

"Oh, Lord, yes, you always get a drink."

"Well, come on and *get* it then—you, too, of course, Mr. Sherwood."

The gambler arose, and began leisurely to fold his paper and to put away his spectacles.

"I see you got Mex Ryan off, Cal," he observed. "You either had extraordinary luck, or you're a mighty fine lawyer. Looked like a clear case to me. He just naturally went in and beat Rucker half to death in his own store. How did you do it?"

"I assure yo' it was no sinecure," laughed the tall, dark youth. "I earned my fee."

"Yes," grumbled Webb, "but he got six months—and I got to take care of him. Cluttering up my jail with dirty beasts like Mex Ryan! Could just as easy have turned him loose!"

"That would have been a little too much!" smiled Bennett. "It was takin' some risk to let him off as easy as we did. It isn't so long since the Vigilantes."

"Oh, hell, we can handle that sort of trash now," snorted Webb.

"Who was backing Mex, anyway?" asked Rowlee curiously.

"Better ask who had it in for Rucker," suggested the fourth member of the group, a man who had not heretofore spoken. This was Dick Blatchford, a round-faced, rather corpulent, rather silent though jovial-looking individual, with a calculating and humorous eye. He was magnificently apparelled, but rather untidy.

"Well, I do ask it," said Rowlee.

But to this he got no response.

"Come on, ain't you got that valuable paper folded up yet?" rumbled Webb to Sherwood.

They all turned down the high-pillared veranda, toward the bar, talking idly and facetiously of last night's wine and this morning's head. A door opened at their very elbow, and in it a woman appeared.

II

She was a slender woman, of medium height, with a small, well-poised head on which the hair lay smooth and glossy. Her age was somewhere between thirty and thirty-five years. A stranger would have been first of all impressed by the imperious carriage of her head and shoulders, the repose of her attitude. Become a friend or a longer acquaintance, he would have noticed more particularly her wide low brow, her steady gray eyes and her grave but humorous lips. But inevitably he would have gone back at last to her more general impression. Ben Sansome, the only man in town who did nothing, made society and dress a profession and the judgment of women a religion, had long since summed her up: "She carries her head charmingly."

This poised, wise serenity of carriage was well set off by the costume of the early fifties—a low collar, above which her neck rose like a flower stem; flowing sleeves; full skirts with many silken petticoats that whispered and rustled; low sandalled shoes, their ties crossed and recrossed around white slender ankles. A cameo locket, hung on a heavy gold chain, rose and fell with her breast; a cameo brooch pinned together the folds of her bodice; massive and wide bracelets of gold clasped her wrists and vastly set off her rounded, slender forearms.

She stood quite motionless in the doorway, nodding with a little smile in response to the men's sweeping salutes.

"You will excuse me gentlemen, I am sure," said Sherwood

Stewart Edward White

formally, and instantly turned aside.

The woman in the doorway thereupon preceded him down a narrow, bare, unlighted hallway, opened another door, and entered a room. Sherwood followed, closing the door after him.

"Want something, Patsy?" he inquired.

The room was obviously one of the best of the Bella Union. That is to say, it was fairly large, the morning sun streamed in through its two windows, and it contained a small iron stove. In all other respects it differed quite from any other hotel room in the San Francisco of that time. A heavy carpet covered the floor, the upholstery was of leather or tapestry, wall paper adorned the walls, a large table supported a bronze lamp and numerous books and papers, a canary, in a brass cage, hung in the sunshine of one of the windows, flitted from perch to perch, occasionally uttering a few liquid notes under its breath.

"Just a little change, Jack, if you have some with you," said the woman. Her speaking voice was rich and low.

Sherwood thrust a forefinger into his waistcoat pocket, and produced one of the hexagonal slugs of gold current at that time.

"Oh, not so much!" she protested.

"All I've got. What are you up to to-day, Patsy?"

"I thought of going down to Yet Lee's—unless there is something better to do."

"Doesn't sound inspiring. Did you go to that fair or bazaar thing yesterday?"

She smiled with her lips, but her eyes darkened.

"Yes, I went. It was not altogether enjoyable. I doubt if I'll try that sort of thing again."

Sherwood's eye suddenly became cold and dangerous.

"If they didn't treat you right—"

She smiled, genuinely this time, at his sudden truculence.

"They didn't mob me," she rejoined equably, "and, anyway, I suppose it is to be expected."

"It's that cat of Morrell's," he surmised.

"Oh, she—and others. I ought not to have spoken of it, Jack. It's really beneath the contempt of sensible people."

"I'll get after Morrell, if he doesn't make that woman behave," said Sherwood, without attention to her last speech.

She smiled at him again, entirely calm and reasonable.

"And what good would it do to get after Morrell?" she asked. "Mrs. Morrell only stands for what most of them feel. I don't care, anyway. I get along splendidly without them." She sauntered over to the window, where she began idly to poke one finger at the canary.

"For the life of me, Patsy," confessed Sherwood, "I can't see that they're an inspiring lot, anyway. From what little I've seen of them, they haven't more than an idea apiece. They'd bore me to death in a week."

"I know that. They'd bore me, too. Don't talk about them. When do they expect the *Panama*—do you know?"

But with masculine persistence he refused to abandon the topic.

"I must confess I don't see the point," he insisted. "You've got more brains than the whole lot of them together, you've got more sense, you're a lot better looking"—he surveyed her, standing in the full light by the canary's cage, her little glossy head thrown back, her pink lips pouted teasingly at the charmed and agitated bird, her fine clear features profiled in the gold of the sunshine—"and you're a thoroughbred, egad, which most of them are not."

"Oh, thank you, kind sir." She threw him a humourous glance. "But of course that is not the point."

"Oh, isn't it? Well, perhaps you'll tell me the point."

She left the canary and came to face him.

"I'm not respectable," she said.

At the word he exploded.

"Respectable? What are you talking about? You talk as though—as though we weren't married, egad!"

"Well, Jack," she replied, a faint mocking smile curving the corners of her mouth, "when it comes to that, we *did* elope, you'll have to acknowledge. And we weren't married for quite a long time afterward."

"We got married as soon as we could, didn't we?" he cried indignantly. "Was it our fault that we didn't get married sooner? And what difference did it make, anyway?"

"Now don't get all worked up," she chided. "I'm just telling you why, in the eyes of some of these people, I'm not 'respectable.' You asked me, you know."

"Go on," he conceded to this last.

"Well, we ran away and weren't married. That's item one.

Then perhaps you've forgotten that I sat on lookout for some of your games in the early days in the mining camps?"

"Forgotten?" said Sherwood, the light of reminiscence springing to his eyes.

The same light had come into hers.

"Will you *ever* forget," she murmured, "the camps by the summer streams the log towns, the lights, the smoke, the freedom—the comradeship—"

"Homesick for the old rough days?" he teased.

"Kind of," she confessed. "But it wasn't 'respectable'—a—well, a *fairly* good-looking woman in a miner's saloon."

He flared again.

"Do you mean to tell me they dare say—"

"They dare say anything—behind our backs," she said, with cool contempt. "It's all drivelling nonsense. I care nothing about it. But you asked me. Don't bother your head about it. Have you anything to suggest doing this morning, instead of Yet Lee's?" She turned away from him toward the door leading into another room. "I'll get my hat," she said over her shoulder.

"Look here, Patsy," said Sherwood, rather grimly, "if you want to get in with that lot, you shall."

She stopped at this, and turned square around.

"If I do—when I do—I will," she replied. "But, John Sherwood, you mustn't interfere—never in the world! Promise!" She stood there, almost menacing in her insistence, evidently resolved to nip this particularly masculine resolution in the bud.

"Egad, Patsy," cried Sherwood, "you are certainly a raving beauty!"

He covered the ground between them in two strides, and crushed her in his arms. She threw her head back for his kiss.

A knock sounded, and almost immediately a very black, very bullet-headed young negro thrust his head in at the door.

"Sam," said Sherwood deliberately, "some day I'm going to kill you!"

"Yes, sah! yes, sah!" agreed Sam heartily.

"Well, what the devil do you want?"

"Th' *Panama* done been, signalled; yes, sah!" said the negro, but without following his head through the door.

"Well, what the devil do you suppose I care, you black limb?" roared Sherwood, "and what do you mean coming in here before you're told?"

"Yes, sah! yes, sah, dat's right," ducked Sam, "Shell I awdah the team, sah?"

"I suppose we might as well go see her docked. Would you like it?" he asked his wife.

"I'd love it."

"Then get the team. And some day I'm going to kill you."

III

Mrs. Sherwood prepared herself first of all by powdering her nose. This simple operation, could it have been seen by the "respectable" members of the community, would in itself have branded her as "fast," In those days cosmetics of any sort were by most considered inventions of the devil. It took extra-ordinary firmness of character even to protect one's self against sunburn by anything more artificial than the shadow of a hat or a parasol.

Then she assumed a fascinating little round hat that fitted well down over her small head. This, innocent of pins, was held on by an elastic at the back. A ribbon, hanging down directly in front, could be utilized to steady it in a breeze.

"All ready," she announced, picking up a tiny parasol, about big enough for a modern doll. "You may carry my mantle."

Near the foot of the veranda steps waited Sam at the heads of a pair of beautiful, slim, satiny horses. Their bay coats had been groomed until they rippled and sparkled with every movement of the muscles beneath. Wide red- lined nostrils softly expanded and contracted with a restrained eagerness; and soft eyes rolled in the direction of the Sherwoods—keen, lithe, nervous, high-strung creatures, gently stamping little hoofs, impatiently tossing dainty heads, but nevertheless making no movement that would stir the vehicle that stood "cramped" at the steps. Their harness carried no blinders; their tails, undocked, swept the ground; but their heads were pulled into the air by the old stupid overhead check reins until their noses pointed almost straight ahead. It gave them rather a haughty air.

Sherwood stepped in first, took the reins in one hand, and offered his other hand to his wife. Sam instantly left the horses' heads to hold a wicker contrivance against the arc of the wheels. This was to protect skirts from dusty tires. Mrs. Sherwood settled as gracefully to her place as a butterfly on its flower. Sam snatched away the wicker guards. Sherwood spoke to the horses. With a purring little snort they moved smoothly away. The gossamerlike wheels threw the light from their swift spokes. Sam, half choked by the swirl of dust, gazed after them. Sherwood, leaning slightly forward against the first eagerness of the animals, showed a strong, competent, arresting figure, with his beaver hat, his keen grim face, his snow-white linen, and the blue of his brass-buttoned-coat. The beautiful horses were stepping as one, a delight to the eye, making nothing whatever of the frail vehicle at their heels. But Sam's eye lingered longest on the small stately figure of his mistress. She sat very straight, her head high, the little parasol poised against the sun, the other hand clasping the hat ribbon.

"Dem's quality foh sure!" said Sam with conviction.

Sherwood drove rapidly around the edge of the Plaza and, so into Kearney Street. From here to the water front were by now many fireproof brick and stone structures, with double doors and iron shatters, like fortresses. So much had San Francisco learned from her five disastrous fires. The stone had come from China, the brick also from overseas. Down side streets one caught glimpses of huge warehouses—already in this year of 1852 men talked of the open-air auctions of three years before as of something in history inconceivably remote. The streets, where formerly mule teams had literally been drowned in mud, now were covered with planking. This made a fine resounding pavement. Horses' hoofs went merrily *klop, klop, klop*, and the wheels rumbled a dull undertone. San Francisco had been very proud of this pavement when it was new. She was very grateful for it even now, for in the upper part of town the mud and dust were still something awful.

Unfortunately the planks were beginning to wear out in places; and a city government, trying to give the least possible for its taxes, had made no repairs.

There were many holes, large or small: jagged, splintered, ugly holes going down to indeterminate blackness either of depth or mud. Private philanthropists had fenced or covered these. Private facetiousness had labelled most of them with signboards. These were rough pictures of disaster painted from the marking pot, and various screeds—"Head of Navigation," "No Bottom," "Horse and Dray Lost Here," "Take Soundings," "Storage, Inquire Below," "Good Fishing for Teal," and the like.

Among these obstructions Sherwood guided his team skilfully, dodging not only them, but other vehicles darting or crawling in the same direction. There were no rules of the road. Omnibuses careered along, every window rattling loudly; drays creaked and strained, their horses' hoofs slipping against wet planks; horsemen threaded their way; nondescript delivery wagons tried to outrattle the omnibuses. The din was something extraordinary—hoofs drumming, wheels rumbling, oaths and shouts, and from the sidewalks the blare and bray of brass bands in front of the various auction shops. Newsboys and bootblacks darted in all directions, shouting raucously as they do to-day. Cigar boys, an institution of the time, added to the hubbub. Everybody was going in the same direction, some sauntering with an air of leisure, some hurrying as though their fortunes were at stake.

A wild shriek arose, and everybody made room for the steam sand shovel on its way to dump the sand hills into the bay. It was called the "steam paddy" to distinguish it from the "hand paddy"—out of Cork or Dublin. It rumbled by on its track, very much like juggernaut in its calm indifference as to how many it ran over. Sherwood's horses looked at it nervously

Stewart Edward White

askance; but he spoke to them, and though they trembled they stood.

Now they debouched on the Central Wharf, and the sound of the hoofs and the wheels changed its tone. Central Wharf extended a full mile into the bay. It was lined on either side its narrow roadway by small shacks, in which were offered fowls, fish, vegetables, candy, refreshments. Some of them were tiny saloons or gambling houses. But by far the majority were the cubicles where the Jewish slop sellers displayed their wares. Men returning from the mines here landed, and here replenished their wardrobes. Everything was exposed to view outside, like clothes hung out after a rain.

The narrow way between this long row of shops was crowded almost dangerously. Magnificent dray horses, with long hair on the fetlocks above their big heavy hoofs, bridling in conscious pride of silver-mounted harness and curled or braided manes, rose above the ruck as their ancestors, the warhorses, must have risen in medieval battle. The crowd parted before them and closed in behind them. Here and there, too, a horseman could be seen—with a little cleared space at his heels. Or a private calash picking its way circumspectly.

From her point of vantage on the elevated seat Mrs. Sherwood could see over the heads of people. She sat very quietly, her body upright, but in the poised repose characteristic of her. Many admiring glances were directed at her. She seemed to be unconscious of them. Nevertheless, nothing escaped her. She saw, and appreciated and enjoyed, every phase of that hetero-geneous crowd—miners in their exaggeratedly rough clothes, brocaded or cotton clad Chinese, gorgeous Spaniards or Chilenos, drunken men, sober men, excited men, empty cans or cases kicking around underfoot, frantic runners for hotels or steamboats trying to push their way by, newsboys and cigar boys darting about and miraculously worming their way through impenetrable places. Atop a portable pair of steps a pale, well-dressed young man was playing thimblerig on his knees with a gilt pea. From an upturned keg a preacher was exhorting. And occasionally, through gaps between the shacks, she caught glimpses of blue water; or of ships at anchor; or, more often, of the tall pile drivers whose hammers went steadily up and down.

Sherwood guided his glossy team and light spidery vehicle with the greatest delicacy and skill. He was wholly absorbed in his task. Suddenly up ahead a wild turmoil broke out. People crowded to right and left, clambering, shouting, screaming. A runaway horse hitched to a light buggy came careering down the way.

A collision seemed inevitable. Sherwood turned his horses' heads directly at an open shop front. They hesitated, their small pointed ears working nervously. Sherwood spoke to them. They moved forward, quivering, picking their way daintily. Sherwood spoke again. They stopped. The runaway hurtled by, missing the tail of the buggy by two feet. A moment later a grand crash marked the end of its career farther down the line. Again Sherwood spoke to his horses, and exerted the slightest pressure on the reins. Daintily, slowly, their ears twitching back and forth, their fine eyes rolling, they backed out of the opening.

Throughout all this exciting little incident the woman had not altered her pose nor the expression of her face. Her head high, her eye ruminative, she had looked on it all as one quite detached from possible consequences. The little parasol did not change its angle. Only, quite deliberately, she had relinquished the ribbon by which she held on her hat, and had placed her slender hand steadyingly on the side of the vehicle.

The bystanders, already leaping down from their places of refuge and again crowding the narrow way, directed admiring eyes toward the beautiful, nervous, docile horses, the calm and dominating man, and the poised, dainty creature at his side. One drunken individual cheered her personally. At this a faint shell pink appeared in her cheeks, though she gave no other sign that she had heard. Sherwood glanced down at her, amused.

But now emerged the Jew slop seller, very voluble. He had darted like a rat to some mysterious inner recess of his burrow; but now he was out again filling the air with lamentations, claims, appeals for justice. Sherwood did not even glance toward him; but in the very act of tooling his horses into the roadway tossed the man some silver. Immediately, with shouts and cheers and laughter, the hoodlums nearby began a scramble.

The end of the long wharf widened to a great square, free of all buildings but a sort of warehouse near one end. Here a rope divided off a landing space. Close to the rope the multitude crowded, ready for its entertainment. Here also stood in stately grandeur the three livery hacks of which San Francisco boasted. They were magnificent affairs, the like of which has never elsewhere been seen plying for public hire, brightly painted, highly varnished, lined with silks, trimmed with solid silver. The harnesses were heavily mounted with the same metal. On their boxes sat fashionable creatures, dressed, not in livery, but throughout in the very latest of the late styles, shod with varnished leather, gloved with softest kid. Sherwood drove skilfully to the very edge of the roped space, pushing aside the crowd on foot. They growled at him savagely. He paid no attention to them, and they gave way. The buggy came to a stop. The horses, tossing their heads, rolling their eyes, stamping their little hoofs, nevertheless stood without need of further attention.

Now the brass bands blared with a sudden overwhelming blast of sound, the crowd cheered noisily; the runners for the hotels began to bark like a pack of dogs. With a vast turmoil of paddle wheels, swirling of white and green waters, bellowing of speaking trumpets, throwing of handlines and scurrying of deck hands and dock hands, the *Panama* came to rest. After considerable delay the gangplank was placed. The passengers began to disembark, facing the din much as they would have faced the buffeting of a strong wind. This was the cream of the entertainment for which the crowd had gathered; for which, indeed, the Sherwoods had made their excursion. Each individual received his meed of comment, sometimes audible and by no means always flattering. Certainly in variety both of character and of circumstance they offered plenty of material. From wild, half-civilized denizens of Louisiana's canebrakes, clinging closely to their little bundles and their long rifles, to the most polished exquisites of fashion they offered all grades and intermediates. Some of them looked rather bewildered. Some seemed to know just what to do and where to go. Most dove into the crowd with the apparent idea of losing their identity as soon as possible. The three magnificent hacks were filled, and managed, with much plunging and excitement, to plow a way through the crowd and so depart. Amusing things happened to which the Sherwoods called each other's attention. Thus a man, burdened with a single valise, ducked under the ropes near them. A paper boy happened to be standing near. The passenger offered the boy a fifty-cent piece.

"Here, boy," said he, "just carry this valise for me."

The paper boy gravely contemplated the fifty cents, dove into his pocket, and produced another.

"Here, man," said he, handing them both to the traveller, "take this and carry it yourself."

One by one the omnibuses filled and departed. The stream of passengers down the gangplank had ceased. The crowd began to thin. Sherwood gathered his reins to go. Mrs. Sherwood suddenly laid her hand on his forearm.

"Oh, the poor thing!" she cried, her voice thrilling with compassion.

A young man and a steward were supporting a girl down the gangplank. Evidently she was very weak and ill. Her face was chalky white, with dark rings under the eyes, her lips were pale, and she leaned heavily on the men. Although she could not have heard Mrs. Sherwood's exclamation of pity, she happened to look up at that instant, revealing a pair of large, dark, and appealing eyes. Her figure, too, dressed in a plain travel ling dress, strikingly simple but bearing the unmistakable mark of distinction, was appealing; as were her exquisite, smooth baby skin and the downward drooping, almost childlike, curves of her lips. The inequalities of the ribbed gangplank were sufficient to cause her to stumble.

"She is very weak," commented Mrs. Sherwood.

"She is—or would be—remarkably pretty," added Sherwood. "I wonder what ails her."

Arrived at the foot of the gangplank the young man removed his hat with an air of perplexity, and looked about him. He was of the rather florid, always boyish type; and the removal of his hat had revealed a mat of close-curling brown hair, like a cap over his well-shaped head. The normal expression of his face was probably quizzically humorous, for already the little lines of habitual half laughter were sketched about his eyes.

"A plunger," said John Sherwood to himself, out of his knowledge of men; then as the young man glanced directly toward him, disclosing the colour and expression of his eyes, "a plunger in something," he amended, revising his first impression.

But now the humorous element was quite in abeyance, and a faint dismay had taken its place. One arm supporting the drooping girl, he was looking up and down the wharf. Not a vehicle remained save the heavy drays already backing up to receive their loads of freight. The dock hands had dropped and were coiling the line that had separated the crowd from the landing stage.

With another exclamation the woman in the carriage rose, and before Sherwood could make a move to assist her, had poised on the rim of the wheel and leaped lightly to the dock. Like a thistledown she floated to the little group at the foot of the gangplank. The steward instantly gave way to her evident intention. She passed her arm around the girl's waist. The three moved slowly toward the buggy, Mrs. Sherwood, her head bent charmingly forward, murmuring compassionate, broken, little phrases, supporting the newcomer's reviving footsteps.

Sherwood, a faint, fond amusement lurking in the depths of his eyes, quietly cramped the wheels of the buggy.

IV

A half hour later the two men, having deposited the women safely in the Sherwoods' rooms at the Bella Union, and having been unceremoniously dismissed by Mrs. Sherwood, strolled together to the veranda. They had not, until now, had a chance to exchange six words.

The newcomer, who announced himself as Milton Keith from Baltimore, proved to have a likable and engaging personality. He was bubbling with interest and enthusiasm; and these qualities, provided they are backed solidly, are always prepossessing. Sherwood, quietly studying him, concluded that such was the case. His jaw and mouth were set in firm lines; his eye, while dancing and mischievous, had depths of capability and reserves of forcefulness. But Sherwood was, by inclination and by the necessities of his profession, a close observer of men. Another, less practised, might have seen here merely an eager, rather talkative, apparently volatile, very friendly, quite unreserved young man of twenty-five. Any one, analytical or otherwise, could not have avoided feeling the attractive force of the youth's personality, the friendly quality that is nine tenths individual magnetism and one tenth the cast of mind that initially takes for granted the other man's friendliness.

At the moment Keith was boyishly avid for the sights of the new city. In these modern days of long journeys, a place so remote as San Francisco, in the most commonplace of circumstances, gathers to its reputation something of the fabulous. How much more true then of a city built from sand dunes in four years; five times swept by fire, yet rising again and better before its ashes were extinct; the resort of all the picturesque, unknown races of the earth—the Chinese, the Chileno, the Mexican, the Spanish, the Islander, the Moor, the Turk—not to speak of ordinary foreigners from Russia, England, France, Belgium, Germany, Italy, and the out-of-the-way corners of Europe; the haunt of the wild and striking individuals of all these races. "Sydney ducks" from the criminal colonies; "shoulder strikers" direct from the tough wards of New York; long, lean, fever-haunted crackers from the Georgia mountains or the Louisiana canebrakes; Pike County desperadoes; long-haired men from the trapping countries; hard-fisted, sardonic state of Maine men fresh from their rivers; and Indian fighters from the Western Reserve; grasping, shrewd commercial Yankees; fire-eating Southern politicians; lawyers, doctors, merchants, chiefs, and thiefs, the well-educated and the ignorant, the high-minded and the scalawags, all dumped down together on a sand hill to work out their destinies; a city whose precedents, whose morals, whose laws, were made or adapted on the spot; where might in some form or another—revolver, money, influence—made its only right; whose history ranged in three years the gamut of human passion, strife, and development; whose background was the fabled El Dorado whence the gold in unending floods poured through its sluices. To the outside world tales of these things had come. They did not lose in the journey. The vast loom of actual occurrences rose above the orizon like mirages. Names and events borrowed a half-legendary quality from distances, as elsewhere from time. Keith had heard of Coleman, of Terry, of Broderick, Brannan, Gwin, Geary, as he had heard of the worthies of ancient history; he had visualized the fabled splendours of San Francisco's great gambling houses, of the excitements of her fervid, fevered life, as he might have visualized the magnificences of pagan Rome; he had listened to tales of her street brawls, her vast projects, the buccaneering raids of her big men, her Vigilance Committee of the year before, as he would have listened to the stories of one of Napoleon's veterans. Now, by the simple process of a voyage that had seemed literally interminable but now was past, he had landed in the very midst of fable. It was like dying, he told Sherwood eagerly, like going irretrievably to a new planet. All his old world now seemed as remote, as insubstantial, as phantomlike, as this had seemed.

"Even yet I can't believe it's all so," he cried, walking excitedly back and forth, and waving an extinct cigar. "I've got to see it, touch it! Why, I know it all in advance. That must be where the Jenny Lind Theatre stood—before the fire—just opposite? I thought so! And the bay used to come up to Montgomery Street, only a block down! You see, I know it all! And when we came in, and I saw all those idle ships lying at anchor, just as they have lain since their crews deserted them in '49 to go to the mines—and I know why they haven't been used since, why they will continue to lie there at anchor until they rot or sink—"

"Do you?" said Sherwood, who was vastly amused and greatly taken by this fresh enthusiasm.

"Yes, the clipper ships!" Keith swept on. "The first cargoes in this new market make the money—the fastest clippers—poor old hulks—but you brought in the argonauts!"

So he ran on, venting his impatience, so plainly divided between his sense of duty in staying near his wife and his great desire to slip the leash, that Sherwood smiled to himself. Once again he mentioned Coleman and the Vigilantes of '51.

"I suppose he's around here? I may see him?"

"Oh, yes," said Sherwood, "you'll see him. But if you would accept a bit of advice, go slow. You must remember that such a movement makes enemies, arouses opposition. A great many excellent people—whom you will know—are a little doubtful about all that."

Keith mentioned other names.

"I know them all. They are among the most influential members of the bar." He glanced at a large watch. "Just at this hour we might find them at the Monumental engine house. What do you say?"

"I should like nothing better!" cried Keith.

"Your wife's illness is not likely to require immediate attendance?" suggested Sherwood inquiringly.

"She's only seasick—horrible voyage—she's always under the weather on shipboard—three weeks of it from Panama—Nan's as strong as a horse," replied Keith, with obvious impatience.

They walked across the Plaza to the Monumental fire engine house, a square brick structure of two stories, with wide folding doors, and a bell cupola apart. Keith paused to admire the engine. It was of the type usual in those days, consisting of a waterbox with inlet and outlet connections, a pump atop, and parallel pump rails on either side, by the hand manipulation of which the water was thrown with force from the box. The vehicle was drawn by means of a long rope, carried on a drum. This could be slacked off at need to accommodate as high as a hundred men or as few as would suffice to move her. So far this engine differed in no manner from those Keith had seen in the East. But this machine belonged to a volunteer company, one of many and all rivals. It was gayly coloured. On the sides of its waterbox were scenic paintings of some little merit. The woodwork was all mahogany. Its brass ornamentation was heavy and brought to a high state of polish. From a light rack along its centre dangled two beautifully chased speaking trumpets, and a row of heavy red-leather helmets. Axes nestled in sockets. A screaming gilt eagle, with wings outspread, hovered atop. Alongside the engine stood the hook and ladder truck and the hose cart. These smaller and less important vehicles were painted in the same scheme of colour, were equally glittering and polished. Keith commented on all this admiringly.

"Yes," said Sherwood, "you see, since the big fires, it has become a good deal a matter of pride. There are eleven volunteer companies, and they are great rivals in everything, political and social, as well as in the line of regular business, so to speak. Mighty efficient. You'll have to join a company, of course; and you better look around a little before deciding. Each represents something different—some different element. They are really as much clubs as fire companies."

They mounted to the upper story, where Keith found himself in a long room, comfortably fitted with chairs, tables, books, and papers. A double door showed a billiard table in action. Sherwood indicated a closed door across the hall.

"Card rooms," said he briefly.

The air was blue with smoke and noisy with rather vociferative conversation and laughter. Several groups of men were gathered in little knots. A negro in white duck moved here and there carrying a tray.

Sherwood promptly introduced Keith to many of these men, and he was as promptly asked to name his drink. Keith caught few of the names, but he liked the hearty, instant cordiality. Remarking on the beauty and order of the machines, loud cries arose for "Taylor! Bert Taylor!" After a moment's delay a short, stocky, very red-faced man, with rather a fussy manner, came forward.

"Mr. Keith," said a tall, dark youth, with a pronounced Southern accent, "I want foh to make you acquainted with Mr. Tayloh. Mr. Tayloh is at once the patron saint of the Monumentals, but to a large extent its 'angel' as well—I hope you understand the theatrical significance of that term, suh. He is motheh, fatheh, guardeen, and dry nurse to every stick, stone, and brick, every piece of wood, brass, or rubbah, every inch of hose, and every man *and* Irishman on these premises." Taylor had turned an embarrassed brick red. "Mr. Keith," went on the dark youth, explanatorily, "was just sayin' that though he had inspected carefully many fire equipments, per'fessional and amateur, he had nevah feasted his eyes on so complete an outfit as that of our Monumentals."

Keith had not said all this, but possibly he had meant it. The brick-red, stocky little man was so plainly embarrassed and anxious to depart that Keith racked his brains for something to say. All he could remember was the manufacturer's nameplate on the machine downstairs.

"I see you have selected the Hunaman engine, sir," said he. The little man's eye brightened.

"It may be, sir, that you favour the piano-box type—of the sort made by Smith or Van Ness?" he inquired politely.

"It is a point on which my opinion is still-suspended," replied Keith with great gravity.

The little man moved nearer, and his shyness fell from him.

"Oh, but really there is no choice, none whatever!" he cried. "I'm sure, sir, I can convince you in five minutes. I assure you we have gone into the subject thoroughly—this Hunaman cost us over five thousand dollars; and you may be certain we went very thoroughly into the matter before making the investment—"

He went on talking in his self-effacing, deprecatory, but very earnest fashion. The other men in the group, Keith felt, were watching with covert amusement. Occasionally, he thought to catch half-concealed grins at his predicament. In less than the five minutes the claims of the piano box were utterly demolished. Followed a dissertation on methods of fighting fire; and then a history of the Monumental Company—its members, its officers, and its proud record. "And our bell—did you know that?—is the bell used by the Vigilantes—" He broke off suddenly in confusion, his embarrassment descending on him again. A moment later he sidled away.

"But I found him very interesting!" protested Keith, in answer to implied apologies.

"Bert is invaluable here; but he's a lunatic on fire apparatus. We couldn't get along without him, but it's sometimes mighty difficult to get on *with* him," said some one.

Keith was making a good impression without consciously trying to do so. His high spirits of youth and enthusiasm were in his favour; and as yet he had no interests to come into conflict with those of any one present. More drinks were ordered and fresh cigars lighted. From Sherwood they now learned that Keith had but just landed, and intended to settle as a permanent resident. As one man they uprose.

"And yo' wastin' of yo' time indoors!" mourned the dark Southerner. "And so much to see!"

Enthusiastically they surrounded him and led him forth. Only a very old, very small, very decadent village is devoid of what is modernly called the "booster" spirit. In those early days of slow transportation and isolated communities, local patriotism was much stronger than it is now. And something about the air's wine of the Pacific slope has always, and probably will always, make of every man an earnest proselyte for whatever patch of soil he calls home. But add to these general considerations the indubitable facts of harbour, hill, health, opportunity, activity, and a genuine history, if of only three years, one can no longer marvel that every man, each in his own way, saw visions.

In the course of the next few hours Keith got confused and mixed impressions of many things. The fortresslike warehouses; the plank roads; the new Jenny Lind Theatre; the steam paddies eating steadily into the sand hills at the edge of town; the Dramatic Museum; houses perched on the crumbling edges of hills; houses sunk far below the level of new streets, with tin cans and ducks floating around them; new office buildings; places where new office buildings were going to be or merely ought to be; land that in five years was going to be worth fabulous sums; unlikely looking spots where historic things had stood or had happened—all these were pointed out to him. He was called upon to exercise the eye of faith; to reconstruct; to eliminate the unfinished, the mean, the sordid; to overlook the inadequate; to build the city as it was sure to be; and to concern himself with that and that only. He admired Mount Tamalpais over the way. He was taken up a high hill—a laborious journey—to gaze on the spot where he would have been able to see Mount Diabolo, if only Mount Diabolo had been visible. And every few blocks he was halted and made to shake hands with some one who was always immediately characterized to him impressively, under the breath—"Colonel Baker, sir, one of the most divinely endowed men with the gift of eloquence, sir"; "Mr. Rowlee, sir, editor of one of our leading journals"; "Judge Caldwell, sir at present one of the ornaments of our bench"; "Mr. Ben Sansome, sir, a leadin' young man in our young but vigorous social life"; and so on.

These introductions safely and ceremoniously accomplished, each newcomer insisted on leading the way to the nearest bar.

"I insist, sir. It is just the hour for my afternoon toddy."

After some murmuring of expostulation, the invitation was invariably accepted.

There was always a barroom immediately adjacent. Keith was struck by the number and splendour of these places. Although San Francisco was only three years removed from the tent stage, and although the freightage from the centres of civilization was appalling, there was no lack of luxury. Mahogany bars with brass rails, huge mirrors with gilt frames, pyramids of delicate crystal, rich hangings, oil paintings of doubtful merit but indisputable interest, heavy chandeliers of prism glasses, most elaborate free lunches, and white-clad barkeepers—such matters were common to all. In addition, certain of the more pretentious boasted special attractions. Thus, one place supported its ceiling on crystal pillars;

another—and this was crowded—had dashing young women to serve the drinks, though the mixing was done by men; a third offered one of the new large musical boxes capable of playing several very noisy tunes; a fourth had imported a marvelous piece of mechanism: a piece of machinery run by clockwork, exhibiting the sea in motion, a ship tossing on its bosom; on shore, a water mill in action, a train of cars passing over a bridge, a deer chase with hounds, huntsmen, and game, all in pursuit or flight, and the like. The barkeepers were marvels of dexterity and of especial knowledge. At command they would deftly and skilfully mix a great variety of drinks— cocktails, sangarees, juleps, bounces, swizzles, and many others. In mixing these drinks it was their especial pride to pass them at arm's length from one tall glass to another, the fluid describing a long curve through the air, but spilling never a drop.

In these places Keith pledged in turn each of his new acquaintances, and was pledged by them. Never, he thought, had he met so jolly, so interesting, so experienced a lot of men. They had not only lived history, they had made it. They were so full of high spirits and the spirit of play. His heart warmed to them mightily; and over and over he told himself that he had made no mistake in his long voyage to new fields of endeavour. On the other hand, he, too, made a good impression. Naturally the numerous drinks had something to do with this mutual esteem; but also it was a fact that his boyish, laughing, half-reckless spirit had much in common with the spirit of the times. Quite accidentally he discovered that the tall, dark Southern youth was Calhoun Bennett. This then seemed to him a remarkable coincidence.

"Why, I have a letter of introduction to you!" he said.

Again and again he recurred to this point, insisting on telling everybody how extraordinary the situation was.

"Here I've been talking to him for three hours," he exclaimed, "and never knew who he was, and all the time I had a letter of introduction to him!"

This and a warm irresponsible glow of comradeship were the sole indications of the drinks he had had. Keith possessed a strong head. Some of the others were not so fortunate. Little Rowlee was frankly verging on drunkenness.

The afternoon wind was beginning to die, and the wisps of high fog that had, since two o'clock, been flying before it, now paused and forgathered to veil the sky. Dusk was falling.

"Look here," suggested Rowlee suddenly; "let's go to Allen's Branch and have a good dinner, and then drift around to Belle's place and see if there's any excitement to be had thereabouts."

"Belle—our local Aspasia, sah," breathed a very elaborate, pompous, elderly Southerner, who had been introduced as Major Marmaduke Miles.

But this suggestion brought to Keith a sudden realization of the lateness of the hour, the duration of his absence, and the fact that, not only had he not yet settled his wife in rooms of her own, but had left her on the hands of strangers. For the first time he noticed that Sherwood was not of the party.

"When did Sherwood leave?" he cried.

"Oh, a right sma't time ago," said Bennett.

Keith started to his feet.

"I should like to join you," said he, "but it is impossible now."

A chorus of expostulation went up at this.

"But I haven't settled down yet!" persisted Keith. "I don't know even whether my baggage is at the hotel."

They waived aside his objections; but finding him obdurate, perhaps a little panicky over the situation, they gave over urging the point.

"But you must join us later in the evening," said they.

The idea grew.

"I tell you what," said Rowlee, with half-drunken gravity; "he's got to come back. We can't afford to lose him this early. And he can't afford to lose us. The best life of this glorious commonwealth is as yet a sealed book to him. It is our sacred duty, gentlemen, to break those seals. What does he know of our temples of Terpsichore? Our altars to the gods of chance? Our bowers of the Cyprians?"

He would have gone on at length, but Keith, laughingly protesting, trying to disengage himself from the detaining hands, broke in with a promise to return. But little Rowlee was not satisfied.

"I think we should take no chances," he stated. "How would it be to appoint a committee to 'company him and see that he gets back?"

Keith's head was clear enough to realize with dismay that this brilliant idea was about to take. But Ben Sansome, seizing the situation, locked his arm firmly in Keith's.

"I'll see personally that he gets back," said he.

V

"That was mighty good of you; you saved my life!" said Keith to him, gratefully, as they walked up the street.

"You couldn't have that tribe of wild Indians descending on your wife," said Sansome. He had kept pace with, the others, but showed it not at all. Sansome was a slender, languid, bored, quiet sort of person, exceedingly well dressed in the height of fashion, speaking with a slight, well-bred drawl, given to looking rather superciliously from beneath his fine eyelashes, almost too good looking. He liked, or pretended he liked, to view life from the discriminating spectator's standpoint; and remained unstirred by stirring events. He prided himself on the delicacy of his social tact. In the natural course of evolution he would probably never marry, and would become in time an "old beau," haunting ballrooms with reminiscences of old-time belles.

Keith, meeting the open air, began to feel his exhilaration.

"What I need is my head under a pump for about ten seconds," he told Sansome frankly. "Lord! It was just about time I got away."

Arrived at the hotel, Sansome said good-bye, but Keith would have none of it.

"No, no!" he cried. "You must come in, now you've come so far! I want you to meet my wife; she'll be delighted!"

And Sansome, whose celebrated social tact had been slightly obscured by his potations, finally consented. Truth to tell, it would have been a little difficult for him to have got away. Poising his light stick and gloves in his left hand, giving his drooping moustache a last twirl, and settling his heavy cravat in place, he followed Keith down the little hall to the Sherwoods' apartments.

At the knock Keith was at once invited to enter. The men threw open the door. Sansome stared with all his might.

Nan Keith had made the usual miraculous recovery from seasickness once she felt the solid ground beneath, her. The beautiful baby-textured skin had come alive with soft colour, her dark, wide, liquid eyes had brightened.

She had assumed a soft, silken, wrapperlike garment with, a wide sash, borrowed from Mrs. Sherwood; and at the moment was seated in an enveloping armchair beneath a wide-shaded lamp. The firm, soft lines of her figure, uncorseted in this negligee, were suggested beneath the silk. Sansome stopped short, staring, his eyes kindling with, interest. Here was something not only new but different—a distinct addition. Sansome, like most dilettantes, was something of a phrase maker, and prided himself on the apt word. He found it here, to his own satisfaction, at least.

"Her beauty is positively creamy!" he murmured to himself.

At sight of her Keith crossed directly to her, full of a sudden, engaging, tender solicitude.

"How are you feeling now, honey?" he inquired. "Quite recovered? All right now?"

But Nan was inclined to be a little vexed and reproachful. She had been left alone, with strangers, altogether too long. Keith excused himself volubly and convincingly—she had been asleep—she was much better off not being disturbed—that this was true was proven by results—she was blooming, positively blooming—as fresh as a rose leaf—of course it was rather an imposition on the Sherwoods, but the baggage hadn't come up yet, and they were kind people, our sort, the sort for whom the word obligation did not exist—he, personally, had not intended being gone so long, but by the rarest of chances he had run across some of the men to whom, he had introductions, and they had been most kind in making him acquainted—nothing was more important to a young lawyer than to "establish connections"—it did not do to overlook a chance.

He urged all this, and more, with all his usual, vital, enthusiastic force. In spite of herself, she was overborne to a reproachful forgiveness.

In the meantime Mrs. Sherwood had gone over to where Ben Sansome was still standing by the door. Sansome did not like Mrs. Sherwood. He considered that she had no social tact at all. This was mainly—though he id not analyze it—because she was quite apt to speak the direct and literal truth to him; because she had a disquieting self-confidence and competence in place of appropriate, graceful, feminine dependence; but especially because she had never and would never play up to his game.

"Are you making a formal afternoon call, Ben?" she asked in her cool, mocking voice. "Aren't you really a little *de trop?*"

"I did not come of my own volition at this time, I assure you," he replied a trifle stiffly. The thought that he was suspected of a blunder in social custom stung him; as, in a rather lazily amused way, she knew it would.

At this reply she glanced keenly toward Keith, then nodded; slowly.

"I see," she conceded.

Sansome moved to go. But at this Keith's attention was attracted. He sprang forward, seized Sansome's arm, insisted on introducing him to Nan, was over-effusive, over-cordial, buoyant. Both Sansome and Mrs. Sherwood were experienced enough to yield entirely to his mood. They understood perfectly that at the least opposition Keith was in just the condition to reveal himself, perhaps, to break over the frail barrier that separates exhilaration from loss of self-control. They saw also that Nan had no suspicion of the state of affairs. Indeed, following the reaction from her long voyage and her illness, she responded and played up to Keith's high spirits. Neither wanted her to grasp the situation if it could be avoided: Mrs. Sherwood from genuine good feeling, Sansome because of the social awkwardness and bad taste. Besides, he felt that his presence at such a scene would be a very bad beginning for himself.

"No, you're not going," Keith was insisting; "you don't realize what a celebration this is! Here we've pulled up all our roots, haven't we, Nan? and come thousands of miles to a new country, a wonderful country; and the very first day of our landing you want us to act as though nothing had happened!"

Nan nodded a vigorous assent to his implied reference to her.

"And what we're going to do is to celebrate," insisted Keith. "You're all going to dine with us. No, I insist! You're the only friends we have out here, and you aren't going to desert us the very first day we need you."

"I wish you would!" cried Nan, sitting forward eagerly.

They tried to expostulate, to get out of it, but without avail. It seemed easier to promise. Keith rushed out to look for his baggage, to arrange for rooms, leaving the three together to await his return.

VI

Both Mrs. Sherwood and Sansome applied themselves to relieving whatever embarrassment Nan might feel over this unusual situation. Sansome was possessed of great charm and social experience. He could play the game of light conversation to perfection. By way of bridging the pause in events, he set himself to describing the society in which the Keiths would shortly find themselves launched. His remarks were practically a monologue, interspersed by irrepressible gurgles of laughter from Nan. Mrs. Sherwood sat quietly by. She did not laugh, but it was evident she was amused. In this congenial atmosphere Sansome outdid himself.

"They are all afraid of each other," he told her, "because they don't know anything about each other. Each ex-washerwoman thinks the other ex- washerwoman must have been at least a duchess at home. It's terribly funny. If they can get hold of six porcelain statuettes, a half-dozen antimac-assars, some gilt chairs, and a glass bell of wax flowers, they imagine they're elegantly furnished. And their functions! I give you my word, I'd as soon attend a reasonably pleasant funeral! Some of them try to entertain by playing intellectual games—you know, rhyming or spelling games—seriously!" He went on to describe some of the women, mentioning no names, however. "You'll recognize them when you meet them," he assured her. "There's one we'll call the Social Agitator—she isn't happy unless she is running things. I believe she spent two weeks once in London—or else she buys her boots there—anyway, when discussions get lively she squelches them by saying, 'Of course,

Stewart Edward White

my dear, that may be absolutely *au fait* in New York—but in London—' It corks them up every time. And 'pon honour, three quarters of the time she's quite wrong! Then there's the Lady Thug. Square jaw, square shoulder, sort of bulging out at the top—you know—in decollete one cannot help thinking 'one more struggle and she'll be free!'"

"Oh, fie, Mr. Sansome," laughed Nan, half shocked.

Sansome rattled on. The ultimate effect was to convey an impression of San Francisco society—such as existed at all—as stodgy, stupid, pretentious, unattractive. Nan was immensely amused, but inclined to take it all with a grain of salt.

"Mrs. Sherwood doesn't bear you out," she told him, "and she's the only one I've seen yet. I think we're going to have a pretty good time."

But at this point Keith returned. He was quite sobered from his temporary exhilaration, but still most cordial and enthusiastic over his little party, Sansome noted with quiet amusement that his light curly hair was damp. Evidently he had taken his own prescription as to the pump.

"Well," he announced, "I have a room—such as it is. can't say much for it. The baggage is all here; nothing missing for a wonder. I've spoken to the manager about dinner for five." He turned to Nan with brightening interest. "Guess what I saw on the bill of fare! Grizzly bear steak! Think of that! I ordered some."

Sansome groaned comically.

"What's the matter?" inquired Keith.

"Did you ever try it before? Tough, stringy, unfit for human consumption."

But Keith was fascinated by the name of the thing.

"There's plenty else," he urged defensively, "and I always try everything once."

It was agreed that they should all meet again after an hour. Sansome renewed his promises to be on hand.

The room Keith had engaged was on the second story, and quite a different sort of affair from that of the Sherwoods'. Indeed it was little more than a pine box, containing only the bare necessities. One window looked out on an unkempt backyard, now mercifully hidden by darkness.

"This is pretty tough," said Keith, "but it is the very best I could do. And the price is horrible. We'll have to hunt up a living place about the first thing we do."

"Oh, it's all right," said Nan indifferently. The lassitude of seasickness had left her, and the excitement of new surroundings was beginning. She felt gently stirred by the give and take of the light conversation in the Sherwoods' room; and, although she did not quite realize it, she was responding to the stimulation of having made a good impression. Her subconscious self was perfectly aware that in the silken negligee, under the pink-shaded lamp, her clear soft skin, the pure lines of her radiant childlike beauty, the shadows of her tumbled hair, had been very appealing and effective. She moved about a trifle restlessly, looking at things without seeing them. "I'm glad to see the brown trunk. Open it, will you, dear? Heavens, what a mirror!" She surveyed herself in the flawed glass, moving from side to side, fascinated at the strange distortions.

"I call it positive extortion, charging what they do for a room like this," grumbled Keith, busy at the trunk. "The Sherwoods must pay a mint of money for theirs. I wonder what he does!"

Her attention attracted by this subject, she arrested her posing before the mirror.

"They certainly are quick to take the stranger in," she commented lightly.

Something in her tone arrested Keith's attention, and he stopped fussing at his keys. Nan had meant little by the remark. It had expressed the vague instinctive recoil of the woman brought up in rather conventional circumstances and in a conservative community from too sudden intimacy, nothing more. She did not herself understand this.

"Don't you like the Sherwoods?" he instantly demanded, with the masculine insistence on dissecting every butterfly.

"Why, she's charming!" said Nan, opening her eyes in surprise. "Of course, I like her immensely!"

"I should think so," grumbled Keith. "They certainly have been mighty good to us."

But Nan had dropped her negligee about her feet, and was convulsed at the figure made of her slim young body by the distorted mirror.

"Come here, Milt," she gasped.

She clung to him, gurgling with laughter, pointing one shaking finger at the monstrosity in the glass.

"Look—look what you married!"

They dressed gayly. His optimism and enthusiasm boiled over again. It was a shame, his leaving her all that afternoon, he reiterated; but she had no idea what giant strides he had made. He told her of the city, and he enumerated some of the acquaintances he had made—Calhoun Bennett, Bert Taylor, Major Marmaduke Miles, Michael Rowlee, Judge Caldwell, and others. They had been most cordial to him, most kind; they had taken him in without delay.

"It's the spirit of the West, Nan," he cried, "hospitable, unsuspicious, free, eager to welcome! Oh, this is going to be the place for me; opportunity waits at every corner. They are not tied down by conventions, by the way somebody else has done things—"

He went on rapidly to detail to her some of the things he had been told—the contemplated public improvements, the levelling of the sand hills, the building of a city out of nothing.

"Why, Nan, do you realize that only four years ago this very Plaza had only six small buildings around it, that there were only three two-story structures in town, that the population was only about five hundred—there are thirty-five thousand now, that—" he rattled on, detailing his recently acquired statistics. Oh, potent influence of the Western spirit—already, eight hours after his landing on California's shores, Milton Keith was a "booster."

With an expansion of relief that only a woman could fully appreciate, Nan unpacked and put on a frock that had nothing whatever to do with the sea voyage, and which she had not for some time seen. In ordinary accustomed circumstances she would never have thought of donning so elaborate a toilette for a hotel dining-room, but she was yielding to reaction. In her way she was "celebrating," just as was Keith. Her hair she did low after the fashion of the time, and bound it to her brow by a bandeau of pearls. The gown itself was pale green and filmy. It lent her a flowerlike semblance that was very fresh and lovely.

"By Jove, Nan, you certainly have recovered from the sea!" cried Keith, and insisted on kissing her.

"Look how you've mussed me all up!" chided Nan, but without irritation.

They found the other three waiting for them, and without delay entered the dining-room. This, as indeed all the lower

Stewart Edward White

story, was in marked contrast of luxury with the bare pine bedrooms upstairs. Long red velvet curtains, held back by tasselled silken cords, draped the long windows; fluted columns at regular intervals upheld the ceiling; the floor was polished and slippery; the tables shone with white and silver. An obese and tremendous darkey in swallowtail waved a white-gloved hand at them, turned ponderously, and preceded them down the aisle with the pomp of a drum major. His dignity was colossal, awe inspiring, remote. Their progress became a procession, a triumphal procession, such as few of Caesar's generals had ever known. Arrived at the predestined table, he stood one side while menials drew out the chairs. Then he marched tremendously back to the main door, his chin high, his expression haughty, his backbone rigid. This head waiter was the feature of the Bella Union Hotel, just as the glass columns were the feature of the Empire, or the clockwork mechanism of the El Dorado.

The dinner itself went well. Everybody seemed to be friendly and at ease, but by one of those strange and sudden social transitions it was rather subdued. This was for various reasons. Nan Keith, after her brief reaction, found herself again suffering from the lassitude and fatigue of a long voyage; she needed a night's rest and knew it. Keith himself was a trifle sleepy as an after affect to the earlier drinking. Sherwood was naturally reserved and coolly observing; Mrs. Sherwood was apparently somehow on guard; and Sansome, as always, took his tone from those about him. The wild spirits of the hour before had taken their flight. It was, however, a pleasant dinner—without constraint, as among old friends. After the meal they went to the public parlour, a splendid but rather dismal place. Sherwood almost immediately excused himself. After a short and somewhat awkward interval, Nan decided she would go to bed for her needed rest.

"You won't think me rude, I know." said she.

Keith, whose buoyant temper had been sadly divided between a genuine wish to do the proper and dutiful thing by his wife and a great desire to see more of this fascinating city, rose with so evident an alacrity under restraint that Mrs. Sherwood scarcely, concealed a smile. She said her adieux at the same time, and left the room, troubling herself only to the extent of that ancient platitude about "letters to write."

VII

"I think we'll find most of the proper crowd down at the Empire," observed Sansome as the two picked their way across the Plaza. "That is one of the few old-fashioned, respectable gambling places left to us. The town is not what it used to be in a sporting way. It was certainly wide open in the good old days!"

The streets at night were ill lighted, except where a blaze of illumination poured from the bigger saloons. The interims were dark, and the side streets and alleys stygian. "None too safe, either," Sansome understated the case. Many people were abroad, but Keith noticed that there seemed to be no idlers; every one appeared to be going somewhere in particular. After a short stroll they entered the Empire, which, Sansome explained, was the most stylish and frequented gambling place in town, a sort of evening club for the well-to-do and powerful. Keith looked over a very large room or hall, at the lower end of which an alcove made a sort of raised stage with footlights. Here sat a dozen "nigger minstrels" with banjos strumming, and bawling away at top pressure. An elaborate rosewood bar ran down the whole length at one side—an impressive polished bar, perhaps sixty feet long, with a white-clad, immaculate barkeeper for every ten feet of it. Big mirrors of French plate reflected the whole room, and on the shelf in front of them glittered crystal glasses of all shapes and sizes, arranged in pyramids and cubes. The whole of the main floor was carpeted heavily. Down the centre were stationed two rows of gambling tables, where various games could be played—

faro, keeno, roulette, stud poker, dice. Beyond these gambling tables, on the other side of the room from the bar, were small tables, easy chairs of ample proportions, lounges, and a fireplace. Everything was most ornate. The ceilings and walls were ivory white and much gilt. Heavy chandeliers, with the usual glass prisms and globes, revolved slowly or swayed from side to side. Huge oil paintings with shaded top and foot-lights occupied all vacant spaces in the walls. They were "valued" at from ten to thirty thousand dollars apiece, and that fact was advertised. "Leda and the Swan," "The Birth of Venus," "The Rape of the Sabines," "Cupid and Psyche" were some of the classic themes treated as having taken place in a warm climate. "Susannah and the Elders" and "Salome Dancing" gave the Biblical flavour. The "Bath of the Harem" finished the collection. No canvas was of less size than seven by ten feet.

The floor was filled with people. A haze of blue smoke hung in the air. There was no loud noise except from the minstrel stage at the end. A low hum of talk, occasionally accented, buzzed continuously. Many of the people wandering about, leaning against the bar, or integers of the compact groups around the gambling tables, were dressed in the height of fashion; but, on the other hand, certainly half were in the roughest sort of clothes—floppy old slouch hats, worn flannel shirts, top boots to which dried mud was clinging. These men were as well treated as the others.

Fascinated, Keith would, have liked to linger, but Sansome threaded his way toward the farther corner. As Keith passed near one of the close groups around a gambling table, it parted momentarily, and he looked into the eyes of the man in charge, cold, passionless, aloof, eyes neither friendly nor unfriendly. And he saw the pale skin; the weary, bored, immobile features; the meticulous neat dress; the long, deft fingers; and caught the withdrawn, deadly, exotic personality of the professional gambler on duty.

The whole place was unlike anything he had ever seen before.

Whether it was primarily a bar, a gambling resort, or a sort of a public club with trimmings, he could not have determined. Many of those present, perhaps a majority, were neither gambling, nor drinking; they seemed not to be adding to the profits of the place in any way, but either wandered about or sat in the easy chairs, smoking, reading papers, or attending to the occasional outbreaks of the minstrels. It was most interesting.

They joined a group in the far corner. A white-clad negro instantly brought them chairs, and hovered discreetly near. Among those sitting about Keith recognized several he had met in the afternoon; and to several more he was introduced. Of these the one who most instantly impressed him was called Morrell. This was evidently a young Englishman, a being of a type raised quite abundantly in England, but more rarely seen in native Americans—the lean-faced, rather flat-cheeked, high-cheek-boned, aquiline-nosed, florid-complexioned, silent, clean-built sort that would seem to represent the high-bred, finely drawn product of a long social evolution. These traits when seen in the person of a native-born American generally do represent this fineness; but the English, having been longer at the production of their race, can often produce the outward semblance without necessarily the inner reality. Many of us even now do not quite realize that fact; certainly in 1852 most of us did not. Morrell was dressed in riding breeches, carried a short bamboo crop, smiled engagingly to exhibit even, strong, white teeth, and had little to say.

"A beverage seems called for," remarked Judge Caldwell, a gross, explosive, tobacco-chewing man, with a merry, reckless eye. The order given, the conversation swung back to the topic that had occupied it before Keith and Sansome had arrived.

It seemed that an individual there present, Markle by name—a tall, histrionic, dark man with a tossing mane—conceived himself to have been insulted by some one whose name Keith did not catch, and had that very afternoon issued warning that he would "shoot on sight." Some of the older men were advising him to go slow.

"But, gentlemen," cried Markle heatedly, "none of you would stand such conduct from anybody! What are we coming to? I'll get that—as sure as God made little apples."

"That's all right; I don't blame yo'," argued Calhoun. Bennett. "Do not misunderstand me, suh. I agree with yo', lock, stock, an' barrel. My point is that yo' must be circumspect. Challenge him, that's the way."

"He isn't worth my challenge, sir, nor the challenge of any decent man. You know that, sir,"

"Well, street shootings have got to be a little, a little—"

He fell silent, and Keith, looked up in surprise to see why. A man was slowly passing the table. He was a thick, tall, strong man, moving with a freedom that bespoke smoothly working muscles. His complexion was florid; and this, in conjunction with a sweeping blue-black moustache, gave him exactly the appearance of a gambler or bartender. Only as he passed the table and responded gravely to the formal salutes, Keith caught a flash of his eye. It was gray, hard as steel, forceful, but so far from being cold it seemed to glow and change with an inner fire, The bartender impression was swept into limbo forever.

"That's one good reason why," said Calhoun Bennett, when this man had gone on.

But Markle overflowed with a torrent of vituperative profanity. His face was congested and purple with the violence of his emotions. Keith stared in astonishment at the depth of hatred stirred. He turned for explanation to the man next him, Judge Girvin, a gentleman of the old school, weighty, authoritative, a little pompous.

"That is Coleman," Judge Girvin told him. "W.T. Coleman, the leader of the vigilance movement of last year."

"That's why," repeated Calhoun Bennett, with quiet vindictiveness, "lawlessness, disrespect foh law and order, mob rule. Since this strangler business, no man can predict what the lawless element may do!"

This speech was the signal for an outburst against the Vigilance Committee, so unanimous and hearty that Keith was rather taken aback. He voiced his bewilderment.

"Why, gentlemen, I am, of course, only in the most distant touch with these events; but the impression East is certainly very general that the Vigilantes did rather a good piece of work in clearing the city of crime."

They turned on him with a savagery that took his breath. Keith laughing, held up both hands.

"Don't shoot, don't shoot! I'll come down!" he cried. "I told you I didn't know anything about it!"

They checked themselves, suddenly ashamed of their heat. Calhoun Bennett voiced their feeling of apology.

"Yo' must accept our excuses, Mr, Keith, but this is a mattah on which we feel strongly. Our indignation was naturally not directed against yo suh."

But Judge Girvin, ponderous, formal, dignified, was making a pronouncement.

"Undoubtedly, young sir," he rolled forth at Keith, "undoubtedly a great many scoundrels were cleared from the city at that time. That no one would have the temerity to deny. But you, sir, as a lawyer, realize with us that even pure and equitable justice without due process of law is against the interests of society as a coherent whole. Infringement of law, even for a good purpose, invariably brings about ultimate contempt, for all law. In the absence of regularly constituted tribunals, as in a primitive society—such as that prior to the

Constitutional Convention of September, 1849—it may become necessary that informal plebiscites be countenanced. But in the presence of regularly constituted and appointed tribunals, extra-legal functions are not to be undertaken by the chance comer. If defects occur in the administration of the law, the remedy is in the hand of the public. The voter—" he went on at length, elaborating the legal view. Everybody listened with respect and approval until he had finished. But then up spoke Judge Caldwell, the round, shining, perspiring, untidy, jovial, Silenus- like jurist with the blunt fingers.

"We all agree with you theoretically, Judge," said he. "What these other fellows object to, I imagine, is that the law has such a hell of a hang fire to it."

Judge Girvin's eyes flashed, and he tossed back his white mane. "The due forms of the law are our heritage from the ages!" he thundered back. "The so-called delays and technicalities are the checks devised by human experience against the rash judgments and rasher actions by the volatile element of society! They are the safeguards, the bulwarks of society! It is better that a hundred guilty men escape than that one innocent man should suffer!"

The old judge was magnificent, his eyes alight, his nostrils expanded, his head reared back defiantly, all the great power of his magnetism and his authority brought to bear. Keith was thrilled. He considered that the discussion had been lifted to a high moral plane.

By rights Judge Caldwell should have been crushed, but he seemed undisturbed,

"Well," he remarked comfortably, "on that low average we must have quite a few innocent men among us after all."

"What do you mean, sir?" demanded Judge Girvin, halted in mid career and not catching the allusion.

"Surely, Judge, you don't mean to imply that you endorse Coleman and his gang?" put in Calhoun Bennett courteously but incredulously.

"Endorse them? Certainly not!" disclaimed Caldwell. "I need my job," he added with a chuckle.

Bennett tossed back his hair, and a faint disgust appeared in his dark eyes, but he said nothing more. Caldwell lit a cigar with pudgy fingers.

"My advice to you," he said to Markle, "is that if you think you're going to have to kill this man in self-defence"—he rolled an unabashed and comical eye at the company—"you be sure to see our old friend, Sheriff Webb, gets you to jail promptly." He heaved to his feet, "Might even send him advance word," he suggested, and waddled away toward the bar.

A dead silence succeeded his departure. None of the younger men ventured a word. Finally Judge Girvin, with a belated idea of upholding the honour of the bench, turned to Keith.

"Judge Caldwell's humour is a little trying at times, but he is essentially sound."

The young Englishman, Morrell, uttered a high cackle.

"Quite right," he observed; "he'll fix it all right for you, Markle."

At the bad taste of what they thought an example of English stupidity every one sat aghast. Keith managed to cover the situation by ordering another round of drinks. Morrell seemed quite pleased with himself.

"Got a rise out of the old Johnny, what?" he remarked to Keith aside.

Judge Caldwell returned. The conversation became general. Vast projects were discussed with the light touch—public works, the purchase of a theatre for the town hall, the sale by auction of city or state lands, the extension of wharves, the granting of franchises, and many other affairs, involving, apparently, millions of money. All these things were spoken of as from the inside. Keith, sipping his drinks quietly, sat apart and listened. He felt himself in the current of big affairs. Occasionally, men sauntered by, paused a moment. Keith noticed that they greeted his companions with respect and deference. He experienced a feeling of being at the centre of things. The evening drifted by pleasantly.

Along toward midnight, John Sherwood, without a hat, stopped long enough to exchange a few joking remarks, then sauntered on.

"I know him," Keith told Calhoun Bennett. "That's John Sherwood. He's at our hotel. What does *he* do?"

"Oh, don't you know who he is?" replied Bennett. "He's the owner of this place."

"A gambler?" cried Keith, a trifle dashed.

"Biggest in town. But square."

Keith for a moment was a little nonplussed. The sudden intimacy rose up to confront him. They were kind people, and Mrs. Sherwood was apparently everything she should be—but a public gambler! Of course he had no prejudices—but Nan—

VIII

Keith returned to the hotel very late, and somewhat exalted. He was bubbling over with good stories, interesting information, and ideas; so he awakened Nan, and sat on the edge of the bed, and proceeded enthusiastically to tell her all about it. She was very sleepy. Also an exasperated inhabitant of the next room pounded on the thin partition. Reluctantly Keith desisted. It took him some time to get to sleep, as the excitement was seething in his veins.

He came to consciousness after a restless night. The sun was streaming in at the window. He felt dull and heavy, with a slight headache and a weariness in all his muscles. Worst of all, Nan, in a ravishing pink fluffy affair, was bending over him, her eyes dancing with amusement and mischief.

"And how is my little madcap this morning?" she inquired with mock solicitude. This stung Keith to some show of energy, and he got up.

The sun was really very bright. A dash of cold water made him feel better. Enthusiasm began to flow back like a tide. The importance of the evening before reasserted its claims on his imagination. As he dressed he told Nan all about it. In the midst of a glowing eulogy of their prospects, he checked himself with a chuckle.

"Guess what the Sherwoods are," said he.

Nan, who had been half listening up to this time, gave him her whole attention.

"A gambler! A common gambler!" she repeated after him, a little dismayed.

"I felt the same way for a minute or so," he answered her tone cheerfully. "But after all I remembered—you must remember —that society here is very mixed. And anyway, Sherwood is no 'common gambler'; I should say he was a most *un*common gambler!" He chuckled at his little joke. "All sorts of people are received here. We've got to get used to that. And certainly no one could hope anywhere to find nicer—more presentable— people."

She nodded, but with a reservation.

"Surely nowhere would you find kinder people," went on Keith. "See how they took us in!"

"Look out they don't take you in, Milton," she interjected suddenly.

Keith, brought up short, sobered at this.

"That is unjust, Nan," he said gravely.

She said nothing, but showed no signs of having been convinced. After her first need had passed, Nan Keith's natural reserve had asserted itself. This was the result of heredity and training, as part of herself, something she could not help. Its tendency was always to draw back from too great or too sudden intimacies. There was nothing snobbish in this; it was a sort of instinct, a natural reaction. She liked Mrs. Sherwood, admired her slow, complete poise, approved her air of breeding and the things by which she had surrounded herself. The older woman's kindness had struck in her a deep chord of appreciation. But somehow circumstances had hurried her too much. Her defensive antagonism, not to Mrs. Sherwood as a person, but to sudden intimacy as such, had been aroused. It had had, in her own mind, no excuse. She knew she ought to be grateful and cordial; she felt that she was not quite ready. The fact that the Sherwoods had proved to be "common gamblers" gave just the little excuse her conscience needed to draw back a trifle. This, it should be added, was also quite instinctive, not at all a formulated thought.

She said nothing for some time; then remarked mysteriously:

"Perhaps that's why they go to meet boats."

Keith, who was miles beyond the Sherwoods by now, looked bewildered.

Keith had letters of business introduction to Palmer, Cook & Co., a banking firm powerful and respected at the time, but destined to become involved in scandal. The most pressing need, both he and Nan had determined, was a house of their own; the hotel was at once uncomfortable and expensive. Accordingly a callow, chipper, self-confident, blond little clerk was assigned to show them about. He had arrived from the East only six months ago; but this was six months earlier than the Keiths, so he put on all the airs of an old-timer. In a two-seated calash, furnished by the bankers, they drove to the westerly part of the town. The plank streets soon ran out into sand or rutty earth roads. These bored their way relentlessly between sand hills in the process of removal. Steam paddies coughed and clanked in all directions. Many houses had, by these operations, been left perched high and dry far above the grade of the new streets. Often the sand was crumbling away from beneath their outer corners. All sorts of nondescript ramshackle and temporary stairs had been improvised to get their inhabitants in or out. The latter seemed to be clinging to their tenements as long as possible.

"They often cave in," explained the clerk, "and the whole kit and caboodle comes sailing down into the street. Sometimes it happens at night," he added darkly.

"But isn't anybody hurt?" cried Nan.

"Lots of 'em," replied the clerk cheerfully "Git dap!"

They now executed a flank attack on the "fashionable" quarter of the town.

"They're grading the street down below," the clerk justified his roundabout course.

Here were a number of isolated, scattered wooden houses, of some size and of much scroll and jigsaw work. Some of them had little ornamental iron fencelets running along their ridgepoles, or lightning rods on the chimneys or at the corners, although thunderstorms were practically unknown. The clerk at once began to talk of these as "mansions." He drew up before one of them, hitched the horse, and invited his clients to descend. Nan looked at the exterior a trifle doubtfully. It was a high-peaked, slender house, drawn together as though it felt cold; with carved wooden panels over each window, miniature balconies with elaborate spindly columns beneath, and a haughty, high, narrow porch partially clothing a varnished front door flanked with narrow strips of coloured glass.

The clerk produced a key. The interior also was high and narrow. Much glistening varnish characterized the front hall. They inspected one after another the various rooms. The house was partly furnished. In the showrooms hung heavy red curtains held back by cords with gilt tassels. Each fireplace was framed by a mantel of white marble. But the glory was the drawing-room. This had been frescoed in pale blue, and all about the wall and even across part of the ceiling had been draped festoon after festoon of fishnet. Only this was not real fishnet, as a closer inspection showed. It had been cunningly painted! In the dim light, and to a person with an optimistic imagination, the illusion was almost perfect. Nan choked suddenly at the sight of this; then her eyes widened to a baby stare, and she become preternaturally solemn.

They looked it all over from top to bottom; the clerk fairly tiptoeing about with the bent-backed air of one who handles a precious jade vase. From the front windows he showed them a really magnificent view, with the blue waters of the bay shining, and the Contra Costa shore shimmering in the haze.

"In the residence next door to the west dwell most desirable neighbours," he urged, "the Morrells. They are English, or at least he is."

"I met him last night," said Keith to Nan; "he looked like a good sort."

"Who is in the big house over there?" asked Nan, indicating a very elaborate structure diagonally opposite.

"That—oh, that—well, that is in rather a state of transition, as it were," stammered the little clerk, and at once rattled on about something else. This magnificent mansion, he explained, was the only one Palmer, Cook & Co. had on their lists for the moment.

Therefore he drove them back to the Bella Union. Keith departed with him to look up a suitable office downtown,

Nan bowed solemnly to his solemn salutation in farewell, and turned as quickly as she could to the interior of the hotel. Sherwood sat in his accustomed place, his big steel spectacles on his nose, his paper spread out before him. He arose and bowed. She nodded, but did not pause. Once inside the hall, she picked up her skirts and fairly flew up the stairs to her room. Slamming the door shut, she locked it, then sank on the edge of the bed and laughed—laughed until she wiped the tears from her cheeks, rocking back and forth and hugging herself in an ecstasy. Every few moments she would pull up; then some unconsidered enormity would strike her afresh and she would go off into another paroxysm. After a while, much relieved, she wiped her eyes and arose.

"This place will be the death of me yet," she told her distorted image in the mirror.

She rummaged in one of her trunks, produced writing materials, and started a letter to an Eastern friend. This occupied her fully for two hours. At that period it was customary to "indite epistles" with a "literary flavour," a practice that immensely tickled those who did the inditing. Nan became wholly interested and quite pleased with herself. Her first impressions, she found when she came to write them down, were stimulating and interesting. She was full of enthusiasm; but had she been capable of a real analysis she would have found it quite different from Keith's enthusiasm. She looked on this strange, uncouth, vital city from the outside, from the superior standpoint. She appreciated it as she would have appreciated the "quaintness" of the villagers in some foreign town.

About noon Keith returned.

"I've looked into every possibility," he told her. "Honest, Nan, I don't see exactly what we are to do unless we build for ourselves. That Boyle house is the only house in town for rent—that is of any size and in a respectable quarter. You see they are too new out here to have built houses for rent yet; and if you find any vacant at all, it is sheer good fortune of course to stay in this little box is impossible, and—"

She had been contemplating him, her eyes dancing with amusement.

"You've taken it!" she accused him.

"Well—I—yes," he admitted, a little red.

She laughed.

"I knew it," she said. "When can we move in? I want to get started."

IX

Keith's first plunge into the teeming life of the place had to suffice him for all the rest of that week. There seemed so many pressing things to do at home. The Boyle house was only partly furnished. Each morning he and Nan went downtown and prospected for things needed. This was Nan's first experience of the sort; and she confessed to a ludicrous surprise over the fact that pots, pans, brooms, kitchen utensils, and such homely matters had to be thought of and bought.

"I had a sort of notion they grew on the premises," she said.

Mrs. Sherwood gave them much valuable advice, particularly as to auctions. In the Keiths limited experience auctions generally had meant cheap or second-hand articles, but out here the reverse was the case. A madness possessed otherwise conservative Eastern merchants—especially of the staid city of Boston—to send out on speculation immense cargoes of all sorts of goods. These were the despair of consignees. Heavy freights, high interest charges, tremendous warehouse rates, speedily ate up whatever chance of profits a fresh consignment might have. The only solution was to sell out as promptly as possible; and the quickest method was the auction. Therefore, auctions were everywhere in progress, and the professional auctioneers were a large, influential, and skilful class of people. Their advertisements made the bulk of the newspapers. They dressed well, carried an air of consequence, furnished refreshments, brass bands, or other entertainments to their patrons. The era of fabulous prices was at an end, but the era of wild speculation as to what the public was going to want was in full tide. Keith and Nan found these auctions great fun, and piece by piece they accumulated the items of their house furnishing. It was slow work, but amusing. At times Mrs. Sherwood accompanied them, but not often. Her advice was always good.

As to Mrs. Sherwood, Nan Keith found her attitude very vague. There was no doubt that she liked her personally, admired her slow, purposeful, half- indolent movements, the poise of her small, patrician head, the unconscious, easy grace of her body, the direct commonsense quality of her mind. One met her face to face; there were no frills and furbelows of the spirit. Also, Nan was grateful for the other woman's first kindness and real sympathy, and she wanted to "play the game." But, on the other hand, all her social training and her instinct of formalism tended to hold her aloof. She blamed herself intellectually for this feeling; but since it was a feeling, and had nothing to do with intellect, it persisted.

In the auction rooms, also, she seemed to meet—be formally introduced to—a bewildering number of people, most of whom she could not place at all. There seemed to be no reason for meeting them; certainly she would not have met them in the East. Nevertheless, they all shook her by the hand, and bowed to her whenever subsequently they passed her on the street. Keith told her this was all usual and proper in this new and mixed social order; and she was perfectly willing to make the effort. She was really charming to everybody. The consciousness that she was successfully adapting herself to their primitive provincial scope, and her very gracious condescension to all types, filled her with respect for her democracy and breadth of mind.

The afternoon they spent at the house receiving boxes and packages. Keith worked busily, happily, feverishly, in his shirt sleeves. He attacked the job on the principle of a whirlwind campaign, hammering, ripping, throwing papers down, deciding instantly where this or that chair or table was to stand, tearing on to the next, enjoying himself dustily and hugely.

Nan was more leisurely. She found time to gossip with the drayman who brought up the goods, actually came to a liking and a warm friendly feeling for him as a person. This was a new experience for Nan, and she explored it curiously.

John McGlynn was a teamster, but likewise a thoroughly independent and capable citizen. He was of the lank, hewn, lean-faced, hawk-nosed type, deliberate in movement and speech, with a twinkling, contemplative, appraising eye, and an unhurried drawl. He told Nan he had come out in '49.

"No, ma'am," he disclaimed vigorously, "I didn't go to the mines. I am a teamster, and I always did teaming." He did not add, as he might have done, that in those days of the individual he had been an important influence.

His great pride was his team and wagon, and that pride was justified. The wagon was a heavy flat affair, gayly decorated, and on the sides of the box were paintings of landscapes. The horses were great, magnificent creatures, with arching thick necks, long wavy manes and forelocks, soft, intelligent eyes, and with great hoofs and hairy fetlocks. They carried themselves in conscious pride, Their harness was heavy with silver and with many white and coloured rings. In colour they were dapple gray.

"That team," said John McGlynn, "is a perfect match. Took me two years to get them together. Wuth a mint of money. That Kate, there, is a regular character. You'd be surprised how cute she is. I often wonder who Kate *is*. She must be some very famous woman."

John McGlynn was a very wonderful and very accommodating person, Nan thought. He would help carry things in, and was willing to unpack or to carry out the mess Keith's mad career left behind, it. Also he cast an eye on the garden possibilities, and issued friendly, expert advice to which Nan listened, breathless. They held long intimate consultations as to the treatment of the soil.

"A few posies does sort of brighten things up; they're wuth while," quoth John.

Without previous consultation, he appeared one day accompanied by a rotund, bland, gorgeous Chinaman, perched beside him on his elevated seat.

"This is Wing Woh, a friend of mine," he announced. "You got to have a Chink, of course. You can't run that sized house without help. Wing knows all the Chinks in town, and bosses about half of them."

Wing Woh descended and without a word walked into the house. He was a very ornate person, dressed in a skull cap with a red coral button atop, a brocaded pale lavendar tunic of silk, baggy pale green trousers tied close around the ankles, snow-white socks and the typical shoe. Gravely, solemnly, methodically he went over the entire house; then returned and clambered up beside John.

"All light," he vouchsafed to the astonished Nan.

Next morning she found waiting on the veranda a smiling "china boy" dressed all in clean white. A small cloth bundle lay at his feet.

"My name Wing Sam," he announced; "I wo'k you thi'ty dolla' month. Where you keep him bloom?"

That day John McGlynn stopped after unloading his boxes to give a little advice.

"Chinks are queer," said he. "When you show this fellow how to do anything, be sure to show him right, because that's the way he's going to do it forever after. You can't change him.

And show him; don't tell him. And let him do things his own way as much as you can, instead of insisting on your way."

McGlynn also advised Keith as to where he could to the best advantage hire a horse and buggy by the month.

"You want a good safe animal, so Mrs. Keith can drive him; but you don't want a cow. Jump aboard and I'll take you around. Never mind your coat," he told Keith, "it's warm."

So they "jumped aboard" and drove down the street. Nan gurgled with amusement over the episode. She sat on the high seat beside John McGlynn's lank figure, above the broad backs of the great horses; and Keith in his shirtsleeves, his hair every which way, a smudge of black across his nose, balanced in the flat dray body behind. Nan tried to imagine the sensation they would create in Baltimore, and laughed aloud.

"Is sort of funny," commented John McGlynn sympathetically. "But everything goes out here."

Nan, aghast at the uncanny perspicacity of the man, choked silently. In her world there had always been a sort of vague, unexpressed feeling that the "lower classes" were dull.

They used the horse and buggy a great deal. It was delivered at the hotel door every morning and taken from the same place every evening. Innumerable errands downtown for things forgotten kept it busy. At night they returned to the hotel pretty well tired out. It was a tremendous task, much as they might be enjoying it.

"Seems to me the more we do the worse it gets," said Keith. "Let's dig some sort of a hole and move in anyway."

"In a few days," agreed Nan, who as general-in-chief had a much clearer idea of the actual state of affairs than the dusty private.

X

One morning the accumulated fatigue had its way, and they overslept scandalously. It was after ten o'clock before they were ready to drive up the street. As they turned the corner from Kearney Street they were saluted by the ringing of numerous bells.

"Why, it's Sunday!" cried Keith, after a moment's calculation. In the unexpectedness of this discovery he reined in the horse.

"It will never do to work to-day," she answered his unspoken thought. "I suppose we ought to go to church."

But Keith turned the horse's head to the left.

"Church?" he returned with great decision. "We're going on a spree. This is a day of rest, and we've earned it."

"Where?" asked Nan, a trifle shocked at his implication as to church.

"I haven't the remotest idea," said Keith.

They drove along a plank road leading out of town. It proved to be thronged with people, all going in the same direction. The shuffle of their feet on the planks and the murmur of their many voices were punctuated by the *klop, klop* of hoofs and occasional shouts of laughter. All races of the earth seemed to be represented. It was like a Congress of the Nations at some great exposition. French, Germans, Italians, Russians, Dutchmen, British, were to be recognized and to be expected. But also were strange peoples—Turks, Arabs, Negroes, Chinese, Kanakas, East Indians, the gorgeous members of the Spanish races, and nondescript queer people to whom neither Nan nor Keith could assign a native habitat. At every step one or the other called delighted attention to some new exhibit. Most extraordinary were, possibly, the men from the gold mines of the Sierras, These were mostly young, but long haired, bearded, rough, wilder than any mortal man need be. They walked with a wide swagger. Their clothes were exaggeratedly coarse, but they ornamented themselves with bright silk handkerchiefs; with feathers, flowers; with squirrel or buck-tails In their hats; with long heavy chains of nuggets; with glittering and prominently displayed pistols, revolvers, stilettos, knives, or dirks. Some had plaited their beards in three tails; others had tied their long hair under their chins. But even the most bizarre seemed to attract no attention. San Francisco was accustomed to it.

Indeed, the few fashionable strollers were much more stared at. Most of the well dressed were in some sort of vehicle. The Keiths saw many buggies like their own. A few very smart, or rather very ornamental, double rigs dashed by. In these sat generally good-looking but rather loud young women, who stared straight ahead with an assumption of supreme indifference. Hacks or omnibuses careered along. In these the company was generally merry but mixed, though occasionally a good-looking couple had hired an ordinary public conveyance. Horsemen and horsewomen were numerous. Some of these were very dashing indeed, the women with long trailing skirts and high hats from which floated veils; the men with skin-tight trousers strapped under varnished boots, and long split-skirted coats. Others were simply plain a-horseback. The native Californians with their heavy, silver-mounted saddles, braided rawhide reins and bridles, their sombreros, their picturesque costumes, and their magnificent fiery horses made a fine appearance. Occasionally screaming, bouncing Chinese, hanging on with both hands, would dash by at full speed, their horses quite uncontrolled, their garments flying, ecstatically scared and happy, causing great confusion, and pursued by curses.

"Evidently we're headed in the right direction," remarked Keith.

After a drive of two or three miles, never far from the bay they arrived at what had evidently been a sleepy little village. The original low, picturesque, red-tiled adobe buildings still clustered about the Mission. But much had been added. The Keiths found themselves in an immense confusion. Screaming signs cried everywhere for attention—advertising bear pits, cock fights, theatrical attractions, side shows, and the like. Innumerable hotels and restaurants, small, cheap, and tawdry, offered their hospitality, the liquid part of which was already being widely accepted. Men were striking pegs with hammers, throwing balls at negroes' heads thrust through canvas, shooting at targets. A racecourse was surrounded. Dust rose in choking clouds, and the sun beat down heavily.

"Goodness, what a place!" cried Nan in dismay.

Had they known it, there were many quiet, attractive, outlying resorts catering to and frequented by the fashionables, for "the Mission" was at that time in its heyday as a Sunday amusement for all classes. As it was, Keith drove on through the village, and so out to a winding country road.

"This is heavenly," said Nan, and laid aside her veil.

The road wound and meandered through the low hills of the peninsula. The sun beat down on them in a flood, only its heat, no longer oppressive, had become grateful.

"Doesn't it feel good on your back!" exclaimed Nan, recognizing this quality. "One seems to soak it in—just the way a thirsty plant soaks water."

The rounded hills were turning a ripe soft brown. Across their crests the sky looked very blue. High in the heavens some buzzards were sailing. Innumerable quail called. On tree tops perched yellow-breasted meadow larks with golden voices. In the bottom of the narrow valley where the road wound were green willow trees and a little trickle of water. From the ground came upward waves of heat and a pungent clean odour of some weed. Nan was excited and keenly receptive to impressions.

"It's a hot day!" she cried, "and the road is dusty. By rights it ought to e disagreeable. But it isn't! Why is that?"

The little valley widened into a pocket. Back from the road stood a low white much house. Its veranda was smothered in the gorgeousness of bougainvillaea. A grave, elderly, bearded Spaniard, on horseback, passed them at a smooth shuffling little trot, and gave them a sonorous *buenas dias*, The road mounted rapidly. Once when Keith had reined in to breathe the horse, they heard the droning crescendo hum of a new swarm of bees passing overhead.

"Isn't this nice!" cried Nan, snuggling against Keith's arm.

Suddenly, over the crest and down the other side, they came on sand hills. The horse plodded along at a walk. Nan hung far out watching, fascinated, the smooth, clean sand dividing before the wheels and flowing back over the rim, and so over a little rise, and the sea was before them.

"Oh, the Pacific!" exclaimed she, sitting up very straight.

The horse broke into a trot along the smooth hard shore. The wind was coming in from the wide spaces. A taste of salt was in the air. Foam wreaths advanced and receded with the edge of the wash, or occasionally blew in a mass across the flat, until gradually they scattered and dissipated. The horse pricked up his ears, breathed deep of the fresh cool air, expanded his nostrils snorting softly, pretended to shy at the foam wreaths.

The wash advanced and drew back with a soft hissing sound; the wind blew flat and low, so that even on the wet parts a fine, white, dried mist of sand was always scurrying and hurrying along close to the ground. Outside the surges reared and fell with a crash.

After the tepid or heated atmosphere of the hills the air was unexpectedly cool and vital. A flock of sickle-billed curlews stood motionless until they were within fifty yards; then rose and flew just inside the line of the breakers, uttering indescribably weird and lonely cries. A long file of pelicans, their wings outspread, sailed close to the surface of the ocean, undulating over the waves and into the hollows exactly paralleling, at a height of only a few feet, the restless contour of the sea. Occasionally they would all flop their wings two or three times in unison.

"I believe it's a sort of game—they're having fun!" stated Nan with conviction.

Everything seemed to be having fun. Close to the wash were forty or fifty tiny white sanderlings in a compact band. When the wash receded they followed it with an incredibly rapid twinkling of little legs; and when again the wave rushed, shoreward, *scuttle, scuttle, scuttle* went they, keeping always just at the edge of the water. Never were they forced to wing; yet never did they permit the distance to widen between themselves and the inrushing or outrushing wave. There were also sundry ducks. These swam just inside the breakers, and were carried backward and forward by the surges. Always they faced seaward. At the very last instant, as a great curler bent over them, they dipped their heads and dived. If the wave did not break, however, they rode over its top. Their accuracy of eye was uncanny. Time after time they gauged the wave so closely that they just flipped over the crest as it crashed with a roar beneath them. A tenth of a second later would have destroyed them. Keith reined up the horse to watch them and the sanderlings.

"It *is* a game," he agreed after a while, "just like the pelicans. It isn't considered sporting for sanderlings to get more than three inches away from the edge of the wash; or for a duck to dive unless he actually has to. It must be a game; for they certainly aren't catching anything."

At this moment the sanderlings as though at a signal sprang into the air, wheeled back and forth with instantaneous precision, and departed. The ducks, too, dove, and came up only outside the surf.

"Good little sportsmen," laughed Keith; "they play the game for its own sake. They don't like an audience."

After a few miles they came to a cliff reaching down to the beach and completely barring the way. Off shore were rocky islets covered with seals and sea lions. A lone blue heron stood atop a sand dune, absolutely motionless.

"I don't know where we are, or how we get out," said Keith, "but I'm going to take that chap there as a sign post," and he turned his horse directly toward the heron.

Sure enough, a track led them through the sand, and by a zigzag route to the top of the knoll that had barred their way along the shore. They came to an edge. Before them lay an arm of the sea, sweeping and eddying with a strong incoming tide. Over the way stood a great mountain, like a sentinel. Far to their right the arm widened. There was a glimpse of sparkling blue, and of the pearl of far-off hills, and the haze of a distant dim peak.

"It's the Golden Gate!" cried Keith in sudden enlightenment.

He told her that the mountain over the way must be Tamalpais; that the pearl-gray, far-off hills must be Contra Costa; that the distant dim peak was undoubtedly Mount Diabolo. She repeated the syllables after him softly, charmed by their music.

Simultaneously they discovered that they were hungry. The wind whipped in from the sea. An outpost tent or so marked the distant invisible city over the hills. Keith turned his horse's head toward them. They drove back across what are now the Presidio hills.

But in a hollow they came upon another ranch house, like the first—low, white, red roofed, covered with vines. Keith insisted on driving to it. A number of saddled horses dozed before the door, a half-dozen dogs sprawled in the dust, fowls picked their way between the horses' legs or over the dogs' recumbent forms. At the sound of wheels several people came from the shadow of the porch into the open. They proved to be Spanish Californians dressed in the flat sombreros, the short velvet jackets, the slashed trousers, and soft leather *zapatos*. The men, handsome, lithe, indolent, pressed around the wheels of the buggy, showing their white teeth in pleasant smiles.

"Can we get anything to eat here?" asked Keith.

They all smiled again most amiably. The elder swept off his hat with a free gesture.

"*A piedes ouestros, senora,*" he said, "*pero no hablo Ingles. Habla usted Espanol?*"

Keith understood the last three words.

"No," he shook his head violently, "no *Espanol*. Hungry." He pinted to Nan, then to himself: "She, me, hungry."

This noble effort brought no results, except that the Californians looked are distressed and solicitous than ever.

"They don't understand us," murmured Nan; "don't you think we'd better drive on?"

But Keith, who had now descended from the buggy, resorted

to sign language. e rubbed his stomach pathetically and pointed down his open mouth; as an afterthought he rubbed the horse's belly; then, with apparent intention, he advanced toward Nan. A furious red inundated her face and neck, and she held her little parasol threateningly between them. Everybody burst into laughter.

"*Si! si! si!*" they cried.

Several started to unharness the horse. Others held out their hands. After moment's hesitation Nan accepted their aid and descended. Keith's performance was evidently considered a great joke.

On the low veranda were two women, one most enormously fat, the other young and lithe. They were dressed almost exactly alike, their blue—black hair parted smoothly over their foreheads but built up to a high structure behind, filmy *rebosas* over high combs, and skirts with many flowered flounces. They both had soft, gentle eyes, and they were both so heavily powdered that their complexions were almost blue. All the men explained to hem at once. The younger answered gayly; the older listened with entire placidity. But when the account was finished, she reached out to pat Nan's and, and to smile reassuringly.

Various foods and a flask of red wine were brought. There was no constraint, for Keith threw himself with delighted abandon into experiments with sign language.

"*Esta simpatica*," the Californians told each other over and again.

Their manners were elaborate, dignified, deliberate, and beautiful. Keith, ordinarily rather direct and brusque, to Nan's great amusement became exactly like them. They outvied each other. The women touched smilingly the stuff of Nan's gown, and directly admired her various feminine trappings. She, thus encouraged, begged permission to examine more closely the lace of the *rebosas* or the beautiful embroidery on the shawls. A little feeling of intimacy drew them all together, although they understood no word of each other's language.

One of the dogs now approached and gravely laid its nose on Nan's knee, gazing up at her with searching soft eyes. The older woman cried out scandalized, but Nan shook her head, and patted the beast's nose.

"You like?" asked the woman.

"Why, you do talk English!" cried Nan.

But either these two words were all the woman had, or she was unwilling to adventure further.

"You like?" she repeated again, after a moment, and then, observing Nan's interest, she uttered a command to one of the numerous ragged small boys standing about. The urchin darted away, to return after a moment with a basket, which he emptied on the ground. Four fuzzy puppies rolled out.

"Oh, the darlings!" cried Nan.

The little animals proceeded at once to roll one another over, growling fiercely, charging uncertainly about, gazing indeterminately through their blue infantile eyes. The mother left her position at Nan's knee to hover over them; turning them over with her nose, licking them, skipping nimbly sidewise when they charged down upon her with an idea of nourishment.

Nan was enchanted. She left the bench to stoop to their level, tumbling them over on their backs; playfully boxing their ears, working them up to a wild state of yapping enthusiasm.

"The little darlings!" she cried; "just see their fat little tummies! And their teeth are just like needles. No, no, you mustn't! You'll tear my flounces! Look, Milton, see this little rascal pull at my handkerchief!"

Stewart Edward White

Her cheeks were flushed, and as she looked up laughing from beneath her at, she made a very charming picture.

"You like," stated the Californian woman with conviction.

After a while it became time to go. Vaqueros brought out the horse and harnessed it to the buggy. Keith made a movement to offer payment, but correctly interpreted the situation and refrained. They mounted the vehicle.

"*Muchas gracias!*" Nan enunciated slowly.

This effort was received with an admiring acclaim that flushed Nan with an inordinate pride. She had picked up the phrase from hearing it used at able. The fat woman came forward, one of the puppies tucked under her arm. In spite of her apparently unwieldy size she moved gracefully and lightly. "You like?" she inquired, holding the squirming puppy at arm's length.

"*Si, si, muchas gracias!*" cried Nan eagerly, and employing at once all her Spanish vocabulary. She deposited the puppy in her lap and reached out o shake hands. Keith flicked the horse with his whip. He, too, had recollected a word of Spanish, and he used it now.

"*Adios!*" he shouted.

But their hosts had a better phrase.

"*Vaya Con Dios!*" they cried in chorus.

Nan was in raptures over the whole episode, but especially over the puppy. The latter, with the instantaneous adaptability of extreme youth, had nuggled down into a compact ball, and was blinking one hazy dark blue eye pward at his new mistress.

"Weren't they nice people," cried Nan, "and wasn't it an adventure? And isn't he just the dearest, cutest little thing?

You're not a little Spanish dog any more, you know. You're a—what is it they call us?—oh, yes! You're a gringo now. Why, that's a fine idea! Your name is Gringo!"

And Gringo he became henceforth.

"What kind of a dog is he?" she asked.

Keith grinned sardonically.

"Of course I do not know his honoured father," said he, "so I cannot offer an opinion as to that half of him. But on his mother's side he is bloodhound, bulldog, collie, setter, pointer, St. Bernard, and Old English sheepdog."

"Which?" asked Nan puzzled.

"All," asserted Keith.

Now suddenly the sun was blotted out. They looked back: a white bank of fog was rolling in from the sea. It flowed over the hills like a flood, reaching long wisps down into the hollows, setting inertly in the flats and valleys, the upper part rolling on and over in a cascade. Beneath its shadow the warmth and brightness of the world had died.

"It strikes me we're going to be cold," remarked Keith, urging forward the horse.

The roadbed became more solid, and they trotted along freely. The horse, also, was anxious to get home. Signs of habitations thickened. The wide waste hills of the ranchos had been left behind. Here and there were outlying dwellings, or road houses, the objectives of pleasure excursions of various sorts and degrees of respectability from the city. From one of the latter came a hail.

"Oh, Keith! I say, Keith!"

From a group of people preparing to enter a number of vehicles two men came running. Ben Sansome and Morrell, somewhat out of breath, came alongside. They were a little flushed and elevated, but very cordial, and full of reproaches that Keith had so entirely dropped out of sight during the past week.

"I tell you, you must come over to our house for supper," said Morrell finally. "Everybody comes."

"The Morrells' Sunday night suppers are an institution," supplemented Sansome.

"I wish I could persuade you," urged Morrell. "I wonder where Mimi is. I know Mrs. Morrell ought to call, and all that sort of thing, but this is not a conventional place. We live next door, y'know. Do be delightful and neighbourly, and come!"

Nan hesitated; but the lure of the well-dressed company, so thoroughly at ease with one another, was irresistible in the reaction. She accepted.

XI

The Keiths arrived to find the Morrells' informal party in full blast. The front parlour was filled with a number of people making a great noise. Out of the confusion Mrs. Morrell arose and came to them, as they stood where the China-man had abandoned them.

"Mimi" Morrell was a tall woman, not fat, but amply built, with a full bust and hips. Her hair was of the peculiar metallic golden blond that might or might not have been natural; her skin smooth and white, but coarse in grain, would look better at night than by daylight. Her handsome, regular features were rather hard and set in their expression when in absolute repose, but absolute repose was rare to them. In action they softened to a very considerable feminine allurement. She moved with decision, and possibly her general attitude smacked the least bit of running things. She gave the impression of keeping an eye open for everything going on about her. To Nan she seemed tremendous, overwhelming, and a little magnificent.

Immediately, without introductions, the whole party moved through the double doors into the dining-room. There they took their places at a table set out lavishly with food and drink in great quantity. Mrs. Morrell explained in her high level voice that servants and service were always dispensed with at her Sunday nights. She rather carelessly indicated a seat to Mrs. Keith, and remarked to Keith that he was to sit next herself Otherwise the party distributed itself. Ben Sansome promptly annexed the chair next to Nan, and started in to

Stewart Edward White

make himself agreeable.

A complete freemasonry obtained among all the party. There was a great deal of shouting back and forth, from one end of the table to the other. Each seemed to have a nickname. One young man was known exclusively as "Popsy," another answered as "Zou-zou," a third was called "Billy Goat"; a very vivid, flashing young woman was "Teeny," and so on. They conversed, or rather shouted, to a great extent by means of catch words or phrases, alluding evidently to events the purport of which the Keiths could by no possibility guess. There were a great many private jokes, the points of which were obvious to only one or two. Every once in a while some one would say "Number Seven!" and everybody would go off into convulsions of laughter. The vivid young woman called Teeny suddenly shrieked, "How about Friday, the twenty-third?" at Popsy, to Popsy's obvious consternation and confusion. Immediately every one turned on either Popsy or Teeny, demanding the true inwardness of the remark. Popsy defended himself, rather pink and embarrassed. The young woman, a devilish knowing glint in her eyes, her red underlip caught between her teeth, refused to answer.

Keith warmed to this free and easy atmosphere. He was friendly and sympathetic with the lively crowd. But in vain he tried for a point of contact. All this badinage depended on a previous knowledge and intimacy, and that, of course, he lacked. Mrs. Morrell, sitting beside him very straight and commanding, delivered her general remarks in a high, clear voice, turning her attention impartially now to one part of the noisy table, now to another.

Suddenly she abandoned the company to its own devices, and leaning her left elbow on the table, she turned squarely to Keith, enveloping him with a magnetic all-for-you look.

"Do you know," she said abruptly, "something tells me you are musical."

"Why, I am, a little," admitted Keith, surprised. "But how could you tell?"

"La, now, I was sure you had a voice the first time I heard you speak. I adore music, and I can always tell."

"Do you sing, too?" asked Keith.

"I? No, unfortunately. I have no more voice than a crow. I strum a bit, but even that has been a good deal neglected lately. There's no temptation to keep up one's music here. I don't know a single soul in all this city who cares a snap of their finger for it."

"We'll have to have some music together," suggested Keith.

"I'd adore it. Isn't it lucky we're neighbours? I've been so interested"—she said it as though she had almost intended to say "amused"—"in watching you this past week. You are the most domestic man I know. I never saw a man work so singlemindedly at his house and home. Domesticity is a rare outworn virtue here, I assure you. It is really quite touching to see a man so devoted these days."

She said these things idly, a little disjointedly, looking at him steadily all the while. Her manner was detached, and yet somehow it impelled him strongly to protest that he was really not a bit domestic.

"Have you met any of the people of the place?" she shifted suddenly,

"Well—I really haven't had much chance yet—a few of the men."

"Well—you'll find things pretty mixed. Don't expect much; one has to take things pretty much as one finds them."

To this simple speech was appended one gesture only—a

slight raising of the eyebrows. Yet the effect was to sweep Keith into the intimacy of an inner circle, to suggest that she, too, found society mixed, and to imply—very remotely—that at least certain members of the present company itself were not quite what he—or she—would choose in another environment. In unconscious response to this unspoken thought, Keith glanced about the table. There was a good deal of drinking going on; and the fun was becoming even more obvious and noisy. Mrs. Morrell occasionally sipped at her champagne. She emitted a slight but rather disturbing perfume.

"Why did you come out here, anyway?" she asked him. "I can't make out. I'm curious."

"Why shouldn't I?" demanded Keith.

"Well, men come here either for money, for adventure, or to make a career." She marked each on the tablecloth with the end of a fork. "Which is it?"

"Guess," laughed Keith.

"You don't need money—or else you have a wonderful nerve to take the Boyle house. I believe you have the nerve, all right. Men with your sort of close curly hair are never—bashful!" she laughed shortly.

"Boyle's rent is safe—for a while," admitted Keith.

"Career?" she went on, looking him in the eyes speculatively, and allowing her gaze to sink deep into his. He noticed that her eyes were a gray green, like semi-precious stones of some sorts, with surface lights, but also with grayer radiations that seemed to go below the surface to smouldering depths— disturbing eyes, like the perfume. "Career?" she repeated. "I think you hold yourself better—a career in the riff-raff of this town." She shook her head archly. "But adventure! Oh, la! There's plenty of that—all sorts!" She gave the impression of meaning a great deal more than she said. "I wish I were a man!" she exclaimed, and laughed.

"I'm glad you're not," rejoined Keith sincerely.

She tapped him lightly on the arm with her fan.

"Oh, la!" she cried.

Keith laughed meaningly and mischievously. He was feeling entirely at home—in his mental shirtsleeves—thoroughly at ease.

"You're a lawyer, are you not?" she asked him.

"Try to be."

"Going to practise?"

"If any practice comes my way."

She looked at him, smiling slowly.

"Oh, it'll come fast enough." She seized her glass and held it to him. "Here's to your career!" she cried. "Bottoms up!"

They clinked glasses and drank.

"You must meet people—influential people," she told him. "We must see what we can do; I'll have some of them in."

"You're simply fine to take all this trouble for me!"

She tapped him again on the arm.

"Silly! We take care of our own people, of *course!* Let's plan it. Have you any connections in town at all?"

"Well, I've met quite a few people about town, and I have

some letters."

"Casual acquaintances are well enough, but your letters?"

"I have one to Calhoun Bennett, and to Mr. Dempster, and Mr. Farwell, and Truett—"

But she was making a wry face.

"What's the matter with, them?" he demanded.

"Cal Bennett's all right—but the others—oh, I suppose they're all right in a business way—but—"

"But, what?"

She made a helpless little gesture.

"I can't describe it—you know—the sort that are always so keen on doing their *duty!*"

She laughed; and to his subconscious surprise Keith found himself saying sympathetically:

"I know the sort of people who always pay their debts!"

They looked into each other's eyes and laughed in comradeship. In sober life Keith did his duty reasonably well, and was never far behind financially.

She fell silent for a moment; then with a muttered "excuse me," she leaned directly across his shoulder to impart something low-voiced and giggly to the woman on his right. To do this she leaned her breast against his arm and shoulder. The conversation lasted some seconds. Keith could not hear a word of it; but he was disturbingly aware of her perfume, the softness of her body, and the warmth that struck even through the intervening clothing. She drew back with a half apology.

"Feminine nonsense," she told him. "Mere man couldn't be expected to understand." She was herself a little flushed from leaning over, but she appeared not to notice Keith's rather breathless state. He muttered something, and gulped at his champagne.

"Do you know Mrs. Sherwood?" he asked, merely to say something,

But to his surprise Mrs, Morrell answered him shortly, her manner changing:

"No, I don't. We draw the line *somewhere*!"

Again she addressed the woman on the right, but this time without leaning across:

"Oh, Amy, the fair Patricia has another victim!" and laughed rather shrilly. Suddenly she rapped the table with the handle of a knife. "Stop it!" she cried to the company at large. "You're making too much noise!"

They all turned to her except one youth who was too noisily busy with his partner to have heard her. Failing in another attempt to get his attention, Mrs. Morrell picked up a chunk of French bread and hurled it at him.

"Good shot!" "Bravo!" "Encore!" came a burst of applause, as the bread, largely by accident, took him squarely between the eyes.

The youth, though astonished, was game. He retaliated in kind. Keith whipped up an empty plate and intercepted it. The youth's partner came to his assistance. Keith, a plate in either hand, deftly protected Mrs. Morrell from the flying missiles. The implied challenge was instantly accepted by all. The air was full of bread. Keith's dexterity was tested to the utmost, but he came through the battle with flying colours. Everybody threw bread. There was much explosive laughter, that soon became fairly exhausting. The battle ceased, both because the combatants were out of ammunition, and because they were too weak from mirth to proceed. Keith with elaborate mock gallantry turned and presented Mrs. Morrell with the two plates.

"The spoils of war!" he told her.

"He should be decorated for conspicuous gallantry on the field of battle!" cried some one.

The idea took. But they could find nothing appropriate until Teeny McFarlane deliberately stepped up on the table and broke from the glass chandelier one of its numerous dangling prisms. This called forth a mild protest from Morrell—"Oh, I say!"—which was drowned in a wild shriek of delight. The process of stepping down from the table tilted Teeny's wide skirts so that for an instant a slim silken leg was plainly visible as far as the knee. "Oh! oh!" cried every one. Some pretended to be shocked, and covered their faces with spread fingers; others feigned to try for another look. Teeny was quite unperturbed.

Keith was the centre of attention and a great success. But there were no more tete-a-tetes. Mrs. Morrell managed to convey the idea that she was displeased, and Keith was of a sufficiently generous and ingenuous disposition to be intrigued by the fact. He had no chance to probe the matter. In a moment or so Mrs. Morrell rose and strolled toward the drawing-room. The others straggled after her. She rather liked thus to emphasize her lack of convention as a hostess, making a pose of never remembering the proper thing to do. Now she moved here and there, laughing her shrill rather mirthless laugh, calling everybody "dearie," uttering abrupt little platitudes. Keith found himself left behind, and rather out in the cold. The company had quite frankly segregated itself into couples. The room was well adapted to this, filled as it was with comfortable chairs arranged with apparent carelessness two by two. The men lighted cigars. Keith saw Nan's eyes widen at this. She was sitting near the fire, and Sansome had penned her in beyond the possibility of invasion by a third. At this date smoking was a more or less doubtfully considered habit, and in the best society men smoked only in certain rigidly specified circumstances. In a drawing-room such an action might be considered the fair equivalent to powdering the feminine nose.

In such a condition, Keith was left rather awkwardly alone, and was fairly thrust upon a fictitious interest in a photograph album, at which he glowered for some moments. Then by a well-planned and skilfully executed flank movement he caught Mrs. Morrell.

"Look here," he demanded; "what has the standing army done to deserve abandonment in a hostile country?"

But she looked at him directly, without response to his playful manner.

"My friend," she said, "this is a pretty free and easy town, as no doubt you have observed, and society is very mixed. But we haven't yet come to receiving women like Mrs. Sherwood, or relishing their being mentioned to us."

"Why, what's the matter with her?" demanded Keith, astonished. "Is she as far from respectability as all that?"

"Respectable! That word isn't understood in San Francisco." She appeared suddenly to soften. "You're a dear innocent boy, so you are, and you've got a dear innocent little wife, and I'll have to look out for you."

Before the deliberate and superior mockery in her eyes as well as in her voice, Keith felt somehow like a small boy. He was stung to a momentary astonishing fury.

"By God——" he began, and checked himself with difficulty.

She smiled at him slowly.

"Perhaps I didn't mean all of that," she said; "perhaps only half of it," she added with significance. "My personal opinion is that you are likely to be a curly haired little devil; and when you look at me like that, I'm glad we're not alone."

She looked at him an enigmatic moment, then turned away from the table near which they had been standing. "Come, help me break up some of this 'twosing,'" she said.

Shortly after this the party dispersed. Mrs. Morrell said good-bye to them carelessly, or not at all, according as it happened.

"You must come again, come often," she told the Keiths. "It's pretty dull unless you make your own fun." She was half sleepily conventional, her lids heavy. "Perhaps we can have some music soon," she added. The words were careless, but she shot Keith an especial gleam.

The Keiths walked sociably home together, almost in silence. Keith, after his habit, superexcited with all the fun, the row, and the half-guilty boyish feeling of having done a little something he ought not to have done, did not want to seem too enthusiastic.

"Jolly crowd," he remarked.

"They were certainly noisy enough," said Nan indifferently; then after a moment, "Where *do* you suppose some of them get their clothes?"

Keith's mind was full of the excitement of the evening. He found himself reviewing the company, appraising it, wondering about it. Was Teeny McFarlane as gay as she appeared? He had never seen women smoke before; but that dark girl with the red thing in her hair puffed a cigarette. Perhaps she was Spanish—he had not met her. And Mrs. Morrell—hanged if he quite dared make her out—it wouldn't do to jump to conclusions nor too hastily to apply Eastern standards; this was a new country, fatal to make a fool mistake;

well-built creature, by gad—

Nan interrupted his thoughts. He came to with a start.

"I think we'd better put the big armchair in the front room, after all," she was saying.

XII

Next morning Keith allayed what little uneasiness his conscience might harbour by remarking, as he adjusted his collar:

"Mrs. Morrell is an amusing type, don't you think? She's a bit vulgar, but she seems good hearted. Wonder what colour her hair used to be?"

"I suppose they are all right," said Nan. "They are a little rowdy. They gave me a headache."

Illogically rehabilitated in his own self-esteem, Keith went on dressing. He was "on" to Mrs. Morrell; her methods were pretty obvious. Wonder if she thought she had really fooled him? Next time he would be on guard and beat her at her own game. She was not a woman to his taste, anyway—he glanced admiringly at Nan's clean profile against the light—but she was full of vitality, she was keen, she was brimming with the joy of life.

The long drive over the Peninsula to the sea and back, the episode of the Spanish people, the rowdy supper party, had one effect, however: it had made so decided a break in the routine that Keith found himself thrust quite outside it. He had worked feverishly all the week, at about double speed; and in ordinary course would have gone on working feverishly at double speed for another week. Now, suddenly, the thought was irksome. He did not analyze this; but, characteristically, discovered an irrefutable reason for not going on with it. They rescued Gringo from Sam's care, and drove up to the house. On the way Keith said:

"Look here, Nan; do you suppose you and Wing can get on all right this morning? All the heavy work is done. I really ought to be settling the office and getting some lines laid for business."

"Why, of course we can get on, silly!" she rejoined. "This isn't your job, anyway. Of course you ought to attend to your business."

Keith again consulted Palmer, Cook & Co. The same clerk showed him offices. He was appalled at the rents. Even a miserable little back room in the obscurer blocks commanded a sum higher than he had anticipated paying. After looking at a dozen, he finally decided on a front room in the Merchants' Exchange Building. This was one of the most expensive, but Keith was tired of looking. The best is the greatest economy in the long run, he told himself, and with a lawyer, new-come, appearances count for much in getting clients. Must get the clients, though, to support this sort of thing! The rest of the morning he spent buying furniture.

About noon he walked back to the Bella Union. His horse and buggy were not hitched to the rail, so he concluded Nan had not yet returned for lunch. Mrs. Sherwood, however, was seated in a rocker at the sunny end of the long veranda. She looked most attractive, her small smooth head bent over some sort of fancywork. Before she looked up Keith had leisure to note the poise of her head and shoulders, the fine long lines of her figure, and the arched-browed serenity of her eyes. Different type this from the full-breasted Morrell, more— more patrician! Rather absurd in view of their respective places in society, but a fact. Keith found himself swiftly speculating on Mrs. Sherwood's origin and experience. She was endowed with a new glamour because of Mrs. Morrell's enigmatic remark the evening before, and also—for Keith was very human—with a new attraction. Feeling vaguely and boyishly devilish, Keith. stopped.

She nodded at him, laying her work aside.

"You are practically invisible." she told him. "Making ourselves a habitation. Seen Mrs. Keith?"

"No. I don't think she's come in."

Keith hesitated, then:

"I think I'll go up to the house for her."

Mrs. Sherwood nodded, and resumed her work calmly, without further remark.

At the house Keith found Nan, her apron on, her hair done up under a dust cap, very busy.

"Noon?" she cried, astonished. "It can't be! But I can't stop now. I think I'll have Wing pick me up a lunch. There's plenty in the house. It's too much bother to clean up."

Keith demurred; then wanted to stay for the pick-up lunch himself. Nan would have none of it. She was full of repressed enthusiasm and eagerness, but she wanted to get rid of him.

"There's not enough. I wouldn't have you around. Go away, that's a good boy! If you'll leave Wing and me entirely alone we'll be ready to move in to-morrow."

"Where's Gringo?" asked Keith by way of indirect yielding— he had really no desire for a picked-up lunch.

"The little rascal! He started to chew everything in the place, so I tied him in the backyard. He pulls and flops dreadfully. Do you think he'll strangle himself?"

Keith looked out the window. Gringo, all four feet planted, was determinedly straining back against his tether. The collar had pulled forward all the loose skin of his neck, so that his eyes and features were lost in wrinkles.

"He doesn't yap," volunteered Nan.

Keith gave it as his opinion that Gringo would stop short of suicide, commended Gringo's taciturnity and evident perseverance, and departed for the hotel. In the dining-room he saw Mrs. Sherwood in a riding habit, eating alone. Keith hesitated, then took the vacant seat opposite. She accorded this permission cordially, but without coquetry, remarking that Sherwood often did not get in at noon. Immediately she turned the conversation to Keith's affairs, inquiring in detail as to how the settling was getting on, when they expected to get in, how they liked the house, whether they had bought all the furniture. "You remember I directed you to the auctions?" she said.

She asked all these questions directly, as a man would, and listened to his replies.

"I suppose you have an office picked out?" she surmised.

At his mention of the Merchants' Exchange Building she raised her arched eyebrows half humorously.

"You picked out an expensive place."

Keith went over his reasoning, to which she listened with a half smile.

"You may be right," she commented; "the reasoning is perfectly sound. But that means you must get the business in order to make it pay. What are your plans?"

He confessed that as yet they were rather vague; there had not been time to do much—too busy settling.

Stewart Edward White

"The usual thing, I suppose," he added: "get acquainted, hang out a shingle, mix with people, sit down and starve in the traditional manner of young lawyers."

He laughed lightly, but she refused to joke.

"There are a good many lawyers here—and most of them poor ones," she told him. "The difficulty is to stand out above the ruck, to become noticed. You must get to know all classes, of course; but especially those of your own profession, men on the bench. Yes, especially men on the bench, they may help you more than any others—"

He seemed to catch a little cynicism in her implied meaning, and experienced a sense of shock on his professional side.

"You don't mean that judges are—"

"Susceptible to influence?" She finished the sentence for him with an amused little laugh. She studied him for an instant with new interest, "They're human—more human here than anywhere else—like the rest of us—they respond to kind treatment—" She laughed again, but at the sight of his face her own became grave. She checked herself. "Everything is so new out here. In older countries the precedents have all been established. Out here there are practically none. They are being made now, every day, by the present judges. Naturally personal influence might get a hearing for one point of view or the other—"

"I see what you mean," he agreed, his face clearing.

"Join a good fire company," she advised him. "That is the first thing to do. Each company represents something different, a different class of men."

"Which would you advise?" asked Keith seriously.

"That is a matter for your own judgment. Only, investigate

well. Meet all the people you can. Know the newspaper men, and the big merchants. In your profession you must cultivate men like Terry, Girvin, Shattuck, Gwin. Keep your eyes open. Be bold and use your wits. Above all, make friends; that's it, *make friends*—everybody, everywhere. Don't despise anybody. You will get plenty of chances." She was sitting erect, and her eyes were flashing. Her usual slow indolent grace had fallen from her; she radiated energy. Her slender figure took on a new appearance of knit strength. "Such chances! My heavens! if I were a man!"

"You'd make a bully man!" cried Keith. Mrs. Morrell, uttering the same wish, had received from him a different reply, but he had forgotten that.

She laughed again, the tension broke, and she sank back into her usual relaxed poise.

"But, thank heavens, I'm not," said she.

XIII

Affairs for the Keiths passed through another week of what might be called the transition stage. It took them that long to settle down in their new house and into some semblance of a routine—two days to the actual installation, and the evenings full of small matters to arrange. Nan was busy all day long playing with her new toy. The housekeeping was fascinating, and Wing Sam a mixture of delight and despair. Like most women who have led the sheltered life, she had not realized as yet that the customs of her own fraction of one per cent, were not immutable. Therefore, she tried to model the household exactly in the pattern of those to which she had been accustomed. Wing Sam blandly refused to be moulded.

Thus Nan spent all one morning drilling him in the proper etiquette of answering doors. Mindful of John McGlynn's advice, she did this by precept, ringing her own door bell, presenting a card as though calling on herself. Wing Sam's placid exterior changed not. half hour later the door bell rang, but no Wing Sam appeared to answer it. It rang again, and again, until Nan herself opened the door. On the doorstep stood Wing Sam himself.

"I foolee you, too," he announced with huge delight.

Painstakingly Nan conveyed to him that this was neither an amusing game nor a practical joke. Later in the day the door bell rang again. Nan, hovering near to gauge the result of her training, saw Wing Sam plant himself firmly in the opening.

"You got ticket?" he demanded sternly of the deliveryman outside. "You no got ticket, you no get in!"

Which, Nan rather hysterically gathered, was what Wing Sam had gained of the calling-card idea. After that, temporarily as she thought, Nan permitted him to go back to his own method, which, had she known it, was the method of every Chinese servant in California. The visitor found his bell answered by a blandly smiling Wing Sam, who cheerfully remarked: "Hullo!" It was friendly, and it didn't matter; but at that stage of her development Nan was more or less scandalized.

Nan's sense of humour always came to her assistance by evening, and she had many amusing anecdotes to tell Keith, over which both of them laughed merrily. Gringo added somewhat to the complications in life. He was a fat, roly-poly, soft-boned, ingratiating puppy, with a tail that waved energetically but uncontrolledly. Gringo at times was very naughty, and very much in the way. But when exasperation turned to vengeance he had a way of keeling over on his back, spreading his hind legs apart in a manner to expose his stomach freely to brutal assault, and casting one calm china-blue eye upward.

"Can there anywhere exist any one so hard-hearted as to injure a poor, absolutely defenceless dog?" he inquired, with full confidence in the answer.

The iniquities of Gringo and the eccentricities of Wing Sam Nan detailed at length, and also her experiences with the natives. She as yet looked on every one as natives. Only later could she expand to the point of including them in her cosmos of people. Nan was transplanted, and her roots had not yet struck down into the soil. In her shopping peregrinations she was making casual acquaintance, and she had not yet become accustomed to it.

"I bought some darling little casseroles at Phelan's to-day," she said. "The whole Phelan family waited on me. Where do you suppose the women get their perfectly awful clothes? Mrs. Phelan offered to take me to her milliner!" or "You know Wilkins—the furniture man where we got the big armchair? I was in there to-day, and he apologized because his wife hadn't called!"

They went to bed early, because they were both very tired.

Keith also had generally passed an interesting day. Immediately after breakfast he went to his office, and conscientiously sat a while. Sometimes he wrote letters or cast up accounts; but there could not be much of this to do. About ten or eleven o'clock his impatient temperament had had enough of this, so he drifted over to the Monumental engine house. After considerable thought he had decided to join this company. It represented about the class of men with whom he wanted to affiliate himself—the influential men of the lawyer, Southern-politician, large business men type. There were many of these volunteer organizations. Their main purpose was to fight fire; but they subserved other objects as well—political, social, and financial. David Broderick, for example, already hated and feared, partly owned and financed a company of ward-heelers who were introducing and establishing the Tammany type of spoils politics. Casey, later in serious trouble, practically manipulated another.

Among the Monumentals, Keith delighted especially in Bert Taylor. Bert Taylor likewise delighted in Keith. The little chubby man's enthusiasm for the company, while recognized as most valuable to the company's welfare, had ended by boring most of the company's members. But Keith was a new listener and avid for information. He had had no notion of how complicated the whole matter could be. Bert Taylor dissertated sometimes on one phase of the subject, sometimes on another.

"It's drills we need, and the fellows won't drill enough!" was Bert Taylor's constant complaint. "What do they know about hose? They run it out any way it comes; and roll it up anyhow, instead of doing a proper job."

"How should you do it?" asked Keith.

"It ought to be laid right—so there's no bends or sharp angles in it; it should never be laid over heaps of stones, or any kind of uneven surface—it all increases the water resistance. If there are any bends or curves they should be regular and even. The hose ought never to rest against a sharp edge or angle. And when you coil it up you ought to reverse the sides every time, so it will wear even and stretch even. Do they do it? Not unless I stand over them with a club!"

He showed Keith the hose, made of India rubber, a comparatively new thing, for heretofore hose had been made of riveted leather. Bert Taylor made him feel the inside of this hose with his forefinger to test its superlative smoothness.

"Mighty little resistance there!" he cried triumphantly.

The nozzles, all in racks, he handled with almost reverent care.

"These are the boys that cost the money," said Taylor. "If the inside isn't polished like a mirror the water doesn't come smooth. And the least little dent makes the stream ragged and broken. Nothing looks worse—and it isn't as effective on the fire. It ought to be thrown like a solid rod of water. I can't get the boys to realize that the slightest bruise, dent, or burr throws the stream in a ragged feathery foam. The result of that is that a lot of water is dissipated and lost."

Keith, who had taken hold of the nozzle rather negligently, returned it with the reverent care due crown jewels.

"How long a stream will it throw?" he asked.

"With thirty men on a side she's done a hundred and twelve feet high, and two hundred and eighteen for distance," said

Bert with simple pride.

He picked up the nozzle again.

"See here. Here's an invention of my own. Cost money to put it in, too, because every other nozzle on earth is made wrong."

He explained that other nozzles are made so that the thread of the hose screwed into the nozzle; while in his, the thread of the nozzle screwed into the hose.

"If there's a leak or a bad connection," explained Bert, "with the old type, the water is blown back into the fireman's face, and he is blinded. His whole efficiency depends on a close joint. But with my scheme the leak is blown forward, away from the lineman. It's a perfectly sound scheme, but I can't make them see it."

"Sounds reasonable," observed Keith, examining perfunctorily a device to which later he was to owe his life.

Item by item they went over the details of equipment—the scaling ladders, the jumping sheets, the branch pipes, the suction pipes, the flat roses, standcocks, goose necks, the dogtails, dam boards, shovels, saws, poleaxes, hooks, and ropes. From a consideration of them the two branched off to the generalities of fire fighting. Keith learned that the combating of a fire, the driving it into a corner, outflanking it, was a fine art.

"I say always, *get in close*," said Taylor. "A fire can be *put* out as well as just drowned out."

It struck Keith as interesting that in a room a stream should always be directed at the top of a fire, so that the water running down helps extinguish the flames below, whereas in attack at the bottom or centre merely puts out the immediate blaze, leaving the rest to spread upward or sideways. Taylor put himself on record against fighting fire from the street.

"Don't want a whole lot of water and row," he maintained. "Get in close quarters and make every drop count."

When Bert's enthusiasm palled, Keith always found men in the reading-room. The engine house was a sort of clearing house for politics, business schemes, personal affairs, or differences.

Once a day, also, as part of his job in his profession, Keith went to the courthouse. There he sat in the enclosure reserved for lawyers and listened to the proceedings, his legal mind alert and interested in the technical battles. At no time in the world's history has sheer technicality unleavened by common sense been carried further than in the early California courts. Even in the most law-ridden times elsewhere a certain check has been exercised by public opinion or the presence of business interests. But here was as yet no public opinion; and business interests, their energies fully taxed by the necessities of a new country, were willing to pay heavily to be let alone. Consequently, lawyers were permitted to play out their fascinating game to their hearts' content, and totally without reference to expedience or to the justice of the case. The battles were indeed intensely technical and shadowy. Points within points were fought bitterly. Often for days the real case at issue was forgotten.

Only one of the more obvious instances of technical triumph need be cited. One man killed another, on a public street, before many witnesses. The indictment was, however, thrown out and he released because it stated only that the victim was killed by a pistol, and failed to specify that his death was due to the discharge of said pistol. The lawyer who evolved this brilliant idea was greatly admired and warmly congratulated.

The wheels of the law ground very slowly. One of the simplest and most effective expedients of defence was delay. A case could be postponed and remanded, often until the witnesses were scattered or influenced. But there were infinite numbers of legal expedients, all most interesting to a man of Keith's profession. His sense of justice was naturally strong and warm, and an appeal to it outside a courtroom or a law office always got an immediate and commonsense response. But inside the law his mind automatically closed, and a "case" could have only legal aspects. Which is true of the majority of lawyers today.

On the adjournment of court Keith generally drifted over to the El Dorado or the Empire, where he spent an hour or so loafing with some of his numerous acquaintances. He was of the temperament that makes itself quickly popular, the laughing, hearty sort, full of badinage, and genuinely liking most men with whom he came in contact. There was always much joking in the air, but back of it was a certain reserve, a certain wariness, for every second man was a professed "fire-eater," given to feeling insulted on the slightest grounds, and flying to the duel or the street fight instanter.

This hour was always most pleasant to Keith; nevertheless, he went home about five o'clock in order to enjoy an hour or so of daylight about the place. He performed prodigies of digging in the new garden: constructing terraces, flower beds, walks, and the like. While the actual construction work was under way he was greatly interested, but cared nothing for the finished product or the mere growing of the flowers.

Gringo received his share of training, at first to his intense disgust. Twice he refused obedience, and the matter being pressed, resorted to the simple expedient of retiring from the scene. Keith dropped everything and pursued. Gringo crawled under things, but was followed even to the dustiest and cob-webbiest farthest corner under the porch; he tried swiftness and dodging, but was trailed in all his doublings and twistings at top speed; he tried running straight away over the sand hills, and at first left his horrible master behind, but the horrible master possessed a horrible persistence. Finally he shut his eyes and squatted, expecting instant annihilation, but instead was haled back to the exact scene of his disobedience, and the command repeated. Nan laughed until the tears came, over the large, warm, red-faced man after the small, obstinate, scared pup, but Keith refused to joke.

"If he finds he can't get away, no matter what happens, I'll never have to do it again," he panted. "But if he wins out, even once, it'll be an awful job."

Gringo tried twice. Then, his faith in his ability to escape completely shattered, he gave up. After that he adored Keith and was always under his feet.

Keith saw nothing of any of the women. Mrs. Sherwood seemed to have dropped from their ken when they left the hotel. Once Keith inquired casually about Mrs. Morrell.

"She's been over twice to see the place," replied Nan.

"We ought to go over there to call," proffered Keith vaguely; but there the matter rested.

XIV

One night Keith was awakened by Nan's suddenly sitting up in bed. There came to his struggling consciousness the persistent steady clangour of many deep bells. Slowly recognition filtered into his mind—the fire bells!

He hastily pulled on some clothes and ran down the front stairs, stumbling over Gringo, who uttered an outraged yelp. From the street he could see a red glow in the sky. At top speed he ran down the street in the direction of the Monumental. In the half darkness he could make out other figures running. The deep tones of the bells continued to smite his ear, but now in addition he heard the tinkling and clinking of innumerable smaller bells—those on the machines. He dashed around a corner to encounter a double line of men, running at full speed, hauling on a long rope attached to an engine. Their mouths were open, and they were all yelling. The light engine careened and swayed and bumped. Two men clung to the short steering tongue, trying to guide it. They were thrown violently from side to side, dragged here and there, tripping, hauling, falling across the tongue, but managing to keep the machine from dashing off at a tangent. Above them, high and precarious, swayed the short stout figure of Bert Taylor. He was in full regalia—leather helmet, heavy leather belt, long-tailed coat, and in his free hand the chased silver speaking trumpet with the red tassels that usually hung on the wall. He was in his glory, dominating the horde. His keen eye, roving everywhere, seeing everything, saw Keith.

"Catch hold!" he roared through the trumpet.

Keith made a flying grab at a vacant place on the line, caught it, was almost jerked from his feet, recovered himself, and charged on, yelling like the rest.

But now Bert Taylor began to shriek something excitedly. It became evident, from glimpses caught down the side streets, but especially through the many vacant lots, that another engine was paralleling their own course a block away.

"Jump her, boys, jump her!" shrieked Bert Taylor. "For God's sake, don't let those Eurekas beat you!"

He danced about on top of the waterbox of the engine, in imminent peril of being jerked from his place, battering his silver trumpet insanely against the brake rods, beseeching, threatening profanely. And profanity at that time was a fine art. Men studied its alliteration, the gorgeousness of its imagery, the blast of its fire. The art has been lost, existing still, in a debased form, only among mule drivers, sailors, and the owners of certain makes of automobiles. The men on the rope responded nobly. The roar of their going over the plank road was like hollow thunder. A man dropped out. Next day it was discovered he had broken his leg in a hole. At tremendous speed they charged through the ring of spectators, and drew up, proud and panting, victors by a hundred feet, to receive the plaudits of the multitude. A handsome man on a handsome horse rode up.

"Monumentals on the fire! Eurekas on cistern number twenty!" he commanded briefly.

This was Charles Duane, the unpaid fire chief; a likable, efficient man, but too fond of the wrong sort of friends.

Now it became evident to Keith why Bert Taylor had urged them so strongly in the race. The fire was too distant from the water supply to be carried in one length of hose. Therefore, one engine was required to relay to another, pumping the water from the cistern, through the hose, and into the waterbox of the other engine. The other engine pumped it from its own waterbox on to the fire. The latter, of course, was the position of honour.

The Eurekas fell back grumbling, and uttering open threats to wash their rivals. By this they meant that they would pump water into the Monumentals faster than the latter could pump it out, thus overflowing and eternally disgracing them. They dropped their suction hose into the cistern, and one of their number held the end of the main hose over a little trapdoor in the Monumental's box. The crews sprang to the long brake handles on either side, and at once the regular *thud, thud, thud* of the pumps took up its rhythm. The hose writhed and swelled; the light engines quivered. Bert Taylor and the Eureka foreman, Carter by name, walked back and forth as on their quarterdecks, exhorting their men. Relays, in uniform assumed on the spot, stood ready at hand. Nobody in either crew knew or cared anything whatsoever about the fire. As the race became closer, the foremen got more excited, begging their crews to increase the stroke, beating their speaking trumpets into shapeless battered relics. An astute observer would now have understood one reason why the jewellery stores carried such a variety of fancy speaking trumpets. They were for presentation by grateful owners after the fire had been extinguished, and it was generally necessary to get a new one for each fire.

Keith, acting under previous instructions, promptly seized a helmet and poleaxe and made his way to the front. The fire had started in one of many flimsy wooden buildings, and had rapidly spread to threaten a whole district. Men from the hook and ladder companies were already at work on some of the hopeless cases. A fireman or two mounted ladders to the eaves, dragging with them a heavy hook on the end of a long pole. Cutting a small hole with their axes, they hooked on this apparatus and descended. As many firemen and volunteers as could get hold of the pole and the rope attached to it, now began to pull.

"Yo, heave ho!" they cried.

The timbers cracked, broke, the whole side of the house came out with a grand and satisfying crash. An inferno of flame was thereby laid open to the streams from the hose lines. It was grand destructive fun for everybody, especially for the boys of all ages, which included in spirit about every male person present.

This sort of work was intended, of course, to confine or check the fire within the area already affected, and could accomplish nothing toward saving the structures already alight. The roar of the flames, the hissing of firebrands sucked upward, the crash of timbers, the shrieks of the foremen through their trumpets, the yells of applause or of sarcasm from the crowd, and the *thud, thud, thud, thud* of numerous brake bars made a fine pandemonium. Everybody except the owners or tenants of the buildings was delighted.

Keith, with two others, was instructed to carry the Monumental nozzle to the roof of a house not afire. Proudly they proceeded to use their scaling ladders. These were a series of short sections, each about six feet long, the tops slightly narrower than the bottoms. By means of slots these could be fitted together. First, Keith erected one of them against the wall of the building, at an angle, and ascended it, carrying another section across his shoulder. When he reached a certain rung, which was painted red, he thrust his foot through the ladder and against the wall, pushed the ladder away from the wall, and fitted the section he was carrying to the top of the section on which he was standing. He then hauled up another section and repeated. When the ladder had reached to the eaves, he and his companions dragged the squirting, writhing hose up with them, chopped footholds in the roof, and lay flat to look over the ridgepole as over a breastwork. All this to the tune of admiring plaudits and with a pleasing glow of heroism. There was a skylight, but either they overlooked or scorned that prosaic expedient.

At the other end of the ridgepole Keith made out the dark forms of two men from another company. His own companions, acting under orders, now descended the ladder, leaving him alone.

The next building was a raging furnace, and on it Keith directed the heavy stream from his nozzle. It was great fun. At first the water seemed to have no effect whatever, but after a little it began to win. The flames were beaten back, broken into detachments. Finally, Keith got to the point of chasing down small individual outbreaks, driving them into their lairs, drowning them as they crouched. He was wholly interested, and the boy in him, with a shamefaced half apology to the man in him, pretended that he was a soldier directing a battery against an enemy.

Along the ridgepole cautiously sidled the two men of the other company, dragging their hose. Keith now recognized them. One was a vivid, debonair, all-confident, magnetic individual named Talbot Ward, a merchant, promoter, speculator, whom everybody liked and trusted; the other a fair Hercules of a man, slow and powerful in everything, called Frank Munro.

"Look here," said Ward, "does it strike you this roof's getting hot?"

Recalled to himself, Keith immediately became aware of the fact.

"The house is afire beneath us," said Ward; "we've got to get out."

"What's the matter with your ladder?" asked Keith.

"They took it away."

"We'll use mine."

They let themselves cautiously down the footholds that had been chopped in the roof, and looked over. A blast of smoke and flame met them in the face.

"Good Lord, she's all afire!" cried Keith, aghast.

The flames were licking around the scaling ladder, which was already blazing. Keith directed the stream from his hose straight down, but with no other result than to break the charred ladder.

They crawled back to the ridgepole, and worked their hose lines around to the end of the building, out of the flames. Here a two-story drop confronted them.

"This thing is going to fall under us if we don't do something," muttered Ward.

"Duane's forgotten us, and those crazy idiots at the engines are too busy trying to keep from being washed," surmised Keith.

"Look here," said Munro suddenly; "I'll brace against a chimney and hang on to the hose, and you can slide down it like a rope."

"How about you?" demanded Ward crisply.

"You can run for more ladders, once you're on the ground."

At this moment the water failed in Keith's hose. He stared at the nozzle, then rapidly began to unscrew it.

"Cistern empty or hose burst," surmised Munro.

But Talbot Ward, cocking his ear toward a distant pandemonium of cheering, guessed the true cause.

"Sucked," said he. By this he meant that the Monumental crew had succeeded in emptying their water box in spite of the

Eureka's best efforts.

"Get off your nozzle quick!" urged Keith.

Munro, without stopping to ask why, bent his great strength to the task; and it was a task, for in his hose the pressure of the water was tremendous. It spurted back all over him, and at the last the nozzle was fairly blown away from him.

"Now couple my hose to yours quick, quick, before my hose fills!" cried Keith.

"They won't go—" Munro began to object.

"Yes, they will, mine's a special thread," urged Keith, who had remembered Bert Taylor's reversed nozzle.

All three bent their energies to catching the threads. It was a fearful job, for the strength of the water had first to be overcome. Keith was terribly excited. Time was precious, for not only might the roof give way beneath them, but at any moment the water might come again in Keith's hose. Then it would be physically impossible to make the coupling. All three men concentrated their efforts on it, their feet gripping the irregularities of the roof or slipping on the shingles. Frank Munro bent his enormous back to the task, the veins standing out in his temples, his face turning purple with the effort. Keith helped him as well as he was able. Talbot Ward, coolly, deliberately, delicately, as though he had all the time in the world, manipulated the coupling, feeling gingerly for the thread. The water spurted, fanned, sprayed, escaping with violence, first at one point, then at another, drenching and blinding them.

"There!" breathed Ward at last, and with a few twists, of his sinewy hands brought the couplings into close connection. Munro relaxed, drawing two or three deep breaths. Without the aid of his great strength the task could not have been accomplished.

"Hook her over the chimney," gasped Keith.

With some difficulty they lifted the loop of the throbbing hose over the chimney.

"Down we go!" cried Keith, and slid hand over hand down the way thus made for them. The others immediately followed, and all three stood looking back. It was a wonder the building had stood so long, for in both stories it was afire, and the walls had apparently burned quite through. Indeed, a moment later the whole structure collapsed. A fountain of sparks and brands sprang upward in the mighty suction.

"There goes our good hose!" said Keith.

The remark brought them to wrath and a desire for vengeance.

"I'm going to lick somebody!" cried Keith, starting determinedly in the direction of the engine.

"We'll help," growled Munro.

But when they came in sight of the engine their anger evaporated, and they clung to each other, weak with mirth.

For the Monumental was "washed," and washed aplenty. This was natural, for now the water was pouring into her box from *both* directions, and would continue so to pour until the hose coupled to Ward's engine had burned through. The water was fairly spouting up from the box, not merely overflowing. Her crew were still working, but raggedly and dispiritedly. Bert Taylor, his trumpet battered beyond all recognition, was fairly voiceless with rage. An interested and ribaldry facetious crowd spared not its sarcasm.

"My crowd must be in the same fix!" gurgled Ward; "the back pressure has 'washed' them, too." Then the full splendour of the situation burst on him, and he fell again on Munro for support.

"Don't you see," he gasped. "They'll never know! The hose will burn through. Unless we tell, they'll never know! We've got even, all right."

At this moment Duane rode up, foaming at the mouth, and desiring to know what the assorted adjectives they were doing there. The crews awoke to their isolation and general uselessness. Bert Taylor, still simmering, descended from his perch. They followed the hose lines to glowing coals!

"Here, this won't do," said Talbot; so they reported themselves before the news of a tragedy had had time to spread.

The fire was now practically under control. It had swept a city block pretty clean, but had been confined to that area. An hour later they dragged their engine rather dispiritedly back to the house. Ordinarily they would have been in high spirits. Fires were to these men a good deal of a lark. The crews were very effective and well drilled, and the saving of property was as well done as possible, but that was all secondary to the game of it. But to-night they had been "washed," they had lost the game, and the fact that they had put out the fire cut very little figure. There was much bickering. It seemed that Bert Taylor, in his enthusiasm, had, out of his own pocket, hired extra men who appeared at the critical moment to relieve the tired men at the brakes; and it was under their fresh impetus that the Monumental had so triumphantly "sucked." Now Bert Taylor was freely blamed. The regular men stoutly maintained that if they had been left alone this would never have happened.

"These whiskey bummers never can last!" they said. Everybody trooped upstairs to the main rooms, where refreshments were served. After some consideration Keith decided to tell his story in explanation of how it was that the Monumentals were washed. Instantly the company cheered up, A clamour broke out. This was great! With Talbot Ward and Munro to corroborate, no one could doubt the story. Taylor ran about jubilantly, returning every few moments to pat Keith on the shoulder.

"Fine! fine!" he cried. "We've got those *Eurekas*! I can't wait for morning!"

Stewart Edward White

XV

Keith got home about daylight to find Nan, terribly anxious, waiting up for him. He brushed away her anxiety with the usual masculine impatience at being made a fuss over, gave a brief account of the fire—omitting mention of his narrow escape—and insisted that she go to bed. After a few moments she obeyed, and immediately fell asleep. Keith bathed himself and changed, made a cup of coffee, and wandered about rather impatiently waiting for time to go downtown. Wing Sam appeared, the morning paper came. The sun gained strength, and finally tempted him outside.

For some time he prowled around, examining Nan's efforts at gardening. There was not much to show as yet, but Keith had already the eye of faith so essential to the Californian, and saw plainly trees, shrubs, and flowers where now only spears of green were visible. The Morrells' garden next door was already well grown, and he cast on it an appraising eye. No sign of life showed about the place except a thread of smoke from the kitchen chimney. It was still early.

Nevertheless, five minutes later Mrs. Morrell opened the side door and stepped forth. She had on a wide leghorn hat, and carried a basket and scissors as though to gather flowers. Immediately she caught sight of Keith and waved him a gay greeting. He vaulted the fence and joined her.

"Aren't these early morning hours perfect? Isn't this glorious sunshine?" she greeted him.

As a matter of fact Mrs. Morrell seldom rose before noon, and detested early morning hours and glorious sunshine. She was inclined to consider the usual remarks in their praise as sheer affectation. But she adored fires, and often went to them when they promised well enough. Sometimes she attended in company with certain of her men friends; and sometimes alone, cloaked as a man. She liked the destruction and stimulation of them. She had been to the fire just extinguished, and seeing Keith in the garden, had put on her fluffiest and gone out to him. It was time this most attractive young man next door paid her more attention.

"How does the hero of the fire survive?" she asked him archly.

"Hero?"

"Don't pretend ignorance. Charles told me all about it. He heard your tale at the Monumental."

"It's hardly heroism to get out of a scrape the best way possible."

"It's heroic to save lives, I think; but especially heroic to keep your head in an emergency."

"Mr. Morrell all right?" asked Keith, to change the subject.

"He is sleeping off the fire—and the after effects. You men need watching every minute—even when we think you must be in danger of your lives."

She laughed and clipped a few flowers at random.

"Have you been moving furniture all these days? We've seen nothing of you. I thought we were going to have some music. I do my little five-finger exercises all by myself and nobody knows but I am playing Beethoven. You ought in Christian charity to help me out—whether you want to or not. What do you think of our garden? Don't you adore flowers?"

"No, I don't believe I do," replied Keith bluntly. "I like to see a pretty woman amongst 'em," he went on gallantly, "they set her like dresses. No good to show me pretty frocks—unless they're filled."

"La! You are so clever; at times I'm really afraid of you," said she.

She went on tossing a few blooms into her basket. Under the stimulus of the fire she had acted on impulse in going out into the garden. She realized it as perhaps a mistake. Keith's early morning freshness and fitness made her feel less sure of herself than usual. She had an uneasy impression that she was not at her best, and this reacted on her ability to exercise her usual magnetism. In fact, Keith, the least observant of men in such things, could not avoid noticing her rather second-hand looking skin, and that her features were more pronounced than he had thought.

"Do come over this evening for some music," she begged. "You can take a nap this afternoon, and you can go home early."

Keith had been just a little uneasy over this second interview with Mrs. Morrell. His straightforward nature was inclined to look back on the impression she had made on him at the supper party with a half-guilty sense of some sort of vague disloyalty he could not formulate. Now he felt much satisfied with himself, and quite relieved. Therefore, he accepted.

"I shall be very glad to," said he.

At breakfast, which was rather late, he told Nan of the meeting and the invitation. Nan's clear lines, fresh creamy skin, bright young eyes, looked more than usually attractive to him.

"Perhaps she *can* play," he said. "Let's go find out. And you must wear your prettiest gown; I'm proud of my wife, and I want her to look her very best."

A little later he remarked:

"I wonder if she isn't considerably older than Morrell."

Stewart Edward White

XVI

When he had at last reached downtown after his late breakfast, Keith found it in a fair turmoil. Knots of men stood everywhere arguing, sometimes very heatedly. Eureka members were openly expressing their anger over what they called Taylor's "dirty trick" in putting hirelings on the brakes, men who did not belong to the Monumental organization at all. If it had not been for that the Monumentals could never have "sucked" at all. On the other hand, the Monumentals and their friends were vehemently asserting that they were well within their rights. Fists were brandished. Several fights started, but were stopped before they had become serious.

Keith avoided these storm centres, waving a friendly hand, but smilingly refusing to be drawn in. Near the Merchants' Exchange, however, he came on a quieter, attentive group, in the centre of which stood Calhoun Bennett. The Southerner's head was thrown back haughtily, but he was listening with entire courtesy to a violent harangue from a burly, red-faced man in rough clothes.

"And I tell you that sort of a trick won't go down with nobody, and the story of why you were washed won't wash itself. It's too thin."

"I have the honah, suh," said Bennett formally, "to info'm yo' that yo' do not know what yo' are talkin' about."

His silken tones apparently enraged the man.

"You silk-stockinged—of a—!" said he.

Without haste Calhoun Bennett rapped the man across the face with his light rattan cane. Venting a howl of rage, the Eureka partisan leaped forward. Calhoun Bennett, quick as a flash, drew a small derringer and fired; and the man went down in a heap. Superbly nonchalant, Bennett, without a glance at his victim, turned away, the ring of spectators parting to let him through. He saw Keith, and at once joined him, drawing the young man's arm through his own. Keith, looking back, saw the man already sitting up, feeling his shoulder and cursing vigorously.

Bennett was fairly radiating rage, which, however, he managed to suppress beneath a well-bred exterior calm.

"These hounds, suh," he told Keith, "profess not to believe us, suh! They profess, suh, that our explanation of how we were washed is a fabrication. You will oblige me, suh, by profferin' yo' personal testimony in the case."

He faced Keith resolutely toward the Eureka engine house. Keith spared a thought to wonder what he was being let in for by this handsome young fire- eater, but he went along unprotesting.

Around the Eureka engine house was a big crowd of men. These fell silent as Bennett and Keith approached. The Eurekas represented quite a different social order from the Monumentals. Its membership was recruited from those who in the East had been small farmers, artisans, or workingmen in the more skilled trades; independent, plain, rather rough, thoroughly democratic, a trifle contemptuous of "silk stockings," outspoken, with little heed for niceties of etiquette or conduct. Bennett pushed his way through them to where stood Carter, the chief, and several of the more influential. Keith, looking at them, met their eyes directed squarely into his. They were steady, clear-looking, solid, rather coarse-grained, grave men.

"I have brought Mr. Keith here, who was an eyewitness, to give his testimony as to the events of last evenin'," said Bennett formally.

Keith told his story. It was received in a blank noncommittal silence. The men all looked at him steadily, and said nothing. Somehow, he was impressed. This silence seemed to him, fancifully, more than mere lack of words—it conveyed a sense of reserve force, of quiet appraisal of himself and his words, of the experiences of men who have been close to realities, who have *done* things in the world. Keith felt himself to be better educated, to own a better brain, to have a wider outlook, to be possessed, in short, of all the advantages of superiority. He had never mingled with rough men, and he had always looked down on them. In this attitude was no condescension and no priggishness, Now he felt, somehow, that the best of these men had something that he had not suspected, some force of character that raised them above his previous conception. They might be more than mere "filling" in a city's population; they might well come to be an element to be reckoned with.

When he had quite finished his story, there ensued a slight pause. Then said Carter:

"We believe Mr. Keith. If Mr. Ward and Frank Munro were there, of course there can be no doubt." Somehow Keith could not resent the implication; it was too impersonally delivered. Carter went on with cold formality and emphasis; "Mr. Keith had a very narrow escape. It was lucky for him that your hired men had 'sucked' your waterbox. In view of that we can, of course, no longer regret the fact."

"It was a dirty trick just the same!" growled a voice out of the crowd.

Carter turned a deliberate look in that direction, and nothing more was said. Bennett ignored the interruption, bowed frigidly, and turned away. The Eureka leaders nodded. In dead silence Keith and Bennett withdrew.

"That settles *that*!" observed Bennett, when at a little distance. "A lot of cheap shopkeepers! It makes me disgusted every time I have anythin' to do with them!"

As they walked away, one of the hangers-on of the police court approached, touching his hat.

"For you, Mr. Bennett," he said most respectfully, proffering a paper.

"Me?" observed Bennett, surprised. He unfolded the paper, glanced at it, and laughed. "I'm arrested for wingin' that 'shoulder-striker' up the street a while back," he told Keith.

"Anything I can do?" asked Keith anxiously.

"Not a thing, thank you. There'll be no trouble at all—just a little nuisance. May call you for a witness later."

He went away with the officer, but shortly after Keith saw him on the street again. The matter had been easily arranged.

Keith went to his office. In spite of himself he could not entirely take Bennett's point of view. Several of the men at Eureka headquarters looked interesting—he would like to know them—perhaps more than interesting, the potentiality of a reasoning and directed power.

XVII

The afternoon nap suggested by Mrs. Morrell was not enjoyed, and Keith returned home feeling pretty tired and inclined to a quiet evening. Nan had to remind him of his engagement.

"Oh, let's send a note over by Wing," he said, a little crossly. "I don't feel like making an effort to-night."

But Nan's convention could not approve of anything quite so radically a last-minute decision.

"It's a little late in the day for that," she pointed out. "She may have stayed in just to see us. We can leave early."

Keith went, grumbling. They found Mrs. Morrell in full evening dress, showing her neck and shoulders, which were her best points, for she was full bosomed and rounded without losing firmness of flesh. Nan was a trifle taken back at this gorgeousness, for she had not dressed. Keith, with his usual directness, made no secret of pretending to be utterly overwhelmed.

"I didn't know we were expected to dress for a real concert with flowers!" he cried, laughing.

Mrs. Morrell shrugged her fine shoulders indifferently.

"This old rag!" she said. "Don't let that bother you. I always like to put on something cool for the evening. It's such a relief."

It developed that Morrell had an engagement, and could not stay.

"He was so disappointed," purred Mrs. Morrell.

She was all eager for the music, brushing aside this and other preliminaries.

"You play, sing?" she asked Nan. "What a pity! I'm afraid you're going to be terribly bored."

She turned instantly to Keith, hurrying him to the piano, giving the impression of being too eager to wait—almost the eagerness of a drunkard in the presence of drink. And this in turn conveyed a vibrating feeling of magnetism, of temperament under restraint, of possibilities veiled. The impact struck Keith's responsive nature full. He waked up, approached the piano with reviving interest. She struck idle chords and flashed at him over her shoulder a brilliant smile.

"What shall it be?" she demanded, still with the undercurrent of eagerness. "You choose—a man's song—something soulful. I'm just in the mood."

"Do you know the 'Bedouin Love Song?'" he inquired.

"The 'Bedouin Love Song?' No—I'm afraid not. We are so far out of the world."

"It's a new thing. It goes like this."

He hummed the air, and she followed it hesitatingly, feeling out the accompaniment. Mrs. Morrell knew her instrument and had a quick ear. Occasionally Keith leaned over her shoulder to strike for her an elusive chord or modulation. In so doing he had to press close, and for all his honest absorption in the matter at hand, could not help becoming aware of her subtle perfume, the shine of her flesh, and the brightness of her crown of hair.

"You play it," she said suddenly.

But he disclaimed the ability.

"I don't know it any better than you do, and you improvise wonderfully."

They became entirely absorbed in this most fascinating of tasks, the working out little by little of a complicated accompaniment.

"There!" she cried gayly at last. "I believe I have it. Let's try."

Keith had a strong smooth baritone, not too well trained, but free from glaring faults and mannerisms. It filled the little drawing-room ringingly. He liked the song, and he sang it with fire and a certain defiance that suited it. At its conclusion Mrs. Morrell sprang to her feet, breathing quickly, her usual hard, quick artificiality of manner quite melted.

"It's wonderful!" she cried. "It lifts one right up! It makes me feel I'd run away—" She checked herself abruptly, and turned to where Nan sat in an armchair outside the circle of light, "Don't you just *adore* it?" she asked in a more restrained manner, and turned back to Keith, who was standing a little flushed and excited by the song, "You have just the voice for it—with that vibrating deep quality." She reseated herself at the piano and struck several loud chords. Under cover of them she added, half under her breath, as though to herself, but distinctly audible to the man at her shoulder; "Luck for us all that you are already taken."

Keith would have been no more than human if he had not followed this cue with a look. She did not lower her eyes, but gave him back his gaze directly. It was as though some secret understanding sprang up between them, though Keith,—in half-angry confusion, could not have analyzed it.

After this they compared notes until they found several songs they both knew. Mrs. Morrell brushed aside Keith's suggestion that she herself should sing, but she did it in a way that left the implication that he was the important one vocally.

"No, no! I've been starved too long. I'm as tired of my little reed of a voice as of the tinkle of a musical box."

The close of the evening was brought about only by the return of Morrell from his engagement. Keith had utterly forgotten his fatigue, and was tingling with the enthusiasm to which his nature always rose under stimulus. The English-man, very self-contained, clean-cut, incisive, brought a new atmosphere. He was cordial and polite, but not expansive. Keith came down from the clouds. He remembered, with compunction, Nan sitting in the armchair, the lateness of the hour, his own fatigue.

"You should hear Mr. Keith's new song, Charley," said Mrs, Morrell. "It's the most wonderful thing! The 'Bedouin Love Song,' You must surely sing it at the Firemen's Ball. It will make a great hit. No, you surely must. With a voice like yours it is selfish not to use it for the benefit of all. Don't you agree with me, Mrs. Keith?"

"I'll sing it, if you will play my accompaniment," said Keith.

On their way home Keith's enthusiasm bubbled up again.

"Isn't it great luck to find somebody to practise with?" he cried—"Unexpected luck in a place like this! I wish you cared for music."

"Oh, I do," said Nan. "I love it. But I just can't do it, that's all."

"Did you like it to-night?"

"I liked it when you really *sang*" replied Nan with a little yawn, "but it always took you such a time to get at it."

A short silence fell.

"Are you really going to sing at the Firemen's Ball?" she asked curiously.

"I haven't been asked yet," he reminded her. "Don't you think it good idea?"

"Oh, I don't know," said Nan, but her voice had a little edge. Keith felt it, and made the usual masculine blunder. He stopped short, thunderstruck at a new idea.

"Why, Nan," he cried reproachfully, "I don't believe you like her!"

"Like her!" she flashed back, her anger leaping to unreasonable proportions—"that old frump!"

No sooner had the door closed after them than Morrell's conventional smile faded, and his countenance fell into its usual hard, cold impassivity.

"Well, what is the game there?" he demanded.

"There is no game," she replied indifferently.

"There is very little money there, I warn you," he persisted.

She turned on him with sudden fury.

"Oh, shut up!" she cried. "I know my own business!"

"And I know mine," he told her, slowly and dangerously. "And I warn you to go slow unless I give the word."

She stared at him a moment, and he stared back. Then, quite

deliberately, she walked over to him until her breast almost touched him. Her eyes were half closed, and a little smile parted her full lips.

"Charley," she drawled wickedly, "I warn *you* to go slow. And I warn you not to interfere with me—or I might interfere with you!"

Morrell shrugged his shoulders, and turned away with an assumption of indifference.

"Please yourself. But I can't afford a scandal just now."

"*You* can't afford a *scandal!*" she cried, and laughed hardly.

"Not just now," he repeated.

Stewart Edward White

XVIII

Perhaps this unwise antagonizing by her husband, perhaps the idleness with which the well-to-do woman was afflicted, perhaps a genuine liking for Keith, gave Mrs. Morrell just the impulse needed. At any rate, she used the common bond of music to bring him much into her company. This was not a difficult matter. Keith was extravagantly fond of just this sort of experimental amateur excursions into lighter music, and he liked Mrs. Morrell. She was a good sort, straightforward and honest and direct, no nonsense in her, but she knew her way about, and a man could have a sort of pleasing, harmless flirtation to which she knew how to play up. There was not, nor could there be—in Keith's mind—any harm in their relations. Nan was the woman for him; but that didn't mean that he was never to see anybody else, or that other women might not—of course in unessential and superficial ways—answer some of his varied needs.

Mrs. Morrell was skilful at keeping up his interest, and she was equally skilful in gradually excluding Nan. This was not difficult, for Nan was secretly bored by the eternal practising, and repelled by Mrs. Morrell's efforts to be fascinating. She saw them plainly enough, but was at first merely amused and faintly disgusted, for she was proud enough to believe absolutely that such crude methods could have no effect on Milton, overlooking the fact that the crudities of women never appear as plainly to a man as they do to another woman. For a woman is in the know. At first she offered one excuse or another, in an attempt to be both polite and plausible. She much preferred a book at home, or a whole free evening to work at making her house attractive. Later, Keith got into the habit of taking her attitude for granted.

"I promised to run over to the Morrells' this evening," he would say, "More music. Of course you won't care to come. You won't be lonely? I won't be gone late."

"Of course not," she laughed. "I'm thankful for the chance to get through with the blue room."

Nevertheless, after a time she began to experience a faint, unreasonable resentment; and Keith an equally faint, equally unreasonable feeling of guilt.

Left to itself this situation would, therefore, have righted itself, but Mrs. Morrell was keen enough to give it the required directing touches:

"Too bad we can't tear your wife away from her house and garden."

"If you only had some one to practise with regularly at home! Your voice ought to be systematically cultivated. It is wonderful!"

And later:

"You ought not to come here so much, I suppose—" rather doubtfully, "Any sort of practice and accompaniment—even my poor efforts—does you so much good! You or I would understand perfectly, but it is sometimes so difficult for the inexperienced domestic type to comprehend! An older woman who understands men knows—but come, we must sing that once more."

The effect of these and a thousand similar speeches injected apparently at random here and there in the tide of other things was at once to intensify Keith's vague feeling of guilt, and to put it in the light somehow of an injustice to himself. He had an unformulated notion that if Nan would or could only understand the situation and be a good fellow that every one would be happy; but as she was a mere woman, with a woman's prejudices, this was impossible. It was absurd to expect him to give up his music just because she wanted to be different! He had really nothing whatever to conceal; and yet it actually seemed that difficulty and concealment would be necessary if this sort of unspoken reproach were kept up. Women were so confoundedly single-minded!

And as the normal, healthy, non-introspective male tends to avoid discomfort, even of his own making, it thus came about that Keith spent less and less time at home. He did not explain to himself why. It was certainly no lessening of his affection for Nan. Only he felt absolutely sure of her, and the mental situation sketched above left him more open to the lure of downtown, which to any live man was in those days especially great. Every evening the "fellows" got together, jawed things over, played pool, had a drink or so, wandered from one place to another, looked with the vivid interest of the young and able-bodied on the seething, colourful, vital life of the new community. It was all harmless and mighty pleasant. Keith argued that he was "establishing connections" and meeting men who could do his profession good, which was more or less true; but it took him from home evenings.

Nan, at first, quite innocently played into his hands. She really preferred to stay at home rather than be bored at the Morrells'. Later, when this tradition had been established, she began to be disturbed, not by any suspicion that Milton's interest was traying, but by a feeling of neglect. She was hurt. And little by little, in spite of herself, a jealousy of the woman next door began to tinge her solitude. Her nature was too noble and generous to harbour such a sentiment without a struggle. She blamed herself for unworthy and wretched jealousy, and yet she could not help herself. Often, especially at first, Keith in an impulse would throw over his plans, and ask her to go to the theatre or a concert, of which there were any and excellent. She generally declined, not because she did not want to go, but because of that impelling desire, universal in the feminine soul, to be a little wooed to it, to be compelled by gentle persuasion that should at once make up for the past and be an earnest for the future. Only Keith took her refusal at its face value. Nan was lonely and hurt.

Her refusals to respond to his rather spasmodic attempts to be nice to her were adopted by Keith's subconscious needs for comfort. If she didn't want to see anything of life, she shouldn't expect him to bury himself. His restless mind gradually adopted the fiction persistently held before him by Mrs. Morrell that his wife was indeed a domestic little body, fond only of her home and garden. As soon as he had hypnotized himself into the full acceptance of this, he felt much happier, His uneasiness fell from him, and he continued life with zest. If any one had told him that he was neglecting Nan, he probably would have been surprised. They were busy; they met amicably; there were no reproaches; they managed to get about and enjoy things together quite a lot.

The basis for the latter illusion rested on the Sunday excursions and picnics. Both the Keiths always attended them. There was invariably the same crowd—the Morrells; Dick Blatchford, the contractor, and his fat, coarse-grained, good-natured Irish wife; Calhoun Bennett; Ben Sansome: Sally Warner, a dashing grass widow, whose unknown elderly husband seemed to be always away "at the mines"; Teeny McFarlane, small, dainty, precise, blond, exquisite, cool, with very self-possessed manners and decided ways, but with the capacity for occasionally and with deliberation outdoing the worst of them, about whom were whispered furtive things the rumour of which died before her armoured front; her husband, a fat, jolly, round-faced, somewhat pop-eyed man who adored her and was absolutely ignorant of one side of her. These and a sprinkling of "fast" youths made the party.

Sometimes the celebrated Sam Brannan went along, loud, coarse, shrewd, bull voiced, kindly when not crossed, unscrupulous, dictatorial, and overbearing, They all got to know each other very well and to be very free in one another's society,

The usual procedure was to drive in buggies, sometimes to the beach, sometimes down the peninsula, starting rather early, and staying out all day. Occasionally rather elaborate lunches were brought, with servants to spread them; but the usual custom was to stop at one of the numerous road houses. No man drove, walked, or talked with his own wife; nevertheless, these affairs though rowdy, noisy, and "fast" enough, were essentially harmless. The respectable members of the community were sufficiently shocked, however. Gay dresses, gay laughter, gay behaviour, gay scorn of convention, above all, the resort to the mysterious naughty road houses were enough. It must be confessed that at times things seemed to go a bit far; but Nan, who was at first bewildered and shocked, noticed that the women did many things in public and nothing in private. As already her mind and tolerance were adapting themselves to new things, she was able to accept it all philosophically as part of a new phase of life.

These people had no misgivings about themselves, and they passed judgment on others with entire assurance. In their slang all with whom they came into contact were either "hearses" or "live Mollies." There was nothing racial, local, or social in this division. A family might be divided, one member being a live Molly, and all the rest the most dismal of hearses. Occasionally a stranger might be brought along. He did not know it, but always he was very carefully watched and appraised: his status discussed and decided at the supper to which the same people—minus all strangers—gathered later. At one of these discussions a third estate came into being.

Teeny McFarlane had that day brought with her a young man of about twenty-four or twenty-five, well dressed, of pleasant features, agreeable in manner, well spoken, but quiet.

"He isn't a live Molly," stated Sally positively.

"Well, Sally took a walk with him," observed Sam Brannan dryly; "she ought to know!"

"Don't need to take a walk with him," countered Sally; "just take a talk with him—or try to.".

"I did try to," interpolated Mrs. Morrell.

"May as well make it unanimous, looks like," said Sam. "He goes for a hearse."

But Teeny McFarlane interposed in her positive, precise little way.

"I object," she drawled. "He certainly isn't as bad as all that. He's a nice boy, and he never bored anybody in his life. Did he bore you, Sally?"

"I can't say he did, now you mention it. He's one of those nice doggy people you don't mind having around."

They discussed the matter animatedly. Teeny McFarlane developed an unexpected obstinacy. She did not suggest that the young man was to be included in any of the future parties; indeed, she answered the direct question decidedly in the negative; no, there was no use trying to include anybody unless they decidedly "belonged."

"You wouldn't call him a live Molly, now would you, Teeny?" implored Cal Bennett.

"No," she answered slowly, "I suppose not. But he is *not* a hearse."

The men, all but Popsy McFarlane, were inspecting Teeny's cool, unrevealing exterior with covert curiosity. She was always an enigma to them. Each man was asking himself why her interest in the mere labelling of this stranger.

"He isn't a live Molly and she objects to his being a hearse," laughed Sally. "He must be something between them. What," she inquired, with the air of propounding a conundrum, "is between a live Molly and a hearse?"

"Give it up!" they cried unanimously.

Sally looked nonplussed, then shrieked: "Why, the pall-bearers, of course!"

The silly phrase caught. Thereafter, those who were acknowledged to be all right enough but not of their feather were known as "pallbearers."

The Keiths were live Mollies. He was decidedly one. His appearance alone inspired good nature and high spirits, he looked so clean, vividly coloured, enthusiastic, alive to his finger tips. He was always game for anything, no matter how ridiculous it made him, or in what sort of a so-called false position it might place him. When he had reached a certain state of dancing-eyed joyous recklessness, Nan was always athrill as to what he might do next. And Nan, spite of her quieter ways and the reserves imposed on her by her breeding, was altogether too pretty and too much of a real person ever to be classed as a hearse. With her ravishing Eastern toilettes, her clear, creamy complexion, and the clean-cut lines of her throat, chin, and cheeks, she always made the other women look a little too vividly accented. The men all admired her on sight, and at first did their best to interest her. They succeeded, for in general they were of vital stuff, but not in the intimately personal way they desired. Her nature found no thrill in experiment. One by one they gave her up in the favour of less attractive but livelier or more complaisant companions; but they continued to like her and to pay her much general attention. She never, in any nuance of manner, even tried to make a difference; nevertheless, their attitude toward her was always more deferential than to the other women.

Ben Sansome was the one exception to the first part of the

above statement. Her gentle but obvious withdrawals from his advances piqued his conceit. Ben was a spoiled youth, with plenty of money; and he had always been a spoiled youth, with plenty of money. Why he had come to San Francisco no one knew. Possibly he did not know himself; for as his affairs had always been idle, he had drifted much, and might have drifted here. Whatever the reason, the fact remained that in this busy, new, and ambitious community he was the one example professionally of the gilded youth. His waistcoats, gloves, varnished boots, jewellery, handkerchiefs were always patterns to the other amateur, gilded youths who had also other things to do. His social tact was enormous, and a recognized institution. If there had been cotillons, he would have led them; but as there were no cotillons, he contented himself with being an *arbiter elegantiarum.* He rather prided himself on his knowledge of such things as jades, old prints, and obscure poets of whom nobody else had ever heard. Naturally he had always been a great success with women, both as harmless parlour ornaments, and in more dangerous ways. In San Francisco he had probably carried farther than he would have carried anywhere else. He had sustained no serious reverses, because difficult game had not heretofore interested him. Entering half interestedly with Nan into what he vaguely intended as one of his numerous, harmless, artistic, perfumed flirtationlets, he had found himself unexpectedly held at arm's length. Just this was needed to fillip his fancy. He went into the game as a game. Sansome made himself useful. By dint of being on hand whenever Keith's carelessness had left her in need of an escort, and only then, he managed to establish himself on a recognized footing as a sort of privileged, charming, useful, harmless family friend.

Outside this small, rather lively coterie the Keiths had very few friends. It must be confessed that the mothers of the future leaders of San Francisco society, and the bearers of what were to be her proudest names, were mostly "hearses." Their husbands were the forceful, able men of the city, but they themselves were conventional as only conventional women can be when goaded into it by a general free-and-easy, unconventional atmosphere. That was their only method of showing disapproval. The effect was worthy but dull. It was a pity, for among them were many intelligent, charming women who needed only a different atmosphere, to expand. The Keiths never saw them, and gained their ideas of them only from the merciless raillery of the "live Mollies."

All this implied more or less entertaining, and entertaining was expensive. The Boyle house was expensive for that matter; and about everything else, save Chinese servants, and, temporarily, whatever the latest clipper ship had glutted the market with. Keith had brought with him a fair sum of money with which to make his start; but under this constant drainage, it dwindled to what was for those times a comparatively small sum. Clients did not come. There were more men practising law than all the other professions. In spite of wide acquaintance and an attractive popular personality, Keith had not as yet made a start. He did not worry—that was not his nature—but he began to realize that he must do one of two things: either make some money, somehow, or give up his present mode of living. The latter course was unthinkable!

XIX

One morning Keith was sitting in his office cogitating these things. His door opened and a meek, mild little wisp of a man sidled in. He held his hat in his hand, revealing clearly sandy hair and a narrow forehead. His eyebrows and lashes were sandy, his eyes pale blue, his mouth weak but obstinate. On invitation he seated himself on the edge of the chair, and laid his hat carefully beside him on the floor.

"I am Dr. Jacob Jones," he said, blinking at Keith. "You have heard of me?"

"I am afraid I have not," said Keith pleasantly.

The little man sighed.

"I have held the City Hospital contract for three years," he explained, "and they owe me a lot of money. I thought you might collect some of it."

"I think if you'd put in a claim through the usual channels you'd receive your dues," advised Keith, somewhat puzzled. He had not heard that the city was refusing to pay legitimate claims.

"I've done that, and they've given me these," said Doctor Jones, handing Keith a bundle of papers.

Keith glanced at them.

Stewart Edward White

"This is 'scrip,'" he said. "It's perfectly good. When the city is without current funds it issues this scrip, bearing interest at 3 per cent. A month. It's all right."

"Yes, I know," said the little man ineffectually, "but I don't want scrip."

Keith ran it over. It amounted to something like eleven thousand dollars.

"What do you want done about it?" he asked,

"I want you to collect the money for me."

But Keith, had recollected something.

"Just wait a minute, please," he begged, and darted across the hall to a friend's office, returning after a moment with a file of legislative reports. "I thought I'd heard something about it; here it is. The State Legislature has voted an issue of 10 per cent. bonds to take up the scrip."

"I don't understand," said Doctor Jones.

"Why, you take your scrip to the proper official and exchange it for an equal value of State bonds."

"But what good does that do me?" cried Jones excitedly. "It doesn't get me my money. They don't guarantee I can sell the bonds at par, do they? And answer me this: isn't it just a scheme to cheat me of my interest? As I understand it, instead of 3 per cent. a month I'm to get 10 per cent. A year?"

"That's the effect," corroborated Keith.

"Well, I don't want bonds, I want money, as is my due."

"Wait a minute," said Keith. He read the report again slowly. "This says that holders of scrip *may* exchange, for bonds; it does not say they *must* exchange," he said finally. "If that interpretation is made of the law, suit and judgment would lie against the city. Do you want to try that?"

"Of course I want to try it!" cried Jones.

"Well, bring me your contract and vouchers, and any other papers to do with the case, and I'll see what can be done."

"I have them right here," said Doctor Jones.

This, as Keith's first case, interested him more than its intrinsic worth warranted. It amused him to bring all his powers to bear, fighting strongly for the technical point, and finally establishing it in court. In spite of the evident intention of the Legislature that city scrip should be retired in favour of bonds, it was ruled that the word *may* in place of the word *must* practically nullified that intention. Judgment was obtained against the city for eleven thousand dollars, and the sheriff was formally instructed to sell certain water-front lots in order to satisfy that judgment. The sale was duly advertised in the papers.

Next morning, after the first insertion of this advertisement, Keith had three more callers. These were men of importance: namely, John Geary, the first postmaster and last *alcalde* of the new city; William Hooper, and James King of William, at that time still a banker. These were grave, solid, and weighty citizens, plainly dressed, earnest, and forceful. They responded politely but formally to Keith's salute, and seated themselves.

"You were, I understand, counsel for Doctor Jones in obtaining judgment on the hospital scrip?" inquired Geary.

"That is correct," acknowledged Keith.

"We have called to inform you of a fact that perhaps escaped your notice: namely, that these gentlemen and myself have been appointed by the Legislature as commissioners to manage the funded debt of the city; that, for that purpose, title of all city lands has been put in our hands."

"No, I did not know that," said Keith.

"Therefore, you see," went on Geary, "the sheriff cannot pass title to any lots that might be sold to satisfy Doctor Jones's judgment."

Keith pondered, his alert mind seizing with avidity on this new and interesting situation.

"No, I cannot quite see that," he said at last; "the actual title is in the city. It owns its property. You gentlemen do not claim to own it, as individuals. You have delegated to you the power to pass title, just as the sheriff and one or two others have that power; but you have not the *sole* power."

"We have advice that title conveyed under this judgment will be invalid."

"That is a matter for the courts to settle."

"The courts—" began Hooper explosively, but Geary overrode him.

"If all the creditors of the city were to adopt the course pursued by Doctor Jones, the city would soon be bankrupt of resources."

"That is true," agreed Keith.

"Then cannot I appeal to your sense of civic patriotism?"

"Gentlemen," replied Keith, "you seem to forget that in this matter I am not acting for myself, but for a client. If it were my affair, I might feel inclined to discuss the matter with you more in detail. But I am only an agent."

"But—" interrupted Hooper again.

"That is quite true," interjected James King of William.

"Well, we shall see your client," went on Geary, "But I might state that on the side of his own best interests he would do well to go slow. There is at least a considerable doubt as to the legality of this sale. It is unlikely that people will care to bid."

After some further polite conversation they took their leave. Keith quickly discovered that the opinion held by the commissioners was shared by most of his friends. They acknowledged the brilliance of his legal victory, admired it heartily, and congratulated him; but they considered that victory barren.

"Nobody will buy; you won't get two bits a lot bid," they all told him.

Little Doctor Jones came to him much depressed. The commissioners had talked with him.

"Do you want my advice?" asked Keith, "Then do this: stick to your guns."

But little Jones was scared.

"I want my money," said he; "perhaps I'd better take those bonds after all."

"Look here," suddenly said Keith, who had been making up his mind. "I'll guarantee you the full amount in cash, within, say, two weeks, but only on this condition: that you go out now, and spread it about everywhere that you are going to stand pat. Tell 'em all you are going to push through this sale."

"How do I know—"

"Take a chance," interrupted Keith. "If at the end of two

Stewart Edward White

weeks I don't pay you cash, you can do what you please. Call off the sheriff's sale at the last minute; I'll pay the costs myself. Come, that's fair enough. You can't lose a cent."

"All right," agreed Jones after a minute.

"Remember: it's part of the bargain that you state everywhere that you're going to force this sale, and that you don't let anybody bluff you."

The affair made quite a little stir. Men like Sam Brannan, Dick Blatchford, the contractor, and Jim Polk discussed Keith and his ability.

"Got a pretty wife, too," added Brannan."—never heard of the fall of man."

"Well, she's going to, if the Morrell woman has her way," observed Ben Sansome dryly.

Polk stretched his long legs, and smiled his desiccated little smile.

"He's a pretty enterprising youngster—more ways than one," said he.

XX

On the evening of the third day after his latest interview with Doctor Jones, Keith threw down his paper with a cry of triumph. He had been scanning the columns of every issue with minute care, combing even the fine print for the auctioneer's advertisements. Here was what he wanted: top of column, third page, where every one would be sure to see it. The commissioners issued a signed statement, calling public attention to the details of their appointment, and warning that titles issued under sheriff's sale would be considered invalid.

Keith read this with great attention, then drew his personal check against Palmer, Cook & Co. for eleven thousand dollars in favour of Doctor Jones. After some search he unearthed the little man in a downtown rookery, and from him obtained an assignment of his judgment against the city. Doctor Jones lost no time spreading the news, with the additional statement that he considered himself well out of the mess. He proceeded to order himself a long-coveted microscope, and was thenceforth lost to sight among low-tide rocks and marine algae. The sheriff's sale came off at the advertised date. There were no bidders; the commissioners' warning had had its effect. Keith himself bought in the lots for $5,000. This check about exhausted his resources. This, less costs, was, of course, paid back to himself as holder of the judgment. He had title, such as it was, for about what he had given Jones.

The bargain amused Keith's acquaintance hugely. Whenever he appeared he was deluged with chaff, all of which he took, good naturedly. He was considered, in a moment of aberration, to have bought an exceedingly doubtful equity. Some thought, he must have a great deal of money, arguing that only the owner of a fat bank account could afford to take such fliers; others considered that he must have very little sense. Keith was apparently unperturbed. He at once began to look about him, considering the next step in his scheme. Since this investment had taken nearly every cent he had left, it was incumbent to raise more money at once.

He called on John Sherwood at the Empire. The gambler listened to him attentively.

"I can't go into it," he said, when Keith had finished. A slight smile sketched itself on his strong, impassive face. "Not that I do not believe it will work; I think it will. But I have long made it a rule never to try to make money outside my own business—which is gambling. I never adopt ordinary honest methods."

Keith's honest but legally trained mind failed to notice the quiet sarcasm of this. "Well, you know everybody in town. Where can I go?"

Sherwood thought a moment.

"I'll take you to Malcolm Neil," he said at last. It was Keith's turn to look thoughtful.

"All right," he said at last. "But not just right away. Give me a couple of days to get ready."

At the appointed time Sherwood escorted Keith to Malcolm Neil's office, introduced and left him. Keith took the proffered wooden chair, examining his man with the keenest attention.

Malcolm Neil, spite of his Scotch name, was a New Englander by birth. He had come out in '49, intending, like everybody else, to go to the mines, but had never gone farther than San

Francisco. The new city offered ample scope for his talents, and he speedily became, not only rich, but a dominating personality among financial circles. He accomplished this by supplementing his natural ability with absolute singleness of purpose. It was known that his sole idea was the making of money. He was reputed to be hard, devoid of sentiment, unscrupulous. Naturally he enjoyed no popularity, but a vast respect. More people had heard of him, or felt his power, than had seen him; for he went little abroad, and preferred to work through agents. John Sherwood's service in obtaining for Keith a personal interview was a very real one. Neil's offices were small, dingy, and ill lighted, at the back of one of the older and cheaper buildings. In the outer of the two were three bookkeepers; the other contained only a desk, two chairs, and an engraving of Daniel Webster addressing the Senate.

The man himself sat humped over slightly, his head thrust a little forward as though on the point of launching a truculent challenge. He was lean, gray, with bushy, overhanging brows, eyes with glinting metallic surfaces, had long sinewy hands, and a carved granite and inscrutable face, His few words of greeting revealed his voice as harsh, grating and domineering.

Keith, reading his man, wasted no time in preliminaries.

"Mr. Neil," he said, "I have a scheme by which a great deal of money can be made."

Neil grunted. If it had not been for the fact that John Sherwood had introduced the maker of that speech, the interview would have here terminated. Malcolm Neil deeply distrusted men with schemes to make large sums of money. After a time, as Keith still waited, he growled;

"What is it?"

"That," said Keith, "I shall not disclose until my standing in the matter is assured."

"What do you want?" growled Neil.

"Fifty per cent of the profits, if you go in."

"What do you want of me?"

"The capital."

"What is the scheme?"

"That I cannot tell you without some assurance of your good intention."

"What do you expect?" rasped Neil, "that I go into this blind?"

"I have prepared this paper," said Keith, handing him a document.

Neil glanced over the paper, then read it through slowly, with great care. When he had finished, he looked up at Keith, and there was a gleam of admiration in his frosty eye.

"You are a lawyer, I take it?" he surmised.

Keith nodded. Neil went over the document for the third time.

"And a good one," added Neil. "This is watertight. It seems to be a contract agreeing to the division you suggest, *providing* I go into the scheme. Very well, I'll sign this." He raised his voice. "Samuels, come in and witness this. Now, what is the scheme?"

Keith produced another paper.

"It is written out in detail here."

Neil reached for it, but Keith drew it back.

"One moment."

He turned it over on the blank side and wrote:

"This is in full the financial deal referred to in contract entered into this 7th of June, 1852, by Malcolm Neil and Milton Keith."

To this he appended his signature, then handed the pen to Neil.

"Sign," he requested.

Neil took the pen, but hesitated for some moments, his alert brain seeking some way out. Finally and grudgingly he signed. Then he leaned back in his chair, eying Keith with rather a wintry humour, though he made no comment. He reached again for the paper, but Keith put his hand on it.

"What more do you want?" inquired Neil in amused tones. His sense of humour had been touched on its only vulnerable point. He appreciated keen and subtle practice when he saw it,

"Not a thing," laughed Keith, "but a few words of explanation before you read that will make it more easily understood. Can you tell me how much water lots are worth?"

"Five to eight thousand for fifty varas."

"All right. I've bought ten fifty vara lots at sheriff's sale for five thousand dollars."

Neil's eye went cold.

"I've heard of that. Your title is no good. The reason you got them so cheaply was that nobody would bid because of that."

"That's for the courts to decide. The fact remains that I've a title, even though clouded, at $500 per lot."

"Proceed."

"Well, the commissioners are now advertising a sale of these same lots at auction on the 15th."

"So I see."

"Well," said Keith softly, "it strikes me that whoever buys these lots then is due for a heap of trouble."

"How so?"

"My title from the sheriff may be clouded, but it will be contested against the title given at that sale. The purchaser will have to defend himself up to the highest court. I can promise him a good fight."

Neil was now watching him steadily,

"If that fact could be widely advertised," went on Keith slowly, "by way of a threat, so to speak, it strikes me it would be very apt to discourage bidding at the commissioners' sale. Nobody wants to buy a lot of lawsuits, at any price. In absence of competition, a fifty vara lot might be sold for as low as—say $500."

Neil nodded, Keith leaned forward.

"Now here's my real idea: suppose *I* buy in against this timid bidding. Suppose *I* am the one who gets the commissioners' title for $500. Then I have both titles. And I am not likely to contest against myself. It's cost me $1,000 per lot—$500 at each sale—a profit of from $4,000 to $7,000 on each lot."

He leaned back. Malcolm Neil sat like a graven image, no expression showing on his flintlike face nor in his eyes. At length he chuckled harshly. Then, and not until then, Keith proceeded:

"But that isn't all. There's plenty more scrip afloat. If you can buy up as much of it as you can scrape together, I'll get judgment for it in the courts, and we can enlarge the deal until somebody smells a rat. We need several things."

"What?"

"Secrecy."

Neil made no reply, but the lines of his mouth straightened.

"Influence to push matters along in official circles."

"Matters will be pushed along."

"A newspaper."

"Leave that to me."

"Agents—not known to be connected with us."

Neil nodded.

"Working capital—but that is provided for in the contract. And"—he hesitated—"it will not harm to have these matters brought before a court whose judge is not unfriendly."

"I can arrange for that, Mr. Keith."

Keith arose.

"Then that is settled." He picked up the duplicate copy of the contract. "There remains only one other formality."

"Yes? What?"

"Your check for $12,000."

"What for?"

"For my expenses in this matter up to date."

"What!" cried Neil.

"The contract specifies that you are to furnish the working capital, Keith pointed out.

"But that means the future—"

"It doesn't say so."

Neil paused a moment.

"This contract would not hold in law, and you know it," he asserted boldly. "It would be held to be an illegal conspiracy."

"I would be pleased to have you point out the illegality in court," said Keith coldly, his manner as frosty as Neil's. "And if conspiracy exists, your name is affixed to it."

Neil pondered this point a moment, then drew his checkbook toward him with a grim little smile.

"Young man, you win," said he.

Keith thawed to sunniness at once.

"Oh, we'll work together all right, once we understand each other," he laughed. "Send your man out after scrip. Let him report to me."

Neil arose rather stiffly, and extended his hand.

"All right, all right!" he muttered, as though impatient. "Keep In Good-day. Good-day."

XXI

The time for the annual Firemen's Ball was now at hand. At this period the Firemen's Ball was an institution of the first social importance. As has been shown, the various organizations were voluntary associations, and in their ranks birds of a feather flocked together. On the common meeting ground of the big annual function all elements met, even—if they did not mingle as freely as they might.

In any case, the affair was very elaborate and very gorgeous. Preparations were in the hands of special committees months in advance. One company had charge of the refreshments, another of the music, a third of the floor arrangements, and so on. There was much jealous anxiety that each should do its part thoroughly and lavishly, for the honour of its organization. The members of each committee were distinguished by coloured ribbons, which they wore importantly everywhere. An air of preoccupied business was the proper thing for days before the event.

It was held this year in one of the armouries. The decoration committee had done its most desperate. Flags of all nations and strips of coloured bunting draped the rafters; greens from the Sausalito Hills framed the windows and doors; huge oiled Chinese lanterns swayed from the roofs. The floor shone like glass. At either end bowers of green half concealed the orchestras—two of them, that the music might never cease. The side rooms were set for refreshments. Many chairs lined the walls. Hundreds of lamps and reflectors had been nailed up in every conceivable place. It took a negro over an hour to light them all. Near the door stood a wide, flat table piled high with programs for the dancers. These were elaborate affairs, and had cost a mint of money—vellum folders, emblazoned in colour outside, with a sort of fireman heraldry and the motto: "We strive to save." Gilded pencils on short silken tasselled cords dangled from their corners.

At eight o'clock the lights were all blazing, the orchestras were tuning, and the floor fluttered with anxious labelled commi-tteemen dashing to and fro. There was nothing for them to do, but they were nervous. By half-past eight the first arrivals could be seen hesitating at the outer door, as though reluctant to make a plunge; herded finally to the right and left of men's and women's dressing-rooms. After a long, chattering interval, encouraged by the slow accumulation of numbers, a little group debouched on the main, floor. Its members all talked and laughed feverishly, and tried with varying success to assume an accustomed ease they did not feel. Most of the women, somehow, seemed all white gloves and dancing slippers, and bore themselves rather like affable, slightly scared rabbits. The men suddenly became very facetious, swapping jokes in loud tones.

The orchestra at the far end immediately struck up, but nobody ventured on the huge and empty floor. Masters of ceremonies, much bebadged, rather conscious of white gloves, strove earnestly with hurried, ingratiating smiles to induce the younger members to break the ice. Ben Sansome, remarkable among them for his social ease and the unobtrusive correctness of his appointments, responsible head of the reception committee, masterfully seized a blushing, protesting damsel and whirled her away. This, however, was merely an informal sort of opening. The real bail could start only with the grand march; and the grand march was a pompous and intricate affair, possible only after the arrival of the city's elite. Partners for the grand march had been bespoken months before.

The Keiths arrived about half-past nine. Nan was looking

particularly well in her girlish fashion. Her usual delicate colour was heightened by anticipation, for she intended ardently to "have a good time." For this occasion, too, she had put on the best of her new Eastern clothes, and was confident of the sensation they would create in the feminine breast. The gown was of silk the colour of pomegranate blossoms, light and filmy, with the wide skirts of the day, the short sleeves, the low neck. Over bodice and skirt had been gracefully trailed long sprays of blossoms. Similar flowers wreathed her head, on which the hair was done low and smooth, with a golden arrow securing it. A fine golden chain spanned her waist. From it dangled smaller chains at the ends of which depended little golden hands. These held up the front of the skirt artistically, at just the right height for dancing and to show flounces and ravishing petticoats beneath. It was an innovation of the sort the feminine heart delights in, a brand-new thing straight from Paris. Nan's gloves were of half length, the backs of the hands embroidered and displaying each several small sparkling jewels. The broad golden bracelets had been clasped outside the gloves. Around her little finger was a ring from which depended, on the end of a chain, a larger ring, and through this larger ring hung her dainty lace handkerchief. This was innovation number two. The men all stared at her proud, delicate, flowerlike effect of fresh beauty; but every woman present, and Nan knew it, noted first, the cut of her gown, second, the dangling little golden hands, and third, the handkerchief ring. She knew that not later than to-morrow at least a half-dozen urgent orders would be booked at Palmerston's; but she knew, also, that at least six months must elapse before those orders could be filled. As for the rest, her stockings were white, her slippers ribboned with cross-ties up the ankles, she carried a stiff and formal bouquet, as big around as a plate, composed of wired flowers ornamented with a "cape" of lace paper; but those things were common.

Altogether, Nan looked extraordinarily well, made a sensation. Keith was pleased and proud of her. He picked one of the blazoned vellum cards from the table and scrawled his initials opposite half a dozen dances.

"I'm going to hold you to those, you know," he said.

They proceeded, leisurely across the floor, and Keith established her in one of the chairs.

"I'll go get some of the men I want you to meet," said he. When he returned with Bernard Black he found Nan already surrounded, Ben Sansome was there, and Calhoun Bennett, and a half-dozen others, either acquaintances made on some of the Sundays, or young men brought up by Sansome in his capacity of Master of Ceremonies. She was having a good time laughing, her colour high, Keith looked about him with the intention of filling his own card.

Mrs, Morrell, surrounded by a hilarious group of the younger fry, was just entering the room. She was dressed in flame colour, and her gown was cut very low, plainly to reveal the swell of her ample bosom. Her evening gloves and slippers were golden, as was a broad metallic woven band around her waist. Altogether, striking, rather a conspicuous effort than an artistic success, any woman would have said; but there could be no doubt that she had provided a glittering bait for the attentions of the men.

Keith immediately made his way across to her.

"You are ravishing this evening," he said, reaching for her card. It was full. Keith was chopfallen.

"Take me to Mrs. Keith," asked Mrs. Morrell, taking the card again, "She looks charming to-night; that simple style just suits her wide-eyed innocence."

She placed her fingers lightly on Keith's arm and moved away, nodding over her shoulder at the rather nonplussed young men who had come in with her. Thus rid of them, she turned again to Keith.

"You didn't think I'd forget you!" she said, as though,

reproachfully. "See, I kept you four dances. I put down those initials myself. Now don't you think I'm a pretty good sort?"

"Indeed I do! Which ones are they?" asked Keith, opening his own card.

"The third, seventh, ninth, and eleventh."

Keith hesitated for an appreciable instant. The seventh and eleventh he had put down for Nan. But somehow in the face of this smiling, cynical-looking, vivid creature, he rather shrank from saying that he had them with his wife. He swiftly reflected that, after all, he had four others with Nan, that she was so surrounded with admirers that she could not go partnerless, and that he would explain.

"Delightful!" he cried, pencilling his program.

Mrs. Morrell fluttered down alongside Mrs. Keith with much small talk. After a moment the music started for the grand march. Everybody took the floor.

"Where can Charley be!" cried Mrs. Morrell in apparent distress. "Don't wait here with me. I assure you I do not in the least mind sitting alone."

But she said it in a fashion that made it impossible, and in this manner Nan lost her first engagement with her husband. Not that it mattered particularly, she told herself, grand marches were rather silly things, and yet she could not avoid a feeling of thwarted pique at being so tied to the wall.

At the close of the march, and after the couples had pretty well resumed their seats, Mrs. Sherwood entered, unattended and very leisurely. She made, in her quieter manner, a greater sensation than had Mrs. Morrell. Quite self-possessed, carrying herself with her customary poise, dressed unobtrusively in black and gold, but with the distinction of an indubitable Parisian model, moving without self-consciousness in contrast to many of the other women, her small head high, her direct gaze a-smoulder with lazy amusement, she glided across the middle of the floor. The eyes of every woman in the ballroom were upon her. The "respectable" element stared shamelessly, making comments aside. Those a little *declasse*, on the fringe of society, or the "faster" women like Mrs. Morrell—who might in a way be considered her rivals—were apparently quite unaware of her. She made her unhasting way to a vacant chair, sat down, and looked calmly about her.

Immediately she was surrounded by a swarm of the unattached men. The attached men became very attentive to their partners.

"Hullo," remarked Keith cheerfully. "There's Mrs. Sherwood. I must go over and say good-evening to her."

On sudden impulse Nan rose with him. She instinctively disliked her present company and the situation; and a sudden pang of conscience had told her that not once since she had left the Bella Union had she laid eyes on the woman who had received her with so much kindness.

"Take me with you," she said to Keith.

"My dear!" cried Mrs. Morrell. "You wouldn't! Take my advice—you're young and innocent!"

She sought one of those exclusive, private-joke glances at Keith, but failed to catch his eye.

"She was very kind to me when I arrived," said Nan serenely. Keith, hesitated; then his impulsive, warm-hearted loyalty spoke.

"Good for you, Nan!" he cried.

They moved away, leaving Mrs. Morrell alone, biting her lip and planning revenges.

The group around Mrs. Sherwood fell away at their approach. Nan sat down next her, leaning forward with a pretty and girlish, impulsiveness.

"It's ages since I have seen you, and I have no excuse to offer," she said. "The days slip by."

"I know," said Mrs. Sherwood. "New house, new Chinaman, even new dog—enough to drive the most important thoughts out of one's head. But you've come out to-night like a flower, my dear. Your gown is charming, and it suits you so well!"

She chatted on, speaking of the floor, the music, the decorations, the crowd.

"I love this sort of thing," she remarked. "People in the mass amuse me. Jack couldn't get away until midnight, but I wouldn't wait for him. I told him it didn't worry me a bit to come without an escort," smoothing away what little embarrassment might linger. The music started up again. The Keiths arose and made their adieux. Mrs, Sherwood looked after them, her bright eyes tender. Mrs. Keith was the only woman who had yet spoken to her.

"Isn't she simply stunning?" cried Keith. "She has something about her that makes most of these others look cheap."

"She's really wonderfully attractive and distinguished looking," agreed Nan.

"If she were only a little less practical—a little softer; more feminine—she'd be a sure-enough man killer. As it is, she needs a little more—you know what I mean—"

"More after Mrs. Morrell's fashion," suggested Nan a trifle wickedly. It popped out on the impulse, and the next instant Nan would have given anything if the words had not been said. Keith was arrested in mid- enthusiasm as though by cold water. He checked himself, looked at her sharply, then accepted the pseudo-challenge.

"Well, Mrs. Morrell, for all her little vulgarities, impresses you as being a very human sort of person."

He felt a sudden and unreasoning anger, possibly because the shot had hit a tender place.

"Shall we dance?" he suggested formally.

"I'm sorry," replied Nan, "I have this with Mr. Sansome; there he comes."

For the first time Keith felt a little irritated at the ubiquitous Sansome; but his sense of justice, while it could not smooth his ruffled feelings, nevertheless made itself heard.

"What I need is a drink," he told himself.

At the buffet he found a crowd of the non-dancing men, or those who had failed to get the early numbers. Here were many of his acquaintances; among them, to his surprise, he recognized the grim features of Malcolm Neil. All were drinking champagne. Keith joined them. They chaffed him unmercifully about his purchases of clouded titles in water lots, and he answered them in kind, aware of Neil's sardonically humorous eye fixed on him. But at the first bars of the next dance he bolted in search of Mrs. Morrell, with whom, he remembered, he had this number.

Mrs. Morrell danced smoothly and lightly for a woman of her size, but was inclined to snuggle up too close, to permit undistracted guidance to her partner. It was almost impossible to avoid collisions with other couples, unless one possessed a Spartan mind and an iron will. In spite of himself, Keith became increasingly aware of her breast pressing against his chest; her smooth arm against his shoulder; the occasional passing contact of her, scarcely veiled from the sense of touch by the thin flame-coloured silk; the perfume she affected; the faint odour of her bright blond hair. In an attempt to break the spell he made some banal remark, but she shook her head impatiently. She danced with her eyes half closed. When the music stopped she drew a deep sighing breath.

"You dance—oh, divinely!" she cried. "I might have known it."

She moved away, and Keith followed her, a trifle intoxicated.

"Let me see your card," she demanded abruptly. "Why, you haven't done your duty; this is hardly a third filled!"

"I hadn't started to fill it—and then you came in," breathed Keith.

They were opposite the door leading into one of the numerous small rooms off the main floor of the armoury.

"Let's sit here—and you can get me a punch," she suggested.

He brought the punch, and she drank it slowly, leaning back in an easy chair. The place was dimly lighted, and her blond, full beauty was more effective than in the more brilliantly lighted ballroom. Mrs. Morrell exerted all her fascination. The next dance was half over before either Keith or—apparently— Mrs. Morrell became aware of the fact.

"Oh, you must run!" she cried, apparently greatly exercised. "Don't mind me; go and find your partner."

Keith replied, that he had this dance free, a fact of which her inspection of his card had perfectly informed her. In answer to his return solicitation as to her own partner, she shrugged her shoulders.

"Oh, he'll find me," she said indifferently. "This is very cozy here."

They resumed what had become an ardent flirtation. Toward the end of the dance Mrs. Morrell's partner came in, looking very flurried. Before he could say a word, Mrs. Morrell began reproachfully to chide him with lack of diligence.

"I've been waiting just *rooted* to this spot!" she said truthfully.

"Shall we dance?" suggested the unfortunate young man.

"It's nearly over," replied Mrs. Morrell carelessly. "Do sit down with us. Get yourself something to drink. *Don't go!*" she commanded Keith fiercely under her breath.

At the beginning of the fourth dance, however, her next partner found her and led her away. She "made a face" over her shoulder at Keith.

When a woman makes up her mind to monopolize a man who has not acquired the fine arts of rudeness and escape she generally succeeds. Keith's cordial nature was incapable of rudeness. Besides, being a perfectly normal man, and Mrs. Morrell experienced and attractive, he liked being monopolized. It crossed his mind once or twice that he might be in for a scolding when he got home. Nan might be absurd. But he was so secure in his essential loyalty to Nan that his present conduct was more in the nature of a delightfully naughty escapade than anything else. He stole the apples now, and later would go dutifully for his licking. Men of Keith's nature are easily held and managed by a wise woman, but the woman must be very wise. Keith loved celebrations. On the wings of an occasion he rose joyfully and readily to incredible altitudes of high-spirited but harmless recklessness. Birthdays, anniversaries, New Years, Christmas, arrivals, departures, he seized upon with rapture. Each had its appropriate ceremonial, its traditional drink, the painstaking brewing of which was a sacred rite. On such occasions he tossed aside the cloak of the everyday. A "celebration" meant that you were different. Humdrum life and habits must be relegated to the background. It was permitted that, unabashed, you be as silly, as frivolous, as inconsequential, as boisterous, as lighthearted, as delightfully irresponsible as your ordinary concealed boyishness pleased. Customary repressions had nothing to do here. This was a celebration! And in the aforementioned our very wise woman would have seen—a safety valve.

Keith was off on a celebration to-night: an unpremeditated, freakish, impish, essentially harmless celebration, with a faint flavour of mischief in it because he had Nan in the back of his head all the time. He played up to Mrs. Morrell with exuberance, with honestly no thought except that he was having a whacking good time, and that old Nan was being teased. It was characteristic that for the time being he fell completely under Mrs. Morrell's fascination. They were together fully half the time, appearing on the floor only occasionally, then disappearing in one or the other of the many nooks. Mrs. Morrell "bolted" her dances shamelessly. Keith thought her awfully amusing and ingenious in the way she managed this. Sometimes they hid in out-of-the-way places. Sometimes she pretended to have mistaken the dance. "The sixth, are you very *sure*? I'm convinced it is only the fifth." Keith's conscience troubled him a little concerning the few names on his own card.

"I have this with Mrs. Wilkins," said he. "I really ought to go and look her up."

She took his card from him and deliberately tore it to small bits which she blew from the palm of her gloved hand. He protested in real dismay, but she looked him challengingly, recklessly, in the eye, until he laughed, too.

All this was, of course, well noticed. Keith, again characteristically, had not taken into consideration the great public. Nan might have remained comparatively indifferent to Keith's philandering about for an evening with the Morrell creature— she had by now a dim but growing understanding of "celebrations"—but that he should deliberately neglect and insult her in the face of all San Francisco was too much. Her high, young enjoyment of the evening fell to ashes. She was furiously angry, but she was a thoroughbred. Only a heightened colour and a sparkling eye might have betrayed her to an astute woman. Observing her, Ben Sansome took heart. It was evident to him that the Keiths had long since reached an absolute indifference in their relations, that they lived the conventional, tolerant, separate lives of the majority of married couples in Ben Sansome's smart acquaintance. He ventured to apply himself more assiduously, and was by no means badly received.

Keith remembered the next dance with his wife. He could not find her, although, a trifle conscience stricken, he searched everywhere. After the music had finished, she emerged from the dressing-room; the next time she could not be found at all. Evidently she was avoiding him with intention.

Mrs. Sherwood, after each dance, returned invariably to the same chair near the middle of one wall. There, owing to the fact that the "respectables" withdrew from the chairs on either side, withdrew gradually and without open rudeness, she held centre of a little court of her own. This made of it a sort of post of observation from which she could review all that was going on. She had no lack of partners, for she danced wonderfully, and in looks was quite the most distinguished woman there. Keith's dance with her came and went, but no Keith appeared to claim it. Mrs. Sherwood smiled a little grimly, and her glance strayed down the wall opposite until it rested on Nan. She examined the girl speculatively. Nan was apparently completely absorbed in Ben Sansome; but there was in her manner something feverish, hectic, a mere nothing, which did not escape Mrs. Sherwood's keen eye.

About midnight Sherwood appeared, and at once made his way to his wife's side. He was punctiliously dressed in the mode: a "swallowtail," bright, soft silk tie of ample proportions, frilled linen, and sparkling studs. He bent with an old-world formality over his wife's hand. She swept away her skirts from the chair at her side, her eyes sparkling softly with pleasure.

"You won't mind," she said carelessly to the young men surrounding her, "I want to talk to Jack for a minute."

They arose, laughing a little.

"That is your one fault, Mrs. Sherwood," said one, "you are altogether too fond of your husband."

"Well, how are things going?" asked Sherwood, as they moved away.

"I'm having a good time. But you're very late, Jack,"

"I know—I wanted to come earlier. Everything all right?"

At the question a little frown sketched itself on her clear brow.

"In general, yes," she said. "But they've got that Lewis boy out in the bar filling him up on champagne."

"That's a pity."

"It's a burning shame!" said she, "And I'd like to shake young Keith. He's dangled after the Morrell woman from start to finish in a manner scandalous to behold."

Sherwood laughed.

"The 'Morrell woman' will do his education good," he remarked.

"Well, she isn't doing that poor little Mrs. Keith's education any good," returned Mrs. Sherwood rather tartly.

Sherwood surveyed Nan and Ben Sansome leisurely.

"I must say she doesn't look crushed," he said, after a moment.

"Do you expect her to weep violently?" asked Mrs. Sherwood.

He accepted good naturedly the customary feminine scorn for the customary masculine obtuseness.

"Well, I don't know that we can help it," said he, philosophically.

Mrs. Sherwood appeared to come to a sudden resolution. She arose.

"You go get that Lewis boy away from the bar," she commanded.

Deliberately she shook and arranged her full skirts. The man with whom she had this dance, and who had been waiting dutifully for the conference to close, darted forward. She shook her head at him smilingly.

"I'm going to let you off," she told him. "You won't mind. I have something extra special to do."

She swept quite alone across the middle of the ballroom, serene, self- possessed; and walked directly toward Keith and Mrs.

Morrell, who were seated together at the other end. A perceptible pause seemed to descend. The music kept on playing, couples kept on dancing, but, nevertheless, suddenly the air was charged with attention. Sherwood looked after her with mingled astonishment and fond pride.

"A frontal attack, egad!" said he to himself.

Keith and Mrs. Morrell pretended, as long as they decently could, not to see her. She swam leisurely toward them. Finally Keith arose hastily; Mrs. Morrell stared straight ahead.

"Young man," accused Mrs. Sherwood, with a faint amusement

in her rich, low voice, "do you know that this is our dance?"

Keith excused his apparent lapse volubly, telling several times over that his program had been destroyed, that he was abject when he thought of the light this put him in.

"It is only when angels like yourself condescend to reach me a helping hand that I have even a chance to right myself," he added. He thought this rather a good touch.

Mrs. Sherwood stood before him easily, in perfect repose of manner, the half smile still sketching her lips. She said just nothing at all in response to his glib excuses; but when he had quite finished she laid her hand in his arm. Mrs. Morrell, her colour high, continued to stare straight ahead, immobile except for the tapping of one foot. To Keith's request to be excused she vouchsafed a stiff half nod, partly in his direction.

They danced. Mrs. Sherwood, like most people who have command enough of their muscles to be able to keep them in graceful repose, danced marvellously well. When she stopped after a single turn of the room, Keith expostulated vigorously.

"You are a perfect partner," he told her.

"Take me in here and get me a sherbet," she commanded, without replying to his protests. "That's good," she said, when she had tasted it. "Now sit down and listen to me. You are making a perfect spectacle of yourself. Don't you know it?"

Keith stiffened to an extreme formality.

"I beg your pardon!" said he freezingly.

"That may be your personal individual right"—went on Mrs. Sherwood's low, rich voice evenly. She was not even looking at him, but rather idly toward the open door into the ballroom. Her fan swung from one finger; every line of her body was relaxed. She might have been tossing him ordinary commonplaces from the surface of a detached mind—"making a spectacle of yourself," she explained; "but you're making a perfect spectacle of your wife as well—and in public. That is not your right at all."

Keith sprang to his feet, furious.

"You are meddling with what is really my own business, madam," said he.

For the first time she looked up at him, dearly and steadily. In the eyes.

"Very well. That is true. Stop a moment and think. Are you attending to your business yourself, even decently? Yes, I understand; you are angry with me. If I were a man, you would challenge me to a duel and all that sort of thing." She smiled indifferently. "Let's take that for granted and get on. Sweep it aside. You are man enough to do it, or I mistake you greatly. Look down into yourself for even one second. Are you playing fair all around? *Aren't you a little ashamed?*"

She held him with, her clear, level gaze. His own did not fall before it, and his head went back, but slowly his face and neck turned red. Thus they stared at each other for a full half minute, she smiling slightly, perfectly cool; he seething with a suppressed emotion of some sort. Then she turned indolently away.

"You're too fine to do things like that," she said, with a new softness in her voice; "we all have too much faith in you. The common tricks would not appeal to you, except in idleness; is it not so?"

She smiled up at him, a little sidewise. Keith caught his breath. For a fleeting instant this extraordinary woman deigned to exert her feminine charms for the first time the coquette looked from her eyes; for the first time he saw mysteriously deep in her veiled nature a depth of possibility, of rich possibility—he could not grasp it—it was gone. But in spite of himself his pulses leaped like a flame. But now she was gazing again at the ballroom door, cool, indolent, aloof, unapproachable. Yet just at that instant, somehow, the other woman looked shallow, superficial, cold. His glance fell on Mrs. Morrell still sitting where he had left her. Something was wrong with her effect—Analysis was submerged in a blaze of anger. This anger was not now against the woman before him; his instinct prevented that. Nor against Mrs. Morrell nor his wife; reluctant justice prevented that.

Nor against himself—where it really belonged. Things were out of joint; he felt cross-grained and ugly. Mrs. Sherwood rose.

"You may take me back now," said she.

As they glided across the floor together, her small sleek head came just above his shoulder. No embarrassment disturbed her manner. Keith could not find in him a spark of resentment against her. She moved by his side with an air of poise and detachment as a woman whose mind had long since weighed and settled the affairs of her own cosmos so that trifles could not disturb her.

Leaving her in her accustomed chair, where Sherwood waited, Keith loyally returned to Mrs. Morrell, who still sat alone. Subconsciously he noticed something wrong with Mrs. Morrell. Her gowning was indeed rather a conspicuous effort than an artistic success. She had badly torn her dress—perhaps that was it.

Mrs. Morrell received him with every appearance of sympathy.

"You poor thing!" she cried. "What a fearful situation! Of course I know you couldn't help it."

But Keith was grumpy and monosyllabic. He refused to discuss the situation or Mrs. Sherwood, returning with an obvious effort to commonplaces. Mrs. Morrell exerted all her fascination to get him back to the former level. A little cold imp sat in the back of Keith's brain and criticized sardonically; Why will big women persist in being kittenish? Why doesn't she mend that awful rent, it's fairly sloppy! Suppose she thinks that kind of talk is funny! I *do* wish she wouldn't laugh in that shrill, cackling fashion! In short, the very tricks that an hour ago were jolly and amusing were now tiresome. Having been distrait, ungallant, masculinely put out for another fifteen minutes, he abruptly excused himself, sought out Nan, and went home.

From her point of observation, Mrs. Sherwood watched them go. Nan looked very tired, and every line of Keith's figure expressed a grumpy moroseness.

"Congratulations," said Sherwood.

"He certainly is a child of nature," returned his wife. "Look at him! He is cross, so he *looks* cross. That this is a ballroom and that all San Francisco is present is a mere detail."

"How did you break it up?" asked Sherwood curiously.

"Men are so utterly ridiculous! He had built up a lot of illusions for himself, but his instincts are true and good. It needed only a touch. It was absurdly simple."

"He'll go back to the Morrell to-morrow," asserted Sherwood confidently.

She shook her head.

"Not to her. He *sees* her now. And not to-morrow. But eventually to somebody, perhaps. He has curly hair."

Sherwood laughed.

"Shear him, like Sampson," he suggested. "But it strikes me he has about the most attractive woman—bar one—in town right at home."

"She'd have no trouble in holding him if she were only *awake*. But she's only a dear little child—and about as helpless. She has very little subtlety. I'm afraid she'll follow the instincts of her training. She'll be too proud to do anything herself to attract her husband, once his attentions to her seem to drop off. She'll just become cold and proud—and perhaps eventually turn elsewhere."

"I don't believe she's a bit that kind," asserted Sherwood positively.

"Nor do I. But, Jack, a woman lonely enough has fancies, that in the long run may become convictions."

XXII

Mrs. Sherwood was completely right. Keith had *seen* Mrs. Morrell. The glamour had fallen from her at a touch. He did not in the least understand how this had happened, and considered that it was his own fault. Mrs. Morrell had not changed in the least, but he had, somehow. He looked upon himself as fickle, disloyal, altogether despicable. Yet for the life of him he could not get up the slightest spark of enthusiasm for musical evenings, Sunday night suppers, or week-end excursions into the country. They had fallen dead to his taste; and with the sudden revolt to which such temperaments as his are subject, he could not bear even the thought of them without a feeling of incipient boredom. The blow administered to his self- respect put him quite out of conceit with himself and the world in general. If he had followed his natural instinct, he would instanter have thrown, overboard all the Morrell episode, bag and baggage.

But that was, of course, impossible. Keith felt his obligations; he was a man of honour; he had respect for the feelings of others; he could not make friendly people the victims of his own outrageous freaks. That was out of the question!

Mrs. Morrell sent for him. She had been puzzled by the episode of the evening before. It would have been absolutely incredible to her that a hundred words from a woman who was not her rival could have destroyed her influence over this man. She had considerable knowledge of men, and she had played her cards carefully. But she realized that something was the matter; and she thought that the time had come to use the power she had gained. A note dispatched by the Chinaman would do.

Keith obeyed the summons. He knew himself well enough to realize that the intimacy, such as it was, must come to a pretty abrupt termination. Otherwise, he would shortly get very bored; and when he got very bored he became, in spite of himself, reserved and self-contained to the point of rudeness. For the exact reason that he saw thus clearly, his conscience was smiting him hard. Mrs. Morrell had done nothing to deserve this treatment. He was a dastard, a coward, ashamed of himself. If she wanted to see him, it was her due that he obey her summons promptly. He went with the vague idea of making amends by doing whatever she seemed to require—for this once.

She entered the dim sitting-room clad in a flowing silken negligee, which she excused on the ground of laziness.

"I'm still a little tired from last night," she said, with a laugh.

The soft material and informal cut clung to and defined the lines of her figure, showing to especial advantage the long sweep of her hips, the pliancy of her waist, the swell of her fine bust. A soft lilac colour set off the glint of her fair hair. She was, in fact, feeling a little languid from the reaction of the ball and in a sudden rush of emotion she admired Keith's crisp freshness. Her eyes swam a little and her breast heaved.

But the preliminary conversation went by jerks. Keith answered her advances with an effort toward ease and cordiality, but with a guarded, unnatural manner that sent a sudden premonitory chill to the woman's heart. Her instinct warned her. As the minutes passed, her uneasiness grew to the point of fear. Was she losing him? Why? This was no time for ordinary methods.

She arose and went to sit by his side.

"What's the matter, dear?" she asked.

"Nothing."

"Why are you acting in this manner? What have I done?"

"I'm not; you haven't done anything—of course."

She suddenly leaned forward, looking into his eyes, projecting all the force of her magnetism. She had before seen him respond, felt him quiver to her tentative, mischievous advances,

"Kiss me," she breathed.

Poor Keith was having a miserable enough time. He clung to his first thought—that this evening was her due, that he was in some way bound, in ending everything, to pay whatever coin he had left. He obeyed her, touching her lips lightly and coldly with his own. Never was chaster caress bestowed on melting mood!

She flung him violently aside, her face writhing and contorted with fury. She was enlightened, completely, as she could have been enlightened in no other manner.

"You can go!" she cried hoarsely. "Get out! Don't dare enter this house again!"

He made some sort of spiritless, feeble protest, trying his best to put some convincing quality into it. But she did not even listen. The ungoverned tiger-cat part of her nature was in the ascendant, the fierce pride of the woman living near the edge of the half-world. She would gladly have killed him. At length he went, very confused, bewildered, miserable— and relieved! He left behind him a bitter enemy.

XXIII

In complete revulsion, Keith scuttled the frivolous world of women. As he expressed it, he was sick of women. They made him tired. Too much fuss trying to keep even with their vagaries. A man liked something he could bite on. He plunged with all the enthusiasm and energy of his vivid personality into his business deal of the water lots and into the fascinating downtown life of the pioneer city. The mere fact that he had ended that asinine Morrell affair somehow made him think he had made it all up to Nan, and he settled back tacitly and without further preliminaries into what his mood considered a most satisfactory domestic basis. That is, he took his home and his home life for granted. It was there when he needed it. He admired Nan greatly, and supplied her with plenty of money, and took her to places when he could get the time. Some day, when things were not quite so lively, they would go somewhere together. In the meantime he never failed to ask her every evening if she had enjoyed herself that day; and she never failed to reply that she had. Everything was most comfortable.

After the Firemen's Ball Nan, somehow relieved of any definite uneasiness, felt that she should be made much of, should be a little wooed, that Keith should make up a little for having been somewhat of a naughty boy. When, instead, she was left more alone than before, she was hurt and depressed. Of course, Milton did not realize—but what was there for her? Wing Sam ran the house; she worked a good deal in the garden, assisted by Gringo. Probably at no time in modern history have wives been left so much alone and so free as during this period. The

Stewart Edward White

man's world was so absorbing; the woman's so empty.

Ben Sansome dropped in quite often. He was always amusing, always agreeable, interested in all sorts of things, ready to give his undivided attention to any sort of a problem, no matter how trivial, to consider it attentively, and to find for it a fair and square deliberate solution. This is exceedingly comforting to the feminine mind. He taught Gringo not to "jump up"; he found out what was the matter with the *Gold of Ophir* cutting; he discovered and took her to see just the shade of hangings she had long sought for the blue room. Within a very short time he had established himself on the footing of the casual old-time caller, happening by, dropping in, commenting and advising detachedly, drifting on again before his little visit had assumed rememberable proportions. He had always the air of just leaning over the fence for a moment's chat; yet he contrived to spend the most of an afternoon. He spoke of Keith often, always in affectionate terms, as of a sort of pal, much as though he and Nan *both* owned him, he, of course, in a lesser degree.

One afternoon, after he had actually been digging away at a bulb bed for half an hour, Nan suggested that he come in for refreshment. Gradually this became a habit. Sansome and Nan sat cozily either side the little Chinese tea table. He visibly luxuriated.

"You don't know what a privilege this is for me—for any lonesome bachelor in this crude city—to have a home like this to come to occasionally."

He hinted at his situation, but made of its details a dark mystery. The final impression was one of surface lightness and gayety, but of inner sadness.

"It is a terrible city for a man without an anchor!" he said. "Keith is a lucky fellow! If I only had some one, as he has, I might amount to something." A gesture implied what a discouraged butterfly sort of person he really was.

"You ought to marry," said Nan gently.

"Marry!" he cried. "Dear lady, whom? Where in this awful mixture they call society could one find a woman to marry?"

"There are plenty of nice women here," chided Nan.

"Yes—and all of them taken by luckier fellows! You wouldn't have me marry Sally Warner, would you—or any of the other half-dozen Sally Warners? I might as well marry a gas chandelier, a grand piano, and a code of immorals—but the standard of such women is so different from the standard of women like yourself."

Nan might pertinently have inquired what Ben Sansome did in this gallery, anyhow; but so cold-blooded and direct an attack would have required a cool detachment incompatible with his dark, good looks, his winning, appealing manners, his thoughtfulness in little things, his almost helpless reliance on her sympathy; in other words, it presupposed a rather cynical, elderly person. And Nan was young, romantic, easily stirred.

"All you need is to believe in yourself a little more," she said earnestly and prettily. "Why don't you undertake something instead of drifting? Some of the people you go with are not especially good for you—do you think so?"

"Good for me?" he laughed bitterly. "Who cares if I go to the dogs? They'd rather like me to; it would keep them company! And I don't know that I care much myself!" he muttered in a lower tone.

She leaned forward, distressed, her eyes shining with expostulation.

"You mustn't hold yourself so low," she told him vehemently. "You mustn't! There are a great many people who believe in you. For their sake you should try. If you would only be just a little bit serious—in regard to yourself, I mean. A gay life is all very well—"

"Gay?" he interrupted, then caught himself. "Yes, I suppose I do seem gay— God knows I try not to cry out—but, really, sometimes I'm near to ending it all—"

She was excited to a panic of negation.

"Oh, no! no!" she expostulated vehemently. ("Egad, she's stunning when she's aroused!" thought Sansome.) "You mustn't talk like that! It isn't fair to yourself; it isn't fair to your manhood! Oh, how you do need some one to pull you up! If I could only help!"

He raised his head and looked directly at her, his dark, melancholy eyes lighting slowly.

"You have helped; you are helping," he murmured. "I suppose I have been weak and a coward, I will try."

"That's right. I am so glad," she said, glowing with sweetness and a desire to aid. "Now you must turn over a new leaf," she hesitated. "Every way, I mean," she added with a little blush.

"I know I drink more than I ought," he supplied in accents of regret.

"Don't you suppose you could do without?" she begged very gently.

"Will you help me?" He turned on her quickly; then, his delicate instincts perceiving a faint, instinctive recoil at his advance, he added: "Just let me come here occasionally, into this quiet atmosphere, when it gets too hard and I can see no light; just to get your help, the strength I shall need to tide me over."

He looked very handsome and romantic and young. He was

apparently very, deeply in earnest. Nan experienced a rash of pity, of protective maternal emotion.

"Yes, do come," she assented softly.

XXIV

All this time Keith was busy every minute of the day. The water-lot matter was absorbing all his attention. Through skilful and secret agents Neil had acquired a great deal of scrip issued by the city for various public works and services which the holders had not yet exchanged for the new bonds. These he turned over to Keith. Very quietly, by prear-rangement, the latter sued and obtained judgments. When all this had been fully accomplished—and not before then—the veil of secrecy was rent. Rowlee's paper advertised a forthcoming sale of water lots to satisfy the judgments.

Then followed, for Keith, an anxious period of three days. But at the end of that time the commissioners issued a signed warning that the titles conveyed by this sale would not be considered legal. On seeing this, Keith at once rushed around to Neil's office.

"Here it is," he announced jubilantly. "They held off so long that I began o be afraid they did not intend to play our game for us. But it's all right."

The matter was widely discussed; but next morning placards, bearing the text of the commissioners' warning, were posted on every blank wall in town and distributed as dodgers. These were attributed by the public to zeal on the part of those officials; but the commissioners knew nothing about it.

"Some anonymous friend of the city must have done it,"

Hooper told his friends, and added, "We are delighted!"

The unknown friend was Malcolm Neil himself.

This warning had its effect. As Keith had predicted, nobody cared to put good money into what was officially and authoritatively announced as a bad title. At the sheriff's sale there were no bona fide bidders except the secret agents of Malcolm Neil. The sheriff's titles—such as they were—went for a song. Immediately the ostensible purchasers were personally warned by the commission; but they seemed satisfied.

So matters rested until, a little later, the commissioners inserted in all the papers the customary legal advertisements setting forth a sale by them, under the State law, of these same water lots to satisfy the interest and fill the sinking fund for the bonds. The next morning appeared a statement signed by all the ostensible purchasers under the sheriff's sale. This stated dearly and succinctly the intention to contest any titles given by the commissioners, even to the highest courts. This was marked *advt*, to indicate the newspaper's neutrality in the matter. Rowlee commented on the situation editorially, He took the righteous and indignant attitude, expressing extreme journalistic horror that such a hold-up should be possible in a modern, civilized community, hurling editorial contempt on the dastardly robbers who were thus intending to shake down the innocent purchasers, etc. In fact, he laid it on thick, But he managed to insinuate a doubt. Between the lines the least astute reader could read Rowlee's belief that perhaps these first purchasers might have a case, iniquitous but legal. He hammered away at this for a week. By the end of that time he had, by the most effective, indirect methods—purporting all the time to be attacking the signers of the warning—succeeded in instilling into the public mind a substantial distrust of the stability of the titles to be conveyed at the commissioners' sale. Malcolm Neil complimented him highly at their final and secret interview.

Again Keith's predictions were fulfilled to the letter. Nobody wanted to buy a lawsuit. There were a few bidders, it is true, but they were faint hearted. Another set of Malcolm's secret agents bid all the lots in at a nominal figure. That very afternoon they all met in Neil's stuffy little back office. Keith had the deeds prepared. All that was necessary was to affix the signatures. The purchasers under both sales conveyed their rights to Neil and Keith. The latter now possessed uncontested and incontestable title.

XXV

Having personally delivered the deeds to the recorder's office, Keith went home. In the relief from pressure, the triumph, and the exaltation, his instinct carried him to the actual background of his life—his genuine but preoccupied affection for Nan. The constraint, that had been so real to her, had never been anything but nebulous to him.

He burst into the house, capered around the room boyishly, seized her, and waltzed her gayly about. Quite taken by surprise, Nan's first thought was that he had been drinking too much; so naturally she failed to rise instantly to the occasion.

"Stop it, Milton!" she cried. "What has got into you! You're tearing me to ribbons!"

He laughed heartily.

"You must think I'm crazy," he acknowledged. "Sit down here, and learn what a great man your husband is." He poured out the story of the transaction, omitting no details of the clever schemes by which it had been worked. He was, above all, proud of his legal address and acumen—there was something in Eastern training, after all; this lay right under their noses, but none of them saw it until he came along and picked it up. "And there are some pretty smart men out here, too, let me tell you that," he added. "They're from all parts of the world, and they've had a hard practical education, their eye teeth are cut!" His egotism over being keener than the acknowledged big men was very fresh and charming. The money gained he mentioned as an afterthought, only when the other aspect of the situation had been exhausted. "The cold hard dollars are pretty welcome just now," he told her. "There's about a quarter million in those lots—and we can realize on all or part of them at any time. All came out of here!" He tapped his forehead, and paused in his rapid pacing to and fro to look down at her In the easy chair, "We are well off now. We needn't scrimp and save"—it did not for the moment occur to him that they had not been doing so—"I'm going to get you eight new gowns, and twelve new hats, and a bushel of diamonds—"

"I'm glad, very glad!" she cried, catching his enthusiasm, her mind for the first time occupying itself seriously with the mechanism of the deal. At first, when he had been explaining, she had not thrown off the impression that he had been drinking, and so had paid little attention to his explanations. "It sounds like magic. Tell me again—how you did it,"

Nothing loath, he went over it again, making clear the double clouding of the titles.

But Nan, being much alone, had the habit, shared with few women of that time, of reading the newspapers. She had followed Rowlee's campaign, and she had taken seriously the editor's diatribes, Rowlee had been talking for effect. The ideals of ultimate civic honesty were yet fifty years in the future, but he had stumbled on their principle. Nan's mind, untrained in any business ethics, caught them; and her sure natural instincts had accepted their essential justice. In recognizing Milton's connection as promoter with just this deal, she was suddenly called upon to make adjustments for which there was no time. She knew Milton would do nothing wrong, and yet—he was waiting in triumph for her response.

"It was very clever. And yet, somehow, it doesn't sound right—" she puzzled, "Are you sure it's honest?"

"Honest?" he snorted, halted in mid-career, "Of course it's

honest! Why isn't it honest?"

Confronted with the direct question, she really did not know. She groped, proffering tentatively some of the arguments half remembered from Rowlee's editorial columns. But she confronted now a lawyer, sure of himself. Keith explosively, and contemptuously demolished her contentions. Everything was absolutely legal, every step of it. If a man hadn't a right to buy in property at any sale and sell it again where he wanted, where in thunder was our boasted liberty? Just the kind of fool notion women get! Keith in his honest pride and triumph had come for sympathy and admiration. Turned back on himself, he became vaguely resentful, and shortly left the house.

Hardly had the front door closed after him when Nan burst into tears. She had not meant it to come out that way at all. Of course she had had no real thought that Milton would do anything dishonest; how absurd of him to take it that way! She had simply expressed a queer instinctive thought that had flashed across her mind; and now she could not for the life of her guess how she had come to do so. Miserably and passionately she realized that she had bungled it.

XXVI

But if Keith missed the appreciation of his triumph at home, he received full meed of it downtown. In a corner of the Empire a dozen of the biggest men in town were gathered. They were Sam Brannan; Palmer, of Palmer, Cook & Co.; Colonel E. D. Baker, the original "silver-tongued orator"; Dick Blatchford, the contractor; Judge Terry, of the Supreme Court; oily, coarse Ned McGowan; Nugent and Rowlee, editors, and some others. They were doing an exceedingly important part of their daily business: sipping their late afternoon cocktails. Calhoun Bennett joined them.

"Little item of news to interest you-all," drawled the Southerner. "I've just come down from the recorder's office. The deeds for the water lots have just been recorded." He paused.

"Have a drink, Cal," urged Dick Blatchford, "and sit down. What of it?"

"They were recorded in the names of Malcolm Neil and young Keith. I'll have a cocktail."

"That so? Pretty shaky title. Which sale did they record under?"

"Both!" said Bennett.

He stood until he saw that the significance of this had soaked in; then he drew out a chair and sat down. Ned McGowan chuckled hoarsely.

"Pretty slick!" said he. "Wonder some of us didn't think of that! I suppose they went around and scared the purchasers until they got them, pretty cheap. Trust old Neil to drive a bargain!"

But Palmer, the banker, who had been thinking, here spoke up:

"The purchasers were undoubtedly their agents," he surmised quietly.

"By God, you're right!" cried Terry. "Old Malcolm is certainly the devil without a tail!"

"Speak of him and you get him," remarked Colonel Baker, pointing out Neil, who had just entered.

They raised a shout at him, until finally the old man, reluctantly and crabbedly, sidled over to join them.

"You're discovered, old fox!" cried Terry; "and the outraged dignity of the law demands a drink."

They plied him with half-facetious, half-envious congratulations. But Neil would have none of them.

"Not my scheme," he growled. "Entirely Keith's. I'm a sleeping partner only. He engineered it all, thought of it all, dragged me in."

"You must have made a good thing out of it, Mr. Neil," suggested Palmer respectfully.

The formidable old man eyed the speaker grumpily for a moment.

"About a quarter million, cool, between us," he vouchsafed finally. He was, for some reason, willing to brag a bit.

This statement was received in admiring silence by all but Terry. Everybody but that devil-may-care and lawless pillar of the law was afraid of Neil. But Terry would joke with anybody.

"I hope you're going to let him have a little of it, Neil," he laughed.

The old man shifted his eyes from Palmer to Terry with much the air of restraining heavy guns. Terry met the impact untroubled.

"Judge," grunted the financier at last, "that young man will get his due share. He has tied me up in a contract that even your honoured court would find difficulty in breaking."

With this parting shot he arose and stumped out.

"If Malcolm Neil acknowledges he is tied up," observed Terry, who had not been in the slightest degree disturbed, "he is certainly tied up!"

"Consider the man who tied him," begged Colonel Baker. "He must, in the language of the poets, be a lallapaloozer."

"He's worth getting hold of," said Dick Blatchford.

Therefore, when, a little later, Keith appeared, he was hailed jovially, and invited to drink. Everybody was very cordial. Within five minutes he was hail fellow with them all, joking with the most august of them on terms of equality. Judge Terry, in whose court he had stood abashed, plied him with cocktails; Colonel Baker told several stories, one of which was new; Sam Brannan, with the mixture of coarseness, overbearing manners, and fascination that made him personally attractive to men and some women, called him "my boy"; and the rest of the party had whole-heartedly taken him in and were treating him as one of themselves. Keith had known all these men, of course, but they had been several cuts above him in importance, and his relations with most of them had been formal. His whole being glowed and expanded. After the first cocktail or two, and after a little of this grateful petting, he had some difficulty in keeping himself from getting too expansive, in holding himself down to becoming modesty, in not talking too much. He quite realized the meaning of this sudden cordiality; but he welcomed it as another endorsement, from the highest, most unimpeachable sources, of his cleverness and legal acumen.

They drank and talked until twilight. Then Keith began to make his excuses.
They shouted him down.

"You're going to dinner with us, my son," stated Brannan. "They've opened an oyster palace down the street, and we're going to sample it."

"But my wife—" began Keith.

"Permit me," interrupted Terry, bending his tall form in courtesy. "I am about to dispatch a messenger to Mrs. Terry, and shall be pleased to instruct him to call at your mansion also."

It was so arranged. Immediately they adjourned to the new "Oyster Palace," a very gaudy white and gilt monstrosity with mirrors and negro minstrels. There were small private rooms, it seemed, and one of these was bespoken from the smiling manager, flattered at the patronage of these substantial men.

San Francisco lived high in those days. It could pay, and for pay the best will go anywhere. The dinner was quite perfect. There were more cocktails and champagne. Under the influence of good fellowship and drinks, Keith was finally prevailed upon to give the details of the whole transaction.

Perhaps this was a little indiscreet, but he was carried away by the occasion. The noisy crowd suddenly became quiet, and listened with the deepest attention. When Keith had finished, there ensued a short silence. Then Judge Terry delivered his opinion.

"Sound as a dollar," he pronounced at last. "Not a hole in it. Is that your opinion, Colonel Baker?"

"Clever piece of work," nodded the orator gravely. After this interim of sobriety the dinner proceeded more and more noisily. The drink affected the different men in different ways. A flush appeared high on the cheek bones of Terry's lean face and an added dignity in his courtly manner. Brannan became louder and more positive. On Blatchford his potations had no appreciable effect except that his round face grew redder. Ned McGowan dropped even his veneer of good breeding, became foul mouthed and profane, full of unpublishable reminiscence to which nobody paid any particular attention. Calhoun Bennett's speech became softer, more deliberate, more consciously Southern. Keith, who was really most unaccustomed to the heavy drinking then in vogue, was filled with a warm and friendly feeling toward everybody. His thoughts were a bit vague, and he had difficulty in focussing his mind sharply. The lights were very bright, and the room warm.

Suddenly they were all in the open air under the stars. There seemed to have been an unexplained interim. Everybody was smoking cigars. Keith was tugging at his pocket and expostulating something about payment—something to do with the dinner. Evidently some part of him had gone on talking and thinking. The fresh air brought him back to the command. Various suggestions were being proffered. Blatchford was for hiring rigs and driving out to the Mission; Calhoun Bennett suggested the El Dorado; but Sam Brannan's bull voice decided them.

"I'm going to Belle's!" he roared, and at once started off up the street. The idea was received with acclamation. They straggled up the street toward the residential portion of town.

Keith followed. The delayed action of the drink had thrown him into a delicious whirling haze. He felt that he could be completely master of himself at any moment merely by making the effort; only it did not at present seem worth while. He knew where Belle's was: it was the ornate house diagonally across the street from his own, the one concerning which the clerk had been so evasive when they were house hunting.

Belle's was a three-story frame building, differing in no outward essential from the fashionable residences around it. On warm evenings there sometimes came through the opened windows the sound of a piano, the clink of glasses, loud laughter or singing. The chance bystander might have heard identically the same from any other house in the neighbour-hood. Only Belle's occasionally—rarely occasionally—contributed a crash or an oath. Such things were, however, quickly hushed. Belle's was run on respectable lines. Men went in and out quite openly, with the tolerance of most, but to the scandal of a few. Those curious, consulting the yellowed files of the newspapers, can read little protests—signed with *nom de plumes*—from young women, complaining that young men of their acquaintance, after calling decorously on them, would cross quite openly to the house over the way. Yet they were powerless, for a year or so at least, to break up the custom.

For Belle's was a carry-over from the 49-51 days when of social life there was none at all. It differed from the merely disreputable house. Belle prided herself on quiet conduct and many friends. In person she was a middle-aged, still attractive Frenchwoman. She had furnished her parlours very elaborately, and she insisted that both her employees and clients should behave in the public rooms with the greatest circumspection.

Indeed, a casual visitor, unacquainted with the character of the place, might well have been deceived. The women sitting about were made up and very decollete, to be sure, but their

Stewart Edward White

conduct, while not always of the highest tone, was nevertheless quite devoid of freedom. Belle permitted no overt word or action; nor was any visitor subjected to another expectation than the occasional opening of a bottle of wine "for the good of the house."

But outside of the one fundamental rule of decency, the caller could make himself comfortable in his own way. He could lounge, pound the piano, joke, play games, smoke where he pleased, and enjoy what was then a rarity—the company and conversation of nimble-witted, well-dressed, beautiful women whose ideas were not narrow. Ultimate possibilities were always kept very much in the background, but that there were possibilities made for present relaxation or freedom.

Twice a year Belle was in the habit of giving a grand party. The invitations were engraved. Entertainment was on a sumptuous scale. There were dancing, all sorts of card games, an elaborate supper, the best of music, often professional entertainers of great merit. Everything was free except wine. Nearly the whole masculine population turned out for Belle's big party—judges, legislators, bankers, merchants, as well as the professional politicians and the gamblers. The most prominent men of the city frequented Belle's at other times openly, without fear of public opinion—many of them merely for the sense of freedom and relaxation they there enjoyed. Everybody was welcome.

Keith, however, knowing the character of the place, had never been inside its doors. Now, enveloped in his rosy haze, exceedingly contented with his company, he followed where they led. At the door a neat coloured maid relieved him of his hat and coat, and smiled a welcome. His dazzled vision took in a long drawing-room, soft red carpets, red brocade curtains of heavy material, with edges of gold fringe and with gold cords, chandeliers of many dangling prisms, a white marble mantel, a grand piano, a few pictures of the nude, and many chairs. Ravishingly beautiful, wonderfully dressed women sat about in indolent attitudes.

The hilarious party at once scattered through the room, Calhoun Bennett went to the piano and began to play sentimental airs. Ned McGowan, his face very red, enthroned himself in an easy chair, clasping girls who perched on either arm. He talked to them in a low voice. They leaned over to hear, and every moment or so they burst into shrieks of laughter. Judge Terry was listening intently to some serious communication Belle herself was making to him. Sam Brannan was roaring for champagne. The others were circulating here and there, talking, playing practical jokes. Altogether, to Keith's rosy vision, a colourful and delightful scene. Nobody paid him the least attention. How long he stood there he did not know. The groups before him shifted and changed confusedly. The lights seemed to blaze and to dim, and then to blaze again. After a long interval he became aware of a touch on his arm. He looked down. A piquant, dark-eyed, tilt-nosed girl was smiling up at him.

"Wat you do?" she was begging. "You come wiz me?"

He focussed his attention on the room. It was almost empty. He saw the back of Judge Terry disappearing into the street. He passed his hand across his eyes.

"Where are the others?" he asked confusedly.

She laughed with significance. He looked down at her again. Her complexion was a sort of dead white, her lips were red and glistening, her eyes were darkened. He turned suddenly and left the house. The coloured maid, disappointed in a tip, stood in the doorway, his hat and coat in her hands, staring after him. The cool air a little cleared his brain. He stopped short in the middle of the street, trying to collect himself.

"I'm drunk," he solved finally, and proceeded very carefully toward his own house. After each dozen steps he paused to collect his thoughts before proceeding. In one of these pauses he distinctly heard a window slam shut; there were plenty of louder things, he heard only the window. He hadn't the least idea of the time of night, except that it must be very late. As a matter of fact, it was not more than half-past ten. Near his own gate he nearly ran into a woman strolling. With some instinct of apology, he turned in her direction. As his bare head was revealed in the dim light, the woman uttered a low laugh.

"And was Belle as charming as ever?" demanded Mrs. Morrell sweetly but icily. "Go in carefully now, so dear little wifey won't know."

She laughed again and moved past him. He stared after her with a vague sense of injustice, somehow; then went on.

XXVII

Keith was sorry next morning, but he was not repentant, in the sense of feeling that he had done anything fatally wrong. He was disgusted with himself. He wasted no regrets, but did register a very definite intention not to let *that* happen again! It was all harmless enough, once in a way, but it was not his sort of thing. Nan would not understand it a bit—why should she? His head ached, and he was feeling a little conscience-stricken about Nan, anyway. He must take her around more, see more of her. Business had been very absorbing lately, but now that this deal had been brought off successfully, it was only due her and himself that he take a little time off. In his present mood he convinced himself, as do most American business or professional men, that he was being driven in his work, and that he wanted nothing better than a let-up from the grind. As a matter of fact, he—and they—love their work.

In this frame of mind he started downtown, rather late. On the street he met a number of his friends. A good many of them chaffed him good-naturedly about the night before. By the time he reached his office he was feeling much better. Things were assuming more of an everyday comfortable aspect. He had not been seated ten minutes before Dick Blatchford drifted in, smoking a black cigar that gave Keith a slight qualmish feeling. Dick seemed quite unaffected by the evening before.

"Hullo, Milt!" he boomed, rolling his heavy form into a chair, his round, red face beaming. "How's the wild Injin this morning? Say, you're a wonder when you get started! You needn't deny it; wasn't I there?" He shook his head, chuckling fatly. "Look here," he went on, "I'm busy this morning—got to get down to North Beach to see Harry Meigs—and I guess you are." He tossed over a package of papers that he produced from an inside pocket. "Look those over at your leisure. I think we better sue the sons of guns. Let me know what you think." He fished about in a tight-drawn waistcoat pocket with a chubby thumb and forefinger, pulled out a strip of paper, and flipped it to Keith as casually as though it were a cigarette pape. "There's a little something as a retainer," said he. "Well, be good!"

After he had lumbered out, Keith examined the check. It was for one thousand dollars. If anything were needed to restore his entire confidence in himself, this retainer would have sufficed. The little spree was regrettable, of course, but it had brought him a client—and a good one!

Two days later Keith, who now had reason to spend more time in his office, received another and less welcome visitor: this was Morrell. The young Englishman, his clean-cut face composed to wooden immobility, his too-close-set eyes squinting watchfully, came in as though on a social call.

"Just dropped around to look at your diggin's," he told the surprised Keith. "Not badly fixed here; good light and all."

He accepted a cigar, and sat for some moments, his hat and stick carefully disposed on his knees.

"Look here, Keith," he broke into a desultory chat after a few minutes. "Deucedly awkward, and all that, of course; but I've been wondering whether you would, be willing to tide me over—remittances late, and all that sort of thing. Stony for the moment. Everything lovely when the mails arrive. Neighbours, see a lot of each other, and that sort, you know."

Keith was totally unprepared for this, and floundered. Morrell, watching him calmly, went on:

"Of course I wouldn't think of coming to you, old chap—
plenty of people glad to bank for me temporarily—but I
wanted you to know just how we stand—Mrs. Morrell and I—
that we feel friendly to you, and all that sort of thing, you
know! You can rely on us—no uneasiness, you know."

"Why, that's very kind of you," returned Keith, puzzled.

"Not a bit! The way I looked at it was that a chap wouldn't
borrow from a man he wasn't friendly with, it isn't done." He
laughed his high, cackling laugh, "So I said to Mimi, 'the dear
man must be worryin' his head off.' It was lucky for you, old
top, that a woman of the world with some sense saw you the
other night instead of some feather-headed gossipin' fool. But
Mimi's not that."

Keith was slowly beginning to suspect, but as yet he considered
his suspicion unjust.

"How much do you need?" he asked,

"Five hundred dollars," replied Morrell coolly.

"I doubt I have that sum free in ready cash."

Morrell looked him in the eye.

"I fancy you will be able to raise it," he said very deliberately.

The men looked at each other.

"This is blackmail, then," said Keith without excitement.

Morrell became very stiff and English in manner.

"Words do not frighten me, sir. This is a personal loan. It is an
action between friends, just as my silence on the subject of
your peccadillo is a friendly action. I mention that silence, not
as a threat, but as an evidence of my own friendly feeling. I see

I have made a mistake."

He arose, his bearing very frigid. Keith was naturally not in the least deceived by this assumption of injured innocence, but he had been thinking.

"Hold on!" he said. "You must forgive my being startled; and you must admit you were a little unfortunate in your presentation. For this loan, what security?"

"My personal note," replied Morrell calmly.

"I must look into my resources. I will let you know to-morrow."

"Not later than to-morrow. I'll call at this hour," said Morrell with meaning.

After the Englishman had gone Keith considered the matter at leisure. Although of a sanguine and excitable temperament When only little things were involved, he was clear headed and uninfluenced by personal feeling in real emergencies.

First, would the Morrells carry out the implied threat? His instinct supplied that answer. Of Morrell himself he had never had any trust. Now he remembered what had never really struck him before: that Morrell, even in this fast and loose society, had never been more than tolerated, and that, appa-rently, only because of the liveliness of his wife. He had the indefinable air of a bad 'un. And Keith's knowledge of women was broad enough to tell him that Mrs. Morrell would be relentless.

Second, would a denial avail against their story? His commonsense told him that if the Morrells started this thing they would carry it through to a finish. There was no sense in it otherwise, for such an attack would mean the burning of most of their social bridges. Morrell could get witnesses from Belle's—say, the coloured maid whom he had not tipped—

and there were his hat and coat.

Third, could he afford to let them tell the tale? As far as his position in the city, either professionally or socially, most decidedly yes. But at home, as decidedly no. In her calmest, most judicial, trusting, loving mood, Nan could never understand. Her breeding and upbringing were against it. She could never comprehend the difference between such a place as Belle's and any disreputable house—if there was a difference. This point needed little argument.

Then he must pay.

Having definitely decided this, he repressed his natural inclinations toward anger, drew the money, laid it aside in his drawer, and went on with his work. When Morrell came, in next morning, very easy and debonair, he handed out the gold pieces and took in return the man's note, without relaxing the extreme gravity and formality of his manner.

"Thanks, old chap!" cried Morrell. "You've saved my life. I won't forget." He paused; then cackled harshly: "Good joke that! No, *I won't* forget!"

Keith bowed coldly, waiting. Morrell, with, a final cackle, made leisurely for the door. As he laid his hand on the knob, Keith spoke:

"By the way, Morrell."

Morrell turned.

"Take care you don't overdo this," advised Keith, very deliberately.

Morrell examined him. Keith's face was grim. He smiled enigmatically.

"Tact is a blessed gift, old top," said he, and went out.

XXVIII

This whole episode proved to be a turning-point in Keith's career. His revulsion against the feminine—hence society—side of life brought about by the affair of Mrs. Morrell, might soon have passed, and he might soon have returned to the old round of picnics, excursions, dinners, and parties, were it not that coincidentally a new and absorbing occupation was thrust upon him. Dick Blatchford's case was only one of many that came to him. He became completely immersed in the fascinating intricacies of the law.

As has been previously pointed out, nowhere before nor since has pure legality been made such a fetish. It was a game played by lawyers, not an attempt to get justice done. Since, in all criminal cases at least, the prosecution was carried on by one man and his associates, poorly paid and hence of mediocre ability, and the defence conducted by the keenest brains in the profession, it followed that convictions were rare. Homicide in various forms was little frowned upon. Duels were of frequent occurrence, and, in several instances, regular excursions, with tickets, were organized to see them. Street shootings of a more informal nature were too numerous to count. Invariably an attempt, generally successful, was made to arrest the homicide. If he had money, he hired the best lawyers, and rested secure. If he had no money, he disappeared for a time. Almost everybody had enough money, or enough friends with money, to adopt the former course. Of 1,200 murders—or "killings" —committed in the San Francisco of those days, there was just *one* legal conviction!

It was a point of professional pride with a lawyer to get his client free. Indeed, to fail would be equivalent to losing a very easy game. The whole battery of technical delays, demurrers, etc., was at his command; a much larger battery than even the absurd criminal courts of our present day can muster. Delays to allow he dispersal of witnesses were easily arranged for, as were changes of venue to courts either prejudiced in favour of the strict interpretation of "law" or frankly venal. Of shadier expedients, such as packing juries, there seemed no end.

Your honourable, high-minded lawyers—which meant the well-dressed and prosperous—had nothing to do with such dirty work; that is, directly. There were plenty of lawyers not so honourable and high minded called in as "counsel." These little lawyers, shoulder strikers, bribe givers and takers, were held in good-humoured contempt by the legal stars—who employed them! Actual dishonesty was diluted through a number of men. Packing a jury was a fine art. Initially was needed connivance at the sheriff's office. Hence lawyers, as a class, were in politics. Neither the stellar lawyer nor the sheriff knew any of the details of the transaction. A sum of money went to the former's "counsel" as expenses, and emerged, considerably diminished, in the sheriff's office as "perquisites." It had gone from the counsel to somebody like Mex Ryan, from him to various plug-uglies, ward heelers, shoulder strikers, from them to one or another of the professional jurymen, and then on the upward curve through the sheriff's underlings who made out the jury lists to Webb himself. The thing was done.

In this tortuous way many influences were needed. The most honest lawyer's limit as to the queer things he would do depended on his individual conscience. It is extraordinary what long training and the moral support of a whole profession will do toward educating a conscience. Do not despise unduly the lawyers of that day. We have all of us good friends in the legal profession who will defend in court a criminal they know to be guilty as charged. They will urge that no man should go undefended; and will argue themselves into a belief that in

Stewart Edward White

such a case "defence" means not merely fair play, but a desperate effort to get him off anyhow—trained conscience. If such sophistries are sincerely believed by honest men nowadays, it cannot be wondered at that queerer sophistries passed current in a community not five years old. It was difficult to draw the line between the men who mistakenly believed themselves honest and those who knew themselves dishonest.

But once in politics there could be no end. In this field the law rubbed shoulders with big contracts, big operations. A city was being built, in a few years, out of nothing, by a busy, careless, and shifting population. The opportunities for making money on public works—either honestly or by jobbery—were almost unlimited. The mood of the times was extravagant. From the still unexhausted placers poured a flood of gold, hard money, tangible wealth; and a large percentage of it paused in San Francisco, changed hands before continuing its journey. Immigrants brought with them a lesser but still significant sum. Money was easy. People could and would pay high taxes without a thought, for they would rather pay well to be let alone than bother with public affairs. The city treasury should have been full to bursting. In addition, the municipality was rich in its real estate. The value of all land had gone up immensely; any time more cash was needed it could quickly be raised by the sale of public lots. The supply seemed inexhaustible.

Like hyenas to a kill the public contractors gathered. Immense public works were undertaken at enormous prices. Paving, sewers, grading, filling, lighting, wharves, buildings Were all voted; and the work completed in the quickest, flimsiest, most slipshod fashion; and at terrible prices. The Graham House, a pretentious frail structure that had failed as a hotel because a swamp lay between it and the city, was bought at a huge price to serve as city hall. It was a veritable white elephant, and even the busy populace spared time to grumble at the flagrant steal. Nobody knew what it would cost to make the thing habitable even. Soon, to every one's relief, it burned down. The property was then swindled over to Peter Smith. The Jenny Lind Theatre, an impossible, ramshackle structure, was purchased over the vigorous protest of every decent citizen, for the enormous sum of $300,000. Another $100,000 was alleged to have been spent in remodeling and furnishing it. Then it was solemnly declared "unsuited to the purpose. "It also burned down in one of the numerous fires. But the money was safe!

To get such deals as these through "legally" it was of course necessary that officials, councilmen, engineers, etc., should be sympathetic .Naturally the big operators, as well as the big lawyers, had to go into politics. Elections came soon to be so many farces. In some wards no decent citizen dared show his face. "Shoulder strikers" were openly hired for purposes of intimidation. Bribery was scarcely concealed. And if things looked doubtful, there were always the election inspectors and judges in reserve who could be relied upon to make things come out right in the final count. The proper men were always returned as elected. If violence or fraud were alleged, lawyers always got the accused off in a strictly legal manner.

In these matters, it must be repeated, no opprobrium ever rested on either the big lawyers or the big operators. "Expenses" went to the underlings, and after some mysterious subterranean manipulation, of which the big fellows remained blandly unconscious, results came back.

In the world of public works Keith rapidly made himself a position. He was leading counsel for Dick Blatchford and one or two others. His job was to know all the rules of the game so well that there were no comebacks; to set the machinery in motion by which the contracts were procured; and to straighten out any irregularities that might arise afterward. His position was almost academic. The matters he fought and decided were so detached from actuality, as far as he was concerned, that they might have been hypothetical cases. When Dick wanted anything specific, Keith instructed Patsy Corrigan to see that the proper officials awarded the contract.

If the matter ever came to the courts, Keith furnished the brains and Patsy somehow "saw" the sheriff and whoever was necessary from the mysterious underworld. Everybody was doing the same thing. In the minds of men profits of any sort were legitimate provided they were "legal," but especially against so vague an entity as a community. Civic consciousness had not been born in them, for the simple reason that the city was constituted perfectly to suit them. Only when men are dissatisfied with their government do they seek to become responsible for it. There was no active public opinion against them. Men were too busy to bother with such things. Occasionally a fairly vigorous protest against some peculiarly outrageous steal made itself heard, but the men who made it were either cranks or it was suspected they had been pinched in some way. They merely represented the opposition any active man expects.

And every last one of these merry, jovial pirates was inordinately proud of the ship he was helping to scuttle! That one fact, attentively considered, explains much.

The city was growing, it was taking on a permanent character. In spite of waste, shoddy work, and frequent fires, its vitality was triumphant. The sand hills had all been graded flat, and the material from them had filled in the water lots of the bay; miles of fireproof brick structures had been built on four or five streets; there were now a half score of long wharves instead of one; omnibuses ran everywhere; fine steamers plied to fashionable watering places about the bay; the planks in the streets were being replaced by cobblestones; telegraph service ad been inaugurated to San Jose and Sacramento; several new theatres had been built; gas lamps were being placed about the streets; huge wooden palaces with much scrollwork ornamentation were being built on Stockton Street and the Rincon Hill. All these things, as well as the climate, the mines, the agricultural resources, the commerce, the scenery, were fully appreciated and enthusiastically made the most of by every mother's son. Any man among them was ready at a moment's notice to wax enthusiastic about the resources and the future of

the place. They were "boosters" in the modern acceptation of
the term.

Stewart Edward White

XXIX

In this eager, fast-living, nervous, high-strung man's world Keith took to himself a prominent part. He was so fully-occupied in other directions that is practice did not lead him into criminal law, so he missed an influence that must have either ended by blunting or repelling him. He corresponded to what nowadays would be called a corporation lawyer. His clients were few, but wealthy, powerful, and remunerative; his cases were subtle and hard fought, He enjoyed the intricate game for its own sake, and he enjoyed his success in it. In the inevitable give and take of a complicated world he knew, of course, of shady doings beneath; but he was not personally involved; he accepted them as part of the make-up of society, human nature, the medium—of work.

But Nan was necessarily left more and more to her own devices. And, further, she was left alone without even the preoccupation furnished her domestic side by such an affair as that with Mrs. Morrell. She knew that Keith was wholly absorbed in his business. She was loyal to his unexpressed idea that in these propitious beginnings he must devote all his energies to his career. She was loyal to his preoccupation. It was the only way in which she could help. And yet, without being given cause for grievance, she was temporarily thrust outside his life, put in cold storage, as it were, until she should be wanted. He bolted immediately after breakfast; often he did not come home to lunch; was quite likely to go out again in the evening.

It followed that Nan had to make her own life out of the materials at hand. This was at first difficult, for all the materials were novel to her. Gradually, however, she fitted herself into the social transformation that was taking place.

Heretofore, society had not existed. Now, vaguely, it was beginning to take coherence and form. A transition period was on. The "nobs" were evolving from chaos. People of the fast Morrell type were losing their influence and ascendency, were being pushed aside to the fringes by the more "solid" elements. Wealth and arrogant dignity were coming into their innings. Formal functions, often on an elaborate scale, were taking the place of the harum-scarum informal parties. There came up some questions of social leadership. In short, social life was developing into the usual game. Lacking other interests, Nan found it amused her to play at it, to contend with the leaders, to form alliances, to declare war, to assume by right and talent her place among the best.

This pleased Keith. Social standing helped him in business; and he enjoyed the sight of his beautiful young wife queening it serenely over the city's best. He was always eager to advance money for new gowns or expensive parties. At first he went out with her, but soon found that three o'clock in the morning meant a next day's brain dulled of its keenest edge. But he would not hear of her staying at home on his account.

"I'm tired, and I'm going to bed right away," he told her. "You go and uphold the splendour of the family. Get Ben to take you."

Ben Sansome was to Keith a tremendous convenience. He was the only idle man in town, always on tap, ready to stay out any and every night until the cocks crowed. Why shouldn't he? He had nothing to do all next day, except, perhaps, to decide which stick he should carry! With a busy man's good-humoured contempt for the mere idler, Keith looked upon Sansome as a harmless household-pet sort of person; good natured, accommodating, pleasant to talk to, good looking, foppish in dress, but beneath any serious human being's notice. Sansome was on easy terms of intimacy with the Keiths. It was mighty good of him to look out for Nan. If he did not, Keith would have to.

In this formative period Ben Sansome was, however, a very important figure in the woman's world. Social construction was a ticklish matter. There were so many things to be decided; small items of etiquette, the "proper thing"— procedure, decorations, good form, larger matters as to whether so-and-so should be received, and if so, how extensively. Ben Sansome was past master of such things. He was the only man in town who knew—or cared—how to "draw lines." He became truly a modern *arbiter elegantiarum.* For San Francisco had begun in real earnest to "draw lines."

They were rather strange lines at times. Of course such people as the Brannans, Montgomerys, Terrys, Bushs, Bakers, Caldwells, and other "old families" (three or four years old), went without saying. Also were included the greater merchants and their feminine representatives, such as Palmer, Cook, Adams, Wilkins, and the like. Also there seemed to be a solid foundation of those respectable and powerful with plenty of wealth—"but hopeless, my dear, absolutely hopeless!" groaned some of the livelier members.

Lightning struck capriciously at those on whom this new society might frown, on those who as lately as last year had ridden the crest of the wave. For example, it spared Sally Warner, with her spotted veils drawn close around her face, her red belts, and her red tufts on her small toques, but it blasted the Morrells. Mrs. Morrell clung tenaciously to the outskirts, but she knew only too well that she did not "belong." In her heart she ascribed this fact to Mrs. Keith. This was unjust, but it added to her bitterness against her neighbours.

Perhaps her suspicions were not unnatural, for Nan won easily in this game. She was undoubtedly the social leader. It seemed eminently fitting that, lacking her husband, she should go out much with Ben Sansome. Most women thought her lucky to have acquired so valuable a social acquisition. Some people, like fat, coarse, sensible Mrs. Dick Blatchford, were a little doubtful.

"Shucks!" snorted Sally Warner, slapping her little riding boot dashingly with her latest novelty, an English hunting crop, "Nan Keith impresses me as one who knows her way about. And, anyway, as long as Mr. Keith is satisfied, I'm sure we should be!"

XXX

To his surprise Ben Sansome found himself warming to what he considered a real passion. At least it was as real a passion as he was capable of feeling. Sansome had always been spoiled. Accustomed as he was to easy conquests, especially of late among the faster San Francisco women of the early days, Nan Keith's very aloofness attracted him. She dwelt in a serene atmosphere of unsuspicion, going about freely with him, taking their right relations for granted, and not thinking about them. Contemplating this, Sansome was clever enough to see that, a false move at the wrong time would do for him. Therefore, he occupied himself at first merely in making himself useful. He accepted Keith's role for him, becoming the friend of the family, dropping in often and informally, happening on the spot at just the right time to relieve Keith of the necessity of escorting Nan to this or that tea or ball. So well did he play his part that at last there came a time when Keith said:

"I'm dead tired to-night, Nan. Seems as if I couldn't stand chatter. Can't you send a note around to Ben and see if he can't get you there and back?"

This came to be a regular thing. If Sansome did not happen to be there, he was sent for. And his engagements were never such that he failed to accept.

He and Keith called each other by their given names; but even after a close intimacy had been established, he never addressed

Nan by hers.

"You sound very formal," she hinted to him at last.

"To me the privilege of calling you by your 'little name' is so great an evidence of friendship, that it actually seems like flaunting that friendship to call you so before others" he replied.

Always after that he called her "Nan" when they were alone together, but "Mrs. Keith" when a third, even Keith himself, was present. In that way their tete-a-tetes were marked off a little. When alone with her he maintained the pose of one struggling manfully against tremendous temptations held back only by her sweet influence. But he never overdid it. As they came to know each other better, he talked ever the more freely of men's mysterious temptations. Nan could not define to herself exactly what they might be.

"Yesterday I couldn't see you," he told her. "I struggled with myself all day. Good God, what does a woman like you know of a man's weaknesses and temptations—But I conquered."

Nan was uneasy. She did not know quite what it was all about, but her instincts warned her.

"I am glad," she replied; and went on hastily, "but you must tell me what you think about having the tea served in the arbour on the seventh, I've been dying to ask you."

With an obvious effort to be cheerful about this fresh subject, he wrenched himself into a new mood. They consulted on the party for the seventh. He broke off abruptly to say: "Do you know you're an extraordinary person—but you are!" he overrode her protests. "Don't I know the ordinary kind? Women have a deep strength of their own that men cannot understand."

He stayed only a few minutes after that. On parting he for

the first time permitted himself a lingering gaze into her eyes as he reluctantly relinquished her hand. She turned away, distinctly uneasy. Yet so skillfully had he woven, his illusion of dependence on her that she shook it off with a tender and maternal smile.

"Poor boy," she murmured. "He is so unhappy and alone!"

Sansome was an accomplished equestrian. Finding that Nan knew nothing whatever about riding, he procured her a gentle horse, and took the greatest trouble and pleasure in teaching her. She proved apt, for she had good natural control of her body .after the first uncertainty and the first stiffness had worn off, she delighted in long rides toward different parts of the peninsula. Gringo, now a full-grown dog inclining toward the shepherd more than anything else, delighted in them, too. He ranged far and wide in front of the horses, exploring every ditch and thicket, wallowing happily in every mudhole, returning occasionally to roll his comical eyes at them as though to say, "Aren't we having a good time?" for Gringo was a dog with a sense of humour. On these excursions she renewed acquaintance with the sand dunes, and the little canons with birds, and the broad beach at low tide on which it was glorious to gallop. Once or twice they even stopped at the little rancho where the Keiths had lunched. There Nan, through Sansome, who talked Spanish, was able to communicate with her kindly hosts; and Gringo met his honoured but rather snappy mother. The mother disowned him utterly. As the days grew shorter they often rode on the Presidio hills, watching the sun set beyond the Golden Gate.

One such evening they had reined up their horses atop one of the hills next the Gate. The sun had set somewhere beyond the headlands. Tamalpais was deep pink with the glow; the water in he Gate was pale lilac; the sky close to the horizon burned orange, but above turned to a pale green that made with its lucent colour alone infinite depths and spaces. Below, the darker waters twisted and turned with the tide. The western headlands were black silhouettes.

"Oh, but it is beautiful!" she said at last.

"Yes, it is beautiful," he agreed somberly; "but when one is lonely, somehow it hurts."

There ensued a short, tense silence, broken only by the soft rolling of the bit wheels in the horses' mouths.

"Yes," she agreed softly, after a moment, "I feel that, too. Yet sometimes I wonder if one doesn't see and feel more keenly when one is not too happy—" She hesitated.

"Yes, yes! Go on!" he urged in a low voice. His tone, his attitude, suddenly seemed to envelop her with understanding. He appeared to offer her aid, chivalrous aid, although no word was spoken. She had not quite meant it that way; in fact, her thought was to offer *him* sympathy. But somehow it was grateful. It would do no harm to enjoy it, secretly, for a moment. His unexpressed sympathy—for what she would have been unable to say—was attractive to her isolation.

Often on returning from these rides she asked him in for a cup of tea. Occasionally, when she was overheated, or damp from the fog, she would excuse herself and slip into a soft negligee. With lamp and fire lit they made a very cozy tete-a-tete. He smoked contemplatively; she stitched at the inevitable embroidery of the period. Occasionally they talked animatedly; quite as frequently they sat in sociable silence. Gringo slept by the fire dreaming of rabbits and things, his hind legs twitching as he triumphantly ran them down. One evening she caught sight of a rip in the sewing of his tobacco pouch. In spite of his protests, she insisted on sewing it up for him. She was conscious of his eyes on her while she plied the needle, and felt somehow very feminine and sure of her power.

"There!" she cried, when she had finished. "You certainly do need somebody to take care of you!

He took it without spoken thanks, and put it slowly away in

his pocket—as though, he would have kissed it. A pregnant silence followed, he sitting staring at her, she jabbing the needle idly into the arm of her chair. Suddenly, as though taking a tremendous resolution, he spoke:

"Nan, I am going to ask you a question. You must not be offended. Do you really love your husband?" At her hasty movement he hurried on: "I imagine I feel something unsatisfied about you—besides, lots of women don't."

As he probably expected, her indignation was thoroughly aroused. He took his castigation and dismissal meekly, and found some interest in the ensuing negotiations toward reconciliation. No one knew better than he how to sue for forgiveness. But he was quite satisfied to have implanted the idea, for Ben Sansome was content with slow coral-insect progress. A busy man, engaged in men's occupations, would never have had the patience for this leisurely establishment of atmosphere and influence; his impatience or passion would have betrayed him to an early outbreak. But with Sansome it was the practice of a fine art. He knew just how far to go. No one could more skilfully ingratiate himself in small ways. He always knew what gown she should wear or had worn, and always commented appreciatively on what she had on. Keith merely knew vaguely whether she looked well or ill. Sansome noticed and praised little things—her well-shod feet, the red lights in her hair, an unusual flower in her belt. He knew every hat she owned, and he had his well-marked preferences. He never made direct love, nor attempted to touch her. She felt the growing attraction, enjoyed it, but did not analyze it. She merely considered Ben Sansome as "nice," as needing guidance, as romantic—

Occasionally, after seeing more than usual of him, some feeling of reaction or some faint stirring of conscience would impel her—perhaps to convince herself of the harmlessness of it all— to make an especial effort to draw her husband out of his preoccupation into more human relations. She dressed with great care, earlier than usual; she gathered flowers for the vases, she fussed about lighting lamps, placing ash trays and chairs, generally arranging the setting for his welcome home. The preparations kindled her own enthusiasm. She became herself quite worked up in anticipation. When she heard his step, she ran to meet him in the hall. Keith happened to be tired to the point of exhaustion.

"Good heavens!" was his comment; "are we having company to-night? Why all the clothes and illumination?"

His relaxed, dispirited manner of removing and hanging up his coat reacted upon her instantly. Her high spirits sank to the depths. They ate their meal in almost complete silence. Nan could not help visualizing Sansome's appreciation of such an occasion.

XXXI

The new coherence in society began to manifest itself in one important way: public gambling declined. In the "old days" it was said that everybody but clergymen frequented the big gambling halls. They were a sort of club. But now the most influential citizens began to stay away. Probably they gambled as much as ever, but they took such pleasures in private. Two or three only of the larger places remained in business. Save for them, open gambling was confined to the low dives near the water front. There was no definite movement against the practice. It merely fell off gradually.

During these busy years the Sherwoods had quite methodically continued to lead their customary lives. He read his morning paper on the veranda of the Bella Union, talked his leisurely politics, drove his horses, and in the evening attended to his business. She drove abroad, received her men friends, gave them impartial advice and help in their difficulties, dressed well, and carried on a life of many small activities. The Sherwoods were always an attractive looking and imposing couple, whenever they appeared. About three or four times a year they drove into the residential part of town and made a half-dozen formal calls—on the Keiths among others. Probably their lives were more nearly ordered on a routine than those of any other people in the new city.

One afternoon Sherwood came in at the usual hour, deposited his high hat carefully on the table, flicked the dust off his boots, and remarked casually:

"Patsy, I've sold the business."

Mrs. Sherwood was pinning on her hat. She stopped short, her hand halfway to her head, as though turned to marble. After a moment she asked in a quick, stifled voice:

"What do you mean?"

"Well," replied Sherwood, continuing methodically to readjust his dress, "I've been thinking for some time that times were changing. The gambling business is losing tone. I don't see the same class of people I used to see. Public sentiment—of the very best people, I mean—is drifting away from it. In the future, in my judgment, it's not going to pay as it ought. I've been thinking these things for some time. So when a bona fide purchaser came along—"

But he got no further. With a smothered cry she let her arms drop. Her customary poise had vanished. She flung herself on him, laughing, crying, gasping.

"Why, Patsy! Patsy!" he cried, patting her small, sleek head as it pressed against his shoulder. "What is it, dearie? Tell me? What's wrong?"

He was vastly perturbed and anxious, for she was not at all the type that loses control readily.

"Nothing! nothing!" she gasped. "I'll be all right in a minute. Don't mind me. Just let me alone. Only you told me so suddenly—"

"Don't you want me to sell?" he asked, utterly bewildered.

Gradually he gathered from her disjointed exclamations that this was just the one thing she had wanted, secretly, for years; the thing she had schooled herself not to hope for; the last thing in the world she had expected. And to his astonishment he gathered further that now she was free she could take her place with the other women—

"But I hadn't the slightest idea you wanted to!" he interrupted at this point. "You've never showed any signs of paying the slightest attention to them before!"

She was drying her eyes, and looking a little happily foolish.

"I knew better than to give them a chance to snub me," she told him. "Now I'm respectable."

But at this Sherwood reared his crest.

"Respectable!" he snorted, "What do you mean? Haven't you always been respectable? I'd like to see anybody who would hint—"

"You're a dear, but you're a man," she broke in more calmly. "Don't you know that a gambler's wife isn't respectable—in their sense of the word?"

"But every mother's son of them gambles!" cried Sherwood. "It's a perfectly legal and legitimate occupation!"

"The men do; we'd always get along if it was only a question of the men. But the women make distinctions—"

"Look here!" he broke out wrathfully. "There's Dick Blatch-ford mixed up in dirty work for dirty money I wouldn't lay my fingers on; and Terry, or Brannan, or McGowan, or all the rest of the boodling, land-grabbing, pettifogging crew! Why, if I made my living or spare cash the way that gang of pirates and cutthroats do I'd carry a pair of handcuffs for myself. Honest! Respectable! I've got no kick on their methods; it's, none of my business. But their wives are all right. I don't see it!"

"It's all names, I acknowledge," she soothed, "just names, I attach no more weight to them than you do. Don't you suppose I'd have said something if I had thought you were doing anything wrong? But that's the way they play the game, and it is their game. If we play it we've got to accept their rules. Don't you see?"

"Well, it's a mighty poor game," grumbled Sherwood, "and they strike me as an exceptionally stupid lot of women. They'd drive me to drink. I don't see what you want to bother with them for."

"They are," she agreed. "They won't amuse me much—you couldn't understand—it's just the *idea* of it—But I won't be looked down on, even by my inferiors! Tell me, Jack, when we sell the business are we going to be wealthy, will we have plenty of money?"

A hurt look came into his fine, straightforward eyes.

"Haven't you always had all you wanted, Patsy?" he inquired.

"Of course I have, you old goose! But I want to know what our resources are before I plan my campaign."

"Going in up to your neck, are you?" he commented ruefully.

She nodded. Her eyes were bright, and a spot of colour glowed in either cheek.

"Course I am. What can I spend?"

"You can have whatever you want."

"That's too vague, too indefinite. How rich—or poor—are we going to be?"

"We'll be rich enough."

"Very?"

"Well—yes, very. The business has paid, investments have

panned out. I got a good cash purchase price."

"How much can I spend a year?" she persisted. "It doesn't matter whether it's much or little, but I want to know."

"What a mercenary little creature!" he cried facetiously, then sobered as he saw by the expression of her face that this, apparently trivial thing meant a great deal to her. "Oh, fifty thousand or so won't cripple us."

A year?" she breathed, awed.

He nodded.

"Oh!" she cried rapidly. "Then we'll have a house—a house built for our very own selves, our very own plans!"

"Why, I thought we were very comfortable here!" he protested, a little dismayed. "Haven't we room enough? I'll make Rebinot cut a door—"

"No! no! no! a house of my own!" She was on fire with excitement, walking restlessly up and down. He watched her a moment or so. His slower imagination was kindling. He was beginning to grasp the symbolism of it, what it meant to her, the release of long-pent secret desires. As she passed him, he seized her and drew her gently to his knee.

"Patsy!" he cried contritely, "I didn't realize! I didn't guess you weren't perfectly contented here!"

She brushed his cheek with hers.

"Of course you didn't," she reassured him.

"If you'd the slightest—"

She threw her head back proudly, her breast swelled.

"I married you to lead your life. Jack, whatever it was," she told him, "to be your *help*mate."

"You're the game little sportsman in this town!" he cried. "And if you want to make those flub-dubs crawl, by God you sail in! I'll back you!"

Ten minutes later she asked him:

"What are you going to do, yourself, Jack? Somehow, I can't imagine you idle."

"Well," said Sherwood, "the boys are organizing a stock exchange, and it struck me that it might be a good idea if I went into that."

She began to laugh softly, in affectionate amusement.

"Stop it!" he commanded indignantly. "I know that laugh, What have I done now?"

"I was just thinking what a nice, *respectable* gambler you are going to be now," she said, "It's in your blood, Jack, and I love it—but it's funny!"

XXXII

But now, at the very sources, the full flood of the somewhat turbid tide of prosperity was beginning to fail. The ebb had not yet reached the civic consciousness. It would have required a philosopher, and a detached philosopher at that, to have connected cause and effect, to have forecast the inevitable trend of events. If there were any philosophers they were not detached! Nobody had discovered the simple truth that extravagance, graft, waste, cost money; and that the money must come from somewhere. Realization on its property and taxes were the twin sources of the city's revenues. The property was now about all sold or swindled away. Remained the taxes. And it is a self-evident truth that people will pay high taxes cheerfully only so long as they themselves are making plenty of money easily.

Up to this period such had been the case. Prices had been high, wages had been high, opportunities had been many. Enormous profits had been the rule. Everybody had invariably made money. These conditions upset the mental balance of the shipping merchants back East. A madness seemed to obsess them for sending goods to California. The mere rumour of a want or a lack was answered by immense shipments of that particular commodity. The first cargo to arrive supplied the want; all the rest simply broke the market. It was a gamble as to who should get there first. The immediate and picturesque consequence was a fleet of beautiful clipper ships, built like racing yachts, with long clean lines and snowy sails. They made extraordinarily fast voyages, and they promptly condemned to death the old- fashioned, slow freight carriers. Indeed, four-hundred odd of these actually rotted at anchor in the bay; it had not paid to move them! Some of these clippers gained vast reputations: the *Flying Cloud*, the *White Squall*, the *Typhoon*, the *Trade Wind*. The markets were continually in a state of glut with goods sold at auction. This condition tightened the money market, which in turn reacted on other branches of industry. Again, the great fires of '49-'53 resulted in the erection of too many fireproof buildings. Storage was needed, and rentals were high, so everybody plunged on storehouses. By '54 many hundreds of them stood vacant presenting loss. At that period the first abundance of the placers began to fall off.

Agriculture was beginning to be undertaken seriously; and while this would be an ultimate source of wealth, its immediate effect was to diminish the demand for imported foodstuffs—another blow to a purely mercantile city.

All this made for excitement, some immediate gain, but a sure ultimate loss. Markets fluctuated wildly. A ship in sight threw operators into a fever. No one knew what she might be carrying, or how she would, affect prices. It was, therefore, positively unsafe to keep-many goods is stock. Quick, immediate sales were the rule. And failures were many.

Now in these middle fifties the pinch was beginning at last to itself felt. Everybody was a little vague about it all, and nobody had gone so far as to formulate his dissatisfactions or his remedies. The tangible result was the formation of two as yet inchoate elements, representing the extremes of ideas and of interests.

The first of these elements—that can with equal justice be called the parasitic or the middleman class—consisted in itself of several sorts of people. The nucleus was a small, intellectually honest set of men who believed, in the law *per se*, in the sacredness of formal institutions in the constitution, and in the subservience of the individual to the institution. This was temperamental. Behind them were many much larger groups of those needed either the interpretation or the protection of the law for their private interests. These were of all sorts from honest literal-minded dealers, through shady contractors and operators, down to grafters and the very lowest type of strong-arm bullies. The tone and respectability came from the first, the practical results from the second. The first class had a genuine intellectual contempt for men whose minds could not see—or at least would not accept—the same subtleties that it did. Its members were fond of such phrases as the "lawless mob," or the "subversion of time-honoured institutions." This small, subjectively honest, conservative, specially trained element must not be forgotten in the final estimate of what later came to be known as the "Law and Order" party.

On the other hand was first of all an equally small nucleus of thinking men whose respect for the law, merely as law, was not so profound; men who were, reluctantly, willing to admit that when law completely broke down in encompassing justice, individualism was justified in stepping in. Behind them was a vast body of more or less unthinking men who recognized the indubitable facts that the law had become a farce, that justice had degenerated to tricks, and who were, therefore, instinctively against law, lawyers, and everybody who had anything to do with them.

Strangely enough this made for lawlessness on both sides. Those who believed in "law and order" committed crime or misdemeanour or mere injustice, sure of escape through some technicality. Those who distrusted courts administered justice illegally with their own hands! Nor was this merely in theory. San Francisco at that time was undoubtedly the most corrupt and lawless city in the world. Street shootings, duels, robberies, ballot-box stuffing, bribery, all the crimes traceable to a supine police and venal or technical courts were actually so commonplace as to command but two or three lines in the daily papers. Justice was completely smothered under technicalities and delays.

The situation would have been intolerable to any people less busy than the people of that time. For political corruption in a vigorous body politic is not, as pessimists would have us believer an indication of incipient decay, but only an indication that a busy people are willing to pay that price to be left alone, to be relieved of the administration of their public affairs, When they get less busy, or the price in corruption becomes too high, then they refuse to pay. The price Francisco was paying becoming very high, not only in money, but in other and spiritual things. She could still afford to pay it; but at the least pressure she would no longer afford it. Then she would act.

Stewart Edward White

XXXIII

In the second year of his residence Keith had a minor adventure that shifted a portion of his activities to other fields. He was in attendance at a council meeting, following the interests of certain clients. The evening was warm, the proceedings dull. Opened windows let in the sounds from the Plaza and a night air that occasionally flared the smoky lamps. The clerk's voice was droning away at some routine when the outer door opened and a most extraordinary quartette entered the chamber. Three of these were the ordinary, ragged, discouraged, emaciated, diseased "bums," only too common in that city. In early California a man either succeeded or he failed into a dark abyss of complete discouragement; the new civilization had little use for weaklings. The fourth man can be no better described than in the words of a chronicler of the period. Says the worthy diarist:

"He was a man of medium stature, slender but very graceful, with almost effeminate hands and feet—the former scrupulously kept, the latter neatly shod—and with a certain air of fragility; very soft blue eyes with sleepy lids; a classically correct nose; short upper lip; rosy, moist lips. His clothes: a claret-coloured coat, neither dress nor frock, but mixed of both fashions, with a velvet collar and brass buttons; a black vest, double breasted; iron-gray pantaloons; fresh, well-starched, and very fine linen; plain black cravat, negligently tied; a cambric handkerchief; and dark kid gloves. He wore gold spectacles, and carried a malacca cane."

Instead of slipping into the seats provided for spectators, this striking individual marched boldly to the open space before the mayor's chair, followed, shamefaced and shambling, by the three bums.

"Your honours and gentlemen," he cried in a clear, ringing voice, to the scandal of the interrupted legislators, "we are very sick and hungry and helpless and wretched. If somebody does not do something for us, we shall die; and that would be bad, considering how far we have come, and how hard it was to get here, and how short a time we have been here, and that we have not had a fair chance. All we ask is a fair chance, and we say again, upon our honour, gentlemen, if somebody does not do something for us, we shall die, or we shall be setting fire to the town first and cutting all our throats."

He stood leaning lightly against his malacca cane, surveying them through his sleepy blue eyes. The first astonishment over, they took up a collection, after the customary careless, generous fashion. The young man saluted with his cane, and herded his three exhibits out.

Keith, much struck, followed them, overtaking the quartette on the street.

"My name is Keith," he said, "I should like to make your acquaintance."

"Mine is Krafft," replied the unknown, "and I am delighted to accept your proffer."

He said nothing more until he had marshalled his charges, into a cheap eating-house, ordered and paid for a supper, and divided the remainder of the amount collected. Then he dusted his fingers daintily with a fine handkerchief, and sauntered out into the street, swinging his malacca cane.

"Incidents of that sort restore one's faith in the generosity of our people," Keith remarked, in order to say something.

"Nobody has been generous," denied Krafft categorically, "and no particular good has been accomplished. Filled their bellies for this evening; given them a place to sleep for this night; that's all."

"That's something," ventured Keith. "It helps."

"The only way to help we have not undertaken. We have done nothing toward finding out why there are such creatures—in a place like this. That's the only way to help them: find out why they are, and then remove the why."

This commonplace of modern charity was then a brand-new thought. Keith had never heard it expressed, and he was much interested.

"I suppose there are always the weak and the useless," he said vaguely.

"If those men were wholly weak and useless, how did they get out here?" countered Krafft. "To compass such a journey takes a crtain energy, a certain sum of money, a certain fund of hope. The money goes, the energy drains, the hope fades. Why?"

They stopped at a corner.

"I live just near here," said Krafft. "If you will honour me."

He led the way down a narrow dark alley, along which they had fairly to grope their way. It debouched, however, into the forgotten centre of the square. All the edges had been built close with brick stores, warehouses, and office buildings. But in the very middle had been left a waste piece of ground, occupied only by a garden and a low one-room abode, with a veranda and a red-tiled roof. Under the moonlight and the black shadows from the modern buildings it slept amid its bright flowers with the ancient air of another world. Krafft turned a key and lighted a lamp. Keith found himself in a small, neat room, with heavy beams, fireplace, and deep embrasured windows. An iron bed, two chairs, a table, a screen, a shelf of books, and a wardrobe were its sole furnishings. In the fireplace had been laid, but not lighted, a fire of sagebrush roots.

Krafft touched a match to the roots, which instantly leaped into eager and aromatic flames. From a shelf he took a new clay pipe which he handed to Keith.

"Tobacco is in that jar," he said.

He himself filled and lighted a big porcelain pipe with wexelwood stem.

"What would you do about it?" asked Keith, continuing the discussion.

"What would you most want, if you were those poor men?" retorted Krafft, blowing a huge cloud.

Keith laughed.

"Drink, food, clothes, bed," he stated succinctly.

"And work wherewith to get them," supplemented Krafft.

Keith laughed again.

"Not if I know their sort! Work is the one thing they *don't* want."

Krafft leaned forword, and tapped the table with one of his long forefingers,

"The lazy part of them, the earthen part of them, the dross of them—yes, perhaps. But let us concede to them a spark that smoulders, way down deep within them—a spark of which they think they are ashamed, which they do not themselves realize the existence of except occasionally. What is the deep need of them? It is to feel that they are still of use, that they amount to something, that they are men. That more than mere food and warmth. Is it not so?"

"I believe you're right," said Keith, impressed.

"Then," said Krafft triumphantly, "it *is* work they want, work that is useful and worth paying for."

"But there's plenty of work to be had," objected Keith, after a moment. "In fact, there's more work in this town than there are men to do it."

"True, But it is the hard work these men have failed at. It is too hard. They try; they are discouraged; they fall again, and perhaps they never get up. Such men must be led, must be watched, be stopped within their strength."

"Who's there to do that sort of dry nursing of bums?" demanded Keith with a half laugh.

"He who would help," said Krafft quietly.

They smoked for some time in silence; then Keith arose to go.

"It is a big idea; it requires thought," said he ruminativeiy. "You are a recent arrival, Mr. Krafft? What is your line of activity?"

The slight, elegant little man smiled.

"I am one of the—what is it you called, them—bums of whom we talk. I try to do what is within my power, within my strength-lest I, too, become discouraged, lest I, too, fall again—and not get up."

"I have not seen you about anywhere," said Keith, puzzled by this speech.

"I do not go anywhere; I should be eaten. You do not understand me, and I am a poor host to talk in riddles. I am a philosopher, not a man of action; egotist, not an egoist; one who cannot swim in your strong waters. As I said, one of that same class your bounty helped this evening."

"Good Lord, man!" cried Keith, looking about the little room. "You're not in want?"

Krafft laughed gently.

"In your sense, no. I have my meals. Enough of me. Go, and think of what I say."

Keith did so, and the result was the first organized charity in San Francisco. Since 1849 men had always been exceptionally generous in responding to appeals for money. Huge sums could easily be raised at any time. Hospitals and almshouses dated from the first. But having given, these pioneers invariably forgot. The erection of the buildings cost more than they should, and management being venal, conditions soon became disgraceful. Alms reached the professional pauper. The miner or immigrant, diseased, discouraged, out of luck, more often died—either actually or morally.

So much had this first interview caught his interest that Keith dropped in on his new acquaintance quite often. It soon became evident that Krafft lived in what might be called decent poverty. The one fine rig-out in which he made his public appearances was most carefully preserved. Indoors he always promptly assumed a dressing-gown, a skull cap with a gold tassel, and his great porcelain pipe. His meals he cooked for himself. Never did he leave his house until about three o'clock. Then, spick and span, exquisitely appointed, he sauntered forth swinging his malacca cane. After a promenade of several hours he returned again to his dressing-gown, his porcelain pipe, and his books. Keith enjoyed hugely his detached, reflective, philosophical, spectator-of-life conversation. They talked on many subjects besides sociology. At his fourth visit Krafft made a suggestion.

"You shall come with me and see," said he.

He led the way to the water front under Telegraph Hill, the newest and the most squalid part of town. The shallow water was in slow process of being filled in by sand from the grading uptown and with all sorts of miscellaneous debris, Pending solidity, this sketchy real estate swarmed with squatters. There were lots sunken below the street level, filled with stagnant water, discarded garments, old boxes, ashes, and rubbish; houses huddled closely together with stale water beneath; there were muddy alleys; murderous cheap saloons; cheaper gambling joints; rickety, sagging tenements. The people corresponded to their habitations. All the low elements lurked here, the thugs, strong-arm men, the hold-ups, the heelers, the weaklings, the bums, the diseased. In ordinary times they here dwelt in a twilight existence; but at periods of excitement—as when the city burned—they swarmed out like rats for plunder.

Krafft held his way steadily to the wharves. There he left the causeway and descended to the level of the beach. Beneath the pilings, and above the high-water mark, was a little hut. It was not over six feet square, constructed of all sorts of old pieces of boxes, scraps of tin, or remnants of canvas. Overhead rumbled continuously the heavy drays, shaking down, through the cracks the dust of the roadway. Against one outside wall of this crazy structure an old man sat, chair tilted in the sun. Even the chair was a curiosity, miraculously held together by wires. The man was very old, and very feeble, his knotted hands clasping a short, black clay pipe. Inside the hut Keith, saw a rough bunk on which lay jumbled a quilt and a piece of canvas.

"Well, John," greeted Krafft cheerfully, "I've brought a friend to see you."

The old man turned on Keith a twinkling blue eye.

"Glad to see you," he said briefly.

"Getting on?" pursued Krafft.

"Fine."

"Here's a new kind of tobacco I want you to try. I should value your opinion."

Keith's hand wandered toward his pocket, but stopped at a sharp look from Krafft. After a moment's chat they withdrew.

"What a pathetic old figure! What utter misery!" cried Keith.

"No!" said Krafft positively. "There you are wrong. Old John is in no need of us. He has his house and his bed, and he gets his food. How, I do not know, but he gets it. The spark is burning clear and steady. He has not lost his grip. He gets his living with confidence. Let him alone."

"But he must be very miserable—especially when it rains," persisted Keith.

Krafft shrugged his shoulders.

"As to that, I know not," he returned indifferently. "That does not matter to the soul. I will now show you another man."

They retraced their steps. On a corner of Montgomery Street Krafft stopped before a one-armed beggar, the stump exposed, a placard around his neck.

"Now here's another John," said Krafft. "What he wants is work, and somebody to see that he does it."

The one-armed beggar, who was fat, with a good-natured countenance, evidently considered this a joke. He grinned cheerfully.

"Don't have to, guvenor," said he.

"How much did you take in yesterday, John?" asked Krafft; then, catching the beggar's look of suspicion, he added, "This is a friend of mine; he's all right."

"Twenty-two dollars," replied the beggar proudly. "Pretty good's day's wages!"

"I'm afraid the spark is about out with you, John," said Krafft thoughtfully. He walked on a few steps, then turned back. "John," he asked, "what is your contribution to society?"

The beggar stared, uncertain of this new chaff.

"The true theory of business, John, is that traffic which does not result In reciprocal advantages to buyer and seller is illegitimate, or at least abnormal."

They walked on, Keith laughing at the expression on the beggar's face.

"That was considerably over his head," he observed.

Nothing more was said for half a block.

"I wonder if it was over yours," then said Krafft, unexpectedly.

"Eh?" ejaculated Keith, bewildered.

These walks with Krafft finally resulted in the institution of a fund which Keith raised and put into Krafft's hands for intelligent use. The effects were so interesting that Keith, thoroughly fascinated, began to pester his friends for positions for some of his proteges. As he was well-liked and in earnest, these efforts were taken good-humourediy.

"Here comes Milt Keith," said John Webb to Bert Taylor. "Bet you a beaver hat he's got a highly educated college professor that he wants a job for."

"A light job, not beyond his powers," quoted Taylor.

"Like cleaning genteel spittoons," supplemented Webb.

"The engine house is full of 'em polishing brass," complained Taylor.

"Well, he's a young felly, and I like him," concluded Webb heartily.

Of course many of the experiments failed, but fewer than might have been anticipated. Part of Krafft's task was to keep in touch with the men. His detached, philosophical method of encouragement and analysis of the situation seemed just the thing they needed.

Stewart Edward White

XXXIV

These activities gave Keith just the required door out into a world other than his own. Were it not for something of the sort he might, like many modern corporation lawyers, have confined himself entirely to his own class. And this, of course, would eventually have meant narrowness.

But through Krafft, and especially through his desire to help Krafft's work, he came in contact with all sorts of people; and, what was more important, he found that he liked a great many of them. So it happened that when it seemed expedient to the ruling caste to put him in as Assistant District Attorney, his inevitable election met with wider approval than such elections usually enjoy.

For it must be understood that in the fifties any candidate selected by the ruling caste was absolutely sure of election. The machinery was thoroughly in their hands. Diplomacy in party caucuses, delicate manipulation at primaries, were backed by cruder methods if need be. Associations were semi-publically formed for the sale of votes; gangs of men were driven from one precinct to another, voting in all; intimidation, and, indeed, open violence, was freely used. Only the most adventurous or the most determined thought it worth while even to try to vote in the rough precincts. And if the first and second lines of defence failed, there was still the third to fall back on when the booths were dosed and the ballots counted: the boxes could still be "stuffed," the count could still be scientifically juggled to bring about any desired result.

This particular election was one of the worst in the history of the place. All day fighting was kept up, and the rowdies swaggered everywhere. Whiskey was to be had for the asking; and the roughs who surrounded the polls fired shots, and in some places started what might fairly be called riots. Yankee Sullivan returned James Casey as elected supervisor, which was probably a mistake, for Casey was not a candidate, his name was on none of the official ballots, and nobody could be found who had voted for him. Everybody was surprised, Casey most of all! The sixth ward count was delayed unconscionably, its returns being withheld until nearly morning. It was more than hinted that this delay was prolonged until the returns had been received from all other precincts, so that any deficiencies might be made up by the sixth. The "slate" went through unbroken.

Of all the candidates, Keith received the most votes, for the simple reason that his total included both the honest and dishonest ballots. Blanchford, Neil, Palmer, Adams, all the political overlords of the city were satisfied, as well they might be, for they had issued the fiat that he be chosen.

"He's one of us," said they.

But what was more unusual, the rank and file of decent, busy, hard-working citizens approved, too.

"Keith is not stuck up," they told each other. "He is the *commonest* man in that bunch. And he's square."

The position carried some social as well as political significance. Society made another effort to take him up. His rare appearances were rather in the nature of concessions. They served to make him more regretted, for he had an easy, jolly way of moving from one group or one woman to another, of paying flattering, monopolizing, brief attention to each in turn, and then disappearing, very early! His bold rather florid countenance radiated energy and quizzical good humour; his tight, closely curled hair crisped with virile alertness; he carried himself taut and eager—altogether a figure to engage the curiosities of women or the interest of men.

Mrs. Sherwood alone was shrewd enough to penetrate to his true feelings. She had experienced no difficulty in pushing to a social leadership shared—indolently and indifferently—with Nan Keith. Already her past was growing dim in a tradition kept alive only by a few whisperers. Her wealth, her natural tact and poise, her calm assumption of the right to rule, her great personal charm, beauty, and taste were more than sufficient to get her what she wanted. The game was almost too easy, when one held the cards.

"Yes, he's very charming," she told her husband, "but that manner of his does not impress me. As a matter of fact, he doesn't care a snap of his finger about any of them. He does it too well. It's a stencil. Only the outside of him does it. He's just as bad as you are; only *he* doesn't hold up a corner of the doorway all the evening, and beam vaguely in general, like a good-natured, dear old owl."

XXXV

A few clear-headed men—not the "chivalry," as the fire-eating professional politicians and lawyers from the South were almost uniformly designated— were able to see exactly the problem that must eventually demand Keith's solution. Some of them talked it over while lounging and smoking in the Fire Queen reading-room. There were present Talbot Ward and his huge satellite, Munro; Coleman, quiet, grim, complacent, but looking, with his sweeping, inky moustache and his florid, complexion, like a flashy "sport"; Hossfros, soon to become an historic character; and the banker, James King of William.

The latter had recently come in for considerable public discussion. He had for some time conducted a banking business, but becoming involved in difficulties, he had turned over all his assets, all his personal fortune, even his dwelling-house, to another bank as trustee to take care of his debts. Almost immediately after, that bank had failed. Opinion in the community divided according to the interests involved. The majority considered that King had been almost quixotically conscientious in stripping himself; but there did not lack those who accused him of sharp practice. In the course of ensuing discussions and recriminations King was challenged to a duel. He declined to fight, basing his refusal on principle. As may be imagined, such an action at such a time was even more widely commented upon than even his refusal to take advantage of the bankruptcy laws. It was, as far as known, the first time any one had had the moral courage to refuse a duel. King had gone quietly about his business, taking an ordinary clerkship with

Palmer, Cook & Co. In the eyes of the discriminating few he had gained prestige, but most people thought him down and out.

"What do you think of our new Assistant District Attorney?" Ward had begun the conversation.

"He's a lawyer," growled Hossfros.

"A pretty fairly honest one, I think," ventured King. "His training may be wrong, but his instincts are right."

"Fat chance anything's got when it mixes up with legalities," supplemented Frank Munro.

"Nevertheless," remarked Coleman seriously, "I believe plain justice has more of a chance with him in charge than with another."

"What sort of justice?" queried King. "Commercial?" He laughed in answer to his own question. "Criminal? I'd like to think it, gentlemen, but I cannot. You know as well as I do that any of us could this evening go into the streets, select our victim, and shoot him down secure in the knowledge that inconvenience is all the punishment we need expect—if we have money or friends. Am I not right, Coleman?"

Coleman smiled sardonically, lifting his blue-black moustache.

"Were Herod for the slaughter of the Innocents brought before a jury of this town, he would be acquitted," he said half-seriously. "Judas Iscariot would pass unscathed so long as any portion of his thirty pieces of silver remained with him."

They laughed at this remarkable pronouncement, but with an undernote of seriousness.

"No man, even exceptionally equipped as this young man seems to be," went on Coleman after a moment, "can accomplish *that*"—he snapped his fingers—"against organized forces such as those of 'Law and Order.'"

"We can't stand this sort of thing forever!" cried Hossfros hotly. "It's getting worse and worse!"

"We probably shall not stand it forever," agreed Coleman equably, "but we are powerless—at present."

They looked toward him for explanation of this last.

"When the people at large find that *they* cannot stand it either, then we shall be no longer powerless. A single man can do something then—a single child!"

"What will happen then?" asked Munro. "Vigilantes? '51 again?"

Coleman, the leader of the Vigilantes of '51, turned on him a grave eye.

"God forbid! We were then a frontier community. We are now an organized, civilized city. We have rights and powers through the regular channels—at the ballot box for example."

Hossfros laughed skeptically.

"It must wait," continued Coleman; "it must wait on public opinion."

"Well," spoke up King, "it's all very well to wait, but public opinion left to itself is a mighty slow growth. It should be fostered. The newspapers—"

"Don't let's lose our sense of humour," cut in Talbot Ward. Can you see Charley Nugent or Mike Rowlee crusading for the right?"

"But my point is good," insisted King. "An honest, fearless

editor, not afraid to call a spade a spade—"

"Would be shot," said Coleman briefly.

"The chances of war," replied King.

"They don't grow that kind around here," grinned Ward.

"Well," concluded Coleman, "this young Keith probably won't help any, but he's going to be interesting to watch, just the same, to see what he'll do the first time they crack the whip over him. That's the vital point as far as he is concerned."

XXXVI

Keith's activities did not immediately confront him with anything in the nature of a test, however. His superiors confined him to the drawing of briefs and the carrying through of carefully selected cases. It was considered well to "work him in" a little before putting responsibility on him.

He enjoyed it, for now he had at his call all the civil and police resources of the city. This gave him a pleasant feeling of power. He was at the centre of things. And through his office he came into contact with ever-widening circles of people, all of whom were disposed, even anxious, to treat him well, to get in his good graces. Possibly most of these were what we would call the worst elements; and by that we would mean not only the roughnecks of the police or sheriff's offices, but also the punctilious, smooth-mannered Southerners who practically monopolized the political offices. These men would have been little considered in the South; in fact, in many cases, they had left their native states under a cloud or even with prison records; but their natural charm, their audacity, and their great punctilio as to "honour" deeply impressed the ordinary citizen. As one chronicler of the times puts it, they had "fluency in harangue, vigour in invective, ostentatious courage, absolute confidence about all matters of morals, politics, and propriety" —which is an excellent thumbnail sketch. Many of these ex-jailbirds rose to wealth and influence, so that to this day the sound of their names means aristocracy and birth to those ignorant of local history. Their descendants may be seen to-day ruffling it proudly on the strength of their "birth!"

They, and the classes they directly and indirectly encouraged, had at last brought the city fairly on the financial rocks. There was no more revenue. Everything taxable had been taxed. The poll tax was out of all reason; property paid 4 per cent. on an actual valuation; theatres, bankers, brokers, freight, miners, merchants, hotel, keepers, incorporationns, every form of industry was levied upon heavily. Still that was not enough. Even labour was paid now in scrip so depreciated that the cost of the simplest public works was terrible.

And to heap up the measure, the year of 1855 was one of financial stringency. The season of '54-'55 had been one of drought. For lack of water most of the mining had ceased. The miners wanted to be trusted for their daily needs; the country stores had to have credit because the miners could not pay; and so on up to the wholesalers in the city. Goods were therefore sold cheap at auction, and the gold went East to pay at the source. Money, actual physical money, became scarce. The gold was gone, and there existed no institution legally entitled to issue the paper money that might have taken its place. All the banking was done by private firms. These took deposits, made loans, issued exchange, but could not issue banknotes.

Still, things had looked a bit squally many times before, but nothing had happened. Men had the habit of optimism. No one stopped to analyze the situation, to realize that the very good reason nothing had happened was that the city had always had behind it the strength of the mines, and that now the mines had withdrawn.

Out of a clear sky came the announcement that Adams & Co. had failed!

At first nobody believed it. Adams & Co. had occupied in men's minds from the start much the same position as the Bank of England. The confirmation of the news caused the wildest panic and excitement. If Adams & Co. were vulnerable, nobody was secure. Small merchants began to call in their credits. The city caught up eagerly every item of news.

All the assets of the bankrupt firm were turned over to Alfred Cohen as receiver. Some interested people did not trust Cohen. They made enough of a fuss to get H. M. Naglee appointed in Cohen's place. Naglee, demanding the assets, was told they had been deposited with Palmer, Cook & Co. The latter refused to give them up, denying Naglee's jurisdiction in the matter. The case was brought into court. Then suddenly it was found that Palmer, Cook & Co. had mysteriously lost their paramount interest in the courts. They had counted on the case being brought before their own judges; but it was cited before Judges Hazen and Park, both of whom, while ultra-technical, were honest. The truth of the matter was that the rats suspected Palmer, Cook & Co. of sinking, too, and had deserted. Judges Hazen and Park called upon the firm to turn over to Naglee the assets of Adams & Co hey still refused. One of the partners, named Jones, and Cohen were imprisoned. Some where $269,000 was missing. Nobody knew anything about it. The books having to do with the transaction had mysteriously disappeared. Two days later an Irishman found them floating in the bay, and brought them to the court. But the crucial pages were missing. And then suddenly, while both Judge Hazen and Judge Park were out of town, application was made to the Supreme Court—of which Judge Terry was head—for the release of Jones and Cohen. The application was granted.

So an immense sum of money disappeared; nobody was punished; it was all strictly legal; and yet the dullest labourer could see that the whole transaction amounted to robbery under arms. Failures resulted right and left. Wells Fargo & Co. closed their doors, but resumed within a few days. A great many pocketbooks were hit. There was much talk and excitement.

XXXVII

On an evening in October, returning home at an early hour, Keith found Nan indignant and excited. She held in her hand a tiny newspaper, not half the usual size, consisting only of a single sheet folded.

"Have you seen this?" she burst out as Keith entered. "Isn't it outrageous!"

Keith was tired, and sank into an easy chair with a sigh of relaxation.

"No, what is it?" he asked, reaching his hand for the paper. "Oh. I saw them selling it on the street yesterday."

It was the *Bulletin*, Vol. 1, No. 2. Like all papers of that day, and like some of the English papers now, its first page was completely covered with small advertisements. A thin driblet of short local items occupied a column on the third and fourth pages, a single column of editorial on the second.

"Seems a piffling little sheet," he observed, "to be read in about eight seconds by any one not interested in advertisements. What is it that agitates you, Nan?"

"Read that." She pointed to the editorial.

The article in question proved to be an attack on Palmer, Cook & Co. It said nothing whatever about the Cohen-Naglee robbery. Its subject was the excessive rentals charged the public by Palmer, Cook & Co. for postal boxes. But it mentioned names, recorded specific instances, avoided generalities, and stated plainly that this was merely beginning at the beginning in an expose of the methods of these "Uriah Heeps."

"Why do they permit such things?" cried Nan, scarcely waiting for Keith to finish his reading, "What is Mr. Palmer going to do about it?"

"Survive, I guess," replied Keith, with a grin. "I take back my opinion of the paper. It certainly has life." He turned to the head of the page. "Hullo!" he cried in surprise. "James King of William running this, eh?" He whistled, then laughed. "That promises to be interesting, sure. He was in business with that crowd for some time. He ought to have information from the inside!"

"Mrs. Palmer is simply furious," said Nan.

"I'll bet she is. Are we invited out this evening?"

"The Thurstons' musicale. I thought you'd be interested in that."

"Let me off, Nan, that's a good fellow," pleaded Keith, whose weariness had vanished. "I'd be delighted to go at any other time. But this is too rich. I must see what the gang has to say."

"I suppose I could drop Ben Sansome a note," assented Nan doubtfully.

"Do! Send the Chink around with it," urged Keith, rising. "I'll get a bite downtown and not bother you."

The gang—as indeed the whole city—took it as a great joke. Of those Keith met, only Jones, the junior partner, failed to see the humour, and he passed the affair off in cavalier fashion. That did not save him from the obligation of setting up the drinks.

"I'm going to fix this thing up in the morning," he stated confidently. "Between you and me, there's evidently been a slip somewhere. Of course it ought never to have been allowed to go so far. I'll see this man King first thing in the morning, and buy him off. Undoubtedly that's about the only reason his paper exists. Wonder where he got the money to start it? He's busted. It can't last long."

"If it keeps up the present gait, it'll last," said Judge Caldwell shrewdly. "Me—I'm going to send in a subscription tomorrow. Wouldn't miss it for anything."

"It'll last as long as he does," growled Terry, "and that'll be about as long as a snowball in hell. What you ought to do, Jones, is what any man of spirit ought to do—call him out!"

"He announces definitely that he won't fight duels," said Calhoun Bennett.

"Then treat him like the cowardly hound he is," flared the uncompromising Terry. "Take the whip to him; and if that isn't effective, shoot him down as you would any other mad dog!"

"Surely, that's a little extreme, Judge," expostulated Caldwell. "He hasn't done anything worse than stir up Jonesy a little."

"But he will, sir," insisted Terry, "you mark my words. If you give him line, he'll not only hang himself, but he'll rope in a lot of bystanders as well."

"I'll bet he sells a lot of papers to-morrow, anyhow," predicted Keith.

"I hope so," bragged Jones. "There'll be the more to read his apology."

Evidently Jones fulfilled his promise, and quite as evidently Keith's prediction was verified. Every man on the street had a copy of the next day's *Bulletin* within twenty minutes of issue.

A roar of delight went up. Jones's visit was reported simply as an item of news, faithfully, sarcastically, and pompously. There was no comment. Even the most faithful partisans of Palmer, Cook & Co. had to grin at the effectiveness of this new way of meeting the impact of such a visit,

"It's clever journalism," Terry admitted, "but it's black-guardly; and I blame Jones for passing it over."

The fourth number—eagerly purchased—proved more interesting because of its hints of future disclosures rather than for its actual information. Broderick was mentioned by name. The attention of the city marshal was succinctly called to the disorderly houses and the statutes concerning them; and it was added, "for his information," that at a certain address a structure was actually building at a cost of $30,000 for improper purposes. Then followed a list of personal bonds and sureties for which Palmer, Cook & Co. were standing voucher, amounting to over two millions.

The expectations of disclosures, thus aroused, were not immediately gratified, except in the case of Broderick. His swindles in the matters of the Jenny Lind Theatre and the City Hall were traced out in detail. Every one knew these things were done, but nobody knew just how; so these disclosures made interesting reading if only as food for natural curiosity. However, the tension somewhat relaxed. It was generally considered that the coarse fibre of the ex-stone-cutter, the old Tammany heeler, and the thick skins of his political adherents could stand this sort of thing. Nobody with a sensitive honour to protect was assailed.

The position of the new paper was by now firmly established. It had a large subscription list; it was eagerly bought on the streets; and its advertising was increasing. King again turned his attention to Palmer, Cook & Co. Each day he treated succinctly, clearly, without rhetoric, some branch of their business. By the time he had finished with them he had not only exposed their iniquities, he had educated the public to an understanding of the financial methods of the times. His tilting at this banking firm had inevitably led him to criticism of certain of their subterfuges to avoid or take advantage of the law; and that as inevitably brought him to analysis and condemnation of the firm's legal advisers, James, Doyle, Barber & Boyd, a firm which had heretofore enjoyed a good reputation. Incidentally he called attention to duelling, venal newspapers, city sales, gambling, Billy Mulligan, Wooley Kearney, Casey, Cora, Yankee Sullivan, Martin Gallagher, Tom Cunningham, Ned McGowan, Charles Duane, and many other worthies, both of high and low degree. Never did he fear to name names and cite specific instances plainly. James King of William dealt in no innuendoes. He had found in himself the editor he had wished for, the man who would call a spade a spade.

The *Bulletin* twice enlarged its form. It sold by the thousand. Its weap of defence was the same as its weapon of offence— pitiless and complete publicity. Measures of reprisal, either direct or underhand, undertaken against him, King published often without comment.

At the first some of the cooler heads thought it might be well to reason with him.

"The man has run a muck," said old Judge Girvin, "and while I am far from denying that In many—perhaps in most —cases his facts are correct, still his methods make for lawlessness among the masses. It might be well to meet him reasonably, and to expostulate."

"I'd expostulate—with a blacksnake," growled the fiery Terry.

A number waited on King. Keith was among them. They found his office in a small ramshackle frame building, situated in the middle instead of alongside one of the back streets. It had probably been one of the early small dwelling-houses, marooned by a resurvey of the streets, and never since moved. King sat in his shirtsleeves before a small flat table. He looked up at them uncompromisingly from his wide-apart steady eyes.

"Gentlemen," he greeted them tentatively.

Judge Girvin seated himself impressively, his fat legs well apart, his beaver hat and cane poised in his left hand; the others, grouped themselves back of him. The judge stated the moderate case well. "We do not deny any man the right to his opinion," he concluded, "but have you reflected on the effect such an expression often has on the minds of those not trained to control?"

King listened to him in silence.

"It seems to me, sir," he answered, when Judge Girvin had quite finished, "that if abuses exist they should be exposed until they are remedied; and that the remedy should come from the law."

"What is your impelling motive?" asked the judge. "Why have you so suddenly taken up this form of activity? Do you feel aggrieved in any way—personally?"

"My motive in starting a newspaper, if that is what you mean, is the plain one of making an honest if modest living. And, incidentally, while doing so, I have some small idea of being of public use. I have no personal grievance; but I am aggrieved, as every decent man must be, at the way the lawyers, the big financial operators, and the other blackguards have robbed the city," stated King plainly.

Judge Girvin, flushing, arose with dignity,

"I wish you good-day, sir," he said coldly, and at once withdrew.

Keith had been watching King with the keenly critical, detached, analytical speculation of the lawyer. He carried away with him the impression of a man inspired.

At the engine house, to which the discomfited delegation withdrew, there was more discussion.

"The man is within his legal rights so far," stated Judge Girvin. "If any of his statements are libellous, it is the duty of the man so libelled to institute action in the courts."

"He's too smooth for that," growled Jones.

"He'll bite off more than he can chew, if he keeps on," said Dick Blatchford comfortably. "He's stirring up hornets' nests when he monkeys with men like Yankee Sullivan. He's about due for an awful scare, one of these days, and then he'll be good."

"Do you know, I don't believe he'll scare," said Keith suddenly, with conviction.

XXXVIII

As Keith surmised, intimidation had no effect. In such a city of fire-eaters it was promptly tried. A dozen publically announced that they thirsted for his blood, and intended to have it; and the records of the dozen were of determination and courage in such matters. In the gambling resorts and on the streets bets were made and pools formed on the probable duration of King's life. He took prompt notice of this fact. Said the *Bulletin's* editorial column:

> Bets are now being offered, we are told, that the editor of the *Bulletin* will not be in existence twenty days longer, and the case of Doctor Hogan, of the Vicksburg paper, who was murdered by gamblers of that place, is cited as a warning. Pah! War, then, is the cry, is it? War between the prostitutes and gamblers on one side, and the virtuous and respectable on the other! Be it so, then! Gamblers of San Francisco, you have made your election, and we are ready on our side for the issue!

Keith read this over John Sherwood's shoulder at the Monumental. The ex-gambler, his famous benign spectacles atop his nose, chuckled over it.

"He doesn't scare for a cent, does he?" was his comment. "Strikes me I got out of the ranks of the ungodly just in time. If I were still gambling, I believe I'd take some of those bets he speaks of. He won't last—in this town. But I like his pluck— kind of. Only he's damn bad for business!"

Saying which, John Sherwood, late gambler but now sincerely believing himself a sound and conservative business man, passed the sheet over to Keith.

From vague threats the situation developed rapidly to the definite and personal. One Selover sent a challenge to King, which was refused. Selover then announced his intention of killing King on sight. The *Bulletin* published this:

> Mr. Selover, it is said, carries a knife. We carry a pistol. We hope neither will be required, but if this encounter cannot be avoided, why will Mr. Selover insist on imperilling the lives of others? We pass every afternoon, about half-past four to five o'clock, along Market Street from Fourth to Fifth streets. The road is wide, and not so much frequented as those streets farther in town. If we are to be shot or cut to pieces, for heaven's sake let it be done there. Others will not be injured, and in case we fall, our house is but a few hundred yards beyond, and the cemetery not much farther.

These detailed attacks and bold defiances had the effect of greatly angering those who were the specific objects of attention; of making very uneasy the class to which these victims belonged; of focussing on public matters a public sentiment that was just becoming conscious of itself because of the pinch of hard times; and of rendering contemptuously indignant all of "higher" society.

To this latter category Keith would undoubtedly have belonged—as did his wife and practically all his friends—had it not been for his association with Krafft. Through him the young lawyer came into intimate personal touch with a large class of people who would otherwise have been remote from him. He heard of their difficulties and problems at first hand, saw the actual effect of abuses that, looked at from above, were abstract or academic. Police brutality as a phrase carried little significance; police brutality as a clubbing of Malachi Hogan, who was brought in with his skull crushed, and whose blood stained Keith's new coat, meant something. Waste of public funds, translated before his eyes into eviction for nonpayment of taxes, took on a new significance. Keith saw plainly that a reform was needed. He was not, on that account, in the least sympathetic with King's methods. Like Judge Govin, he felt them revolutionary and subversive. But he could not share the contempt of his class; rather he respected the editor as a sincere but mistaken man. When his name came up for discussion or bitter vituperation, Keith was silent. He read the *Bulletin* editorials; and while he in no way endorsed their conclusions or recommendations, he could not but acknowledge their general accuracy. Without his knowing it, he was being educated. He came to realize the need for better administration by the city's officers and a better enforcement of the laws. Very quietly, deep down within himself, he made up his mind that in the Assistant District Attorney's office, at least, the old order of things should cease.

Stewart Edward White

XXXIX

One afternoon Keith walked down Kearney Street deep in discussion of an important Federal case with his friend, Billy Richardson, the United States Marshal. Although both just and official, Richardson was popular with all classes save those with whom his duty brought him into conflict. They found their way deliberately blocked, and came out of the absorption of their discussion to recognize before them Charles Cora, an Italian gambler of considerable prominence and wealth. Cora was a small, dark man, nervously built, dressed neatly and carefully in the height of gambler fashion. He seemed to be terribly excited, and at once launched a stream of oaths at Richardson.

"What's the matter with you, Charley?" asked the latter, as soon as he had recovered from his surprise.

Cora, evidently too incoherent to speak, leaped at the marshal, his fist drawn back. Keith seized him around the body, holding his arms to his sides.

"Hold on; take it easy!" he panted. "What's up, anyway?"

Cora, struggling violently, gritted out:

"He knows damn well what's up."

"I'll swear I don't!" denied Richardson.

"Then what do you mean telling every one that my Belle insulted your wife last night at the opera house?" demanded Cora, ceasing to struggle.

"Belle?" repeated Richardson equably. "I don't know what you're talking about. Be reasonable. Explain yourself."

"Yes, I got it straight," insisted the Italian. "Your wife says it insults her to sit next to my Belle, and you go everywhere telling it. What right you got to do that? Answer me that!"

"Now look here," said Richardson. "I was with Jim Scott all last evening. My wife wasn't with me. If you don't believe me, go ask Scotty."

Cora had apparently cooled off, so Keith released him. He shook his head, grumbling, only half convinced. After a moment he moved away. The two men watched him go, half vexed, half amused.

"He's crazy as a pup about that woman," observed Richardson.

"Who is she?" inquired Keith.

"Why, Belle—you know Belle, the one who keeps that, crib up your way."

"That woman!" marvelled Keith.

He spent the afternoon in court and in his office. About half-past six, on his way home, he saw Cora and Richardson come out of the Blue Wing saloon together. They were talking earnestly, and stopped in the square of light from the window. Richardson was explaining, and Cora was listening sullenly. As Keith passed them he heard, the marshal say, "Well, is it all right?" and Cora reply, "Yes." Something caused him to look back after he had gone a dozen yards. He saw Cora suddenly seize Richardson's collar with his left hand, at the same time drawing a derringer with his right.

"What are you going to do?" cried Richardson loudly and steadily, without straggling, "Don't shoot; I am unarmed!"

Without reply Cora fired into his breast. The marshal wilted, but with iron strength Cora continued for several moments to hold up his victim by the collar. Then he let the body drop, and moved away at a fast walk, the derringer still in his right hand.

Keith ran to his friend, and with others carried him into a nearby drug store. The sound of the shot almost immediately brought out a crowd. Keith, bending over the body of the murdered man, could see them pressing about the windows outside, their faces showing white from the lamps in the drug-store window or fading into the darkness beyond. They crowded through the doorway until driven out again by some of the cooler heads. Conjectures and inquiries flew thick. All sorts of reports were current of the details, but the crowd had the main facts—Cora had shot Richardson, Richardson was dead, Cora had been taken to jail.

"Then he's safe!" they sneered savagely.

Men had been shot on the streets before, many men, some of them as well known and liked as Richardson; but not after public sentiment had been aroused as the *Bulletin* had aroused it. The crowds continued to gather. Several men made violent street-corner speeches. There was some talk of lynching. A storm of yes and no burst forth when the question was put. Bells rang. A great mob surged to the jail, were firmly met by a strong armed guard, and fell back muttering.

"Who will be the next victim?" men asked. "What a farce!" cried some, in deep disgust. "Why, the jailer is Cora's especial crony!" stated others, who seemed to know. "If the jury is packed, hang the jury!" advised certain far-seeing ones. A grim, quiet, black-bearded man expressed the undercurrent of opinion: "Mark my words," said he, "if Charles Cora is left for trial, he will be let loose on the community to assassinate his third victim!" It seemed that Cora had been involved in a previous shooting scrape. But to swing a mob to action there must be determined men at its head, and this mob had no leaders. Sam Brannan started to say something in his coarse, roaring voice, and was promptly arrested for inciting a riot. Nobody cared enough seriously for the redoubtable Sam to object to this. The situation was ticklish, but the police handled it tactfully for once, opposing only a passive opposition, leaving the crowd to fritter its energies in purposeless cursing, surging to and fro, and in harmless threats.

Keith did not join the throngs on the streets. Having determined that Richardson was dead, he accompanied the body home. He was deeply stirred, not only by the circumstances of the murder, but also by the scene at which he had to assist when the news must be broken to Mrs. Richardson. From the house he went directly to King's residence, where he was told that the editor had gone downtown. After considerable search and inquiry he at last got sight of his man standing atop a wooden awning overlooking the Plaza in front of the jail. King nodded to him as he climbed out of the second-story window to take his position at the newspaper man's side.

The square was a wild sight, filled, packed with men, a crowd of men tossed in constant motion. A mumbling growl came from them continuously, and occasionally a shout. Many hands were upraised, and in some of them were weapons. Opposite, the blank front of the jail.

King's eyes were shining with interest and a certain quiet exultation, but he seemed not at all excited.

"Will they storm the jail?" asked Keith.

King shook his head.

"No, these people will do nothing. But they show the spirit of the time. All it needs now is organization, cool, deliberate organization—to-morrow."

"That's just what I've hunted you out to talk about," said Keith earnestly. "There is much talk of a Vigilance Committee. As you say, all it needs is the call. That means lawlessness, bloodshed."

"Conditions at present are intolerable," said King briefly.

"I agree with you," replied Keith. King stared. "But in this case I assure you the law will do its duty. It is an absolutely open and shut case. Acquittal is impossible. Why, I myself was witness of the affair."

King looked skeptical.

"Hundreds of such cases have been acquitted, or the indictment quashed."

"But this is entirely different. In the first place, the case will come before Judge Norton and Judge Hazen, both of whom you will acknowledge are honest. In the second place, this case will be in my hands as Assistant District Attorney. I myself shall do the prosecuting, and I promise you on my honour that every effort will be made for a deserved and speedy conviction. I acknowledge justice has sometimes gone wrong in the past; but that has not been the fault of the law, but of the administration of the law. If you have the least confidence in Judge Norton and Judge Hazen, and if you can be brought to believe me, you will see that this one case of all cases should not be taken from the constituted authorities or made the basis for a movement outside the law."

"Well?" said King, half convinced.

"The *Bulletin* has the greatest influence with these people. Use it. Give the law, the honest law, a chance. Do not get back of any Vigilante movement. In that way, I am convinced, you will be of the greatest public service."

Next day the *Bulletin* came out vigorously counselling dependence on the law, expressing confidence in the integrity of Hazen and Norton, and enunciating a personal belief that the had passed when it would be necessary to resort to arbitrary measures. The mob's anger had possessed vitality enough to keep it up all night; but the attitude of the *Bulletin*, backed by responsible men like Ward, Coleman, Hossiros, Bluxome, and others, averted a crisis. Nevertheless, King added a paragraph of warning:

Hang Billy Mulligan! That's the word! If Mr. Sheriff Scannell does not remove Billy Mulligan from his present post as keeper of the county jail, and Mulligan lets Cora escape, hang Billy Mulligan, and if necessary to get rid of the sheriff, hang him— hang the sheriff!

XL

The popular excitement gradually died. It had no leaders. Coleman and men of his stamp, who had taken command of similar crises in former times, counselled moderation. They were influenced, partly by the fact that Richardson had been a public official and a popular one. Conviction seemed certain.

Keith applied himself heart and soul to the case. Its preparation seemed to him, at first an easy matter. It was open and shut. Although at the moment of the murder the street had not been crowded, a half-dozen eye-witnesses of the actual shooting were easily found, willing to testify to the essential facts. No defence seemed possible, but Cora remained undisturbed. He had retained one of the most brilliant lawyers of the time, James McDougall. This fact in itself might have warned Keith, for McDougall had the reputation of avoiding lost causes and empty purses. The lawyer promptly took as counsel the most brilliant of the younger men, Jimmy Ware, Allyn Lane, and Keith's friend, Calhoun Bennett. This meant money, and plenty of it, for all of these were expensive men. The exact source of the money was uncertain; but it was known that Belle was advancing liberally for her lover, and that James Casey, bound by some mysterious obligation, was active in taking up collections. Cora lived in great luxury at the jail. He had long been a personal friend of Sheriff Webb and his first deputy, Billy Mulligan.

Several months passed before the case could be forced to trial. All sorts of legal and technical expedients were used to defer action. McDougall and his legal assistants were skilful players at the game, and the points they advanced had to be fought out according to the rules, each a separate little case with plenty of its own technicalities. Some of Keith's witnesses were difficult to hold; they had business elsewhere, and naturally resented being compelled, through no fault of their own, to remain. Keith had always looked on this play of legal rapiers as a part—an interesting part—of the game; but heretofore he had always been on the obstructing side. He worried a great deal. At length, by superhuman efforts, he broke through the thicket of technicalities and brought the matter to an issue. The day was set. He returned home so relieved in spirit that Nan could not but remark on his buoyancy.

"Yes," he responded, "I've managed to drive that old rascal, McDougall, into the open at last."

Nan caught at the epithet.

"But you don't mean that—quite—do you?" she asked. "The McDougalls are such delightful people."

"No, of course not. Just law talk," said Keith, quite sincerely. "He's handled his case well up to now. I'm just exasperated on that account, that's all."

But setting the day irrevocably was only a beginning. The jury had to be selected. Sheriff Webb had in his hands the calling of the venire. While it was true that the old-time, "professional jurymen"—men who hung around the courthouse for no other purpose—were no longer in existence, it can be readily seen that Webb was able, if it were worth while, to exercise a judicious eye in the selection of "amenables." The early exhaustion of Keith's quota of peremptory challenges was significant, for McDougall rarely found it desirable to challenge at all! Keith displayed tremendous resource in last-moment detective work concerning the records of the panel. In this way he was enabled to challenge several for cause, after all his peremptory challenges had been used. At first he had great difficulty in getting results, for the police detectives proved supine. It was only after he had hired private agents, paying for them from his own pocket, that he obtained information on which he could act. The final result was a jury better than he had dared hope for, but worse than he desired. He had gone through a tremendous labour, and realized fully the difference between being for or against the powers.

The case came to trial, Keith presented six witnesses—respectable, one of them well-known. These testified to the same simple facts, and their testimony remained unshaken under cross-examination. McDougall offered the plea of self-defence. He brought a cloud of witnesses to swear that Cora had drawn his weapon only after Richardson had produced and cocked a pistol. By skilful technical delays Keith gained time for his detectives, and succeeded in showing that two of these witnesses had been elsewhere at the time of the killing, and therefore had perjured themselves. He recalled his own witnesses, and found two willing to swear that Richardson's hands had been empty and hanging at his sides, The defence did not trouble to cross-examine this statement.

At last, with a perfunctory judicial charge, the case went to the jury. Keith, weary to the bone, sat back in grateful relaxation. He had worked hard, against odds, and had done a good job. He was willing now to spare a little professional admiration for McDougall's skilful legal manoeuvring. There could be no earthly doubt of the result. He idly watched the big bland-faced clock, with its long second hand moving forward by spaced jerks. The jury was out a very long time for so simple a verdict, but that was a habit of California juries. It did not worry Keith. He was glad to rest. The judge stared at the ceiling, his hands clasped over his stomach. Cora's lawyers talked together in a low voice. Flies buzzed against dusty window-panes. The spectators watched apathetically. Belle, in a ravishing toilet, was there.

The opening of the door broke the spell almost rudely. Keith sat up, listening to the formal questions and answers. They had disagreed!

For a moment the import of this did not penetrate to Keith's understanding. Then he half rose, shouted "What!" and sank back stunned. His brain was in confusion. Only dimly did he hear the judge dismissing the jury, remanding Cora for retrial, adjourning court. Instantly Cora was surrounded by a congratulatory crowd. Keith sat alone. McDougall, gathering up his papers from the table assigned to counsel, made some facetious remark. Keith did not reply. McDougall looked at him sharply, and as he went out he remarked to Casey:

"Keith takes this hard."

"He does!" cried Casey, genuinely astonished. "They were trying to tell me he was altogether too active in this matter; but I told them he was young and had his way to make, and was playing to the gallery."

He sauntered across the room.

"Well, Milt," he cried in a jovial voice, but watching the young lawyer narrowly, "the Lord's on the side of true virtue, as usual."

Keith came to himself, scowled, started to say something, but refrained with an obvious effort.

Casey wandered back to McDougall.

"You're right, Mac," he said. "I guess he's got the swell head. We'll have to call him off gently, or he'll make a nuisance of himself at the next trial. He makes altogether too much trouble."

But McDougall was tolerant.

"Oh, let him alone, Jim. He's got his way to make. Let him alone. We can handle the situation."

Stewart Edward White

XLI

Keith left the courtroom in a daze of incredulity. This was his first serious defeat; and he could not understand it. The case was absolutely open and shut, a mere question of fact to which there were sufficient and competent witnesses. For the moment he was completely routed.

As he emerged to the busy crowds on Kearney Street a sudden repugnance to meeting acquaintances overcame him. He turned off toward the bay, making his way by the back streets, alleys, and slums of that unsavoury quarter. But even here he was not to escape. He had not gone two blocks before he descried Krafft's slight and elegant figure sauntering toward him. Keith braced himself for the inevitable question.

"Well," it came, "how goes the trial?"

The words released Keith's pent flood of bitterness. Here was an outlet; Krafft was "safe." He poured out his disappointment, his suspicion, his indignation. The little man listened to him in silence, a slight smile, sketching his full, red lips. When Keith had somewhat run down, Krafft, without a word, took him by the arm and led him by devious ways down to the water-front portion of the city. There he planted him near the entrance of a dark alley.

"Now you wait here," Keith was told.

Keith obeyed. The interval was long, but he had much to

occupy his mind. After a time Krafft returned in company with a slouching, drink-sodden bummer of powerful build and lowering mien, the remains of a forceful personality. This individual shambled along in the wake of the dapper little Krafft quite meekly and submissively.

"Here you are," said the latter briskly, and with a sort of nonchalant authority. "Come, now, Mex, tell Mr, Keith what you know about the Cora trial. Go on!" he urged, as the man hesitated. "He's not going to 'use' you—he doesn't even know who you are or where you're to be found, and I'm not going to tell him. Speak up, Mex! I tell you I want him to know how things stand."

Keith by now was acquainted with many of Krafft's proteges, but he had never met the delectable Mex. Evidently the latter had long known Krafft, however, for he acknowledged his authority unquestioningly.

"It's like this, boss," he began in a hoarse voice. "You don't know me, like Mr. Krafft says, but there's plenty that do. I got a lot of infloonce down here, and when anybody wants anything they know where to come to get it, which is right to headquarters—here," he slapped his great chest.

"Get on," interrupted Krafft impatiently. "We'll take it for granted that you are a great man."

Mex looked at him reproachfully, but went on:

"About this Cora trial: they come to me for good, reliable witnesses, and I got 'em, and drilled 'em. There ain't nobody in it with me for making any witness watertight."

"How many witnesses?" prompted Krafft.

"Eight," replied Mex promptly.

"How much?"

"Well, they give me five thousand fer to git the job done," admitted Mex, with some reluctance.

"Hope they got some of it," commented Krafft.

"Who gave you the money?" demanded Keith.

But Krafft interposed.

"Hold on, my son, that isn't ethics at all! You mustn't ask questions like that, must he, Mex? Very bad form!" He turned to Keith with a crisp air of decision. "That's what was the matter with your trial; I just thought I'd show you. Go on, Mex, get out," he commanded that individual, good-humouredly. "I'm not particularly proud of you, but I suppose I've got to stand you. Only remember this: Mr. Keith is my friend. Swear him out of the high seats of heaven—if you can—because that's the nature of you; but let him walk safely. In other words, no strong-arm work; do you understand?"

The man mumbled and growled something.

"Nonsense, Mex," interrupted Krafft sharply. "Do as I say.

"It's a matter of a tidy sum," blurted out Mex at last.

Krafft laughed.

"You see, you were already marked for the slaughter," he told Keith; then to Mex:

"Well, you let him alone; he's my friend."

"All right, if you say so," growled the man.

"You're safe—as far as Mex and all his people are concerned," said Krafft to Keith. "Our word is always good, when given to a friend; isn't it, Mex?"

The man nodded, awkwardly and slouched away.

Keith's depression had given place to anger. He had been beaten by unfair means; his opponent had cheated at the game, and his opponent enjoyed the respect of the community as a high-minded, able, dignified member of the bar. It was unthinkable! A man caught cheating at cards would most certainly be expelled from any decent club.

"I'll disbar that man if it's the last act of my life!" He cried, "He's not fit to practise among decent men!"

He left Krafft standing on the corner and smiling quietly, and hurried back to his office.

XLII

It was unfortunate for everybody that Morrell should have chosen that particular afternoon to pay one of his periodical calls. Morrell had been tactful and judicious in his demands. Keith was not particularly afraid of his story or the effect of it if told, but he disliked intensely the fuss and bother of explanations and readjustments. It had seemed easier to let things drift along. The transactions were skilfully veiled, notes were always given, Morrell was shrewd enough to take care that it did not cost too much. There existed not the slightest cordiality between the men, but a tacit assumption of civil relations.

But this afternoon the sight of Morrell, seated with what seemed to Keith a smug, superior, supercilious confidence in the best of the office chairs, was more than Keith could stand. He was bursting with anger at the world in general.

"You here?" he barked at Morrell, without waiting for a greeting. "Well, I'm sick of you! Get out!"

Morrell stared at him dumbfounded.

"I don't believe I understand," he objected.

"Get out! Get out! Get out! Is that plain enough?" shouted Keith.

Morrell arose with cold dignity.

"I cannot permit—" he began.

Keith turned on him abruptly.

"Look here, don't try to come that rot. I said, get out—and I mean it!"

So menacing was his aspect that Morrell drew back toward the door.

"I suppose you know what this means?" he threatened, an ugly note in his quiet voice.

"I don't give a damn what it means," rejoined Keith with deadly earnestness, "and if you don't get out of here I'll throw you out!"

Morrell went hastily.

Keith slammed his papers into a drawer, locked it and his office door, and went directly to the office of the *Bulletin*. There, seated in all the chairs, perched on the tables and window ledges, he found a representative group. He recognized most of them, including James King of William, Coleman, Hossfros, Isaac Bluxome, Talbot Ward, and others. A dead silence greeted his appearance. He stopped by the door.

"You have, of course, heard the news," he said. "I have come here to state unequivocally, and for publication, that the Cora trial will be pushed as rapidly and as strongly as is in the power of the District Attorney's office. And if legal evidence of corruption can be obtained, proceedings will at once be inaugurated to indict the bribe givers."

A short silence followed this speech. Several men looked toward one another. The tension appeared to relax a trifle.

"I am glad to hear this, sir, from your own lips," at last said Coleman formally, "and I wish you every success."

Another short and rather embarrassed silence fell.

"I should like to state privately to you gentlemen, and not for publication"—Keith, paused and glanced toward King, who nodded reassuringly—"that I have evidence, but unfortunately not legal, that James McDougall has been guilty, either personally or through agents, of bribery and corruption; and it is my intention to undertake his disbarment if I can possibly get proper evidence."

"Whether he bribed or didn't bribe, he knew perfectly well that Cora was guilty," stated King positively. "And he had no right to take the case."

But at that period this was an extreme view, as it still is in the legal mind.

"I suppose every man has a moral right to a defence," said Coleman doubtfully. "If every lawyer should refuse to take Cora's case, as you say McDougall should have refused, why the man would have gone undefended!"

"That's all right," returned King, undaunted, "He ought to have a lawyer—appointed by the court—to see merely that he gets a fair trial; not a lawyer—hired, prostituted, at a great price—to try by every technical means to get him off."

"A lawyer must, by the ethics of his profession, take every case brought him, I suppose," some one enunciated the ancient doctrine.

"Well, if that is the case," rejoined King hotly, "the law warps the thinking and the morals of any man who professes it. And if I had a son to place in life, I most certainly should not put him in a calling that deliberately trains his mind to see things that way!"

"I am sorry you have so low an opinion," spoke up Keith from the doorway. "I am afraid I must hold the contrary as to the nobility of my chosen profession. It can be disgraced, I admit. That it has been disgraced, I agree. That it can be redeemed, I am going to prove."

He bowed and left the office.

XLIII

Morrell went directly from Keith's office to Keith's house. He was not particularly angry; for some time he had expected just this result, but since he had threatened, he intended to accomplish. Finding Nan Keith at home, he plunged directly at he subject in his most direct and English fashion. She listened to him steadily until he had finished.

"Is that all?" she then asked him quietly,

"That's all," he acknowledged.

She arose.

"Then I will say, Mr. Morrell, that I do not believe you. I know my husband thoroughly, and I am beginning to know you. I believe that is my only comment. Good afternoon."

He made a half attempt to point to her the way to corroborative evidence, but she swept this superbly aside, Finally he took his correct leave, half angry, half amused, wholly cynical, for to his mind the reason for her indifference to the news he brought lay in what he supposed to be her relations with Ben Sansome.

"Bally ass!" he apostrophized himself. "Might have known how she'd take it."

His reading of Nan's motives was, of course, incorrect. Her

first feeling was merely a white heat of anger against Morrell, whom she had never liked. Perhaps after a little this emotion might have carried over into, not distrust, but an uneasiness as to the main issue; but before she had arrived at this point Keith came in to deliver an ill-timed warning. As ill luck would have it, and as such coincidences often come about in the most perverse fashion, Keith had, down the street, met some malicious fool who had dropped a laughing remark about Sansome. It was nothing in itself. Ordinarily, Keith would have paid no attention   it. To-day it clashed with his mood. Even now his jealousy was not stirred in the least, but his sense of appearances was irritated. By the time he had reached home he had worked up a proper indignation.

"Look here, Nan," he blurted out as soon as he had closed the door behind him, "you're seeing too much of Sansome. Everybody's talking."

"Who is everybody?" she asked very quietly.

"Of course I know it's all right," he blundered ahead tactlessly—the gleam in her eye should have warned him that he might have omitted that reassurance—"but just the looks of the thing. And he's such a weak and wishy-washy little nonentity!"

Her sense of justice aroused by this, she sprang to the defence of Sansome.

"You are quite mistaken there," she said with dignity. "Men of that type are never understood by men of yours. He is my friend—and yours. And he has been very kind to both of us."

"Well, just the same, you ought not to get yourself talked about," repeated Keith stubbornly.

"Do you distrust me?" she demanded.

"Heavens, no! But you don't realize how it looks to others.

He's coming here morning, noon, and night."

"It seems to me I may be the best judge of my own conduct."

"Well," said Keith deliberately, "I don't know that you are. You must remember that you are my wife, and that you bear my name. I have something to say about it. I'm telling you; but if you cannot manage the matter properly, I'll just have to drop a hint to Sansome."

At that she blazed out.

"Do that and you will regret it to the last day of your life!" she flared. "If you'd be as careful with the name of Keith as I am, it would not suffer!"

"What do you mean by that?" he asked? after a blank pause.

She had not intended to use that weapon, but now she persisted placidly.

"I mean that if our name has been talked about, it has not been because of any action of mine."

His heart was beating wildly. In the multiplicity of fighting interests he had actually forgotten (for the moment) all about his office visitor. But he, too, had pluck.

"I see you have had a call from our friend Morrell," he ventured.

"Well!" she challenged.

Her head was back, and her breath was short. This crisis had come upon them swiftly, unexpectedly, unwanted by either. Now it loomed over them in a terrible, because unknown, portent. Each realized that a misstep might mean irreparable consequences, but each felt constrained to go on. The situation must now be developed. Keith, faced with this new problem, lost his heat, and became cool, careful, wary, as when in court his faculties marshaled themselves. Nan, on the other hand, while well in control of her mind, poised on a brink.

"I don't know what he told you," said Keith, the blood suffusing his face and spreading over his ears and neck, "but I'm going to tell you everything he would be justified in telling you. One evening a number of years ago, in company with a crowd, I went inside the doors of a disreputable place, and immediately came out again. It was part of a spree, and harmless. That was all there was to it. You believe me?" In spite of his iron control, a deep note of anxiety vibrated in his voice as he proffered the question.

Her heart gave a leap for pride as he made this confession, his face very red, but his head back, She knew he spoke the truth, the whole truth.

"Of course I believe you," she said, trying to speak naturally, but with a mad impulse to laugh or cry. She swallowed, gripped her nerves, and went on. "But, naturally," she told him,

"I consider myself as good a custodian of the family reputation as yourself."

There the matter rested. By mutual but tacit consent they withdrew cautiously from the debated ground, each curiously haunted by a feeling that catastrophe had been fortunately and narrowly averted.

Stewart Edward White

XLIV

Keith immediately moved for a retrial, and began anew his heartbreaking labours in forcing a way to definite action through the thorn thicket of technicalities. At the same time, on his own account, and very secretly, he commenced a search for evidence against the attorneys for the defence. By now he possessed certain private agents of his own whom he considered trustworthy.

Early in his investigations he abandoned hope of getting direct evidence against McDougall himself. That astute lawyer had been careful to have nothing whatever to do with actual bribery or corruption, and he was crafty enough to disassociate himself from direct dealing with agents. Indeed, Keith himself was in some slight doubt as to whether McDougall had any actual detailed knowledge of the underground workings at all. But McDougall's. associates were a different matter. Here, little by little, real evidence began to accumulate, until Keith felt that he could, with reasonable excuse, move for an official investigation. To his genuine grief Calhoun Bennett seemed to be heavily involved. He could not forget that the young Southerner had been one of his earliest friends in the city, nor had he ever tried to forget the real liking he had felt for him. It was not difficult to recognize that according to his code Cal Bennett had merely played the game as the game was played, carrying out zealously the intentions of his superiors, availing himself of time-honoured methods, wholeheartedly fighting for his own side. Yet there could be no doubt that he had made himself criminally liable. Keith brooded much over the situation, but got nowhere, and so resolutely pushed it into the back of his mind in favour of the need of the moment.

But quietly as he conducted his investigations, some rumour of them escaped. One afternoon he received a call from Bennett. The young man was evidently a little embarrassed, but intent on getting at the matter.

"Look heah, Keith," he began, dropping into a chair, and leaning both arms on the table opposite Keith, "I don't want to say anything offensive, or take any disagreeable implications, or insult you by false suspicions, but there are various persistent rumours about, and I thought I'd better come to you direct."

"Fire away, Cal," said Keith.

"Well, it's just this: they do say yo're tryin' to fasten a criminal charge of bribery on me. You and I have been friends—and still are, I hope—but if yo're goin' gunnin' foh me, I want to know it."

His face was slightly flushed, but his fine dark eyes looked hopefully to his friend for denial. Keith was genuinely distressed. He moved an inkwell to and fro, and did not look up; but his voice was steady and determined as he replied:

"I'm not gunning for you, Cal, and I wish to heaven you weren't mixed up in this mess." He looked up. "But I *am* gunning for crooked work in this Cora case!"

Bennett took his arms from the table, and sat erect.

"Do you mean to imply, suh, that I am guilty of crooked work?" he inquired, a new edge of formality in his voice.

"No, no, of course not!" hastened Keith. "I hadn't thought of you in that connection! I am just looking the whole matter up—"

"Well, suh, I strongly advise you to drop it," interrupted Bennett curtly.

"But why?"

"It isn't ethical. You will find great resentment among yo' colleagues of the bar at the implication conveyed by yo' so-called investigation, suh."

Calhoun Bennett had become stiff and formal. Keith still tried desperately to be reasonable and conciliatory.

"But if there proves to be nothing out of the way," he urged, "surely no one could have anything to fear or object to."

"Nobody has anything to fear in any case," said Bennett, "but any gentleman—and I, most decidedly—would object to the implication."

At this Keith, stiffened a little in his turn.

"I am sorry we differ on that point, I have good reason to believe there has been crooked work somewhere in this Cora trial. I do not know who has done it; I accuse nobody; but in the public office I hold it seems my plain duty to investigate."

"Yo' public duty is to prosecute, that is all," argued Bennett. "It is the duty of the grand jury to investigate or to order investigations."

Here spoke the spirit of the law, for technically Bennett was correct.

"Whatever the rigid interpretation"—Keith found himself uttering heresy—"I still feel it my duty to deal personally with whatever seems to me unjustly to interfere with, proper convictions." Then he stopped, aghast at the tremendous step he had taken. For to a man trained as was Keith, in a time when all men were created for the law, and not the law for men, in a society where the lawyer was considered the greatest citizen, and subtle technicality paramount to justice or commonsense, this was a tremendous step. At that moment, and by that spontaneous and unconsidered statement, Keith, unknown to himself, passed from one side to the other in the great social struggle that was impending.

"I wa'n you, suh," Bennett was repeating, "yo' course will not meet with the approval of the members of the bar."

"I am sorry, Cal," said Keith sadly.

Bennett rose, bowed stiffly, and turned to the door. But suddenly he whirled back, his face alight with feeling,

"Oh, see heah, Milt, be sensible!" he cried. "I know just how yo're feelin' now. Yo're sore, and I don't blame you. You put ap a hard fight, and though you got licked, I don't mind tellin' you that the whole bar appreciates yo're brilliant work. You must remember you had to play a lone hand against pretty big men—the biggest we've got! We all appreciate the odds. Cora has lots of friends. You'll never convict him, Milt; but go in again for another trial, if it will do yo're feelin's any good, with our best wishes. Only don't let gettin' licked make you so sore! Don't go buttin' yo're haid at yo're friends! Be a spo't!"

A half hour ago this appeal might have gained a response if not a practical effect, but the spiritual transformation in Keith was complete.

"I'm sorry," he replied simply, "but I must go ahead in my own way."

Calhoun Bennett's face lost its glow, and his tall figure stiffened.

"I must wa'n you not to bring my name into this," said he. "I do not intend to have my reputation sacrificed to yo' strait-laced Yankee conscience. If my name is ever mentioned, I shall hold you responsible, *personally* responsible. You understand, suh?"

He stood stiff and straight, staring at Keith. Keith did not stir. After a moment Calhoun Bennett went out.

XLV

After this interview Keith experienced a marked and formal coldness from nearly all of his old associates, Those with whom he came into direct personal contact showed him scrupulous politeness, but confined their conversation to the briefest necessary words, and quit him as soon as possible. He found himself very much alone, for at this period he had lost the confidence of one faction and had not yet gained that of the other.

His investigations encountered always increasing difficulties. In his own department he could obtain little assistance. A dead inertia opposed all his efforts. Nevertheless, he went ahead doggedly, using Krafft and some of Krafft's proteges to considerable effect.

But soon pressure was brought on him from a new direction: his opponents struck at him through his home.

For some days Nan had been aware of a changed atmosphere in the society she frequented and had heretofore led. The change was subtle, defied analysis, but was to the woman's sensitive instincts indubitable. At first she had been inclined to consider it subjective, to imagine that something wrong with herself must be projecting itself through her imagination; but finally she realized that the impression was well based. In people's attitude there was nothing overt; it was rather a withdrawl of intimacy, a puzzling touch of formality. She seemed overnight to have lost in popularity.

Truth to tell, she paid little attention to this. By now she was experienced enough in human nature to understand and to be able to gauge the slight fluctuations, the ebbs and flows of esteem, the kaleidoscopic shiftings and realignments of the elements of frivolous and formal society. Mrs. Brown had hired away Mrs. Smith's best servant; for an hour they looked askance on Mrs. Brown; then, the episode forgotten, Mrs. Brown's cork bobbed to the surface company of all the other corks. It was very trivial. Besides, just at this moment, Nan was wholly occupied with preparations for her first "afternoon" of the year. She intended as usual to give three of these formal affairs, and from them the season took its tone. The list was necessarily far from exclusive, but Nan made up for by the care she gave her most original arrangements. She prided herself on doing things simply, but with a difference, calling heavily on her resources of correspondence, her memory, and her very good imagination for some novelty of food or entertainment. At the first of these receptions, too, she wore always for the first time some new and marvellous toilet straight from Paris, the style of which had not been shown to even her most intimate friends. This year, for example, she had done the most obvious and, therefore, the most unlikely thing: she had turned to the contemporaneous Spanish for her theme. Nobody had thought of that. The Colonial, the Moorish, the German, the Russian, the Hungarian—all the rest of the individual or "picturesque"—but nobody had thought to look next door. Nan had decorated the rooms with yellow and red, hung the walls with riatas, strings of red peppers and the like, obtained Spanish guitar players, and added enough fiery Mexican dishes to the more digestible refreshments to emphasize the Spanish flavour. She wore a dress of golden satin, a wreath of coral flowers about her hair, and morocco slippers matched in hue.

The afternoon was fine. People were slow in coming. A few of the nondescripts that must be invited on such occasions put in an appearance, responded hastily to their hostess's greeting, and wandered about furtively but interminably. Patricia Sherwood, who had come early, circulated nobly, trying to break up the frozen little groups, but in vain. The time passed. More non-descripts—and not a soul else! As five o'clock neared, a cold fear clutched at Nan's heart. No one was coming!

She worked hard to cover with light graciousness the cold-hearted dismay that filled her breast as the party dragged its weary length away. All her elaborate preparations and decorations seemed to mock her. The Spanish orchestra tinkled away gayly until she felt she could throw something at them; the caterer's servants served solemnly the awed nondescripts. Nan's cheeks burned and her throat choked with unshed tears. She could not bear to look at Patsy Sherwood, who remained tactfully distant.

About five-thirty the door opened to admit a little group, at the sight of whom Nan uttered a short, hysterical chuckle. Then she glided to meet them, both hands outstretched in welcome, Mrs. Sherwood watched her with admiration. Nan was game.

There were three in the party: Mrs. Morrell, Sally Warner, and Mrs. Scattergood. Sally Warner was of the gushing type of tall, rather desiccated femininity who always knows you so much better than you know her, who cultivates you every moment for a week and forgets you for months on end, who is hard up and worldly and therefore calculating, whose job is to amuse people and who will therefore sacrifice her best, perhaps not most useful, friend to an epigram, whose wit is barbed, who has a fine nose for trouble, and who is always in at the death. Mrs. Scattergood was a small blond woman, high voiced, precise in manner, very positive in her statements which she delivered in a drawling tone, humourless, inquisitive about petty affairs, the sort of "good woman" with whom no fault can be found, but who drives men to crime. Mrs. Morrell we know.

These three, after greeting their hostess gushingly, circulated compactly, talking to each other in low voices. Nan knew they were watching her, and that they had come for the sole purpose of getting first-hand details of her fiasco for later recounting in drawing-rooms where, undoubtedly, even now awaited eager auditors. She came to a decision. The matter could not be worse. When, the three came to make their farewells, she detained them.

"No, I'm not going to let you go yet," she told them, perhaps a little imperiously. "I haven't had half a visit with you. Wait until this rabble clears out."

She hesitated a moment over Mrs. Sherwood, but finally let her go without protest. When the last guest had departed she sank into a chair. As she was already on the verge of hysterics, she easily kept up an air of gayety.

"Girls, what an awful party!" she cried. "I could tear my hair! It was a perfect nightmare." Struggling to control her voice and keep back her tears, she added abruptly: "Now tell me what it is all about."

Mrs. Morrell and Sally Warner were plainly uneasy and at a loss how to meet this situation, but Mrs. Scattergood remained quite composed in her small, compact way.

"What's what all about, Nan, dear?" asked Sally Warner in her most vivacious manner. She keenly felt the dramatic situation and was already visualizing herself in the role of raconteuse.

"You know perfectly well. Why this funeral? Where are they all? Why did they stay away? I have a right to know."

"I'm sure there's nothing *I* can think of!" replied Sally artificially "The idea!"

But Mrs. Scattergood, with all the relish of performing a noble and disagreeable duty, broke in:

"You know, dear," she said in her didactic, slow voice, "as well as we do, what the world is. Of course *we* understand, but people will talk!"

"In heaven's name what are you driving at? What are they talking about?" demanded Nan, as Mrs. Scattergood apparently came to a full stop.

A pause ensued while Sally and Mrs, Scattergood exchanged glances with Mrs. Morrell.

"Well," at last said Sally, judicially, buttoning her glove, her head on one side, "if I had a nice husband like yours, I wouldn't let him run around getting himself disliked for nothing."

"You ought to use your influence with him before it is too late," added Mrs. Morrell.

Nan looked helplessly from one to the other, too uncertain of her ground now to risk another step,

"So that's it," she ventured at last. "Some one has been telling lies about us!"

"Oh, dear no!" disclaimed Mrs. Scattergood, "It is only that your friends cannot understand your taking sides against them. Naturally they feel hurt. Forgive me, dear—you know I say it with all affection—but don't you think it a mistake?"

Nan was thoroughly dazed and mystified, but afraid to press the matter further. She had a suspicion Mrs. Morrell was again responsible for her difficulties, but was too uncertain to urge them to stay for further elucidation. They arose. These were the days of hoop skirts, and the set of the outer skirt had to be carefully adjusted before going out. As they posed in turn before the hall pier glass they chattered. "How lovely the house looks." "You certainly have worked hard, and must be tired, poor dear!" "Well, we'll see you to-morrow at Mrs. Terry's. You're *not asked*? Surely there is some mistake! Well, those things always happen in a big affair, don't they?" "See you soon." "Good-bye." "Good-bye."

Outside the house they paused at the head of the steps.

"Well, what do you think of that?" said Sally. "I really believe the poor thing doesn't know, I believe I'll just drop in for a minute at Mrs. Caldwell's. Sorry you're not going my way."

After a fashion Nan felt relieved by this interview, for she thought she discerned only Mrs. Morrell's influence, and this, she knew, she could easily overcome. While she waited for Keith's return from whatever inaccessible fastnesses he always occupied during these big afternoon receptions, she reviewed the situation, her indignation mounting. Downstairs, Wing Sam and his temporary assistants were clearing things away. Usually Nan superintended this, but to-day she did not care. When Keith finally entered the room, she burst out on him with a rapid and angry account of the whole situation as she saw it; but to her surprise he did not rise to it. His weary, spiritless, uninterested: acceptance of it astonished her to the last degree. To him her entanglement with the Cora affair— for at once he saw the trend of it all—seemed the last straw. Not even his own home was sacred. His spirit was so bruised and wearied that he actually could not rise to an explanation. He seemed to realize an utter hopelessness of making her see his point of view. This was not so strange when it is considered that this point of view, however firmly settled, was still a new and unexplained fact with himself. He contented himself with saying: "The Morrells had nothing whatever to do with it." It was the only thing that occurred to him as worth saying; but it was unfortunate, for it left Nan's irritation without logical support. Naturally that irritation was promptly transferred to him.

"Then what, in heaven's name, is it?" she demanded. "My friends are all treating me as if I had the smallpox."

"Cheerful lot of friends we've made in this town!" he

said bitterly.

"What is the matter with them?" she persisted.

"The matter is they've taken me for a fool they could order around to suit themselves. They found they couldn't. Now they're through with me, even Cal Bennett," he added in a lower tone that revealed his hurt.

She paused, biting her underlip.

"Is the trouble anything to do with this Cora case?" she asked, suddenly enlightened by some vague, stray recollection.

"Of course!" he replied crossly, exasperated at the nagging necessity of arousing himself to explanations. "There's no use arguing about it. I'm going to see it through in spite of that hound McDougall and his whole pack of curs!"

"But why have you turned so against your friends?" she asked more gently, struck by his careworn look as he sprawled in the easy chair under the lamp. "I don't see! You'll get yourself disliked!"

She did not press the matter further for the moment, but three days later she brought up the topic again. In the interim she had heard considerable direct and indirect opinion. She selected after dinner as the most propitious time for discussion. As a matter of fact, earlier in the day would have been better, before Keith's soul had been rubbed raw by downtown attrition.

"I don't believe you quite realize how strongly people feel about the Cora case," she began. "Isn't it possible to drop it or compromise it or something, Milton?"

In the reaction from argument and—coldness downtown he felt he could stand no more of it at home.

"I wish you'd let that matter drop!" he said decidedly. "You couldn't understand it."

She hesitated. A red spot appeared in either cheek.

"I must say I *don't* understand!" she countered. "It is inconceivable to me that a man like you should turn so easily against his class!"

"My class?" he echoed wearily.

"What do such creatures as Cora and Yankee Sullivan amount to?" she cried hotly, "I suppose you'll say *they* are in your class next! How you can consider them of sufficient importance to go dead against your best friends on their account!"

"It is because I am right and they are wrong."

She was a little carried beyond herself.

"Well, they all think the same way," she pointed out. "Aren't you a little —a little—"

"Pig-headed," supplied Keith bitterly.

"—to put your opinion against theirs?" she finished.

Keith did not reply.

This was Nan's last attempt. She did not bring up the subject again. But she withdrew proudly and completely from all participation in society. She refused herself to callers. Once the situation was thoroughly defined, she accepted it. If her husband decided to play the game in this way, she, too, would follow, whether she approved or not. Nan was loyal and a thoroughbred. And she was either too proud or too indifferent to fight it out with the other women, in the rough and tumble of social ambition.

XLVI

In this voluntary seclusion Nan saw laterally only two persons. One of these was Mrs. Sherwood. The ex-gambler's wife called frequently; and, for some reason, Nan never refused to see her, although she did not make her visitor particularly welcome. Often an almost overmastering impulse seized her to open her soul to this charming, sympathetic, tactful woman, but something always restrained her. Her heart was too sore. And since an inhibited impulse usually expresses itself by contraries, her attitude was of studied and aloof politeness. Mrs. Sherwood never seemed to notice this. She sat in the high-ceilinged "parlour," with its strange fresco of painted fish-nets, and chatted on in a cheerful monologue, detailing small gossipy items of news. She always said goodbye cordially, and went out with a wonderful assumption of ignorance that anything was wrong. Her visits did Nan good, although never could the latter break through the ice wall of reserve. Nan's conscience often hurt her that she could answer this genuine friendship with so little cordiality. She wondered dully how Mrs. Sherwood could bring herself to be so good to so cross-grained a creature as herself. As a matter of fact, the women were marking time in their relations—Mrs. Sherwood consciously, Nan unconsciously—until better days.

The other regular caller was Ben Sansome. His attitude was in some sense detached. He was quietly, deeply sympathetic in his manner, never obtrusive, never even hinting in words at his knowledge of the state of affairs, but managing in some subtle manner to convey the impression that he alone fully

　　　　Stewart Edward White

understood. Nan found that, without her realization, almost in spite of herself, Sansome had managed to isolate her with himself on a little island of mutual understanding, apart from all the rest of the world.

Her life was now becoming circumscribed. Household, books, some small individual charities, and long afternoon walks filled her days. At first Sansome had accompanied her on these tramps, but the unfailing, almost uncanny insight of the man told him that at such times her spirit really craved solitude, so he soon tactfully ceased all attempts to join her. Her usual walk was over the cliffs toward the bay, where, from some of the elevations near Russian Hill, she could look out to the Golden Gate, or across to Tamalpais or the Contra Costa shores. The crawl of the distant blue water, the flash of wing or sail, the taste of salt rime, the canon shadows of the hills, the flying murk, or the last majestic and magnificent blotting out of the world as the legions of sea fog overtoiled it, all answered or soothed moods in her spirit. Sometimes she forgot herself and overstayed the daylight. At such times she scuttled home half fearfully for the great city, like a jungle beast, was most dangerous at night.

One evening, returning thus in haste, she was lured aside by the clang of bells and the glare of a fire. No child ever resisted that combination, and Nan was still a good deal of a child. Almost before she knew, it she was wedged fast in a crowd. The pressure was suffocating; and, to her alarm, she found herself surrounded by a rough-looking set of men. They were probably harmless workingmen, but Nan did not know that. She became frightened, and tried to escape, but her strength was not equal to it. Near the verge of panic, she was fairly on the point of struggling, when she felt an arm thrown around her shoulder. She looked up with a cry, to meet Ben Sansome's brown eyes.

"Don't be afraid; I'm here," he said soothingly.

In the revulsion Nan fairly thrilled under the touch of his

manly, protection. This impulse was followed instantly, by an instinct of withdrawal from the embrace about her shoulder, which was in turn succeeded by a fierce scorn of being prudish in such circumstances. Sansome masterfully worked her out through the press. At the last tactful moment he withdrew his arm. She thanked him, still a little frightened.

"It was certainly lucky you happened to be here!" she ended.

"Lucky!" he laughed briefly. "I knew that sooner or later you'd need me."

He stopped at that, but allowed her questions to elicit the fact that every afternoon he had followed her at a discreet distance, scrupulously respecting her privacy, but ready for the need that sooner or later must surely arrive. Nan was touched.

"You have no right to endanger yourself this way!" he cried, as though carried away. "It is not just to those who care for you!" and by the tone of his voice, the look of his eye, the slight emphasizing pressure of his hand he managed to convey to her, but in a manner to which she could not possibly object, his belief that his last phrase referred more to himself than to any one else in the world.

It was about this period that John Sherwood, dressing for dinner, remarked to his wife:

"Patsy, the more I see of you the more I admire you. Do you remember that Firemen's Ball when you started in to break up that Keith-Morrell affair? He dropped her so far that I haven't heard her *plunk* yet! I don't know what made me think of it—it was a long time ago."

"Yes, that was all right," she replied thoughtfully, "but I'm not as pleased as I might be with the Keith situation."

Sherwood stopped tying his cravat and turned to face her.

"He's perfectly straight, I assure you," he said earnestly. "I don't believe he knows that any other woman but his wife exists. I *know* that. But I wish he'd go a little easier with the men."

"Oh, I wasn't thinking of him. She's the culprit now."

"What!" cried Sherwood, astonished, "that little innocent baby!"

"That 'little innocent baby' is seeing altogether too much of Ben Sansome."

Sherwood uttered a snort of masculine scorn.

"Ho! Ben Sansome?"

"Yes, Ben Sansome."

"Why, he's a notorious butterfly."

"Well, it looks now as though he intended to alight."

"Seriously?"

She nodded. Sherwood slowly went on with his dressing.

"I like that little creature," he said at last. "She's the sort that strikes me as born to be treated well and to be happy. Some people are that way, you know; just as others are born painters or plumbers." She nodded in appreciation. "And if you give the word, Patsy, I'll go around and have a word with Keith— or spoil Sansome—whichever you say—"

She laughed.

"You're a dear, Jack, but if you love me, keep your hands off here."

"Are you bossing this job?" he asked gravely.

"I'm bossing this job," she repeated, with equal gravity.

He said nothing more for a time, but his eyes twinkled.

XLVII

Keith's investigations proceeded until at last he felt justified in preferring before the Bar Association charges of irregular practice against James Ware, Bernard Black, and—to his great regret—Calhoun Bennett. He conceived he had enough evidence to convict these men legally, but he as yet shrank from asking for an indictment against them, preferring at first to try for their discipline before their fellow lawyers. If the Bar Association failed, however, he had every intention of pressing the matter in the courts.

Almost immediately after the filing of the complaint he was waited on in his office by a man only slightly known to him, Major Marmaduke Miles. The major's occupation in life was obscure. He was a red-faced, tightly buttoned, full-jowled, choleric Southerner of the ultra-punctilious brand, always well dressed in quaint and rather old-fashioned garments, with charming manners, and the reminiscence of good looks lost in a florid and apoplectic habit. This person entered Keith's office, greeted him formally, declined a chair. Standing very erect before Keith's desk, his beaver hat poised on his left forearm, he said:

"I am requested, suh, to enquiah of yo' the name of a friend with whom I can confer."

"If that means a challenge, Major, I must first ask the name of your principal," returned Keith.

"I am actin' fo' Mr. Calhoun Bennett, suh," stated the major.

"Tell Cal Bennett I will not fight him," said Keith quietly.

The major was plainly flabbergasted, and for a moment puffed his red cheeks in and out rapidly.

"You mean to tell me, suh, that yo' refuse the satisfaction due a gentleman after affrontin' him?"

"I won't fight Cal Bennett," repeated Keith patiently.

The major turned even redder, and swelled so visibly that Keith, in spite of his sad realization of the gravity of the affair, caught himself guiltily in a boyish anticipation that some of the major's strained buttons would pop.

"I shall so repo't to my principal, suh. But I may add, suh, that in my opinion, suh, yo' are conductin' yo'self in a manner unbecomin' to a gentleman; and othuh gentlemen will say so, suh! They may go even farthah and stigmatize yo' conduct as cowardly, suh! And it might even be that I, suh, would agree with that expression, suh!"

The major glowered. Keith smiled wearily. It did not to him at the moment that this would be so great a calamity.

"I am sorry to have forfeited your good opinion, Major," he contented himself with saying.

The major marched straight back to the Monumental, where Bennett and a number of friends were awaiting the result of his mission. The major's angry passions had been rising, every foot of the way.

"He won't fight, suh!" he bellowed, slamming his cane across the table. "He won't fight! And I stigmatized him to his face as a white-livered hound!"

Calhoun Bennett sank back pale, and speechless. His companions deluged him with advice.

"Horsewhip the craven publicly." "Warn him to go heeled, and then force the issue!" "Shoot him down like the dog he is!"

But the major's mighty bellow dominated everything.

"I claim the privilege!" he roared. "Egad, I *demand* the privilege! It is my right! I am insulted by such a rebuff! Now that I have acquitted myself of Cal's errand, I will call him out myself. Ain't that right, Cal? I'll make the hound fight!"

The old major looked redder and fiercer than ever. There could be no doubt that he would make any one fight, once he started out to do so, and that he would carry the matter through. He was brave enough.

But little Jimmy Ware, who had been doing some thinking, here spoke up. It seemed to him a good chance to get a reputation without any risk. Since James King of William had uncompromisingly refused to fight duels, his example had been followed. A strong party of those having conscientious scruples against the practice had come into being. Keith's refusal to fight Bennett, to Ware's mind, indicated that he belonged to this class. It looked safe.

"Pardon me, Major," he broke in suavely; "but each in turn. I claim the right. Cal had first chance because he had personally warned the man of the consequences. But I am equally accused. You must admit my prior claim."

The major came off the boil. Puffing his red cheeks in and out he considered.

"Yo're right, suh," he conceded reluctantly.

After considerable persuasion, and some flattery as to his familiarity with the niceties of the Code, the major consented to bear Jimmy's defiance. He entered Keith's office again, stiffer than a ramrod. Keith smiled at him.

"There's no use, Major, I won't fight Cal Bennett," he greeted his visitor.

"I am the bearer of a challenge from Mistah James Ware," he announced.

"What!" yelled Keith, so suddenly and violently that Major Miles recoiled a step.

"From Mistah James Ware," he repeated.

Keith laughed savagely.

"Oh, I'll fight him," he growled; "gladly; any time he wants it."

The major's face lit up.

"If you'll name yo' friend, suh," he suggested.

"Friend? Friend? What for? I'm capable of arranging this. I haven't time to hunt up a friend."

"It's customary," objected the major.

"Look here," Keith swept on, "I'm the challenged party and I have the say- so, haven't I?"

"Yo' can name the weapons," conceded Major Marmaduke Miles.

"All right, we'll call this revolvers, navy revolvers—biggest there are, whatever that is. And close up. None of your half-mile shooting."

"Ten yards," suggested Major Miles with unholy joy.

"And right away—this afternoon," went on Keith. "If that little runt wants trouble, egad he's going to have all his little skin will hold."

But the major would not have this. It was not done. He waived conducting his negotiations through a second, but that was as far as his conventional soul would go. He held out for three o'clock the following afternoon.

"And I wish to apologize, Mistah Keith," he said, on part- ing, "fo' my ill-considered words of a short time ago. I misunder- stood yo' reasons fo' refusin' to fight Mistah Bennett."

He bowed his rotund, tightly buttoned little figure and departed, to strike Jimmy Ware with complete consternation.

Duels in the fifties were almost an acknowledged public institution. Although technically illegal, no one was ever convicted of any of the consequences of such encounters. They were conducted quite openly. Indeed, some of the more famous were actively advertised by steamboat men, who carried excursions to the field. Keith's acceptance of Ware's challenge aroused the keenest interest. Outside the prominence of the men involved, a vague feeling was current that in their persons were symbolized opposing forces in the city's growth. As yet these forces had not segregated to that point where champions were demanded, or indeed would be recognized as such, but vague feelings of antagonism, of alignments, were abroad. Those who later would constitute the Law and Order class generally sympathized with Ware; those whom history was to know as the Vigilantes felt stirrings of partisanship for Keith. Therefore, the following afternoon a small flotilla set sail for the Contra Costa shore, and a crowd of several hundred spectators disembarked at the chosen duelling ground.

Nan knew nothing of all this. Keith was now in such depths of low spirits that his wearied soul did not much care what became of him. He put his affairs in shape, shrugged his shoul- ders, and went to the encounter with absolute indifference.

The preliminaries were soon over. Keith found himself facing Jimmy Ware at the distance he had himself chosen. A double line of spectators stood at a respectful space on either side. Major Miles and an acquaintance of Keith's who had volunteered to act for him were posted nearer at hand. Keith had listened attentively to the instructions. The word was to be given—*one, two, three. Fire!* Between the first and last words the duellists were to discharge the first shot from their weapons. After that they were to fire at will. One shot would have sufficed Jimmy Ware; but Keith, without emotion, filed with a dead indifference to any possible danger and a savage contempt for the whole proceedings, had insisted on the full measure. He was totally unaccustomed to weapons. At the word of command he raised the revolver and fired, carelessly but coolly, and without result. One after the other he discharged the six chambers of his weapon, aiming as well as he knew how. It did not occur to him that Ware was firing at him. After the sixth miss he threw the revolver away in cold disgust.

"This is a farce," said he, "and I'm not going to be fool enough to take part in it any longer."

Jimmy Ware, delighted at finding himself unharmed, and confident now that bluff would go, started to say something lofty and disdainful. Keith whirled back on him.

"If you want 'satisfaction,' as you call it, you'll get it, and you'll get it plenty! I'm sick of being made a fool of. Just open your ugly head to me again, and I'll knock it off your shoulders!" His eye smouldered dangerously, and Jimmy Ware, very uncertain in his mind, took refuge in a haughty look. Keith glared at him moment, then turned to the crowd: "I'll give all of you fair warning," said he. "I'm going to do my legal duty in all things; and I'm not going to fight duels. Anybody who interferes with me is going to get into trouble!"

An uproar ensued. All this was most irregular, unprecedented, a disgrace to a gentlemen's meeting. The major roared like a bull. If a man would not fight, would not defend his actions, how could a gentleman get at him except by street brawling or assassination, and both of these were repugnant to finer feelings. A dozen fire-eaters felt themselves personally insulted. The crowd surrounded Keith, shouting at him, jostling him, threatening. A cool, somewhat amused voice broke in.

"Gentlemen," said Talbot Ward, in so decided a tone that they turned to hear. "I am a neutral non-partisan in this little war, I am for neither party, for neither opinion, in the matter. I, like Mr, Keith, never fight duels. But may I suggest—merely in the interest of fair play—that for the moment you are forgetting yourselves? My opinion coincides with Mr. Keith's that duelling is a foolish sort of game, but it is a game, and recognized; and if you are going to play it, why not stick to its rules? Mr. Keith, and Mr. Ware have exchanged shots. Mr. Ware has therefore had 'satisfaction.' Now Mr. Keith and I going to walk—quietly—to the boat. We do not expect to be molested."

"By God, Tal!" cried Major Miles in astonishment, "ye' don't mean to tell me yo're linin' yourself up on the side of that blackleg!"

"Well," put in a new voice, a very cheerful voice, "I don't pretend to be neutral, and I'd just as lief fight duels as not, and I'm willing to state to you all that though I don't know a damn thing about this case nor its merits, I like this man's style. And I'm ready to state that I'll take his place and fight any—or all of you—right here and now. You, Major?"

All eyes turned to him. He was a dark, eager youth, standing with his slouch hat in his hand, his head thrown back, his mop of shiny black hair tossed from his forehead, his eyes glowing. The major hummed and fussed.

"I have absolutely no quarrel with you, suh!" he said.

"Nor with my friend yonder?" insisted the newcomer.

"I should esteem it beneath my dignity to fight with a craven and a coward, suh!" the major saved his face.

The stranger glanced at Keith, an amused light in his eyes.

"We'll let it go at that," he conceded. "Anybody else?" he challenged, eying them.

Every one seemed busy getting ready to go home, and appeared not to hear him. After a moment he put on his felt hat and joined Keith and Ward, who were walking slowly toward the landing.

"Well," remarked a rough-looking Yankee—our old friend Graves of the Eurekas to his friend Carter—"I didn't know anything would cool off the major like that!"

"I reckon the major knew who he was talking to," replied Carter.

"Who is the cuss? I never saw him before."

"Don't you know him? I reckon you must have heard of him, anyway. He's just down from the Sierra. That's the express rider, Johnny Fairfax—Diamond Jack, they call him."

Graves whistled an enlightened whistle.

XLVIII

Johnny Fairfax accompanied Keith all the way back to his office, although Talbot Ward said good-bye at the wharves. He bubbled over with conversation and enthusiasm, and seemed to have taken a great fancy to the lawyer. The theme of his glancing talk was the duel, over which he was immensely amused; but from it he diverged on the slightest occasion to comment on whatever for the moment struck his notice.

"That was certainly the rottenest shooting I ever saw!" he exclaimed over and over, and then would go off into peals of laughter. "I don't see how twelve shots at that distance could miss! After the second exchange I concluded even the side line wasn't safe, and I got behind a tree. Pays to be prompt In your decision; there were a hundred applicants for that tree a moment later, The bloodless duel as a parlour amusement! You ought to have charged that large and respectable audience an admission fee! That's a good idea; I'll present it to you! If you ever have another due, you must have a good manager! There's money in it!"

Keith laughed a trifle ruefully,

"I suppose it was funny," he acknowledged.

"Now don't get huffy," begged Johnny Fairfax. "What you ought to do is to learn to shoot. You'll probably need to know how if you keep on living around here," His eye fell on a shooting gallery. "Come in here," he urged impulsively.

The proprietor was instructed to load his pistols and for a dozen shots Keith was coached vehemently in the elementals of shooting—taught at least the theory of pulling steadily, of coordinating various muscles and psychological processes that were not at all used to cooerdination. He learned that mere steady aiming was a small part of it.

"Anybody can do wonderful shooting with an empty pistol," said Johnny contemptuously. "And anybody can hold as steady as a rock—until he pulls the trigger."

"It's interesting," conceded Keith; "mighty interesting. I didn't know there was so much to it."

"Of course it's interesting," said Johnny. "And you're only at the rudiments. Look here!"

And, to the astonishment of Keith, the worshipful adoration of the shooting-gallery proprietor, and the awe of the usual audience that gathered at the sound of the reports, he proceeded to give an exhibition of the skill that had made him famous. The shooting galleries of those days used no puny twenty-twos. Derringers, pocket revolvers, and the huge "navies" were at hand—with reduced loads, naturally—for those who in habitual life affected these weapons. Johnny shot with all of them, displaying the tricks of the gunman with all the naive enthusiasm of youth. His manner throughout was that engaging mixture of modesty afraid of being thought conceited and eager pride in showing his skill so attractive to everybody. At first he shot deliberately, splitting cards, hitting marbles, and devastating whole rows of clay pipes. Then he took to secreting the weapons in various pockets from which he produced and discharged them in lightning time. His hand darted with the speed and precision of a snake's head.

"I've just been fooling with shooting things tossed in the air," he said, exuberant with enthusiasm. "But I'm afraid we can't try that here."

"I'm afraid not," agreed the proprietor regretfully.

"It really isn't very hard, once you get the knack."

"Oh, no," said the proprietor with elaborate sarcasm. "Say," he went on earnestly, "I suppose it ain't no use trying to hire you—"

Johnny shook his head, smiling.

"I was afraid not," observed the proprietor disappointedly. "You'd be the making of this place. Drop in any time you want practice. Won't cost you a cent. Would you mind telling me your name?"

"Fairfax," replied Johnny, gruffly embarrassed.

"Not Diamond Jack?" hesitated the proprietor.

"I'm sometimes called that," conceded Johnny, still more gruffly. "How much is it?"

"Not one gosh-danged continental red cent," cried the man, "and I'm pleased to meet you."

Johnny shook his extended hand, mumbled something, and bolted for the street. Keith followed, laughing.

"It seems you're quite a celebrity," he observed.

But Johnny refused to pursue that subject.

"You come with me and buy you a pistol," he growled. "You ought not to be allowed loose. You're as helpless as a baby."

Johnny picked out a small .31 calibre revolver and a supply of ammunition.

"Now you practise!" was his final warning and advice.

Keith went home with a new glow at his heart. He was ripe for a friend.

Johnny seemed to have little to do for the moment. He never volunteered information as to his business or his plans, and Keith never inquired. But the young express rider fell into the habit of dropping in at Keith's office. He was always very apologetic and solicitous as to whether or no he was interrupting, saying that he had stopped for only ten seconds; but he invariably ended in the swivel chair with a good cigar. Keith was at this time busy; but he was never too busy for Johnny Fairfax. The latter was a luxury to which he treated himself. Johnny was not only welcome because he was practically Keith's only friend, but also his frank and engaging comments on men and things were gradually giving the harassed lawyer a new point of view on the society in which he found himself. Keith, as a newcomer in a community already established, had naturally accepted the prominent figures in that community as he would have accepted prominent figures anywhere: that is, as respectable, formidable, admirable, solid, unquestioned pillars of society. He was of a modest disposition and disinclined to question. He respected them as any modest young man respects those older and more successful than himself. For the same reason he accepted their views and their authority; or, if he questioned them, he did so sadly, almost guiltily, with many heart-searchings.

But Johnny Fairfax held no such attitude. Not he! The city's great names had scant respect from him! Not for an instant did he hesitate to criticize or analyze the most renowned. It was not long before he learned all about the Cora trial and Keith's subsequent efforts to discipline McDougall and his associates.

"I hope you get 'em!" said he; "the whole lot! I don't know much about this McDougall; but I do know his friends, and most of 'em aren't worth thinkin' about. They're big people here, but back where I came from, in old Virginia, the best of em wouldn't be overseers on a plantation. That's why they like it so much out here. Look at that gang! Casey has been in the penitentiary, Rowlee ran some little blackleg sheet down South until they run him out——I tell you, sir, as a Southerner I'm not proud of the Southerners out here. They're a cheap lot, most of 'em. They were a cheap lot home. The only difference is that back there everybody knew it, and out here everybody thinks they're great people because they get up on their hind legs and say so out loud. That old bluff, Major Miles, he was put out of a Richmond club, sir, for cheatin' at cards—I know that for a fact!"

Somehow, this frank criticism was like a breeze of fresh air to Keith: it put new courage into him. Johnny Fairfax had no interests in the city; he had no fear; his viewpoint was free from all sham; he was newly in from the outside. Through his eyes things fell into perspective. Suddenly San Francisco upper society became to Keith what it really was: a welter of cheap, bragging, venal, self-seeking men, with here and there an honest fine character standing high above. And he began, but dimly, to see that the real men of the place were not—as yet— well known. Probably one of the most impressive and typical figures of the time was Justice of the Supreme Court Terry. In the eyes of those too close to events to have a clear sense of proportion, he was one of the great men of his period. Courtly handsome, with haughty manners, of aristocratic bearing, fiercely proud, touchily quarrelsome on "points of honour," generous but a bitter hater, hea nd his equally handsome, proud, and fiery wife were considered by many people of the time as embodying the ideal of Southern chivalry. But Johnny Fairfax would have none of it.

"He a typical Southern gentleman!" he laughed, "As being born in the South myself, I repudiate that! I know too much about Terry. Why, look here: he's a good sport, and he's got ability, and he makes friends, and he isn't afraid of anything, But then you stop. He's not a gentleman! It shows most particularly when he gets mad. Then he'll throw over anything —anything—to have his own way. He's a big man now, but he won't be knee-high to a June bug before he gets done."

Johnny's prediction was long in fulfilment, but a score of years later it came to pass, and Judge Terry's reputation has sunk almost to the level of that of his brother on the bench—Judge "Ned" McGowan.

"They're all a bad lot," Johnny finished, "and I hope you lick them! You don't know all the good folks in this town yet!"

XLIX

Calhoun Bennett dropped the matter, and contented himself with cutting Keith dead whenever they happened to meet. Jimmy Ware and Black were men of a different sort; indeed McDougall had made them his associates mainly because of heir knowledge of the city's darker phases and their unscrupulousness. In the admirable organization thus sketched Calhoun Bennett had acted as a sort of go-between.

After the duel these two precious citizens held many anxious consultations. They could not tell just how much evidence Keith had succeeded in gathering, but they knew that plenty of it existed. If the matter came to an issue, they suspected the consequences might be serious. Either Keith or his evidence must in some way be got rid of. Black, who was inclined by instinct and training to be direct, was in favour of the simple expedient of hiring assassins.

"Won't do," negatived the more astute Ware. "The thing will be traced back to us—not legally, of course, but to a moral certainty, and while they won't be able to prove anything on us, the state of the public mind is such that hell would pop."

"He says he won't fight another duel," said Black doubtfully.

"No."

"We've got to kill him in a street quarrel, then."

"He's got to be killed in a street quarrel," amended Ware, "that's certain; but nobody even remotely connected with this Cora trial must seem to have anything to do with it. It must have the appearance of a private quarrel from away outside. Otherwise—"

"Got anybody in mind?" asked the practical Black.

"Yes, and he ought to be here at any moment."

As though Jimmy Ware's words had been the cue for which he waited, Morrell here entered the room.

L

At three o'clock in the afternoon of May 14, 1856, the current issue of the *Bulletin* was placed on sale. A very few minutes later a copy found its way into the hands of James Casey. Casey at that time, in addition to his political cares, was editor of a small sheet he called the *Sunday Times*. With this he had strenuously supported the extreme wing of the Law party, which, as has been explained, comprised also the gambling and lawless element. It was suspected by some that his paper was more or less subsidized for the purpose, though the probability is that Casey found his reward merely in political support. This Casey it was who, to his own vast surprise, had at a previous election been returned as elected supervisor; although he was not a candidate, his name was not on the ticket, and no man could be found who had voted for him. Indeed, he was not even a resident of the district. However, Yankee Sullivan, who ran the election, said officially the votes had been cast for him; so elected he was proclaimed. Undoubtedly he proved useful; he had always proved useful at elections elsewhere, seldom appearing in person, but adept at selecting suitable agents. His methods were devious, dishonest, and rough. He was head of the Crescent Fire Engine Company, and was personally popular. In appearance he was a short, slight man, with a bright, keen face, a good forehead, a thin but florid countenance, dark curly hair, and light blue eyes, a type of unscrupulous Irish adventurer with a dash of romantic ideals. Like all the gentlemen rovers of his time, he was exceedingly touchy on the subject of "honour."

In the *Bulletin* of the date mentioned James Casey read these words, apropos of the threat of one Bagby to shoot Casey on sight:

It does not matter how bad a man Casey had been, or how much benefit it might be to the public to have him out of the way, we cannot accord to any one citizen the right to kill him, or even beat him, without justifiable provocation. The fact that Casey has been an inmate of Sing Sing prison in New York is no offence against the laws of this State; nor is the fact of his having stuffed himself through the ballot box, as elected to the Board of Supervisors from a district where it is said he was not even a candidate, any justification for Mr. Bagby to shoot Casey, however richly the latter may deserve to have his neck stretched for such fraud on the public.

Casey read this in the full knowledge that thousands of his fellow-citizens would also read it. His thin face turned white with anger. He crumpled the paper into a ball and hurled it violently into the gutter, settled his hat more firmly on his head, and proceeded at once to the *Bulletin* office with the full intention of shooting King on sight. Probably he would have done so, save for the accidental circumstance that King happened to be busy at a table, his back squarely to the door. Casey could not shoot a man in the back without a word. He was breathless and stuttering with excitement. King was alone, but an open door into an adjoining office permitted two witnesses to see and hear.

"What do you mean by that article?" cried Casey in a strangled voice.

King turned slowly, and examined his visitor for a moment.

"What article?" he inquired at last.

"That which says I was formerly an inmate of Sing Sing!"

King gazed at him with a depth of detached, patient sadness in his dark yes.

"Is it not true?" he asked finally.

"That is not the question," retorted Casey, trying again to work himself up to the rage in which he had entered. "I do not wish my past acts rated up: on that point I am sensitive."

A faint smile came and went on King's lips.

"Are you done?" he asked still quietly; then, receiving no reply, he turned in his chair and leaned forward with a sudden intensity. His next words hit with the impact of bullets: "There's the door! Go! Never show your face here again!" he commanded.

Casey found himself moving toward the open door. He did not want to do this, he wanted to shoot King, or at least to provoke a quarrel, but he was for the moment overcome by a stronger personality. At the door he gathered himself together a little.

"I'll say in my paper what I please!" he asserted, with a show of bravado.

King was leaning back, watching him steadily.

"You have a perfect right to do so," he rejoined. "I shall never notice your paper."

Casey struck himself on the breast.

"And if necessary I shall defend myself!" he cried.

King's passivity broke. He bounded from his seat bristling with anger.

"Go!" he commanded sharply, and Casey went.

LI

People had already read King's article in the *Bulletin*. People had seen Casey heading for the *Bulletin* office with blood in his eye. The news had spread. When the Irishman emerged he found waiting for him a curious crowd. His friends crowded around asking eager questions. Casey answered with vague but bloodthirsty generalities: he wasn't a man to be trifled with, and egad some people had to find that out! blackmailing was not a healthy occupation when it was aimed at a gentleman! He left the impression that King had recanted, had apologized, had even begged—there would be no more trouble. Uttering brags of this sort, Casey led the way to the Bank Exchange, a fashionable bar near at hand. Here he set up the drinks, and was treated in turn. His bragging became more boastful. He made a fine impression, but within his breast the taste of his interview with King curdled into dangerous bitterness. Casey could never stand much alcohol. The well-meant admiration and sympathy of his friends served only to increase his hidden, smouldering rage. His eyes became bloodshot, and he talked even more at random.

In the group that surrounded him was our old acquaintance, Judge Edward McGowan—Ned McGowan—jolly, hard drinking, oily, but not as noisy as usual. He was watching Casey closely. The Honourable Ned was himself a fugitive from Pennsylvania justice. By dint of a gay life, a happy combination of bullying and intrigue, he had made himself a place in the new city, and at last had "risen" to the bench. He was apparently all on the surface, but his schemes ran deep.

Some historians claim that he had furnished King the documents proving Casey an ex-convict! Now, when he considered the moment opportune, he drew Casey from the noisy group at the bar.

"All this talk is very well," he said contemptuously to the Irishman, "but I see through it. What are you going to do about it?"

"I'll get even with the—, don't you worry about that!" promised Casey, still blustering.

This McGowan brushed aside as irrelevant. "Are you armed?" he asked. "No, that little weapon is too uncertain. Take this." He glanced about him, and hastily passed to Casey a big "navy" revolver. "You can hide it under your cloak—so!" He fixed Casey's eyes with his own, and brought to bear on the little man all the force of his very vital personality, "Listen: King comes by here every evening. Everybody knows that, and everybody knows what has happened."

He stared at Casey significantly for a moment, then turned abruptly away. Casey, become suddenly quiet, his blustering mood fallen from him, his face thoughtful and white, his eyes dilated, said nothing. He returned to the bar, took a solitary drink, and walked out the door, his right hand concealed beneath his long cloak. McGowan watched him intently, following to the door, and looking after the other's retreating form. Casey walked across the street, but stopped behind a wagon, where he stood, apparently waiting. McGowan, with a grunt of satisfaction, sauntered deliberately to the corner of the Bank Exchange. There he leaned against the wall, also waiting.

For nearly an hoar the two thus remained: Casey shrouded in his cloak, apparently oblivious to everything except the corner of Merchant and Montgomery streets, on which he kept his eyes fixed; McGowan lounging easily, occasionally speaking a low word to a passerby. Invariably the person so addressed came to a stop. Soon a little group had formed, idling with

Judge McGowan. A small boy happening by was commandeered with a message for Pete Wrightman, the deputy sheriff,
and shortly Pete arrived out of breath to join the group.

At just five o'clock the idlers stiffened to attention. King's
figure was seen to turn the corner of Merchant Street into
Montgomery. Head bent, he walked toward the corner of the
Bankers' Exchange, the men on the corner watching him.
When nearly at that point he turned to cross the street
diagonally.

At the same instant Casey stepped forward from behind the
wagon, throwing back his cloak.

LII

The same afternoon Johnny Fairfax and Keith were sitting together in the Monumental's reading-room. They happened to be the only members in the building with the exception of Bert Taylor, who was never anywhere else. Of late Keith had acquired the habit of visiting the reading-room at this empty hour. He was beginning to shrink from meeting his fellowmen. Johnny Fairfax was a great comfort to him, for the express rider was never out of spirits, had a sane outlook, and entertained a genuine friendship for the young lawyer. Although yet under thirty years of age, he was already an "old-timer," for he had come out in '49, and knew the city's early history at first hand.

"This old bell of yours is historical," he told Keith. "Its tolling called together the Vigilantes of '51."

They sat gossiping for an hour, half sleepy with reaction from the fatigues of the day, smoking slowly, enjoying themselves. Everything was very peaceful—the long slant of a sunbeam through dust motes, the buzz of an early bluebottle, the half-heard activities of some of the servants in the pantry beyond, preparing for the rush of the cocktail hour. Suddenly Johnny raised his head and pricked up his ears.

What the deuce is that!" he exclaimed.

They listened, then descended to the big open engine-room doors and listened again. From the direction of Market Street came the dull sounds of turmoil, shouting, the growl and roar of many people excited by something. Across the Plaza a man appeared, running. As he came nearer, both could see that his face had a very grim expression.

"Here!" called Johnny, as the man neared them. "Stop a minute! Tell us what's the matter!"

The man ceased running, but did not stop. He was panting but evidently very angry. His words came from between gritted teeth.

"Fight," he said briefly. "Casey and James King of William. King's shot."

At the words something seemed to be stilled in Keith's mind. Johnny seized the man by the sleeve.

"Hold on," he begged. "I know that kind of a fight. Tell us."

"Casey went up close to King, said 'come on,' and instantly shot him before King knew what he was saying."

"Killed?"

"Fatally wounded."

"Where's Casey?"

"In jail—of course—where he's safe—with his friends."

"Where you headed for?"

"I'm going to get my gun!" said the man grimly, and began again to run.

They watched his receding figure until it swung around the corner and disappeared. Without warning a white-hot wave of anger swept over Keith. All the little baffling, annoying delays, enmities, technicalities, chicaneries, personal antagonisms, evasions that had made up the Cora trial were in it. He seemed to see clearly the inevitable outcome of this trial also. It would be another Cora-Richardson case over again. A brave spirit had been brutally blotted out by an outlaw who relied confidently on the usual exoneration. With an exclamation Keith darted into the engine house to where hung the rope ready for an alarm. An instant later the heavy booming of the Monumental's bell smote the air.

LIII

Having given this alarm. Keith, Johnny at his elbow, started toward the centre of disturbance, From it arose a dull, menacing roar, like the sound of breakers on a rocky coast. Many people, with much excitement, shouting, and vituperation, were converging toward the common centre. As this was approached, it became more difficult, at last impossible, to proceed. The streets were packed, jammed. All sorts of rumours were abroad—King, was dead—King was only slightly hurt—Casey was not in jail at all—Casey had escaped down the Peninsula—the United States warships had anchored off the foot of Market Street and were preparing to bombard the city. There was much rushing to and fro without cause. And over all the roar could be distinguished occasionally single cries, as one may catch fragments of conversation in a crowded room, and all of these were sinister: "Hang him!" "Where is he?" "Run him up on a lamp post!" "Bring him out!" "He'll get away if left to the officers!" And over all the cries, the shouts, the curses, the noise of shuffling feet, the very sound of heavy breathing—hat—the numbers of the mob magnified to a muffled, formidable undernote, pealed louder and louder the Monumental bell, which now Bert Taylor—or some one else—was ringing like mad.

Keith's eyes had become grim and inscrutable, and his mouth had settled into a hard, straight line. Johnny's interest had at first centred in the mob, but after a few curious glances at his companion he transferred it entirely to him, Johnny Fairfax was a judge of men and of crises; and now he was invaded with a great curiosity to see how the one and the other were here to work out. With a determination that would not be gainsaid, Keith thrust himself through the crowd until he had gained an elevated coping. Here he stood watching. Johnny, after a glance at his face, joined him.

Suddenly in the entrance of Dunbar Alley, next the city jail, a compact group of men with drawn pistols appeared. They made their way rapidly to a carriage standing near, jumped in, and the driver whipped up his horses. With a yell of rage the crowd charged down, but recoiled instinctively before the presented pistols. The horses reared and plunged, and before anybody had gathered his wits sufficiently to seize the bridles, the whole equipage had disappeared around the corner of Kearney Street.

"I must say that was well done," said Johnny.

"North and Charles Duane, with Casey, inside," commented Keith, as dispassionately as though reading from a catalogue. "Billy Mulligan and his deputies outside. That is to be remembered."

A great mob had surged after the disappearing vehicle, but at least fifty yards in the rear. The remainder were following at a more leisurely pace. Almost immediately the street was empty. Keith climbed slowly down from his coping.

"What do you intend doing?" asked Johnny curiously.

"Nothing yet."

"But they're getting him away!"

"No," said Keith, out of his local knowledge. "They're merely taking him to the county jail; it's stronger."

They followed the crowd to the wide open space below the county jail. The latter was at that period a solidly built one-story building situated atop a low bluff. Below it the marshal had drawn up his officers. They stood coolly at ease. The mob, very excited, vociferated, surged back and forth. North and his men, busily and coolly, but emphatically, were warning them, over and over again, not to approach nearer. A single, concerted rush would have overwhelmed the few defenders; but the rush was not made. Nevertheless, it could not be doubted that this time the temper of the people was very determined. The excitement was growing with every minute. Cries again took coherence.

"Hang him!" "Arrest the officers!" "Good, that's it!" "Let's take the jail!"

A man burst through the front ranks, clambered up the low bluff on which stood the jail, turned, and attempted to harangue the crowd. He was instantly torn down by the officers. He fought like a wild cat, and the crowd, on the hair trigger as it was, howled and broke forward. But Marshal North, who really handled the situation intelligently, sharply commanded his men to desist, and instantly to release the orator. He knew better than to allow the matter to come to an issue of strength. Intensely excited, the man shouldered his way through the crowd, and, assisted by many hands, mounted the balcony of a two-story house. Thence he began to harangue, but so great was the confusion that he could not be heard.

"Who is he?" "Who is that man?" voices cried from a dozen points.

George Frank, a hotel keeper, possessed of a great voice, shouted back:

"That is Thomas King—"

An officer seized Frank hastily by the collar. "Stop or I'll arrest you!" he threatened.

Stewart Edward White

"—brother of James King of William!" bellowed Frank, undaunted.

"Bully for you!" muttered Johnny Fairfax, whose eyes were shining.

Keith was watching the whole scene from beneath the brim of his hat, his eyes sombre and expressionless. Johnny glanced at him from time to time, but said nothing.

From the balcony Thomas King continued to harangue the crowd. Little of what he said could be heard, but he was at a white heat of excitement, and those nearest him were greatly aroused. An officer made a movement to arrest him, but a hasty message from the sapient North restrained that.

At that moment a great cheer burst out from the lower end of the street. Over the heads of the crowd could be distinguished the glint of file after file of bayonets.

"That's the ticket!" cried an enthusiast near Keith and Johnny. "Here come the militia boys! Now we'll soon have the jail!"

The bayonets bobbed steadily through the crowd, deployed in front of the jail, and turned to face the mob. A great groan went up.

"Sold!" cried the enthusiast.

These were volunteers from the Law and Order party, hastily armed from the militia armouries, and thrown in front of the jail for its protection.

Immediately they had taken position the jail door opened, and there appeared a rather short, carefully dressed man, with side whiskers, carrying his hat in his hand. He stood for a moment, appealing for attention, one arm upraised. Little by little the noise died down.

"Who is that?" inquired Johnny.

He received no reply from Keith, but the enthusiast informed him:

"That's our beloved mayor—Van Ness," said he.

When quiet had at length been restored, Van Ness addressed them:

"You are here creating an excitement," he said, "which may lead to occurrences this night which will require years to wipe out. You are now labouring under great excitement, and I advise you quietly to disperse. I assure you the prisoner is safe. Let the law have its course and justice will be done."

Up to this point Van Ness had been listened to with respect, but at the last word he received such a chorus of jeers and cat calls that he retired hastily.

"How about Richardson?" they demanded of him. "Where's the law in Cora's case?" "To hell with such justice!"

"Not the popular orator," observed Johnny Fairfax.

More soldiers came, and then more, at short intervals, until the square was filled with shining bayonets. Johnny was frankly disgusted. As a man of action he too well understood that this particular crisis was practically over. From this mob the jail was safe.

"They lost their chance talking," he said. "They ought to have rushed the jail first pop. Now the whole thing will fizzle out slowly. Let's go get supper."

Without reply Keith descended from his perch. They hunted some time for a restaurant. All were closed for the sufficient reason that their staffs were on the streets. Finally they discovered a Chinese chop house prepared to serve them, and here they ate. Johnny was voluble in his scorn for the manner in which a golden opportunity had been allowed to slip by. Keith was very taciturn.

"Let's get out of here," he said abruptly at last. "Let's get some news."

They learned that King was still alive, though badly wounded in the left breast; that he could not be moved; that he was attended by Dr. Beverly Cole and a half score of the best surgeons of the city; that a mass meeting had been called at the Plaza. Indeed, there could be no doubt that the centre of excitement had been shifted to the Plaza. Men by thousands, all armed, were marching in that direction. Johnny and Keith found the square jammed, but the latter led the way by devious alleys to the rear of the Monumental headquarters, and so out to a little second-story balcony.

Below them the faces of the packed mass of humanity showed white in the dim light from the street lamps and the buildings. Arms gleamed. Every roof top, every window, every balcony was crowded. From the latter vehement orators held forth. All wanted to talk at once. Some of these people were, as our chronicler of the time quaintly expresses it, "considerably tight." Keith looked them all over with an appraising eye, listening at the same time to incendiary speeches advising the battering down of the jail and the hanging of all its inmates. Occasionally one of the cooler headed would get in a few words, but invariably was interrupted by some well-meaning hot head.

There seemed to be a great diversity of opinion both among the people on the balcony and those below. Keith listened attentively for a time, then, with the abruptness that had characterized his movements and decisions since the moment he had heard the news of King's assassination, he turned away.

"Let's go," he said briefly.

"Oh, hold on!" cried Johnny, aghast. "It's just the shank of the evening! We'll miss all the fun."

"There'll be nothing done," said Keith with decision.

"I'm more in hopes," persisted Johnny. "I'll bet there are ten thousand men here, armed and angry, and getting angrier every minute. They could fairly eat up that lot at the jail."

"They won't," said Keith.

"I'll bet one good man could turn them loose in a minute."

Suddenly Keith's dour taciturnity broke. "You're perfectly right," he conceded; "but the point is that good men won't lead a rabble. If we're to have good leaders we must have something for them to lead. If we're to cure these conditions, we must do things in due order. This cannot be remedied by mere excitement nor by deeds done under excitement. I have not yet seen anything that promises either satisfaction or reform."

"What do you propose doing, then?" asked Johnny, his intuitions again satisfying him that here was the man to tie to.

"Walk about," replied Keith.

They walked about. In the course of the evening they looked in on a dozen meetings of which they had news—in the Pioneer Club, in rooms over the old Bella Union, in a saloon off Montgomery Street, at the offices of various merchants. Keith looked carefully over the personnel of each of these various meetings, listened a minute or so, and went out. By some of the men so gathered Johnny was quite impressed, but Keith shook his head.

"These meetings are being held by clubs or cliques," he explained his disbelief in them. "They influence a certain following, but not a general following. This must be a general

Stewart Edward White

movement or none at all. The right people haven't taken hold."

About midnight he unexpectedly announced that he was going home and to bed. Johnny was frankly scandalized,

"I think nothing will happen in this matter," said Keith,

"The time for mob violence has passed. If an attack were now to be made, I should consider it unfortunate, and should not want to be mixed up in it, anyway. A mob attack is nothing but a manifestation of sheer lawlessness."

"And you're keen for the dear law, of course," said Johnny with sarcasm.

"There is a difference between mere laws and the law. There is a time—either here or coming soon—when laws may be broken that justice may be done. But no popular movement will succeed unless it has behind it the solemn, essential human law. Good-night."

LIV

On this same afternoon of King's assassination Nan Keith, was expecting Sansome in for tea. Afternoon tea was then an exotic institution, practically unknown in California society. Ben Sansome was about the only man of Nan's acquaintance who took it as a matter of course, without either awkwardness, embarrassment, or ill-timed jest. The day had been fine, and several times she had regretted her promise as she cast an eye at the glow over the gilt-edged tops of the western hills. The sunset through the Golden Gate must to-day be very fine.

And Ben Sansome had failed her! She had made certain little especial preparations—picked flowers, herself cut the sandwiches thin, put on her most becoming tea gown. As time passed she became more and more annoyed. She was disappointed not so much at the absence of Ben Sansome as a person as at the waste of her efforts.

But at six o'clock, when she had given him up, and was about to change from her tea gown, he came in, full of apologies, very flustered, and bursting with news.

"King was shot on the street by Casey," he told her, trying not unsuccessfully for his habitual detached manner. "I stopped to get the news for you. King is not dead, but probably fatally wounded. Casey is in jail. There is a great public excitement— a mob is forming. I've been expecting something of the sort. King has been pretty free with his comments."

At seven o'clock Nan jumped to her feet in a sudden panic.

"Why, I wonder where Milton is!" she cried. "He's never been late as this before!"

"He's probably stayed downtown to follow the course of the excitement. Naturally he would. He may not get home to supper at all."

Wing Sam announced supper. He was unheeded. Even Gringo, his ears cocked, watched the door, getting up uneasily, whining, sniffing inquiringly, and lying down again. At half-past seven Sansome firmly intervened.

"You're going to make yourself ill," he insisted, "if you don't eat something. I am hungry, anyway, and I'm not going to leave you until he comes back."

"Oh, you must be starved! How thoughtless I am!" she cried.

Sansome, who, it must be confessed, had been somewhat chagrined at the apparent intensity of her anxiety, was, within the next two hours, considerably reassured. Nan never did things halfway. For the moment she had forgotten her guest. He was certainly very kind, very thoughtful—as always—to stay here with her. She must not oppress his spirits. But the inner tension was terrible. She felt that shortly something must snap. And after supper, when they had returned to the drawing-room, a queer, low, growling, distant roar, borne on a chance shift of wind, broke one of her sentences in the middle.

"What's that?" she cried, but before Sansome had replied, she knew what It was, the roar of the mob! And Milton was somewhere there!

Suddenly a wave of reaction swept her, of anger. Why was he there? Why wasn't he at home? Why had he made no attempt to relieve her cruel anxiety? A messenger—it would have been very simple! And Ben Sansome was so kind— as always. She turned to him with a new decision.

"I know you are dying to go see what is going on," she said. "You simply must not stay here any longer on my account. I insist! Indeed, I think I'll go to bed." But Ben Sansome, his manner becoming almost caressingly protective, would not listen.

"It isn't safe to leave you alone," he told her. "All the worst elements of the city will be out. No woman should be left alone in times of such danger. I should feel most uneasy at leaving you before your husband comes in."

His words were correct enough, but he managed to convey his opinion that he was only fulfilling what should have been Keith's first and manifest duty. She made no reply. The conversation languished and died. They sat in the lamplight opposite each other, occasionally exchanging a word or so. Sansome was content and enjoying himself. He conceived that the stars were fighting for him, and he was enjoying the hour. Nan, a prey alternately to almost uncontrollable fits of anxiety and flaming resentment, could hardly sit still.

About midnight Gringo pricked up his ears and barked sharply. A moment later Keith came in.

He was evidently dead tired and wholly preoccupied. He hung up his hat absently. Nan had sprung to her feet.

"Oh, how could you!" she cried, the pent exasperation in her voice. "I've been so anxious! I didn't know what might have happened!"

"I'm all right," replied Keith briefly. "Sorry you were worried. No chance to send you word."

His apparent indifference added fuel to Nan's irritation.

"If it hadn't been for Ben, I should have been stark, staring crazy, here all alone!".

Keith for the first time appeared to notice Sansome's presence. He nodded at him wearily.

"Mighty good of you," said he. "I appreciate it."

"I thought *some* man ought to be in the house at a time of such public excitement," rejoined Sansome significantly.

Keith failed to catch, or elected not to notice, the implication. Nan's cheeks turned red.

Without further remark Keith walked across to lock the window; returning, he extinguished a small lamp on the side table. He was tired out, knew he must be up early, and wanted above everything to get to bed. The hint was sufficiently obvious. Sansome rose. Nan's flush deepened with mortification.

"Well, I'll just run along," said Sansome cheerfully. He did not ask for news of the evening, nor did Keith volunteer it. Keith nodded at him briefly and indifferently. He did not mean to be rude, but his wearied mind was filled to the exclusion of everything else with the significance of this day.

Nan, feeling that she must make amends, followed Sansome into the hall. Her anxiety for Keith's safety relieved, her whole reaction was indignantly toward Sansome.

"I'm sorry to have you go," she said, with a feeling that other circumstances could not have called out, "I don't know what I'd have done without you!"

Sansome's sensitive intuitions thrilled to the feeling.

"Your husband is here to take care of you—now," he murmured. "I must be off." He took her hand, and bent over her, gazing into her eyes with the concentration of a professional hypnotist, "Good-night," he said, with a world of unexpressed meaning. "Try to get some sleep—Nan," He said her name in a lower tone, almost lingeringly, then turned abruptly and went out.

Nan stood looking for a moment at the closed door. The effect of his personality was on her spirit, the mantle of his care for her, his consideration for her every mood, wrapped her about gratefully.

She found the lights all out, and Keith already half undressed.

"I must say, Milton," she said, "you might have been a little less rude to Mr. Sansome. It would have only been decent after he had sat up here until all hours."

Keith, whose wide eyes would have showed him to be wholly preoccupied with some inner vision or problem, answered impatiently from the surface of his mind:

"What in the world did I do to Sansome?"

"You didn't do anything, that's the trouble. Do you realize he waited here over six hours for you to come in?"

"Oh, I guess he'll pull through," said Keith a little contemptuously.

Nan became indignant.

"At least," she retorted, "you ought to be grateful that he stayed to protect the place!"

"The place was in no danger," said Keith, yawning.

She checked herself, and made a fresh start.

"What's it all about? What's happened? Where have you been?" she asked.

Keith roused himself with an effort.

"I've been a little of everywhere. Lord, I'm tired! There's a mob about trying to get up nerve to hang Casey. I suppose you've heard that Casey shot King this afternoon?"

"Yes, I heard that."

"Well, when I saw nothing was going to happen, I came home, though I'm not sure the trouble is over."

Having said this, Keith fell gratefully to his pillow. Nan was nervous, wide-awake, curious. She asked a number of questions. Keith answered with extreme brevity. He was temporarily exhausted. Shortly he fell asleep between two sentences.

LV

The following morning Keith woke early, slipped to the kitchen where he was fed by Wing Sam, and was downtown before Nan, who had not so promptly fallen asleep, had yet stirred. Even at that hour the streets were crowded. Many—and the majority of these were "considerably tight," or otherwise looking the worse for wear—had been up all night, unable to tear themselves away from the fascinating centres of excitement. The majority, however, had, like Keith, snatched some repose, and now were out eager to discover what a new day might bring forth.

The morning newspapers had been issued. Each man held a copy of one of them open at the editorial column, and others tucked away under his arm. Never had there been such a circulation; and in the case of the *Herald* never would so many be sold again. For that ill-starred sheet, mistaking utterly the times, held boldly along the way of its sympathies. It spoke of the assassination as an "affray"; held forth violently against the mob spirit of the evening before; and stated vehemently its opinion that, now that "Justice is regularly administered" there was no excuse for even the threat of public violence. If there had been any doubt as to the depth to which public opinion was at last stirred, the reception of the *Herald's* editorial would have settled it. Actually, for the moment, indignation seemed to run more strongly against that sheet than against Casey himself.

Keith glanced over this editorial with a half smile, tossed the

Stewart Edward White

paper in the gutter, and opened the *Alta* for news. King, still living, had been removed from the office of the Express Company to a room in the Montgomery Block. There, attended by his wife, Dr. Beverly Cole, and a whole corps of volunteer physicians, he was making a fight for life. The bullet had penetrated his left breast. That was all that was to be reported at present. Keith glanced at the third page. His eye was caught by this notice:

THE VIGILANCE COMMITTEE

The members of the Vigilance Committee in good standing will please meet at No. 105-1/2 Sacramento Street, this day, Thursday, 15th instant, at nine o'clock A.M.

By order of the

COMMITTEE OF THIRTEEN.

While he was still gazing thoughtfully at this Johnny Fairfax, fresh as the morning, appeared at his elbow.

"Hello, wise man," he greeted him cheerily. "You were a good prophet—and you got some sleep. I hung around all night, but nothing new was done."

"Look here," said Keith, placing his finger on the notice, "do you suppose this genuine?"

Johnny read the notice.

"Couldn't say."

"Because if this is actually the old Committee of '51, it means business."

"There's one way to find out."

"How's that?"

"Go and see," advised Johnny.

Number 105-1/2 Sacramento Street proved to be a big three-storied barnlike structure that had been built by a short-lived political party called the Know Nothings. Already the hall was packed to its full capacity, the entrance ways jammed, and a big crowd had gathered in the streets.

"Fine chance we have here!" observed Johnny ruefully.

They stood well free of the press for a few moments, watching. More men were coming from all directions. But Johnny was resourceful, and likewise restless.

"Let's prowl around a little," he suggested to his companion.

They prowled to such good purpose that they discovered, at the rear of the building, opening into a blind alley, a narrow wooden stairway. It was unguarded and untenanted.

"Here we are," pronounced Johnny.

They ascended it, and immediately found themselves In a small room back of the stage or speaker's platform, It contained about a score of men. Their aspect was earnest, serious, grave. Although there was a sufficiency of chairs, they were all afoot, gathered in a loose group, in whose centre stood William Coleman, his massive shoulders squared, his large bony, hands clenched at his side, his florid complexion even more flushed than usual, his steady eye travelling slowly from one face to another, Again the strange contradictions in, his appearance struck Keith with the impact of a distinct shock—the low smoothed hair, the sweeping blue-black moustache, the vivid colour, and high cheek bones of the typical gambler —the clear eye, firm mouth, incisive, deliberate speech, the emanation of personality that inspired confidence. Next him, talking earnestly, stood Clancey Dempster, a small man, mild of manner, blue eyed, with light, smooth hair, the last man in the room one would have picked for great firmness and courage, yet destined to play one of the leading roles in this crisis. The gigantic merchant, Truett, towered above him, he who had calmly held two fighting teamsters apart by their collars; and homely, stubborn, honest Farwell, direct, uncompromising, inspired with tremendous single-minded earnestness, but tender as a girl to any under dog; and James Dows, rough and ready, humorous, blasphemous, absolutely direct, endowed with "horse sense," eccentric, but of fundamentally good judgment: Hossfros of '51; Dr. Beverly Cole, high spirited, distinguished looking, courtly; the excitable, active, nervous, talkative, but staunch Tom Smiley, Isaac Blucome whose signature as "33, Secretary" was to become terrible; fiery little George Ward, willing—but unable—to whip his weight in wild cats. As Keith recognized these men, and others of their stamp, he nodded his head contentedly.

Johnny Fairfax must have caught the same impression, for he leaned across to whisper to Keith, his eyes shining:

"We've hit it!"

Their entrance had passed unnoticed in the absorption of discussion. Coleman was speaking, evidently in final decision.

"It is a serious business," said he. "It is no child's play. It may prove very serious. We may get through quickly, so safely, or we may so involve ourselves as never to get through."

"The issue is not of choice, but of expediency," urged Dempster. "Shall we have vigilance with order or a mob with anarchy?"

Coleman pondered a moment, then threw up his head.

"On two conditions I will accept the responsibility—absolute obedience, absolute secrecy."

Without waiting for a reply to this he threw open a door, and followed by the others, stepped out on the platform. A roar greeted their appearance. Johnny and Keith, remaining modestly in the background, lingered near the open door.

The hall was filled to its utmost capacity. Every inch of floor space was occupied, and men perched on sills, clung to beams. Coleman raised his hand and obtained an immediate dead silence.

"In view of the miscarriage of justice in the courts," he announced briefly, "it has been thought expedient to revive the Vigilance Committee. An Executive Council was chosen by a representative of the whole body. I have been asked to take charge. I will do so, but must stipulate that I am to be free to choose the first council myself. Is that agreed?"

A roar of assent answered him.

"Very well, gentlemen. I shall request you to vacate the hall. In a short time the books will be open for enrollment."

He turned and reentered the anteroom followed by the others. In so doing he came face to face with the intruders.

"This is not your place, gentlemen," he told them courteously.

They retired down the narrow back stairs and joined the huge throng that filled the streets, waiting patiently and quietly, its eyes fixed on the closed doors of the hall. In a remarkably short time these doors were thrown open. Those nearest surged forward. Inside the passage were twelve men, later to be known as the Executive Committee. These held back the rush, admitting but one man at a time. The crowd immediately caught the idea. There was absolutely no excitement. Every man was grimly in earnest. Cries of "Order! Order! Line up!" came from different parts of the throng. A rough quadruple queue was formed extending down the street. There was no talk nor smiles, none of the usual rough joking. Each waited his turn without impatience.

Johnny Fairfax and Keith, owing to the chance that they had, entered the crowd from the nearby alley and found themselves close to the head of the line. As they neared the entrance, and so could hear what was there going on, they found that each applicant was being closely scrutinized and interrogated. The great majority passed this ordeal, but several men were peremtorily turned back with a warning not to try again.

Keith's turn came. He was conscious of the scrutiny of many eyes; he heard the word "pass" pronounced by some one in the background, and climbed the stairs. At the top he was directed to an anteroom at the left. Here behind a table sat Coleman, Dempster, and a third man unknown to him. To them he repeated the words of an oath of secrecy, and then was passed into another room where Isaac Bluxome sat behind a ledger. In this he wrote his name.

"Your number is 178," said Bluxome to him, "By that number, and not by your name, you are henceforth to be known here. Never use names, always their numbers, in referring to other members."

Thence Keith was directed to the main hall where were those already admitted. These were gathered in groups discussing the situation. In a moment Johnny Fairfax joined him.

"179, I am," said Johnny. His eyes swept the hall. "Not much mob spirit about this; it looks like business."

They hung around for an hour. The hall slowly filled. Finally, learning that nothing further was to be done until the enrollment had finished, they wandered out again into the street. The unbroken lines of applicants extended as far down the street as the eye could see.

All that day the applicants, orderly and grim with purpose, were passed through in line. By mid-day it was seen that the Know-Nothing Hall was going to be too small for the meeting that would later take place. Therefore, a move was made to the

Turnverein Hall. After enrolling, no man departed from the vicinity for long. Short absences for hastily snatched meals were followed by hurried returns lest something be missed. From time to time reports were circulated as to the activities of the Executive Committee, which had been in continuous session since its appointment. Thus it was said that an Examining Committee had been appointed to scrutinize the applicants; that the members of the Executive Committee had been raised to twenty-six, that Oscar Smith had been appointed chief of police. The latter rumour was immediately verified by the energetic activities of that able citizen. He, or his messengers, darted here and there searching for individuals wanted as doorkeepers, guards, or police officers. His regulations also began to be felt. By evening only registered members of the committee were allowed on the floor of the hall, even the expostulating reporters being gently but firmly ejected.

Nobody manifested the least excitement or impatience. At eight o'clock Coleman came out of one of the side rooms, and, mounting a table, called for order.

"A military organization is deemed necessary," he said crisply. "Numbers one to one hundred will please assemble in the southwest corner of the room; numbers one hundred and one to two hundred will take the first window; numbers two hundred and one to three hundred the second window, and so on." He hesitated and looked over the assembly. "*Que les Francais, se mettent au centre,*" he ended.

This command in a foreign language was made necessary by the extraordinary number of Frenchmen who had first answered the call of gold in the El Dorado of '49; and then with equal enthusiasm responded to this demand for essential justice.

Coleman waited while the multitude shifted here and there. When the component parts had again come to rest he made his next announcement:

"Now each company will elect its own officers, but those officers are subject to the orders of the Executive Committee."

Numbers one hundred and one to two hundred inclusive, the company in which Keith and Johnny Fairfax found themselves, were for the most part strangers to one another, They exchanged glances, hesitating as to how to begin. Then a small, spectacled, man spoke up.

"Gentlemen," said he, "we must get organized as rapidly as possible, Mr, Coleman is waiting. We need for a leader a man who is experienced in active life. I nominate John Fairfax as captain of this company."

Johnny gasped and turned red.

"Who's your little friend?" Keith whispered.

"Never saw him before in my life," replied Johnny.

The announcement was received with indecision. Nobody immediately replied or commented aloud on the nomination, but men were asking each other in undertones. The little spectacled man saw this, and spoke up again: "Perhaps I should say that Mr. Fairfax is better known as Diamond Jack."

Faces cleared, heads nodded. A murmur of recognition replaced the puzzled frowning, "Good man," "The express rider," "Danny Randall's man," they told each other.

"I do not know Mr. Fairfax," the spectacled man was saying, "but I saw his name just before mine on the register."

"This is Fairfax," said Keith, thrusting the reluctant Johnny forward. He was elected to the post by acclamation.

"Nominations for a lieutenant?" suggested the spectacled man, but Keith interrupted.

"If you all have as much confidence in Mr. Fairfax as I have," said he, "perhaps you'll give him free hand and let him pick his own officers."

This seemed a good idea, and was instantly adopted.

"Well, I thank you, gentlemen," said Johnny, "and we'll do our best to become efficient. Report your names and addresses to this gentleman here—"

"Willey," supplied the little man.

"We shall drill to-morrow at eight sharp. Bring whatever weapons—"

But Coleman was again speaking and on this very subject:

"The committee have arranged with George Law," he was saying, "to supply or hire muskets to the number of several thousands. These weapons will be at this hall to-morrow morning early. Company captains can then make their requisitions."

A murmur of inquiry swept the hall. "George Law? Where did *he* get several thousand muskets?" And the counter current of information making its way slowly—they were only flintlocks, perfectly efficient though, had bayonets—superseded government arms—brought out some time ago by Law to arm some mysterious filibustering expedition that had fizzled.

In this manner, without confusion, an organization of two thousand men was formed, sixteen military companies officered and armed.

Shortly after Coleman dismissed the meeting. Its members dispersed to their homes. Absolute quiet descended on the city, which slept under the moon.

LVI

To the thoughtful bystander all this preparation had its significance and its portent, which became the stronger when he contemplated the dispositions of the Law and Order party. The latter had been not less vigorous, and its strength could not be doubted. The same day that marked the organization of the Vigilantes saw the regular police force largely increased. In addition, the sheriff issued thousands of summonses to citizens, calling on them for service on a *posse*. These were in due form of the law. To refuse them meant to put one's self outside the law. A great many of them were responded to, for this reason only, by men not wholly in sympathy with either side. Once the oath was administered, these new deputies were confronted by the choice between perjury and service. To be sure the issuance of these summonses forced many of the neutral minded into the ranks of the Vigilantes. The refusal to act placed them on the wrong side of the law; and they felt that joining a party pledged to what practically amounted to civil war was only a short step farther. The various military companies were mustered, reminded of their oaths, called upon solemnly to fulfil their sworn duty, and marched to various strategic points about the jail and elsewhere. Parenthetically, their every appearance on the streets was well hissed by the populace. The governor was informally notified of a state of insurrection, and requested to send in the State militia. By evening all the forces of organized society were under arms. The leaders of the Law and Order party were jubilant. Their position appeared to be impregnable. They felt that back of them was all the weight of constituted authority, reaching, if need be, to the Federal Government at Washington. Opposed to them was lawlessness. Lawlessness had occasionally become dignified revolution, to be sure, but only when a race took its stand on a great issue; never when a handful espoused a local quarrel. Civil war it might be; but civil war, the wise politicians argued, must spread to become effective; and how could a civil war based on the shooting of an obscure editor in a three-year-old frontier town spread anywhere? Especially such an editor as James King of William.

For King had made many bitter enemies. In attacking individual members of a class he had often unreasonably antagonized the whole class. Thus he had justly castigated the *Times* and other venal newspapers; but in so doing had by his too general statements drawn the fire of every other journal in town. He had with entire reason attacked a certain scalawag of a Roman Catholic priest—a man the church itself must soon have taken in hand—but had somehow managed to offend all Roman Catholics in doing so; likewise, there could be no question that his bitter scorn for "the chivalry" was well justified, but the manner of its expression offended also the decent Southerners. And all these people saw the Vigilantes, not as a protest against a condition that had become intolerable, but as the personal champions of King. The enemies of King, many of them worthy citizens, quite out of sympathy with the present methods of administering the law, became the enemies of the Vigilantes.

No wonder the Law and Order party felt no uneasiness. They did not underestimate the determination of their opponents. It was felt that fighting, severe fighting, was perhaps inevitable. The Law and Order party loved fighting. They had chosen as their commander William Tecumseh Sherman, later to gain his fame as a great soldier. His greatness in a military capacity seems to have been exceeded only by his inability to remember facts proved elsewhere by original historical documents. This is the only possible explanation for the hash of misstatements comprising those chapters in his "Memoirs" dealing with this time. In writing them the worthy general evidently forgot that original documents existed, or that statements concerning historical events can often be checked.

And as a final source of satisfaction, the Vigilantes had placed themselves on record. Every man could be apprehended and made to feel the weight of the law. A mob is irresponsible and anonymous. These fools had written down their names in books!

LVII

Now a new element was injected into the situation in the person of the governor of the State, one J. Neely Johnson, a politician who would long since have been utterly forgotten had not his unlucky star risen just at this unlucky time. A more unfortunate man for a crisis it would have been difficult to find. His whole life had been one of trimming; he had made his way by trimming; he had gained the governor's chair by yielding to the opinions of others. This training combined perfectly with the natural disposition of a chameleon. He was, or became, a sincere trimmer, taking his colour and his temporary beliefs from those with whom he happened to be. His judgment often stuck at trifles, and his opinions were quickly heated but as quickly cooled. His private morals were none of the best, which gave certain men an added hold.

On receipt of the message sent by the Law and Order party— but not, be it noted, by the proper authorities—requesting the State militia, Governor Johnson came down post-haste from Sacramento. Immediately on arriving in the city he sent word to Coleman requesting an interview. Coleman at once followed the messenger to the Continental Hotel. He was shown to a private room where he found Johnson pacing up and down alone. Coleman bowed gravely in response to the governor's airy greeting. Johnson sat down, offered cigars, made every effort to appear amiable and conciliatory.

"This is bad; this is bad, Coleman," he began the interview. "What is it you want?"

Stewart Edward White

"Peace," replied Coleman, "and if possible without a struggle."

"That's all very well," said Johnson pettishly, "to talk about peace with an army of insurrection newly raised. But what is it you actually wish to accomplish?"

Coleman looked at him steadily, then leaned forward.

"The law is crippled," he told the governor in measured tones. "We want merely to accomplish what the crippled law should do but cannot. This done, we will gladly retire. Now, Governor, you have been asked by the mayor, and certain others, to bring out the militia and crush this movement. I assure you, it cannot be done; and if you attempt it, it will cause you and us great trouble. Do as Governor McDougall did in '51. See in this movement what he saw in that: a local movement for a local reform, in which the State is not concerned. We are not a mob; we demand no overthrow of institutions. We ask not a single court to adjourn; we ask not a single officer to vacate his position; we demand only the enforcement of the law—which, after all, we have made!" He extended his strong fist and laid it on the table. "If you deem it the conscientious duty of your office to discountenance these proceedings—as perhaps you well may—then let your opposition be in appearance only. In your heart you must know the necessity of this measure; you know the standing of the men managing it, You know that this is no mob, no distempered faction. It is San Francisco herself who speaks! Let California stand aside; let her leave us to our shame and sorrow; for, as God lives, we will cleanse this city of her corruption or perish with her! So we have sworn!"

This long speech, delivered with the solemnity of absolute conviction, profoundly impressed Johnson's volatile nature.

"But ," he objected uncertainly, "Coleman, you must understand! This is against the law—and I have sworn to uphold the law!"

"That is a matter for your own conscience," rejoined Coleman a little impatiently. "Issue your proclamation, if you feel that the dignity of the law may be best maintained by frowning on justice—but confine yourself to that! Leave us alone in our righteous purposes!"

Johnson, his chameleon soul aglow with enthusiasm, leaped to his feet and seized Coleman's two hands. In his eye stood a tear.

"Sir," he cried, "go on with your work! Let it be done as speedily as possible! You have my best wishes!"

Coleman did not relax his formal gravity.

"I am glad you feel that way, and that we understand each other," he contented himself with saying.

The heroic moment past, Johnson's restless mind began to glance among anxieties.

"But hasten the undertaking as much as you can," he begged. The opposition is stronger than you suppose. The pressure on me is going to be terrible. What about the prisoners in the jail?" asked Johnson anxiously. "What is your immediate plan?"

"That is in the hands of the committee," evaded Coleman.

He left the governor, again pacing up and down.

Stewart Edward White

LVIII

Coleman returned at once to the hall to resume his interrupted labours with the committee. The results of his conference with the governor seemed very satisfactory,

"We can now go ahead with free minds," said Clancey Dempster.

The business was astonishingly varied in scope. Charles Doane —not to be confused with Duane, the ex-fire chief—was appointed military commander- in-chief; Colonel Johns, captain of artillery; Olney was given the task of guarding the jail from the outside "with a force numerous enough to prevent escape." After considerable discussion Aaron Burns was made head of a civilian committee to take charge of all prisoners. It was moved and carried that no city or county official should be admitted to membership, a striking commentary on the disesteem in which such men were held. Permanent headquarters were arranged for; committees appointed for the solicitation of funds. A dozen other matters of similar detail were taken up, intelligently discussed, and provided for with the celerity of men trained in crises of business or life. At length it was moved the "committee, as a body, shall visit the county jail at such time as the Executive Committee might direct; and take thence James P. Casey and Charles Cora, give them a fair trial, and administer such punishment as justice shall demand."

This was the real business, for the transaction of which all these lesser businesses had been prepared. A slight pause followed its introduction, as though each member present were savouring the significance of the moment.

"Are you ready for the question?" asked Coleman in grave tones. "Those in favour—"

"Aye," came the instant response from every man present.

A messenger opened the door to announce that Governor Johnson was in the anteroom requesting speech with Coleman. The latter, handing his gavel to Dempster, immediately answered the summons.

He found Johnson, accompanied by Sherman, Garrison, and two strangers, lounging in the anteroom. The governor sprawled in a chair, his hat pulled over his eyes, a cigar in the corner of his mouth. His companions arose and bowed gravely as Coleman entered the room, but he remained seated, nodding at Coleman with an air of cavalier bravado that was plainly intended to conceal his nervousness. Without waiting for the exchange of spoken greetings, he burst out:

"We have come to ask what you intend to do," he demanded truculently of Coleman, as though he had never seen or talked to him before.

Coleman stared at him for an instant, completely surprised; read him; set his mouth grimly.

"Outrages are of constant occurrence," he recited briefly; "our suffrages are profaned, our fellow-citizens shot down in the street, our courts afford us no redress, we will endure it no longer."

"I agree with you as to the grievances," rejoined the governor, almost as though reciting a learned lesson; "but I think the courts are the proper remedy. The judges are good men, and there is no necessity for the people to turn themselves into a mob and obstruct the execution of the laws."

A flush mounted Coleman's cheek.

"Sir!" he cried indignantly, "this is no mob! You know this is no mob!"

Johnson looked at him from between half-closed lids, as though from a great distance.

"The opposition is stronger than you imagine," he said. "There is danger to the city—great danger of bloodshed—which should be prevented if possible." He paused, focussed his whole attention on Coleman, and went on with deliberate significance: *"It may be necessary to bring out all the force at my command.* I strongly advise you to leave the case of Casey to the courts; and I pledge myself to his fair and speedy trial."

Although realizing fully what a formidable element this change of front threw into the situation, Coleman's expression did not change: Sherman, watching him closely, could not see that his eyes even flickered,

"That will not satisfy the people," he told the governor, coldly and formally. "However they might consider your intention, they will doubt your ability to keep such a promise," He was going to say more, but checked, himself abruptly. The silent but intent attitude of the governor's four companions had struck his attention. "They are present as witnesses!" he told himself. Aloud he said, "Sir, I will report your remarks to my associates," Coleman wanted witnesses, too.

He returned to the committee, interrupting the proceedings,

"The governor has flopped over the fence." he informed them. "He is out there with Sherman and some others threatening to bring in the State troops unless we turn Casey over to the courts and disband. He personally guarantees a fair and speedy trial."

"What did you tell him?" demanded Hossfros.

"I haven't told him anything. It suddenly occurred to me that I ought to have witnesses for my side of the conversation, What do you think?"

"Same as I've always thought," replied Ward.

A murmur of assent greeted this.

After a remarkably brief discussion, considering the delicacy of the crisis, Coleman with others returned to the anteroom.

"Sorry to have kept you waiting," he said blandly, "but some consideration of the question was necessary. Let us understand each other clearly. As I understand your proposal, it is that, if we make no move, you guarantee no escape, immediate trial, and instant execution?"

"That is it," agreed Johnson, after a moment's focussing of his mind. For the first time it became evident to Coleman that the man had a trifle too much aboard.

"We doubt your ability to do this," went on Coleman, "but we are ready to meet you halfway. This is what we will promise: we will take no steps without first giving you notice. But in return we insist that ten men of our own selection shall be added to the sheriff's force within the jail."

"And," added Isaac Bluxome, "that they be fed and kept and treated well. That's part of the bargain."

"Why, that sounds fair and reasonable, gentlemen!" the governor cried heartily. "I see no objection to that! I was sure we could come to an agreement!"

He was suddenly all cordiality, all smiles, shaking each man's hand in turn. His companions retained their manner of glacial formality, however. He shortly withdrew, full of spirits, very much relieved at the lifting of what seemed to him a cloud of unjust oppression for a poor official who merely wanted peace. The real situation, evident enough to the keener brains on either side, was veiled to him. For poor Johnson had thus far stepped from one blunder into another. If Coleman were completely outside the law, then he, as an executive of the law, had no business treating or making agreements with him at all. Furthermore, as executive of the State, he had no legal right to interfere with city affairs unless formally summoned by the authorities—a procedure that had not been adopted. And to cap it all, he had for the second time treated with "rebels" and to their advantage. For, as the astute Coleman well knew, the final agreement was all to the benefit of the committee. They gained the right to place a personal guard over the prisoners; they gave, practically, only a promise to withdraw that guard before attacking the jail—a procedure eminently sensible if they cared anything for the guard.

This little weakness was immediately and vigorously pointed out to Johnson when he returned triumphantly to his hotel. Keen minds were plenty in the Law and Order party. Johnson was crestfallen. Like all men of little calibre elevated by expediency to high office, he wanted above everything to have peace, to leave things as they were, to avoid friction.

"Upon my word, gentlemen!" cried the governor, dismayed, "I did it for the best; and I assure you I am still convinced that this agreement—entered into in all faith, and sincerity—"

"Bosh!" boomed Judge Caldwell.

"I beg your pardon!" said Johnson, flushing.

"I said 'bosh,'" repeated the judge, bringing the point of his cane against the floor. "You've muddied it, as every sensible man can see. Best thing is to put a bold face on it. Take it for granted that the committee has promised to surrender all right of action, and that they have promised definitely to leave the case to the courts."

"I hardly think they intended that," murmured Johnson.

"Meant!" snorted the judge. "The words will bear that interpretation, won't they? Who cares what they meant!"

The following morning this version was industriously passed about. When Coleman heard of it he pulled his long moustache,

"The time has come," he said with decision. "After that, it is either ourselves or a mob."

He went immediately to the hall.

"Call Olney," he told a messenger. The head of the guard was soon before him.

"Olney," said his chief, "will you accept the command of a picked company in an important but somewhat perilous movement?"

Olney's tall form stiffened with pleasure.

"I will—with thanks!"

"Well, then, pick out from all the forces, of whatever companies, sixty men. Accept none but men—of the very highest bravery. Let them know that they are chosen for the post of danger, which is the post of honour, and permit none to serve who does not so esteem it."

Olney saluted, and went at once to the main floor, which, for drilling purposes, was shared by four companies. He stood still until his eye fell on Johnny Fairfax—him he called aside. "You can get the whole sixty right here if you want to," Johnny told him. "But if you want to distribute things—"

"I do," said Olney.

"Then I'd take Keith, Carter, that teamster McGlynn, and Salisbury."

Together they went the rounds of the impromptu armouries, going carefully over the rolls, picking a man here and there. By eight o'clock the sixty, informed, equipped, and ready, were gathered at the hall. Olney dismissed all others, and set himself to drilling his picked body.

"I don't care whether you can do 'shoulder arms' or not," he said, "but you've got to learn simple evolutions so I can handle you. And you must learn one another's faces. Now, come on!"

At two o'clock in the morning he expressed himself as satisfied. From the stock of blankets with which the headquarters were already provided they elected, bedding, and turned in on the floor. At six o'clock Olney began to send out detachments for breakfast.

"Feed up," he advised them. "I don't know what this is all about, but it pays to eat well."

By eight o'clock every man was in his place, lined up to rigid attention as Coleman entered the building.

"There they are!" said Olney proudly. "Every man of them of good, tough courage, and you can handle them as well as any old soldiers!"

Other men came into the hall, some of them in ranks, as they had fallen in at their own company headquarters outside, others singly or in groups. Doorkeepers prevented all exit; once a man was in, he was not permitted to go out. Some of the leaders and captains, among whom were Doane, Olney, and Talbot Ward, were summoned to Coleman's room. Shortly they emerged, and circulated through the hall giving to each captain of a company detailed and explicit directions. Each was instructed as to what hour he and his command were to start; from what given point; along exactly what route; and at exactly what time he was to arrive at another given point—not a moment sooner or later. Each was ignorant as to the instructions given the others. Never was a plan better laid out for concerted action, and probably never before had such a plan been so well carried out. Each captain listened attentively, returned to head his company, thoughtful with responsibility.

Olney gave the orders to his picked, company in person. They were told to leave their muskets. Armed only with pistols, they were to make their way by different routes to the jail.

Keith, and Johnny Fairfax started out together, "This is a mistake, as far as I am concerned," observed Keith to his companion. "I can't shoot a pistol. I ought to be in the rank and file, not with this picked lot. They chose me merely because I was your friend."

"You can make a noise, anyway," replied Johnny, whose eyes were alight with excitement. "I wonder what's up? This looks like business! I wouldn't miss it for a million dollars!"

Apparently the general populace had no inkling that anything was forward. The streets were much as usual except that an inordinate amount of street- corner discussion seemed to be going on; but that in view of the circumstances was normal. A broad-beamed Irish woman, under full sail alone accosted them. Her face Keith vaguely recognized, but he could not have told where he had seen it.

"I hear Mr. King, God rest him, is better," she said. "And what are the men going to do with that villain, Casey? If the men don't hang him, the women will!".

A little farther Keith stopped short at sight of two men hurrying by.

"Hold on, Watkins!" he called.

The four of them drew aside a little, out of the way.

"Weren't you in the jail guard?" asked Keith.

Watkins nodded.

"How does it happen you're outside?"

"The committee sent notice that the truce was over."

Johnny uttered an exultant yell, which he cut short shame-facedly when a dozen passersby looked around.

LIX

It happened on this day that Nan Keith had refused an invitation to ride with Ben Sansome, but had agreed as a compromise to give him a cup of tea late in the afternoon. Nan's mood was latterly becoming more and more restless. It was an unconscious reflection of the times, unconscious because she had no real conception of what was going on. In obedience to Keith's positively expressed request she had kept away from the downtown districts, leaving the necessary marketing to Wing Sam. For the moment, as has been explained, her points of touch with society were limited. It happened that before the trouble began the Keiths had been subscribers to the Bulletin and the Herald, and these two journals continued to be delivered. Neither of them gave her much idea of what was really going on. For a moment her imagination was touched by the blank space of white paper the Bulletin left where King's editorials had usually been printed, but Thomas King's subsequent violence had repelled her. The Herald, after rashly treating the "affray" as a street brawl, lost hundreds of subscribers and most of its advertising. It shrunk to a sheet a quarter of its usual size. Naturally, its editor, John Nugent, was the more solidly and bitterly aligned with the Law and Order party. The true importance of the revolt, either as an ethical movement or merely as regards its physical size, did not get to Nan at all. She knew the time was one of turmoils and excitements. She believed the city in danger of mobs. Her attitude might be described as a mixture of fastidious disapproval and a sympathetic restlessness.

Stewart Edward White

About the middle of the afternoon Mrs. Sherwood came up the front walk and rang the bell. Nan, sitting behind lace curtains, was impressed by her air of controlled excitement. Mrs. Sherwood hurried. She hurried gracefully, to be sure, and with a reminiscence of her usual feline indolence; but she hurried, nevertheless. Therefore, Nan herself answered the bell, instead of awaiting the deliberate Wing Sam.

"My dear," cried Mrs. Sherwood, "get your mantle, and come with me. There's something going to happen-something big!"

She refused to answer Nan's questions.

"You'll see," was all the reply she vouchsafed. "Hurry!"

They crossed by the new graded streets where the sand hills had been, and soon found themselves on the low elevations above the county jail. Mrs. Sherwood led the way to the porch of a onestory wooden house that appeared to be unoccupied.

"This is fine!" she said with satisfaction.

The jail was just below them, and they looked directly across the open square in front of it and the convergence of two streets. The jail was buzzing like a hive: men were coming and going busily, running away as though on errands, or darting in through the open door. Armed men were taking their places on the flat roof.

In contrast to this one little spot of excited activity, the rest of the scene was almost superlatively peaceful. People were drifting in from all the side streets, but they were sauntering slowly, as though without particular interest; they might have been going to or coming from church. A warm, basking, Sunday feel was in the sunshine. There was not the faintest breeze. Distant sounds carried clearly, as the barking of a dog—it might have been Gringo shut up at home—or the crowing of a distant cock. From the square below arose the murmur of a multitude talking. The groups of people increased in frequency, in numbers. Black forms began to appear on roof tops all about; white faces at windows. It would have been impossible to say when the scattered groups became a crowd; when the side of the square filled; when the converging streets became black with closely packed people; when the windows and doors and balconies, the copings and railings, the slopes of the hills were all occupied, but so it was. Before she fairly realized that many were gathering, Nan looked down on twenty thousand people. They took their positions quietly, and waited. There was no shouting, no demonstration, so little talking that the low murmur never rendered inaudible the barking of the dog or the crowing of the distant cock. The doors of the jail had closed. Men ceased going in and out. The armed forces on the roof were increased.

Nan had left off asking questions of Mrs. Sherwood, who answered none. The feeling of tense expectation filled her also. What was forward? Was this a mob? Why were these people gathered? Somehow they gave her the impression that they, too, like Mrs. Sherwood and herself, were waiting to see.

After a long time she saw the closely packed crowd down the vista of one of the converging streets move in the agitation of some disturbance. A moment later the sun caught files of bayonets. At the same instant the same thing happened at the end of the other converging street. The armed columns came steadily forward, the people giving way. Their men were dressed in sober citizens' clothes. The shining steel of the bayonets furnished the only touch of uniform. Quietly and steadily they came forward, the snake of steel undulating and twisting like a living thing. The two columns reached the convergence of the street together. As they entered the square before the jail, a third and fourth column debouched from side streets, and others deployed into view on the hills behind. The timing was perfect. One minute the prospect was empty of all but spectators, the next it was filled with grim and silent armed men.

Near the two women and among chance spectators on the

Stewart Edward White

piazza of the deserted house a well-known character of the times leaned against one of the pillars. This was Colonel Gift. Our chronicler, who has an eye for the telling phrase, describes him as "a tall, lank, empty-bowelled, tobacco- spurting Southerner, with eyes like burning black balls, who could talk a company of listeners into an insane asylum quicker than any man in California, and whose blasphemy could not be equalled, either in quantity or quality, by the most profane of any age or nation." In this crisis Colonel Gift's sympathies may be guessed. He watched the scene below him with a sardonic eye. As the armed columns wheeled into place and stood at attention, he turned to a man standing near.

"I tell you, stranger," said he, "when you see those damned psalm-singing Yankees turn out of their churches, shoulder their guns, and march away of a Sunday, you may know that hell is going to crack shortly!"

Mrs. Sherwood turned an amused eye in his direction. The colonel, for the first time becoming aware of her presence, swept off his black slouch hat and apologized profusely for the "damn."

The armed men stood rigid, four deep all around the square. Behind them the masses of the people watched. Even the murmur died. Again everybody waited.

Now, at a command, the ranks fell apart and from the side street marched the sixty men chosen by Olney dragging a field gun at the end of a rope. Their preliminary task of watching the jail for a possible escape finished, they had been again gathered. With beautiful military precision they wheeled and came to rest facing the frowning walls of the jail, the cannon pointed at the door.

Nan gasped sharply, and seized Mrs. Sherwood's arm with both hands. She had recognized Keith standing by the right wheel of the cannon. He was looking straight ahead, and the expression on his face was one she had never seen there before.

Suddenly something swelled up within her breast and choked her. The tears rushed to her eyes.

Quite deliberately, each motion in plain sight, the cannon was loaded with powder and ball. A man lit a slow match, blew it painstakingly to a glow, then took his position at the breech. The slight innumerable sounds of these activities died. The bustle of men moving imperceptibly fell. Not even the coughing and sneezing usual to a gathering of people paying attention was heard, for the intense interest inhibited these nervous symptoms. Probably never have twenty thousand people, gathered in one place, made their presence so little evident. A deep, solemn stillness brooded over them. The spring sun lay warm and grateful on men's shoulders; the doves and birds, the distant dogs and roosters, cooed and twittered, barked and crowed.

Nothing happened for full ten minutes. The picked men stood rigid by the gun in the middle of the square; the slow match burned sleepily, a tiny thread of smoke rising in the still air; the sunlight gleamed from the ranks of bayonets; the vast multitude held its breath, the walls of the jail remained blank and inscrutable.

Then a man on horseback was seen pushing his way through the crowd. He rode directly up to the jail door, on which he rapped thrice with the handle of his riding whip. Against the silence these taps, but gently delivered, sounded sharp and staccato. After a moment the wicket opened. The rider, without dismounting, handed through it a note; then, with a superb display of the old-fashioned horsemanship, backed his horse half the length of the square where he, too, came to rest.

"Who is he?" whispered Nan. Why she whispered she could not have told.

"Charles Doane," answered Mrs. Sherwood, in the same voice.

Another commotion down the street. Again the ranks parted

and closed again, this time to admit three carriages driven rapidly. As they came to a stop the muskets all around the square leaped to the "present." So disconcerting was this sudden slap and rattle of arms after the tenseness of the last half hour, that men dodged back as though from a blow. With admirable precision, Olney's men, obeying a series of commands, moved forward from the gun to form a hollow square around the carriages. Only the man with the burning slow match was left standing by the breech.

From the carriages then descended Coleman, Truett, Talbot Ward, Smiley, and two other men whom neither Nan nor Mrs. Sherwood recognized. Amid the dead silence they walked directly to the jail door, Olney's Sixty breaking the square and deploying close at their heels. A low colloquy through the wicket now took place. At length the door swung slowly open. The committee entered. The door swung shut after them. Again the people waited, but now once more arose the murmur of low-toned conversation.

LX

Up to this day Casey had been very content with his situation. His quarters were the best the place afforded, and they had been made more comfortable. Scores of friends had visited him, hailing him as their champion. He had been made to feel quite a hero. To be sure it was a nuisance to be so confined; but when he shot King, he had anticipated undergoing some inconvenience. It was a price to pay. He understood that there was some public excitement, and that it was well to lie low for a little until that had died down. The momentary annoyance would be more than offset by later prestige. Casey did not in the least fear the courts. He had before his eyes too many reassuring examples. His friends were rallying nobly to his defence. Over the wines and cigars, with which he was liberally supplied, they boasted of their strength and their dispositions —the whole police force of the city, the militia companies sworn, to act in just such emergencies, hundreds of volunteers, if necessary the whole power of the State of California called to put down this affronting of duly constituted law!

But this Sunday morning Casey was uneasy. There seemed to be much whispering in corners, much bustling to and fro. He paced back and forth, fretting, interrogating those about him. But they could or would tell him little—there was trouble;— and they fussed away, leaving Casey alone. As a matter of fact, the withdrawal of the committee's guard of ten, and the formal notice that the truce was thus promptly ended, had caught the Law and Order party unprepared. With five hours' notice—or indeed by next day, even were no notice given—the jail would

Stewart Edward White

have been impregnably defended. The sudden move of the committee won; as prompt, decisive moves will.

The bustling of the people in the jail suddenly died. Casey heard no shuffle of feet, no whisper of conversation. The building might have been empty save for himself. But he did hear outside the steady rhythmic tramp of feet.

Sheriff Scannell stood before him, the Vigilantes' written communication in his hand. Casey, looking up from the bed on which he had fallen in sudden shrinking, saw on his face an expression that made him cower. For the first time realization came to him of the straits he was in. His vivid Irish imagination leaped instantaneously from the complacence of absolute safety to the depths of terror. He sprang to his feet.

"You aren't going to betray me! You aren't going to give me up!" he cried, wringing his hands.

"James," replied' Scannell solemnly, "there are three thousand armed men coming for you, and I have not now thirty supporters around the jail."

"Not thirty!" cried. Casey, astonished. For a moment he appeared crushed; then leaped to his feet flourishing a long knife he had drawn from his boot. "I'll, not be taken from this place alive!" he shrieked, beside himself with hysteria. "Where are all you brave fellows who were going to see me through this?"

Scannell looked at him sadly. In the pause came a sharp knocking at the door of the jail. The sheriff turned away. A moment later Casey, listening intently, heard the door open and close, heard the sound of talking. He fairly darted to his table, scrawled a paper, and called to attract attention. Marshal North, answered the summons.

"Give this to them—to the Vigilantes," urged Casey, thrusting the paper into his hands. North glanced through the note.

> TO THE VIGILANT COMMITTEE. Gentlemen: I am willing to go before you if you will let me speak but ten minutes. I do not wish the blood of any man upon my head.
>
> JAS. CASEY

But after North had gone to deliver this, Casey again sprang to his feet, again flourished his bowie knife, again ramped up and down, again swore he would never be taken alive. A deputy passed the door. Casey's demeanour collapsed again.

"Tell them," he begged this man earnestly; "tell them if two respectable citizens will promise me gentlemanly treatment, I'll go peaceably! I will not be dragged through the streets like a dog! If they will give me a fair trial and allow me to summon my witnesses, I'll yield!"

And the deputy left him pacing up and down, waving his knife, muttering wildly to, himself.

On entering the jail door Coleman and his companions bowed formally to the sheriff.

"We have come for the prisoner, Casey," said Coleman. "We ask that he be peaceably delivered us handcuffed, at the door, immediately."

"Under existing circumstances," replied Scannell, "I shall make no resistance. The prison and its contents are yours."

But Truett interrupted pointedly:

"We want only the man Casey, at present," he said. "For the rest we hold you strictly accountable."

Scannell bowed without reply. North and the deputy came in

succession to deliver Casey's messages, and to report his apparent determination. The committee offered no comment. They penetrated to the ulterior of the jail. Many men, apparently unarmed, idling about as though merely spectators, looked at them curiously as they passed. Casey heard them, coming and sprang back from the door, holding his long knife dramatically poised. Coleman walked directly to the door, where he stopped, looking Casey coldly in the eye. The seconds, passed. Neither man stirred. At the end of a full minute Coleman said sharply:

"Lay down that knife!"

As though his incisive tones had broken the spell, Casey moved. He looked wildly to right and to left; then flung the knife from him and buried his face in his hands.

"Your requests are granted," said Coleman shortly; then to Marshal North: "Open the door and bring him out."

LXI

On the veranda of the unoccupied house above the jail Nan Keith stood rigid, her hand upon her heart. During the period of the committee's absence inside the jail she did not alter her position by a hair's breadth. She was in the hypnosis of a portentous waiting. Time fell into the abyss of eternity: whether it were ten minutes or ten hours did not matter in the least.

For this was to Nan in the nature of a revelation so sudden and so complete that it filled her whole soul. Had she known what Mrs. Sherwood was taking her to see, she would have pre-visualized a drunken, disorderly, howling, bloodthirsty mob; a huge composite of brawling antagonisms, of blind fury, of vulgar irrationalisms. Here were men filled with purpose; This was what caught at her breath—the grim silent purpose of it! The orderly progression of events, moving with the certainty of a fate, was like the steady crescendo of solemn music. And this crescendo rose in her as a tide of emotion that overflowed and drowned her. The right and wrong—as she had examined them intellectually or through, the darkened glasses of her caste prejudices—were quite lost. This was merely something primitive, wonderful, beautiful. The spectacle was at the moment of suspense, yet she felt so impatience—the wheel must turn in its own majestic circle—but only an intense expectation. And in this she felt, subconsciously, that she was one with the multitude.

The jail door swung open. The committee came out. In the

Stewart Edward White

middle of their compact group walked a stranger.

"Casey!" breathed a vast voice from the crowd.

An indescribable burst of grateful relief fluttered across the upturned faces as a breeze across water. It was almost timid at first, but gathered strength as it spread. It rolled up the hillside. A great, deep breath seemed to fill the lungs of the throng. The murmur swelled suddenly, was on the point of bursting into the frantic cheering of twenty thousand men.

But Coleman, his hat removed, raised his hand. In obedience to the simple gesture the cheer was stifled. In an instant all was still. The little group entered the carriages, which immediately wheeled and drove away.

Nan, standing bolt upright, her attitude still unchanged, caught her breath at the inhibition of the cheer. She did not even try to wink away the tears that rolled down her cheeks. Through them she saw the troops wheel with the precision of veterans, and march away after the carriages. The crowd melted slowly. Soon were left only the inscrutable jail, the gun still pointed at its door, the rigid ranks of Olney's Sixty, who had evidently been left on guard, and a few stragglers.

Suddenly she turned and walked away. Mrs. Sherwood followed her as rapidly as she could, but did not succeed in catching up with her. At the corner below the Keiths' house she stopped, watched until Nan had gained her own dooryard, hen turned toward home, a smile sketching her lips, a light in her eyes.

Nan flung open her door and went directly to the parlour. She stood in the doorway contemplating the scene. It was very cozy. The afternoon sun slanted through the high-narrow windows of the period, gilding the dust motes floating lazily to and fro. The tea table, set with a snowy doth, glittered invitingly, its silver and porcelain, its plates of dainty sandwiches and thin waferlike cookies—Wing Sam's specialty

—enticingly displayed. Two easy chairs had been drawn close, and, before the unoccupied one a low footstool had been placed. Ben Sansome sat in the other. He was, as usual, exquisitely dressed. All his little appointments were not only correct but worn easily. The varicoloured waistcoat, the sparkling studs and cravat pins, the bright, soft silk tie, were all subdued from their ordinary too-vivid effect by the grace with which they were carried. Nan saw all this, and appreciated it dispassionately, appraising him anew through clarified vision. Especially she noticed the waxed ends of his small moustache. He had, at the sound of her entrance, lighted the tea kettle; and as she came in he smiled up at her brightly.

"You see," he cried gayly, "I am doing your task for you! I have the lamp all lit!"

She paid no attention to this, but advanced two steps into the room.

"Which side are you on, anyway?" she asked abruptly and a little harshly.

Sansome raised his eyebrows in faint and fastidious surprise.

"Dear lady, what do you mean?"

"The only thing I can mean in these times: are you with the Law and Order, or with the Committee of Vigilance?"

Sansome shrugged his shoulders whimsically and sank back into his chair.

"How can you ask that, dear lady?" he begged pathetically. "You would not class me with the rabble, I hope."

But Nan did not in the slightest degree respond to the lightness of his tone. Her own was cold and detached.

"I do not know how to class you," she said. "But I asked you a question."

Sansome arose to his feet again. His manner now became sympathetic, but into it had crept the least hint of resentment,

"I don't understand your mood" he told her. "You are overwrought."

Nan's self-control slipped by ever so little. She did not actually stamp her foot, but her delivery of her next speech achieved that for her.

"Will you answer me?" she demanded. "Which side, are you on?"

"I am on the side every gentleman is on," replied Sansome, a trifle stung. "The side of the law."

"Then," she cried, with a sudden intensity, "why weren't you there—on your side—defending the jail?' Why are you here?"

Ben Sansome's knowledge of women was wide, and he therefore imagined it profound. Here he recognized the symptoms of hysteria; cause unknown. He dopted the lightly soothing.

"I thought I was asked here!" he cried with quizzical mock pathos.

She stared at him a contemplative instant so steadily that he coloured. She was not seeing him, however; she was seeing Keith, standing with his fellows in the open, under the walls of the jail and its hidden guns. With a short laugh she turned away.

"You were," said she. "Help yourself to tea. As you say, I am overwrought. I am going to lie down."

Her one compelling instinct now was to get away from him before something in her brain snapped. He became soothing.

"Won't you have a cup of tea first?" he urged. "It will do you good."

"A cup of tea!" she repeated with deadly calm. It seemed such an ending to such a day! She tried to laugh, but strangled in her throat; and she bolted wildly from the room, leaving Ben Sansome staring.

LXII

Nan's high exaltation of spirit, which still soared at the altitude to which the events of the afternoon had lifted it, next expressed itself in a characteristically feminine manner: she picked flowers in the garden, arranged them, placed them effectively, set the table herself, lighted the lamps, touched a match to the wood fire always comfortable in San Francisco evenings, slightly altered the position of the chairs, visited Wing Sam with fresh instructions. Gringo, who looked on all this as for his especial benefit, took his place luxuriously before the grate. It was a cozy, homelike scene. Then she dressed slowly and carefully in her most becoming gown—the only gown Keith had ever definitely singled out for individual praise—took especial pains with her hair, and finally descended to join Gringo. The latter, as a greeting intended to show his entire confidence, promptly rolled over to expose his vitals to her should it be her pleasure to hurt a poor defenceless dog. He was a ridiculous sight, upside down, his tongue lolling out, his eye rolled up at her adoringly. She laughed at him a little, then leaned swiftly over to confide something in his ear.

But that evening Keith was late. The clock on the mantel chimed clearly the hour, then the quarter and the half. Wing Sam came to protest aggrievedly that "him glub catchum cold—you no wait!" Nan was severe with Wing Sam and his suggestion—so unwontedly severe that Wing Sam returned to the kitchen muttering darkly. He had caught the atmosphere of celebration, somehow, and on his own-initiative had frosted with wonderful white a cake not yet cut, and on the cake had carefully traced pink legends in Chinese and English characters. The former was one of those conventional mottoes seen on every laundry, club, and temple which would have translated "Health, long life, and happiness"; the other Wing Sam had copied from a lithograph he much admired. It read "Use Rising Sun Stove Polish." Glowering with resentment, Wing Sam scraped the frosting from the cake.

At eight o'clock a small boy delivered a note at the door and scuttled back to the centre of excitement. It was a scrawl from Keith, saying that he was detained, would not be home to dinner, might not be in at all. Nan sat down to a cold, belated meal served by a loftily disapproving Chinaman. She tried to think of her pride in Keith, and the work he, in company with his fellows, was doing for the city; to recall some of her exaltation of the afternoon; but it was very difficult. Her little preparations were so much nearer. The table, the flowers, the shaded lamps, the fire on the hearth, her gown, the twist of her hair, all mocked her anticipations. In spite of herself her spirits went down to zero. She could not eat, she could not even sit at the table through the service of the various courses. Midway in the meal she threw aside her napkin and returned abruptly to the drawing- room. The fire was snapping merrily on the hearth. Gringo opened his eyes at her entrance, recognized his beloved mistress, and rolled over as usual, all four legs in the air, his tender stomach confidingly exposed, for Who could be so brutal as to hurt a poor, defenceless dog? Nan kicked him pettishly in the ribs. Gringo stopped panting, and drew in his tongue, but otherwise did not shift his posture. This was, of course, a mistake. Nan kicked him again. Gringo rose deliberately and retired with dignity to the coldest, darkest, most cheerless corner he could find, where he sat and looked dejected.

"You look such a silly fool!" Nan told him relentlessly.

Thus passed the moment of exaltation and expansion. If Keith had come home to dine, it is probable that the barrier between them—of which he was only dimly conscious—would have been broken. But by midnight Nan had, as she imagined, "thought out" the situation. She was able to see him now through eyes purged of self-pity or self-thought. She came to full realization, which she formulated to herself, that she was not now the central point of his interest—that she was "no longer" the central point, as she expressed it. She was right also in her conclusion that all day long he hardly gave her more than a perfunctory thought. So far, her facts were absolutely correct. But Nan was, in spite of her natural good mind and married experience, too ignorant of man psychology to draw the true conclusion. Indeed, very few women ever realize man's possibilities of single-minded purpose and concentration to the temporary exclusion of other things. Keith's whole being was carried by this moral movement in which he was involved. He simply took Nan for granted; and that is something a woman never gets used to, and always misinterprets.

"He no longer loves me!" she said to herself, in this hour of plain thinking. She faced it squarely; and her heart sank to the depths; for she still loved him, and the sight of him that afternoon amid the guns had told her how much.

But her next thought was not of herself, but of him, and the situation in which, he was working out his destiny. "How can I best help?" she asked herself, which showed that the spirit aroused in her that afternoon had not in reality died. And her intellect relentlessly pointed out to her that her only aid would come from her self-effacement, her standing one side. When the great work was done, then, perhaps—

So affairs in the Keith household went on exactly as before. Nobody but Gringo knew that anything had happened; and he only realized that the universe had suffered an upheaval, so that now mistresses might kick their poor defenceless dogs in the stomach.

LXIII

Casey was safely in custody. Cora also had been taken on a second trip to the jail. They had been escorted into the headquarters, the doors of which had closed behind them and behind the armed men who guarded them. The streets were filled with an orderly crowd. They waited with that same absence of excitement, impatience, or tumult so characteristic of all the popular gatherings of that earnest time, save when the upholders of the law were gathered. After a long interval one of the committeemen, Dows by name, appeared at an upper window. He did not have to appeal for attention, and had barely to raise his voice.

"It is not the intention of the committee to be hasty," he announced. "Nothing more will be done to-day."

Silence greeted this statement. At last some one spoke up:

"Where are Casey and Cora?" he asked.

"The committee holds possession of the jail; all are safe," replied Dows.

With this assurance the crowd was completely satisfied, as it proved by dispersing quietly and at once.

Of the three thousand enrolled men, three hundred were retained under arms at headquarters; a hundred surrounded and watched the jail; the rest were dismissed. About midnight a dense fog descended on the city. The streets were deserted. But on the roofs of the jail and the adjacent buildings indistinct figures stalked to and fro in the misty moonlight.

All next day, which was Monday, headquarters remained inscrutable. Small activities went forward. Guards and patrols were changed. The cannon was brought from before the jail. Early in the day a huge crowd gathered, packing the adjacent streets, watching patiently far into the night to see what would happen. Nothing happened.

But about the city at large patrols of armed men moved on mysterious business. Gun shops were picketed, and their owners forbidden to sell weapons. Evidently the committee was carrying out a considered plan.

Toward evening the weather thickened and a rain came on. It turned colder. Still the crowd did not disperse. It stood in its sodden shoes, hugging its sodden cloaks to its shoulders, humped over, About eight o'clock several companies in rigid marching formation appeared. A stir of interest, shivered through the crowd, but died as it became evident that this was only a general relief for those on duty during the day. At midnight, or thereabouts, the crowd went home; but again by first daylight the streets for blocks were jammed full. Still it rained with a sullen, persistence. Still nothing happened.

And all over the city business was practically at a stand. Knots of men stood conferring on every corner. Conversation in mixed company was very wary indeed. No man dared express himself too openly. The courts were empty. Some actually closed, on one excuse or another, but most went through a form of business. Some judges took the occasion to go to White Sulphur Springs on vacations, long contemplated, they said. These things occasioned lively comment. It was generally known that the Sacramento steamer of the evening before had carried several hundred passengers, all with pressing business at the capitol, or somewhere else. As our chronicler tells it: "A good many who had things on their minds left for the country." Still it rained; still the crowd waited; still the headquarters of the Committee of Vigilance remained closed and inscrutable.

LXIV

During all this time the Executive Committee sat in continuous session, for it had been agreed that no recess of more than thirty minutes should be taken until a decision had been reached. The room in which they sat was a large one, lighted by windows on one side only. Coleman sat behind a raised desk at one end. Below it stood a small table accommodating two. On either side six small tables completed three sides of a hollow square. No ornament, no especial comforts— the desk, the thirteen pine tables, the twenty-eight pine chairs, the wooden walls, the oil lamps, the four long windows—that was all.

The prisoners, who, when they had seen the thousands before the jail, had expected nothing less than instant execution by lynch law, began to take heart. After a man has faced what he thinks is the prospect of immediate and unavoidable death, such treatment as this arouses real hope. The prisoners were strictly guarded and closely confined, it is true, but they understood they were to have a fair trial "according to law." That last phrase cheered them immensely. They knew the law. Nor were they entirely cut off from the outside. Casey was allowed to see several men in regard to certain pressing business matters, and was permitted to talk to them freely, although always in the presence of a member of the committee. Cora received visits from Belle. She had spent thousands in his legal defence; now she came to see him faithfully, and tried to cheer him, but was plainly cowed. Her self-control had vanished. She clung to him passionately, weeping. He was forced to what should have been her role; and in cheering her he managed to gain a modicum of self-confidence for himself. She left him at midnight, much reassured.

But on Monday morning Cora's cell door was thrown open, and he was motioned forth by a grave man, who conducted him through echoing gloomy corridors to the committee room, where he was left facing the tables and the men who sat behind them. Cora's natural buoyancy vanished. The men before him met his gaze with rigid, unbending solemnity. The rain beat mournfully against the windows, blurring the glass, casting the high apartment in a half gloom. Nobody moved or spoke. All looked at him. The echo of his footsteps died, and the room was cast in stillness except for the soft dashing of the storm.

"Charles Cora," at last pronounced Coleman in measured tones, "you are here on trial for your life, accused with the murder of United States Marshal Richardson."

Cora, who was a plucky man, had recovered his wits. He must have realized that he was in a tight place, but he kept his head admirably. His demeanour took on alertness, his manner throughout was respectful, and his voice low.

"Do I get no counsel?" he inquired.

"Counsel will be given you."

He put in an earnest plea for counsel outside the tribunal—impartial counsel.

"Our members are impartial," Coleman told him.

Cora hesitated; locking about him.

"If Mr. Truett will act for me," he suggested; "and I beg you earnestly, gentlemen, that the excitement of the time may not be prejudicial to my interests, that I may have a chance for my life!"

"Your trial will be fair," he was assured.

"I shall undertake the defence," Truett agreed briefly; "and petition that Smiley be appointed as my assistant."

This being granted, the three men drew one side for a consultation. In a short time Truett handed to the sergeant-at-arms—the same man who had conducted Cora to the tribunal—a list of the witnesses Cora wished to summon. These were at once sought by a subcommittee outside. In the meantime, witnesses for the prosecution were one by one admitted, sworn, and examined. All ordinary forms of law were closely followed. All essential facts were separately brought out. It was the historic Cora trial over again, with one difference—gone were the technical delays. By dusk Keith, who had been called at three, had all but completed the long tale of his testimony, had finished recounting, not only what he had seen of the quarrel and the subsequent shooting, but also a detailed account of the trial, the adverse influences brought to bear on the prosecution, and his investigations into the question of "undue influence." No attempt was made to confine the investigation to the technical trial.

Keith was the last witness for the prosecution. And the witnesses for the defence, where were they? Of the list submitted by Cora not one could be found! In hiding, afraid, the perjurers would not appear!

The dusk was falling in earnest now. The corners of the room were in darkness. Beneath Coleman's desk Bluxome, the secretary, had lighted an oil lamp the better to see his notes. In the interest of Keith's testimony the general illumination had not been ordered. Outside the tiny patch of yellow light the men of Vigilance sat motionless, listening, their shadows dim and huge against the wall.

The door opened, and Charles Doane, the Grand Marshal of the Vigilantes, advanced three steps into the room.

"Mr. President," he said clearly, his voice cutting the stillness, "I am instructed to announce that James King of William is dead."

LXV

Thursday noon was set for the funeral of the man who had given his life that a city might live. In the room where he had made his brave fight against death he now lay in state. On Wednesday ten thousand people visited him there. Early Thursday morning his remains were transferred to the Unitarian Church where, early as it was, a great multitude had gathered to do him honour. Now through the long morning hours it sat with him silently. The church was soon filled to over-flowing; the streets in all directions became crowded with sober-faced men and women. They knew they would be unable to get into the church, to attend nearer his last communion with his fellowmen, but they stayed, feeling vaguely that their mere presence helped—as, indeed, perhaps it did. Marching bodies from every guild or society in the city stood in rank after rank, extending down the street as far as the eye could reach. Hundreds of horsemen, carriages, foot marchers, quietly, orderly, were already getting into line. They, too, were excluded from the funeral ceremonies by lack of room; they, too, waited to do honour to the cortege. This procession was over two miles in length. Each man wore a band of crepe around his left arm. The time set for the funeral ceremony was yet hours distant.

It seemed that all the city must be there. But those who, hurrying to the scene, had occasion to pass near the Vigilante headquarters found the vacant square guarded on all sides by a triple line of armed men. The side streets, also, were filled with them. They stood in exact alignment, rigid, bayonets fixed, their eyes straight ahead. Three thousand of them were there. Hour after hour they stood, untiring, staring at the building, which gave no sign; just as the other multitude, only a few squares away, stood hour after hour, patiently waiting in the bright sun.

At quarter before one the upper windows of the headquarters building were thrown open, and small platforms, extending about three feet, were thrust from two of them. An instant later two heavy beams were shoved out from the flat roof directly over the platforms. From the ends of the beams dangled nooses of rope. A dead wait ensued. Across the silence could be heard faintly from the open windows of the distant church the chords of an organ, the rise and fall of a hymn, then the measured cadence of oration. The funeral services had begun.

As though this were a signal, the blinds that had partly closed the window openings were swung back, and Charles Cora was conducted to the end of one of the little platforms. His face was covered with a white handkerchief, and his arms and legs were bound with cords. The attendant adjusted the noose, then left him. An instant later Casey appeared. He had petitioned not to be blindfolded, so his face was bare. Cora stood bolt upright, motionless as a stone. Casey's nerve had left him; his face was pale and his eyes bloodshot. As the attendant placed the noose, the murderer's eyes darted here and there over the square. Did he still expect that the boastful promises of his friends would be fulfilled, did he still hope for rescue? If so, that hope must have died as he looked down on those set, grim faces staring straight ahead, on that sinister ring of steel. He began to babble.

"Gentlemen!" he cried at them, "I am not a murderer! I do not feel afraid to meet my God on a charge of murder! I have done nothing but what I thought was right! To-morrow let no editor dare call me a murderer! Whenever I was injured I have resented it. It has been part of my education during twenty-nine years! Gentlemen, I forgive you this persecution!

O God! My poor mother! O God!"

Not one word of contrition; not one word for the man who lay yonder in the church; not one syllable for the heartbroken wife kneeling at the coffin! He ceased. And his words went out into the void and found no echo against that wall of steel.

They waited. For what? Across the intervening housetops the sound of speaking ceased to carry. The last orator had given place. At the door of the sanctuary was visible a slight, commotion: the coffin was being carried out. It was placed in the hearse. Every head was bared. There ensued a slight pause; then from overhead the great bell boomed once. Another bell in the next block answered. A third, more distant, chimed in. From all parts of the city tolled the solemn requiem.

At the first stroke the long cortege moved forward toward Lone Mountain; at the first stroke the Vigilantes, as one man, presented arms; at the first stroke the platforms dropped and Casey and Cora fell into the abyss of eternity.

LXVI

This execution occasioned a great storm of indignation among the adherents of law and order. Serious-minded men, like Judge Shattuck, admitted the essential justice rendered, but condemned strongly the method.

"Of course they were murderers," cried the judge, "and of course they should have been hung, and of course the city is better off without either of them. I'm not afraid of their friends, and I don't care who knows what I think! And some very worthy citizens, wrongly, are involved in this, some citizens whom otherwise I greatly respect. It is better that a hundred criminals should escape than that the whole law of California should be outraged by an act that denies at once the value and the authority of our government. The energy, the talent for organization, that this committee has displayed in the exercise of usurped authority, might have been directed in aid of the courts, consistently with the constitution and the laws, with, equal if not greater efficiency."

But very few were able to see it in this calm spirit. The ruling class, the "chivalry," the best element of the city had been slapped in the face. And by whom? By a lot of "Yankee shopkeepers," assisted by renegades like Keith, Talbot Ward, and others. The committee was a lot of stranglers; they ought to be punished as murderers; they ought to be shot down, egad, as revolutionaries! It was realized that street shooting had temporarily become unsafe; otherwise, there is no doubt that the hotheads would have gone forth deliberately abrawling.

There were many threats made against individuals, many condign—and lawless—punishments promised them.

As an undercurrent, nowhere expressed or even acknowledged, was a strong feeling of relief. Any Law and Order would have fought at the mere suggestion; but every one of them felt it. After all, the law had been surprised and overpowered. It had yielded only to overwhelming odds. With the execution of Cora and Casey accomplished, the committee might be expected to disband. And, of course, when it did disband, then the law would have its innings. Its forces would be better organized and consolidated, its power assured. It could then apprehend and bring to justice the ringleaders of this unwarranted undertaking. Like dogs at the heels of a retreating foe, the hotheads became bolder as this secret conviction gained strength. They were in favour of using an armed force to take Coleman and his fellow-conspirators into the custody of the law. Calmer spirits held this scheme in check.

"Let them have rope," advised Blatchford. "I know mobs. Now that they've hung somebody, their spirit will die down. Give them a few days."

But to the surprise, and indignation of these people, the Vigilantes showed no of an intention to disband. On the contrary, their activities extended and their organization tightened. The various companies drilled daily until they went through evolutions and the manual of arms with all the perfection of regular troops. The committee's books remained open; by the last of the week over seven thousand men had signed the rolls. Vanloads of furniture and various supplies were backed up before the doors of headquarters, and were carried within by members of the organization—no non-member ever saw the inside of the building while it was occupied by the Vigilantes. The character of these furnishings and supplies would seem to argue an intention of permanence. Stoves, cooking utensils, cot beds, provisions, blankets, bulletin boards, arms, chairs, tables, field guns, ammunition, were only some items. Doorkeepers were always in attendance.

Sentinels patrolled the streets and the roof. The great warehouse took on an exceedingly animated appearance.

The Executive Committee was in session all of each day. It became known that a "black list" of some sort was in preparation. On the heels of this orders came for the Vigilante police, instructing them to arrest certain men and to warn certain others to leave town immediately. It was evident that a clean sweep was contemplated.

Among the first of those arrested was the notorious Yankee Sullivan, an ex- prize fighter, ward heeler, ballot-box staffer, and shoulder striker. He had always been a pillar of strength to those engaged in corrupt practices. This man went to pieces completely. He confessed the details of many of his own crimes but, what was more important, implicated many others as well. His testimony was invaluable, not necessarily as final proof against those whom he accused, but as indications for thorough investigations. Finally, unexpectedly, he committed suicide in his cell. It seems he had been accustomed to from sixty to eighty drinks of whiskey a day, and the sudden, complete deprivation had destroyed him. Warned by this, the committee henceforward issued regular rations of whiskey to its prisoners!

Trials in due order, with counsel for defence and ample opportunity to call witnesses, went on briskly. Those who anticipated more hangings were disappointed. It became known that the committee had set for itself the rule that capital punishment would be inflicted only for crimes so punishable by the regular law. But each outgoing ship carried crowds of those on whom had been passed the sentence of banishment. The majority of these were, of course, low thugs, "Sydney ducks," hangers on; but a very large proportion were taken from what had been known as the city's best. In the law courts these men would in many cases have been declared as white as the driven snow. But they were undesirable citizens; the committee so decided them; and bade them begone. Charles Duane, Wooley Kearney, William Carr, Edward

Stewart Edward White

Bulger, Philander Brace, William McLean, J.D. Musgrave, and Peter Wightman were well-known and influential names found on the "black list," Peter Wightman, James White, and our old friend, Ned McGowan, ran away. Hundreds of others left the city. A terror spread among the ignorant and vicious of the underworld. Some of the minor offenders brought in by the Vigilante police were by the Executive Committee turned over to the regular law courts. *Every one of such cases was promptly convicted by those courts!*

This did not look much like disbanding, nor did any opportunity for wholesale arrest of the anarchists seem imminent. The leaders of the Law and Order faction were at last aroused.

"This is more than anarchy; it is revolution," said Judge Caldwell. "It is a successful revolution because it is organized. The people of this city are scattered and powerless. They in turn should be organized to combat the forces of disorder."

In pursuance of this belief—that the public at large needed only to be called together in order to defend its institutions— handbills were printed and newspaper notices published calling a meeting for June and in Portsmouth Square. Elaborate secret preparations, involving certain distributions of armed men were made to prevent what was considered certain interference. This was useless. Immediately after the appearance of the notice the Committee of Vigilance issued orders that the meeting was in no manner to be disturbed, and hung out placards reading:

"Members of the Vigilance Committee: Order must be maintained."

"Friends of the Vigilance Committee: Keep out of the Square," etc.

The meeting was well attended. Enormous crowds gathered, not only in and around the square itself, but in balconies and windows and on housetops. It was a ribald, disrespectful crowd, evidently out for a good time, calling back and forth, shouting question or comment at the men gathered about the speaker's platform.

"What kind of a circus do you call this show, anyway?" roared a huge, bare-armed miner in red shirt.

"This is the Law and Murder meeting," instantly answered some one from a balcony.

This phrase tickled the crowd hugely. The words were passed from man to man. Eventually they became the stereotyped retort. "Stranglers!" sneered one faction. "Law and Murder!" flung back the other.

On the platform stood or sat the owners of many of the city's proud names—judges, jurists, merchants, holders of high political office, men whose influence a month ago had been paramount and irresistible. Among them were famed orators, men who had never failed to hold and influence a crowd. But two hundred feet away little could be heard. It early became evident that, though there would be no interference, the sentiment of the crowd was against them. And, what was particularly maddening, the sentiment was good-humoured. Even the compliment of being taken seriously was denied them!

Colonel Ed Baker came forward to speak. The colonel's gift of eloquence was such that, in spite of his known principles, his lack of scruple, his insincerity, he won his way to a picturesque popularity and fame. Later he delivered a funeral oration over the remains of David Broderick that has gone far to invest the memory of that hard-headed, venal, unscrupulous politician with an aura of romance. But the crowd would have little of him this day. An almost continuous uproar drowned his efforts. Catch words such as liberty, constitution, *habeas corpus*, trial by jury, freedom, etc., occasionally became audible. The people were not interested.

"See Cora's defender!" cried someone, voicing the general suspicion that Baker had been one of the little gambler's hidden counsel. "Cora!" "Ed Baker!" "Ten thousand dollars!" "Out of that, you old reprobate!" jeered the audience. He spoke ten minutes against the storm, then yielded, red faced and angry. Others tried in vain. A Southerner named Benham, while deploring passionately the condition of the city which had been seized by a mob, robbed of its sacred rights, etc., happened inadvertently to throw back his coat, thus revealing the butt of a Colt's revolver. The bystanders caught the point at once.

"There's a pretty Law and Order man!" they shrieked. "Hey, Benham! Don't you know it's against the law to go armed?"

"I carry this weapon," shrieked Benham, passionately shaking his fist, "not as an instrument to overthrow the law, but to uphold it!"

A clear, steady voice from a nearby balcony made itself distinctly heard:

"In other words, sir, you break the law in order to uphold the law," it said. "What more are the Vigilantes doing?"

The crowd went wild over this repartee. The confusion became worse. Old Judge Campbell was thrust forward, in the hope that his age and his senior judgeship would command respect. He was unable to utter consecutive sentences.

"I once thought," he interrupted himself piteously, "that I was the free citizen of a free country, but recent occurrences have convinced me that I am a slave; a slave, gentlemen, more a slave than any on a Southern plantation for they know their masters, but I know not mine!"

But his auditors refused to be affected.

"Oh, yes, you do!" they informed him. "You know your

masters as well as anybody—two of them were hung the other day!"

After this the meeting broke up. The most ardent Law and Order man could not deny that as a popular demonstration it had been a fizzle.

But if this attempt at home to gain coherence failed, up river the partisans had better luck. A hasty messenger with tidings for the ear of the Executive Committee only was followed by rapidly spreading rumours. Five hundred men with two pieces of artillery were coming down from Sacramento to liberate the prisoners, especially Billy Mulligan, or die in the attempt. They were reported to be men from the southeast: Texans, Carolinians, crackers from Pike County, all fire-eaters, reckless, sure to make trouble. Their numbers were not in themselves formidable, but every man knew the city still to be full of scattered warriors needing only leaders and a rallying point. The materials for a very pretty civil war were laid for the match. An uneasiness pervaded headquarters, not for the outcome, but for the unavoidable fighting and bloodshed.

Therefore, when Olney hastily entered the main hall early in the evening, and in a loud voice called for "two hundred men with side arms for especial duty," there was a veritable scramble to enlist. Olney picked out the required number, selecting, it was afterward noticed, only the big men physically. They fell in, and were marched quickly out Market Street. It was dark. Expectations were high. Just beyond Second Street, dimly visible against the sky or in the faint starlight, they saw a mysterious force opposing them, men on foot, horses, the wheels of guns. Each man gripped his revolver and set his teeth. Here, evidently, from this ordinarily deserted and distant part of town, a flanking attack was to have been delivered. As they drew nearer they made out wagons; and nearer still-bale upon bale of gunny sacks, and shovels!

The truth dawned on them, and a great laugh went up. "Sold! Sold! Sold!" they cried.

But they set to work with a will, filled the gunny sacks with sand, piled them on the wagons; and so by morning Fort Gunnybags, as headquarters was thenceforth called, came into existence. Cannon were mounted, breastworks piled, embrasures planned.

The five hundred fire-eaters were no myth. They disembarked, greeted the horde of friends who had come to meet them, marched to Fort Gunnybags, looked it over, thrust their hands in their pockets, and walked peacefully away to the nearest barrooms!

Wise men. By now the Vigilante dispositions were so complete that in the mere interest of examining so sudden yet so thorough an organization, a paragraph or so may profitably be spent on it. Behind headquarters was a long shed stable in which were to be found at all hours saddle horses and artillery horses, all saddled and bridled, ready for instant use. Twenty-six pieces of artillery, mostly sent in by captains of merchant vessels in the harbour, were here parked. Other cannon were mounted for the defence of Fort Gunnybags. Muskets, rifles, and sabres enough to arm 6,000 men had been accumulated— and there were 6,000 men to use them! A French portable barricade had been constructed in the event of possible street fighting, a sort of wheeled framework that could be transformed into litters or scaling ladders. Sutlers' offices and kitchens could feed a small army. Flags and painted signs carrying the emblematic open eye of vigilance decorated the rooms, A huge alarm bell had been mounted on the roof. The mattresses, beds, cots, blankets, and other furniture necessary to sleep four companies on the premises had been provided. A completely equipped armourer's shop and a hospital with all supplies occupied the third story. The forces were divided into four companies of artillery, one squadron and two troops of cavalry, four regiments, and thirty-two companies of infantry; besides the small but efficient police organization. A tap on the bell gathered these men in an incredibly short space of time. "As a rule," says Bancroft, "within fifteen minutes from the time the bell was tapped, on any occasion, seven-tenths of the entire Vigilante forces would be in their places armed ready for battle."

Another corps, not as heroic, but quite as necessary, it was found advisable to appoint. The sacking of which Fort Gunnybags was made was of very coarse texture. When dry, the sand filling tended to run out! Therefore, those bags had to be kept constantly wet, and somebody had to do it. Enemies sneeringly remarked that Fort Gunnybags consumed much more water without than within; but this joke lost its point when it became known that the committee, decades in advance of its period, had prohibited alcohol absolutely!

Realizing from the two lamentable fiascos just recounted that little could be accomplished by private initiative, the upholders of the law turned their attention to Sacramento. Here they had every reason to hope for success. No matter how well organized the Vigilantes might be, or how thoroughly they carried the sympathies of the local public, there could be no doubt that they were acting in defiance of the law, were, in fact, no better than rebels. It was not only within the power, it was the duty of the governor of the State to declare the city in a condition of insurrection.

This being accomplished, it followed logically that the State troops must put down the insurrection; and if they failed, there was still the immense power of the republic to call upon. After all, when you look at it that way, this handful of disturbers amounted to very little.

The first step was to win over the governor. Without him the next step could not be taken. Accordingly all the big guns of San Francisco took the *Senator* for Sacramento. There they met Terry, Volney Howard, and others of the same ilk. No governor of Johnson's sort could long withstand such pressure. He promised to issue the proclamation of insurrection as soon as it was "legally proved" that the committee had acted outside the law. The mere fact that it had already hanged two men and deported a great number of others meant nothing.

That, apparently, was not legal proof.

In order that all things should be legal, then, Terry issued a writ of *habeas corpus* for the body of one William Mulligan, and gave it into the hands of Deputy-sheriff Harrison for service on the committee. Nobody expected the latter to deliver over Mulligan.

"But they'll deny the writ," said Terry, "and that will constitute a legal defiance of the State. The governor will then be legally justified in issuing his proclamation, and ordering out the State troops to enforce the writ."

If the State troops proved inadequate, the plan was then to call on the United States—as locally represented by General Wool and Captain David Farragut—for assistance. With this armed backing three times the Vigilante force could be quickly subdued. As it was all legal, it could not fail.

Harrison took the writ of *habeas corpus* and proceeded to San Francisco. He presented himself at headquarters, produced his writ, and had himself announced to the Executive Committee then in session.

"Tell him to go to hell!" growled someone.

But a half-dozen members saw through the ruse, and interposed vigorous objections.

"I move," said Dempster solemnly, "that our police be permitted to remove all prisoners for a few hours."

This was carried, and put into immediate effect. Deputy Harrison was then politely received, his writ fully acknowledged, and he was allowed to search the premises. Of course he found nothing, and departed much crestfallen. The scheme had failed. The committee had in no way denied his authority or his writ. Harrison was no fool. He saw clearly what he had been expected to do. On his way back to Sacramento he did some thinking. To Terry he unblushingly returned the writ endorsed: "Prevented from service by armed men." For the sake of the cause Harrison had lied!

Johnson immediately issued his proclamation. The leaders turned with confidence to the Federal authorities for assistance. To their blank dismay General Wool refused to furnish arms. His position was that he had no authority to do so without orders from Washington. The sympathies of this doughty old soldier were not with this attempt. Colonel Baker and Volney Howard waited on him, and after considerable conversation made the mistake of threatening to report him to Washington for refusing to uphold the law.

"I think, gentlemen," flashed back the veteran, "I know my duty, and in its performance dread no responsibility."

So saying he bowed them from the room. Farragut equally could not clearly see why he should train the guns of his ship on the city. With this fiasco the opposition for the moment died. The Executive Committee went on patiently working down through its black list. It announced that after June 24th no new cases would be taken, A few days later it proclaimed an "adjournment parade" on July 5th. It considered its work done. The city had become safe.

LXVII

But this peaceful outcome did not suit the aristocratic wing of the Law and Order party in the least. The haughty, supremely individualistic, bold, forceful, often charming coterie of fire-eaters had, in their opinion, been insulted, and they wanted reprisal, punishment, blood. Terry, Baker, Bennett, Miles, Webb, Nugent, Blatchford, Rowlee, Caldwell, Broderick, Ware, Volney Howard, Black—to mention only a few—chafed intolerably. Such men were accustomed to have their own way, to cherish an ultra-sensitive "honour," to be looked up to; had come to consider themselves as especially privileged, to look upon themselves as direct representatives of the only proper government and administration of law. This revolt of the "lower classes," the "smug, psalm-singing Yankees," the "shopkeepers," was intolerable impudence. Because of a series of accidents, proper resentment of such impudence, due punishment of such denial of the law had been postponed. It was not, therefore, abrogated.

When, therefore, the committee announced July 5th as a definite date for disbanding, the lawful authorities and their upholders, blinded by their passions, were distinctly disappointed. Where the common citizen perceived only the welcome end of a necessary job well done, they saw slipping away the last chance for a clash of arms that should teach these rebels their place. It was all very well to talk of arresting the ringleaders and bringing them to justice. In the present lamentable demoralization of the courts it might not work; and even if it did work, the punishment of ringleaders was small satisfaction as compared to triumphant vindication in pitched battle.

Sherman had resigned command of the military in disgust when he found that General Wool and Captain Farragut had no intention of supplying him Federal arms, thus closing—save for later inaccurate writing in his "Memoirs"—an unfortunate phase of his career. In his stead had been chosen General Volney Howard. Howard was a rather fat, very pompous, wholly conceited bombastes furioso with apparently remarkable lack of judgment or grasp of a situation. In the committee's action looking toward adjournment he actually thought he saw a sign of weakening!

"Now is the moment for us to show our power!" he said.

In this he gained the zealous support of Judge Terry and Major Marmaduke Miles, two others with more zeal than discretion. These three managed to persuade Governor Johnson to order a parade of State troops in the streets of San Francisco. Their argument was that such a parade—of legally organized forces—would overawe the citizens; their secret hope, however, was that such a show would provoke the desired conflict. This hope they shared with Howard, after the governor's order had been obtained. Howard's vanity and inclinations jumped together. He consented. Altogether, it was a very pretty little plot.

By now the Law and Order forces had become numerically formidable. The bobtail and rag-tag, ejected either by force or by fright, flocked to the colours. A certain proportion of the militia remained in the ranks, though a majority had resigned. A large contingent of reckless, wild young men, without a care or a tie in the world, with no interest in the rights of the case, or, indeed, in themselves, avid only for adventure, offered themselves as soon as the prospects for a real fight became good. And there were always the five hundred discomfited Texans.

Stewart Edward White

Nor were arms now lacking. Contrary to all expectation, the committee had scrupulously refrained from meddling with the State armouries. All militia muskets were available. In addition the State had now the right to a certain quota of Federal arms, stored in the arsenal at Benicia. These could be requisitioned.

At this point in the planning weasly little Jimmy Ware had a bright idea.

"Look here!" he cried, "how many of those Benicia muskets are there?"

"About a hundred and fifty stand, sir," Howard told him.

"Now they can't help us a whole lot," propounded Ware. "They are too few. But why can't we use them for bait, to get those people on the wrong side of the fence?"

"What do you mean?" asked Terry, who knew Ware intimately.

"Suppose they are shipped from Benicia to the armouries in the city; they are legally Federal property until they are delivered, aren't they?"

"Certainly."

"Well, if the Stranglers should happen to seize them while they're still Federal property, they've committed a definite offence against the United States, haven't they?"

"What do we care about that now?" asked Major Marmaduke Miles, to whom this seemed irrelevant.

But Judge Terry's legal mind was struck with the beauty and simplicity of this ruse.

"Hold on!" he cried. "If we ship them in a boat, the seizure will be piracy. If they intercept those arms, they're pirates, and we can legally call on the Federal forces—*and they'll be compelled to respond, egad!*"

"They're pretty smart; suppose they smell a rat?" asked Miles doubtfully.

"Then we'll have the muskets where we want them, anyway. It's worth trying," replied Ware.

"I know just the man," put in Terry. "I'll send for him."

Shortly appeared a saturnine, lank, bibulous individual known as Rube Maloney. To him Terry explained. He was to charter a sloop, take the muskets aboard—and get caught.

"No resistance, mind you!" warned Terry.

"Trust me for that," grinned Rube. "I ain't anxious for no punctured skin, nor yit a stretched neck."

"Pick your men carefully."

"I'll take Jack Phillips and Jim McNab," said Rube, after a moment's thought, "and possibly a few refreshments?" he suggested.

Terry reached into his pocket.

"Certainly, certainly," said he. "Treat yourself well."

There remained only to see that the accurate details should get to the Committee of Vigilance, but in such a manner as to avoid suspicion that the information had been "planted."

"Is there anybody we can trust on their rolls?" asked Terry.

But it was reluctantly conceded that the Vigilantes had pretty well cleaned out the doubtful ones. Here again, the resourceful Jimmy Ware came to the rescue.

"I know your man—Morrell. He'll get it to them. As far as anybody knows, he hasn't taken sides at all."

"Will you see him?" asked Terry.

"I'll see him," promised Jimmy Ware.

LXVIII

By this time the Vigilante organization had pretty well
succeeded in eliminating the few Law and Order sympathizers
who had been bold enough to attempt to play the part of spy
by signing the rolls. These had not been many, and their
warning had been sufficient. But Morrell had, in a measure,
escaped distrust even if he had not gained confidence. He had
had the sense not to join the organization; and his attitude of
the slightly supercilious, veiledly contemptuous Britisher,
scorning all things about him, was sufficient guarantee of his
neutrality. This breed was then very common. He left his
conference with Jimmy Ware thoroughly instructed, quite
acquiescent, but revolving matters in his own mind to see if
somehow he could not turn them to his advantage. For
Morrell was, as always, in need of money. In addition, he had
a personal score to settle with Keith for, although he had
apparently forgotten their last interview regarding "loans," the
memory rankled. And Morrell had not forgotten that before all
this Vigilante business broke he had been made a good offer by
Cora's counsel to get Keith out of the way. Cora was now very
dead, to be sure; but on sounding Jimmy Ware, Morrell
learned that Keith's removal would still be pleasant to the
powers that pay.

If he could work these things all in together—Cogitating
absorbedly, he glanced up to see Ben Sansome sauntering
down the street, his malacca cane at the proper angle, his
cylindrical hat resting lightly on his sleek locks, his whole
person spick with the indescribably complete appointment of

Stewart Edward White

the dandy. Sansome was mixed up with the Keiths—perhaps he could be used—On impulse Morrell hailed him genially, and invited him to take a drink. The exquisite brightened, and perceptibly hastened his step. Morrell's rather ultra-Anglicism always fascinated him. They turned in at the El Dorado, and there seated themselves at the most remote of the small tables.

"Well," said Morrell cheerfully, after preliminary small talk had been disposed of, "how goes the fair Nancy?"

Sansome's effeminately handsome face darkened. Things had in reality gone very badly with the fair Nancy. Her revulsion against Sansome at the time of the capture of the jail had been complete; and as is the case with real revulsions, she had not attempted to conceal it. Sansome's careful structure, which had gained so lofty an elevation, had collapsed like the proverbial house of cards. His vanity had been cruelly rasped. And what had been more or less merely a dilettante's attraction had been thereby changed into a thwarted passion.

"Damn the fair Nancy!" he cried, in answer to Morrell's question.

Morrell's eyes narrowed, and he motioned quietly to the waiting black to replenish the glasses.

"With all my heart, damn her!" said he. "I agree with you; she's a snippy, cold little piece. Not my style at all. Not worth the serious attention of a man like yourself. Who is it now, you sly dog?"

Sansome sipped at his drink; sighed sentimentally.

"Cold—yes—but if the right man could awaken her—" he murmured.

"Look here, Sansome, do you want that woman?"

Sansome looked at his companion haughtily; his eye fell; he

drew circles with the bottom of his glass.

"By gad!" he cried with a sudden queer burst of fire; "I've got to have her!"

And then he turned slowly red, actually started to wriggle, concealed his embarrassment under cover of his cigar.

"H'm," observed Morrell speculatively, without looking across at Sansome. "Tell me, Ben, does she still care for her husband?"

"No; that I'll swear!" replied Sansome eagerly.

"If you're sure of that one essential little fact, and you really want her, why don't you take her?"

"Damn it, ain't I telling you? She won't see me."

"Tell me about it," urged Morrell, settling back, and again motioning for fresh drinks.

Sansome, whose soul was ripe for sympathy, needed little more urging. He poured out his tale, sometimes rushingly and passionately, again, as his submerged but still conventional self-consciousness straggled to the surface, with shamefaced bravado. "By Gad!" he finished. "You know, I feel like a raw schoolboy, talkin' like this!"

Morrell leaned forward, his reserve of manner laid aside, his whole being radiating sympathetic charm.

"My dear chap, don't," he begged, laying his hand on Sansome's forearm. "A genuine passion is the most glorious thing on earth even in callow youth! But when we old men of the world—" The pause was eloquent. "She's a headstrong filly," he went on in a more matter-of-fact tone, after a moment, " takes a bit of handling. You'll pardon me, old chap, if I suggest that you've gone about things a bit wrong."

"How is that?" asked Sansome. Under the influence of drinks, confession, and sympathy, he was in a glow of fellow-feeling.

"Believe me, I know women and horses! You've ridden this one too much on the snaffle. Try the curb. That high-spirited sort takes a bit of handling. They like to feel themselves dominated. You've been too gentle, too refined. She's gentle and refined for two. What she wants is the brute— 'Rape of the Sabines' principle. Savage her a bit, and she'll come to heel like a dog. Not at once, perhaps. Give her a week."

"That's all very well," objected Sansome, whose eyes were shining, "but how about that week? She'll run to that beast of a husband with her story—"

"And be sorry for it afterward—"

"Too late."

Morrell appeared to think.

"There's something in that. But suppose we arranged to get the husband out of the way, where she couldn't run to him at once—" he suggested.

They had more drinks. At first Morrell was only sardonically amused; but as his imagination got to working and the creative power awoke, his interest became more genuine. It was all too wildly improbable for words—and yet, was anything improbable in this impossible place? At least it was amusing, the whole thing was amusing—this super-refined exquisite awakened, to an emotion so genuine that what judgment he had was now obscured by the eagerness of his passion; the situation apparently so easily malleable; the beautiful safety of it all for himself. And it did not really matter if the whole fantastic plot failed!

"I tell you, no," he broke his thoughts to reply to some ill-considered suggestion, "The good old simple methods are the best—they're all laid out for us by the Drury Lane melodramas. You leave it to me to get rid of him. Then we'll send the usual message to her that he is lying wounded somewhere—say at Jake's road house—"

"Won't that get her to thinking too much of him?" interrupted Sansome anxiously.

Morrell, momentarily taken aback, gained time for a reply by pouring Sansome another drink, "He's more sense left than I thought," he said to himself; and aloud: "All you want is to get her out to Jake's. She'll go simply as a matter of wifely duty, and all that. Don't worry. Once she's there, it's your affair; and unless I mistake my man, I believe you'll know how to manage the situation"—he winked slyly—"she's really mad about you, but, like most women, she's hemmed in by convention. Boldly break through the convention, and she'll come around."

Sansome was plainly fascinated by the idea, but in a trepidation of doubt, nevertheless.

"But suppose she doesn't come around?" he objected vaguely.

Morrell threw aside his cigarette and arose with an air of decision.

"I thought you were so crazy mad about her?" he said in tones that cut. "What are you wasting my time for?"

"No, no! Hold on!" cried Sansome, at once all fire again. "I'll do it—hold on!"

"As a matter of fact," observed Morrell, reseating himself, and speaking as though there had been no interruption, "I imagine you have little to fear from that."

He went into the street a little later, his vision somewhat blurred, but his mind clear. Sansome, by now very pot-valiant, swaggered alongside.

"By the way, Ben," said Morrell suddenly, "I hope you go armed—these are bad times."

"I have always carried a derringer—and I can use it, too!" boasted Sansome, swinging his cane.

Morrell, left alone, stood on the corner for some time diligently engaged in getting control of himself. He laughed a little.

"Regular bally melodrama, conspiracy and all, right off the blood-and- thunder stage," said he. "Wonder if it works in real life? We'll see."

After his head had cleared, he set to work methodically to find Keith, but when he finally met that individual it was most casually. Morrell was apparently in a hurry, but as he saw Keith he appeared to hesitate, then, making up his mind, he approached the young lawyer.

"Look here, Keith, a word with you," he said. "I have stumbled on some information which may be important. I was on my way to the committee with it, but I'm in a hurry. The governor is shipping arms into the city to- morrow night from Benicia, by a small sloop."

"Are you sure of this?" asked Keith.

"Certain."

"Where did you get the information?"

"That I cannot tell you."

Keith still hesitated; Morrell turned on his heel.

"Well, I've told you. You can do as you please, but you'd better let the committee decide whether to take the tip or not."

He walked away without once looking back, certain that Keith would end by reporting the information,

"Chances are he'll go with the capturing party," ran the trend of his thoughts, "and so he'll be out of reach of this little abduction. But I don't care much. If he follows them out to Jake's by any chance, Sansome will shoot him—or he'll shoot Sansome. Doesn't matter which. Shootin's none too healthy these days *for either side!* Oh, Lord, most amusin'!"

He thought a while, then turned up the hill toward his own house. A new refinement of the plot had occurred to the artist's soul too much drink had released in him.

Mrs. Morrell was vastly surprised to see him. She was clad in a formless pink silk wrapper, was reclining on a sofa, and was settling down to relaxation of mind and body by means of French novels and cigarettes,

"Well, what are you doing here at this time of day?" was her greeting.

"Came to bask in the light of your smiles, my dear," he replied with elephantine irony.

"Nonsense!" she rejoined sharply, "You've been drinking again!"

"To be sure; but not enough to hurt." His manner suddenly became businesslike, "Look here," he asked her, "are you game to make a tidy bit of money?"

"Always!" she replied promptly, also becoming businesslike.

He explained in detail. She listened in silence at first with a slight smile of contempt on her lips. As he progressed, however, the smile faded.

"Where do I come in?" she asked finally.

"You must be there when the message comes to her. She might not go out to Jake's alone—probably wouldn't. I don't know her well enough to judge. Hurry her into it."

"I see." She laughed suddenly. "Lord, she'll be surprised when I call on her! Take some doing, that!" She thought a few moments. "My appearance will connect us with it. Won't do."

"If the thing goes through we won't be here," he pointed out. "If it doesn't go through all right, we'll arrange a little comedy. Have you bound and gagged—before her eyes—or something like that."

"Thanks," she replied to this.

Morrell was not entirely open. He did not tell her that money or no money, plot or no plot, he had resolved to flee the city, at least for a time. Investigations were getting too close to some of his past activities. He did not offer in words what he nevertheless knew to be the most potent of his arguments— namely, the implacable hate Mrs. Morrell bore Keith. Morrell's knowledge of this hate was accurate, though his analysis of its cause was faulty. He thought his wife to be Keith's discarded mistress, and did not greatly care. Nor did he mention the possibility which, however, Mrs. Morrell now voiced.

"Suppose Keith follows them out to Jake's?" she suggested.

"One of them will kill, and the Stranglers will hang the other," he said briefly.

She looked up.

"I don't care for that!"

"In that event, you will not be present. Your job will be to duck out." He paused, then went on slowly: "Would you grieve at the demise of either—or all three?"

Her face hardened.

"But," he went on slowly, "the chances of it are very remote. If there is any killing, it will come later. Keith will be kept out of the way."

"And after?"

"You hint of an assignation. I will arrange for witnesses."

"Where does the money come in?" she demanded. Morrell floundered for a moment. He had lost sight of the money.

"It comes from certain parties who want Keith put out of the way," he said.

"And suppose Keith is not put out of the way?" she began, her facile mind pouncing on the weakness of this statement. "Never mind," she interrupted herself. "I'll do it!" Her face had hardened again, "Can you depend on Sansome to go through with it?"

"Only if he's fairly drunk."

"Yes?"

"I'll attend to that. That is my job. You may not see me tomorrow; but go in the evening to call on her."

"It looks absolutely preposterous," she said at last, "but it may work. And, if any part of it works, that'll be enough."

"Yes," said he.

They had both forgotten the money.

LXIX

As Morrell had surmised, Keith decided to pass on the news for what it was worth. The committee believed it, and was filled with consternation at the incredible folly of the projected show of armed force.

"This is not peace, but war," said Coleman, "which we are trying to avert!"

The Executive Committee went into immediate session. It was now evident that the disbanding would have to be indefinitely postponed. An extraordinary program to meet the emergency was discussed piecemeal. One of its details had to do with the shipment of arms from Benicia. The committee here fell neatly into the trap prepared for it. In all probability no one clearly realized the legal status of the muskets, but all supposed them already to belong to the State that was threatening to use them. Charles Doane, instructed to take the steps necessary to their capture, called to him the chief of the harbour police.

"Have you a small vessel ready for immediate service?" he asked this man.

"Yes, a sloop, at the foot of this street."

"Be ready to sail in half an hour."

Doane then turned the job over to a trustworthy, quick-witted man named John Durkee. The latter selected twelve to assist him, among whom was Keith, at the latter's especial request. Morrell, loitering near, saw this band depart for the water front, and followed them far enough to watch them embark, to witness the hoisting of the sloop's sails, and to see the craft heel to the evening breeze and slip away around the point. All things were going well. The committee suspected nothing of the plot to fasten the crime of piracy on it; Keith was out of the way. Morrell turned on his heel and walked rapidly to his rendezvous with Sansome.

Durkee and his sloop beat for some hours against wind and tide; but finally, so strong were both, he was forced to anchor in San Pablo Bay until conditions had somewhat modified. Finally, he was able to get under way again, A number of craft were sailing about, and one by one these were overhauled, commanded to lay to, and boarded in true piratical style. It was fun for everybody. The breeze blew in strongly from the Golden Gate, the waves chopped and danced merrily, the little sloop dipped her rail and flew along at a speed that justified her reputation as a racer, gulls followed curiously. But there were no practical results. Every sailing craft they overhauled proved innocent, and either indignant or sarcastic. The sun dipped, and the short twilight of this latitude was almost immediately succeeded by a brilliant night. Slowly the breeze died, until the little sloop could just crawl along. It grew chilly, and there was no food aboard. A less persistent man than John Durkee would have felt justified in giving it up and heading for home; but John had been instructed to cruise until he captured the arms; and he profanely announced his intention of so doing.

In this he was more faithful to his superiors than the notorious Rube Maloney to his employers. It was to the interest of the Law and Order party that Rube and his precious crew should be promptly and easily captured. They had been instructed to carry boldly and flagrantly, in full daylight, down the middle of the bay. But Terry's permission, to lay in "refreshments" at cost of the conspirators had been liberally interpreted. By six o'clock Rube had just sense enough left to drop anchor off

Pueblo Point. There the three jolly mariners proceeded to celebrate; and there they would probably have lain undiscovered had less of a bulldog than Durkee been sent after them.

As it was, midnight had passed before Durkee's keen eyes caught the loom of some object in the black mist close under the point. Quietly he eased off the sheet and bore down on it. As soon as he ascertained definitely that the object was indeed a boat, he ran alongside. The twelve men boarded with a rush: they found themselves in possession of an empty deck. From the hatch came the reek of alcohol and the sound of hearty snoring. The capture was made.

In a half hour the transfer of the muskets and the three prisoners was accomplished. The latter offered no resistance, but seemed cross at being awakened. Leaving the vessel anchored off the point, the little sloop stood away again for San Francisco, reaching the California Street wharf shortly after daylight. Here she was moored, and one of the crew was dispatched to the committee for further instructions and grub. He returned after an hour, but was preceded somewhat by the grub.

"They say to deliver the muskets at headquarters," he reported, "but to turn the prisoners loose."

"Turn them loose!" cried Durkee, astonished.

"That's what they said," repeated the messenger. "And here's written orders," and he displayed a paper signed by the well-known "33, Secretary," and bearing the Vigilante seal of the open eye.

"All right," acquiesced Durkee. "Now, you mangy hounds, you've got just about twenty-eight seconds to make yourselves as scarce as your virtues. Scat!"

Rube and his two companions had several of the twenty-eight

seconds to spare; but once they had lost sight of their captors, they moderated their pace. They had been much depressed, but now they cheered up and swaggered. A few drinks restored them to normal, and they were able to put a good face on the report they now made to their employers, all of whom, including Terry, had gathered thus early to receive them. After all, things had gone well: they had been actually captured, which was the essential thing, and it did not seem necessary to go into extraneous details.

"Good!" cried Terry, who had come down from Sacramento personally to superintend the working out of this latest ruse.

He was illegally absent from his court, meddling illegally with matters not in his jurisdiction. "Now we must get a warrant for piracy into the hands of the United States Marshal. Send him alone, with no deputies. When he makes his deposition of resistance, then we shall see!"

The marshal found Durkee still at the wharf, seated on an upturned cask.

"I have this warrant for your arrest!" he proclaimed in a voice purposely loud.

"Yes? Let's see it," rejoined Durkee, lazily reaching out his hand.

He read the document through leisurely. His features betrayed no hint of his thoughts, but nevertheless his brain was very active. He read that he was accused of piracy against the might and majesty of the United States Government; and as his eyes slowly followed the involved and redundant legal phraseology, he reviewed the situation. The nature, of the trap became to him, partly evident. There was no doubt that technically he was a pirate, if these arms—as it seemed—belonged to the Government and not to the State. The punishment of piracy was death. Without appreciation of the fact, the committee had made him liable to the death penalty. And he had no doubt that the Federal Courts of California, as then constituted, would visit that penalty on him. He raised his head and looked about him. Within call were lounging a dozen resolute men belonging to the Committee of Vigilance. He had but to raise his voice to bring them to his assistance. Once inside Fort Gunnybags he knew that the committee would stand behind him to the last man.

But John Durkee had imagination as well as bulldog persistency. His mind flashed ahead into the future, envisaging the remoter consequences. He saw the majesty of the law's forces invoked to back this warrant which the tremendous power of the disciplined Vigilantes would repulse; he saw reinforcements, summoned. What reinforce-ments? A smile flitted across his lips, and he glanced up at the warship *John Adams* riding at anchor outside, her guns, their tampons in place, staring blackly at the city. He saw the whole plot.

"That's all right," he told the waiting marshal, folding the warrant and returning it to him. "Put your paper in your pocket. I'll go with you."

By this quietly courageous and intelligent deed John Durkee completely frustrated the fourth and most dangerous effort of the Law and Order party. There was no legal excuse for calling on Federal forces to take one man—who peaceably surrendered!

Undoubtedly, had not matters taken the decided and critical turn soon to be detailed, Durkee would have been immediately brought to trial, and perhaps executed. As it was, even the most rabid of the Law and Order party agreed it was inexpedient to press matters. The case was postponed again and again, and did not come to trial until several months, by which time the Vigilantes had practically finished their work. The law finally saved its face by charging the jury that "if they believed the prisoners took the arms with the intention of appropriating them to their own use and permanently depriving the owner of them, then they were guilty. But if they took them only for the purpose of preventing their being used against themselves and their associates, then they were not guilty." Under which hair-splitting and convenient interpretation the "pirates" went free, and everybody was satisfied!

Stewart Edward White

LXX

After leaving the office where they had made their report to their employers, Rube Maloney and his two friends visited all the saloons. There they found sympathetic and admiring audiences. They reviled the committee collectively and singly; bragged that they would shoot Coleman, Truett, Durkee, and some others at sight; flourished weapons, and otherwise became so publicly and noisily obstreperous that the committee decided they needed a lesson. Accordingly they instructed Sterling Hopkins, with four others, to rearrest the lot and bring them in. Hopkins was a bulldog, pertinacious, rough, a faithful creature.

News of these orders ran ahead of their performance. Rube and his satellites dropped everything and fled to their masters like threatened dogs. Their masters, who included Terry, Bowie, Major Marmaduke Miles, and a few others, happened to be discussing the situation in the office of Richard Ashe, a Texan, and an active member of "the chivalry." The three redoubtables burst in on this gathering, wild-eyed, scared, with, the statement that a thousand stranglers were at their heels.

"Better hide 'em," suggested Bowie.

But hot-headed Terry, seconded by equally hot-headed Ashe, would have none of this.

"By gad, let them try it!" cried the judge. "I've been aching for this chance!"

Therefore when Hopkins, having left his small *posse* at the foot of the stairs, knocked and entered, he was faced by the muzzles of half a dozen pistols, and profanely told to get out of there. He was no fool, so he obeyed. If Terry had possessed the sense of a rooster, or a single quality of leadership, he would have seen that this was not the moment to precipitate a crisis. The forces of his own party were neither armed nor ready. But here, as in all other important actions of his career, he was governed by the haughty and headstrong passions of the moment—as when later he justified himself in attempting to shoot down an old and unarmed man. Hopkins left his men at the foot of the stairs, borrowed a horse from Dr. Beverly Cole, who was passing, and galloped to headquarters. There he was instructed to return, to keep watch, that reinforcements would follow. He arrived at the building in which Ashe's office was located, in time to see Maloney, Terry, Ashe, McNabb, Bowie, and Rowe all armed with shotguns, just turning the far corner. He dismounted and called on his men to follow. The little *posse* dogged the judge's party for some distance. For a time no attention was paid to them, but as they pressed closer Terry, Ashe, and Maloney whirled and presented their shotguns. The movement was probably intended only as a threat; but Hopkins, always bold to the point of rashness, made a sudden rush at Maloney. Judge Terry thrust his gun at the Vigilante officer who seized it by the barrel. At the same instant Ashe pressed the muzzle of his weapon against one Bovee's breast, but hesitated to pull the trigger. It was getting to be unhealthy to shoot men in the open street.

"Are you a friend?" he faltered.

"Yes," replied Bovee, and by a rapid motion struck the barrel aside.

Another of the Vigilantes named Barry covered Rowe with a pistol. Rowe's "chivalry" oozed. He dropped his gun and fled toward the armoury. The others struggled for possession of weapons, but nobody fired. Suddenly Terry whipped out a knife and plunged it into Hopkins's neck. Hopkins relaxed his hold on Terry's shotgun and staggered back.

"I am stabbed! Take them, Vigilantes!" he cried.

He sank to the pavement. Terry and his friends dropped everything and ran toward the armoury. Of the Vigilante *posse* only Bovee and Barry remained, but these two pursued the fleeing Law and Order men to the very portals of the armoury itself. When the door was slammed in their faces, they took up their stand outside, they two holding within several hundred men! At the end of ten minutes a pompous, portly individual came up under full sail, cast a detached and haughty glance at the two quiet men lounging unwarrantedly in his path, and attempted to pass inside.

"You cannot enter here," said Bovee grimly, as they barred his way.

The pompous man turned purple.

"Do you know who I am?" he demanded.

"I don't give a damn who you are," replied Bovee, still quietly.

"I am Major-General Volney E. Howard!"

"You cannot enter here," repeated Bovee, and this time he said it in a tone of voice that sent the major-general scurrying away.

After a short interval another man dashed up very much in a hurry. Mistaking Bovee and Barry for sentinels, he cried as he ran up:

"I am a lieutenant in Calhoun Bennett's company, and I have been sent here to—"

"I am a member of the Committee of Vigilance," interrupted

Barry, "and you cannot enter."

"What!" cried the officer, in astonishment. "Have the Vigilance Committee possession of this building?"

"They have," was the reply of the dauntless two.

The lieutenant rolled up his eyes and darted away faster than he had come. A few moments later, doubtless to the vast relief of the "outside garrison" of the armoury within which five or six hundred men were held close by this magnificent bluff, the great Vigilante bell boomed out: *one, two, three*, rest; then *one, two, three*, rest; and repeat.

Immediately the streets were alive with men. Merchants left their customers, clerks their books, mechanics their tools. Dray-men stripped their horses of harness, abandoned their wagons where they stood, and rode away to their cavalry. Clancey Dempster's office was only four blocks from headquarters. At the first stroke of the bell he leaped from his desk, ran down the stairs, and jumped into his buggy. Yet he could drive only three of the four blocks, so dense already was the crowd. He abandoned his rig in the middle of the street and forced his way through afoot. Two days later he recovered his rig. In the building he found the companies, silently, without confusion, falling into line.

"All right!" he called encouragingly. "Keep cool! Take your time about it!"

"Ah, Mr. Dempster," they replied, "we've waited long! This is the clean sweep!"

James Olney was lying in bed with a badly sprained ankle when the alarm bell began to toll. He commandeered one boot from a fellow-boarder with extremely large feet, and hobbled to the street. There he seized by force of arms the passing delivery wagon of a kerosene dealer, climbed to the seat, and lashed the astonished horse to a run. San Francisco streets ran to chuck holes and ruts in those days, and the vehicle lurched and banged with a grand rattle and scatteration of tins and measures. The terrified driver at last mustered courage to protest.

"You are spilling my kerosene!" he wailed.

"Damn your kerosene, sir!" bellowed the general; then relenting: "I will pay you for your kerosene!"

Up to headquarters he sailed full tilt, and how he got through the crowd without committing manslaughter no one tells. There he was greeted by wild cheering, and was at once lifted bodily to the back of a white horse, the conspicuous colour of which made it an excellent rallying point.

Within an incredibly brief space of time they were off for the armoury; the military companies marching like veterans; the artillery rumbling over the rude pavements; the cavalry jogging along to cover the rear. A huge roaring mob accompanied them, followed them, raced up the parallel streets to arrive before the armoury at the same moment as the first files.

The armoury square was found to be deserted except for the intrepid Barry and Bovee, who still marched back and forth before the closed door. No one had entered or left the building.

Inside the armoury the first spirit of bravado and fight-to-the-last-ditch had died to a sullen stubbornness. Nobody had much, to say. Terry was very contrite as well he might be. A judge of the Supreme Court, who had no business being in San Francisco at all, sworn to uphold the law, had stepped out from his jurisdiction to commit as lawless and idiotic a deed of passion as could have been imagined! Whatever chances the Law and Order party might have had, could they have mobilized their forces, were dissipated. Their troops were scattered in small units; their rank and file were heaven knew where; their enemies, fully organized, had been mustered by the alarm bell to full alertness and compactness. And Terry's was the hand that had struck that bell! For the only time in his recorded history David Terry's ungoverned spirit was humbled. Until he found that nothing immediate was going to happen to him, and while under the silent but scathing disapprobation of his companions, he actually talked of resigning! Parenthetically, the fit did not last long, and he soon reared, his haughty crest as high as ever. But now, listening to the roar of the mob outside, peeping at the grim thousands of armed men deploying before the armoury, he regretted his deed.

"This is very unfortunate; very unfortunate!" he said, "But you shall not imperil your lives for me. It is I they want. I will surrender to them."

Instead of the prompt expostulation he expected, a dead silence greeted these words.

"There is nothing else to do," agreed Ashe at last.

An officer was sent to negotiate.

"We will deliver up the armoury if you will agree not to give us over to the mob," he told the committee.

"We hold, and intend to hold, the mob under absolute control. We have nothing in common with mobs," was Coleman's reply.

The doors were then thrown open, and a company of the Vigilante troops marched in. Within ten minutes, the streets were cleared. The six hundred prisoners, surrounded by a solid body of infantry with cavalry on the flanks, were marched to headquarters. The city was jubilant. This, at last, was the clean sweep! Men went about with shining faces, slapping each other on the back. And Coleman, the wise general, realizing that compromises were useless, peace impossible, came to a decision. Shortly from headquarters the entire Vigilante forces moved in four divisions toward the cardinal points of the compass. From them small squads were from time to time detached and sent out to right or left. The main divisions surrounded the remaining four big armouries; the smaller squads combed the city house by house for arms. In the early morning the armouries capitulated. By sun-up every weapon in the city had been taken to Fort Gunnybags.

LXXI

Up to this time Nan Keith had undergone the experience of nine out of ten married women in early California: that is, she had been neglected. Neglect in some form or other was the common lot of the legally attached feminine. How could it logically be otherwise? In the turbulent, varied, restless, intensely interesting, deeply exciting life of the pioneer city only a poor-spirited, bloodless, nerveless man would have thought to settle down to domesticity. A quiet evening at home stands small chance, even in an old-established community, against a dog fight on the corner or a fire in the next block; and here were men fights instead, and a great, splendid, conflagration of desires, appetites, and passions, a grand clash of interests and wills that burned out men's lives in the space of a few years. It was a restless time, full of neglected women. This neglect varied in degree to be sure. Nan was lucky there. No other woman had thrust her way in, no other attraction lured Keith from her, as had happened to so many others. She possessed all his interest. But at present that interest seemed so attenuated, so remote!

After her revulsion of feeing the afternoon the Vigilantes first rose in their might, she withdrew within her pride. Nan was no meek and humble spirit. But the scales had dropped from her eyes as to affairs about her. San Francisco suddenly became something besides a crude collection of buildings. For the first time she saw it as a living entity, strong in the throes of growth. She devoured eagerly all the newspapers, collected avidly all the rumours. Whenever possible, she discussed the state of affairs; but this was difficult, for nearly every one was strongly partisan for one side or another, and incapable of anything but excitement and vituperation. The Sherwoods were a great comfort to her here. While approving of the new movement, they nevertheless refused to become heated, and retained a spirit of humour. Sherwood was not a member of the Committee of Vigilance, but he had subscribed heavily—and openly—to its funds; he had assisted it with his counsels; and it was hinted that, sub-rosa, he had taken part in some of the more obscure but dangerous operations.

"I am an elderly, peace-loving, respectable citizen," he told Nan, "and I stand unequivocally for law and order and for justice, for the orderly doing of things; and against violence, mob spirit, and high-handedness."

"Why, John Sherwood!" cried Nan, up in arms at once. "I'd never have believed you could be on the side of Judge Terry and that stripe."

"Oho!" cried Sherwood, delighted to have drawn her. "Now we have it! But what made you think I was on that side?"

"Why—didn't you just say—"

"Oh," said Sherwood comfortably, "I was using real meanings, not just word tags. In my opinion real law and order, orderly doing of things, *et cetera*, are all on the other side."

"And the men—" cried Nan, aglow.

"The men are of course all noble, self-sacrificing, patriotic, immaculate demigods who—" He broke off, chuckling at Nan's expression. "No, seriously, I think they are doing a fine work, and that they'll go down in history."

"You're an old dear!" cried Nan, impulsively kissing his cheek. "Take care," he warned, "you're endangering my glasses and making my wife jealous."

Nan drew back, a little ashamed at having shown her feelings; and rather astonished herself at their intensity.

In the course of these conversations the pendulum with her began again to quiver at the descent. Through the calmly philosophical eye of the ex- gambler, John Sherwood, she partly envisaged the significance of what was happening—the struggling forth of real government from the sham. Her own troubles grew small by comparison. She began to feel nearer Keith in spirit than for some time past, to understand him better, even—though this was difficult—to get occasionally a glimpse of his relations toward herself. It was all very inchoate, instinctive, unformed; rather an instinct than a clear view. She became restless; for she had no outlet either for her own excitement or the communicated excitement of the times. It was difficult to wait, and yet wait she must. For what? She did not know!

On the crucial June evening she sat by the lamp trying in vain to concentrate her attention on a book. The sound of the door bell made her jump. She heard Wing Sam's shuffle, and his cheerful greeting which all her training had been unable to eliminate. Wing Sam always met every caller with a smiling "Hello!" A moment later she arose in some surprise as Mrs. Morrell entered the room.

Relations between the women had never been broken off, though the pretence of ordinary cordiality had long since been dropped. When Mrs. Morrell found it expedient to make this call, she spent several hours trying to invent a plausible excuse. She was unable to do so. Finally she gave it up in angry despair.

"As long as it is not too bald, what difference does it make?" she said to herself cynically.

And out of this desperation, and by no means from cleverness, she hit on the cleverest thing possible. Instead of coming to make a friendly call, she pretended to be on an errand of protest.

"It's about your dog," she told Nan, "he's a dear good dog, and a great friend of ours. But cannot you shut him up nights? He's inclined to prowl around under my windows, and just the sound of him there keeps me awake. I know it's foolish; but I am so nervous these days—"

"Why, of course," said Nan with real contrition. "I'd no idea—"

Gringo was at the moment ingratiating himself with Wing Sam *in re* one soup bone of no use to anybody but dogs. If he could have heard Mrs. Morrell's indictment, he would have been both grieved and surprised: Gringo never prowled anywhere. Like most rather meaty individuals, he was a very sound sleeper; and in the morning he often felt a little uneasy in his conscience as to the matter of stray trespassing cats or such small fry. He had every confidence that his instincts would warn him of really important things, like burglars. Still, the important things are not all of life, nor burglars all the duty of a dog.

Having slandered the innocent Gringo, Mrs. Morrell stayed for a chat. Apparently she was always just on the point of departure, but never went. Nan, being, as she thought, in the wrong as to the worthy Gringo, tried her best to be polite, but was miserably conscious of being snippy.

At the end of an hour the door bell rang again. If Nan had been watching, she might have seen Mrs. Morrell's body relax as though from a tension. After a moment Wing Sam shuffled into the room carrying a soiled folded paper.

"Man he tell you lead this chop-chop," said he.

Murmuring an apology, Nan opened the paper. With a cry she sprang to her feet. Her face had gone white.

"What is it?" cried Mrs. Morrell in apparent anxiety.

Without a word Nan extended the paper. Written in pencil were these words:

> MADAM: Your husband has been injured in an attempt at arrest. He wants me to tell you he is at Jake's Place hurt bad. With respects. JOHN Q. ALDER.

For an instant Mrs. Morrell did not dare look up. She was thoroughly angry at what she thought to be her husband's stupidity.

"Why, that wouldn't deceive a child!" she thought contemptuously.

"How dreadful! Who is Alder?" she said, merely to say something.

Nan shook her head.

"I don't know," she replied rather wildly. "One of the Vigilantes, I suppose. I must go out there. At once!"

She ran to the hall where she began to rummage for cloaks. Mrs. Morrell followed her in wonderment. She was going to take this crude bait after all! Mrs. Morrell had not the slightest idea Nan still loved her husband.

"You can't go alone!" she cried in apparent sympathy. "You poor child! Jake's Place—at this time of night!"

"I'd go to hell if he needed me there!" cried Nan.

Mrs. Morrell became suddenly capable and commanding.

"Then I shall go with you," she announced firmly.

"Oh, you're good to me!" cried Nan, full of contrition, and

feeling, beneath her anxiety, that she had misjudged her neighbour's heart.

Mrs. Morrell took charge. She lit the lantern, led the way to the stable, did the most toward harnessing the horse. They made rather a mess of it, but the horse was gentle and reliable. When they had backed the buggy out of the barn, she insisted on driving.

"You're in no fit condition," she told Nan, and Nan obediently climbed in beside her.

The drive was made in silence, except that occasionally Nan urged hurry. She sat bolt upright, her hands clasped in her lap, her figure rigid, trying to keep hold of herself. At Jake's Place a surly hostler appeared and led away their horse. Jake's Place was in darkness save for one lighted room on the ground floor and a dimly illuminated bar at the other end.

It is but just to a celebrated resort that had seen and was still to see much of life to say that it knew nothing of the plot. Sansome had engaged the ground-floor parlour, and ordered a fire and drinks. Morrell had commanded a little supper for later. Now two ladies appeared. This was all normal. Without drinks, little suppers, and the subsequent appearance of ladies, Jake's Place would soon have languished.

Nan leaped over the wheel to the ground as soon as the buggy had stopped, and before the dilatory hostler had cramped aside the wheel.

"Where is he?" she demanded breathlessly. The hostler jerked a thumb at the lighted windows. Without a word Nan ran up the steps and to the door. The hostler looked after her flying figure, then grinned up at Mrs. Morrell.

"Yum! yum!" said he, "but she's the eager little piece!"

Mrs. Morrell gave him a coin, and as he moved away with the

horse, she, too, ran up the steps. Nan had entered the parlour door, leaving it open behind her. Mrs. Morrell closed it again, and locked it. Then, with a certainty that proved her familiarity with the place, she walked down the length of the veranda to a hall, which she entered.

Nan had burst into a parlour with an open fire. Before it stood a small table crowded with bottles and glasses. Sansome rose, rather unsteadily, from one of the easy chairs. Nan uttered an exclamation of relief as she recognized him.

"Oh, I'm glad you're here!" she cried. "This is kind! How is he? Where is he?"

LXXII

Morrell had no easy day with Ben Sansome. He had been forced to spend the whole of it with his protege, save for the hour he had devoted to seeing Keith off on the piratical expedition. It was a terrible bore. In turn he had played on the youth's pique, the supposed insult to his manhood, his desire for the woman. Sansome was not naturally a valiant adventurer; but he had an exceedingly touchy vanity, which, with a little coddling, answered nearly as well. Morrell took the confident attitude that, of course, Sansome was not afraid; therefore Sansome was ashamed to be afraid.

"For the moment," said the Englishman, "she's carried away by the glamour of this Vigilante movement. They seem to her strong men. She contrasts them with us men of the world, and as she cannot see that a polished exterior is not incompatible with strength, she has a faint growing contempt for us. Women like strength, masterfulness. It is the chance of your life to show her that a man *comme il faut* is the equal of these squalid brutes in that respect. She is in love with you already, but she doesn't know it. All that is necessary is a show of masterfulness to make her realize it." He stifled a yawn. "Lord, what dreary piffle!" he confided to himself. He painted Keith as a contemptible renegade from his own class, currying favour with those below him, a cheap demagogue, a turncoat avid for popular power.

"At heart he's a coward—all such men are. And he's so wrapped up in his ambition that his wife is a small matter to him. There's no danger from him, for he's away; and after the first flare-up we'll be able to handle him among us, never fear!" But after impressing this point, Morrell always was most careful to interpose the warning: "If it should come to trouble, don't let him get near you! He's absolutely rotten with a gun— you saw him in that farce of a duel—but he's a strong beggar. Don't let him get his hands on you!"

"I won't," promised Sansome, a trifle shakily.

Then Morrell, lighting a fresh cigar and fortifying his bored soul with another drink, skilfully outlined a portrait of Sansome himself as a hero, a dashing man of the world, a real devil among the ladies, the haughty and proud exponent of aristocratic high-handedness. He laid this on pretty thick, but Sansome had by now consumed a vast number of drinks, and was ready to swallow almost anything in addition. Morrell's customary demeanour was rather stolid, silent, and stupid; but when he was really interested and cared to exert himself, he became unexpectedly voluble and plausible. Mid-evening he drove this creature of his own fashioning out to Jake's Place, and deposited him in the parlour with the open fire, the table of drinks, and the easy chairs.

His plans from this point on were based on the fact that he had started Keith out on an expedition that should last all night. Had there been the slightest chance that the injured husband could appear, you may be sure Morrell would not have been present. Of course witnesses were necessary to the meeting at the road house. With Keith imminent, hirelings would have been arranged for. With Keith safety away, Morrell saw no reason why he should not enjoy the situation himself. Therefore he had arranged a little supper party. Teeny McFarlane and Jimmy Ware were his first thought. Then he added Pop McFarlane. If he wanted Teeny as a witness, the party must be respectable!

At the sound of wheels outside Morrell arose and slipped out the back door of the parlour.

"Now, remember!" he told Sansome from the doorway. "Now's the chance of your life! You've got her love, and you must keep her. She'll cut up rough at first. That's when you must show what's in you. Go right after her!"

As Nan burst into the room by one door he softly closed—and locked—the other behind him.

LXXIII

But Sansome, although he had put up a brave front to the last moment, was not in reality feeling near the hero of romance he looked. In spite of Morrell's cleverness, the Englishman had failed to observe that Sansome had touched the fringe of that second stage of semi-drunkenness when the "drinks were dying on him." While outwardly fairly sober, inwardly he was verging toward the incoherent. First one phase or mood would come to the top, then another, without order; sequence, or logical reason. He was momentarily dangerous or harmless. Nan's abrupt entrance scattered his last coherences. For the moment he fell back on habit, and habit was with him conventional He smiled his best smile.

"Do sit down," he urged in his most society manner.

This immediately convinced Nan that Keith must be badly hurt.

"Tell me at once!" she demanded "Where is Milton? Is he—is—"

"As far as I know," replied Sansome, still in his courtly manner, "Mr. Keith is in perfect health. As to where he is"—he waved an airy hand—"I do not know. It does not matter, does it? The point is we are cozy here together. Do sit down."

"I don't understand," said she, advancing a step nearer, her brows knit, "Don't put me off. I got a note saying—"

"I know; I wrote it," boasted Sansome fatuously.

The blood mounted her face, her fists clenched, she advanced several steps fearlessly.

"I don't, quite understand," she repeated, in hard, crisp tones. "You wrote it?' Isn't it true? What did you do such a thing for?"

"To get you here, my dear, of course," rejoined Sansome gallantly. "I knew your puritanical scruples—I love them every one—but—"

"Do you mean to say you dared decoy me here!" challenged Nan, all aflame. Her whole emotion was one of rage. It did not occur to her to be afraid of Ben Sansome, the conventional, the dilettante exquisite, without the gumption to say boo to a goose!

This Sansome answered her, the habit of society strong within him. He became deprecatory, pleading, almost apologetic. His manners were on top and his rather weak nature quailed before the blaze of her anger.

"I know it was inexcusable," he babbled, "but what could I do? I am mad about you! Do forgive me! Just sit down for a few moments. I don't blame you for being angry—any one is angry at being deceived—but do forgive me. If you'll only consider why I did it, you won't be angry. That's right," he ended soothingly, seeing that she neither spoke nor moved, "Just sit right down here and be comfortable. It must be cold driving. Let me give you a glass of sherry." He fussed about, shoving forward an armchair, arranging pillows, unstopping the decanter.

"You fool!" she ejaculated in a low voice. She looked him all up and down, and turned to go.

The door was locked! For the first time she noticed that Mrs.

Morrell had not followed her in. Her heart fluttered in sudden panic, which she subdued. She moved toward the other door.

The words, and especially the frustration of her intention, brought another mood to the surface of Sansome's intoxication. The polished society man with the habit of external unselfishness disappeared. Another Sansome, whom Nan did not recognize, sprang to take his place.

"No, you don't!" he snarled. "That door's locked, too. You don't get out of here until I choose to let you out!"

"You'll let me out; and you'll let me out right now, or I'll call for help," said Nan determinedly.

Sansome deliberately seated himself, stretching his legs out straight before him, his hands in his pockets. This was the masterful role he had seen himself playing, and he instinctively took the attitude approved by the best melodramatic masters.

"Call all you please," he sneered. "Nobody's going to pay any attention to your calls at Jake's Place!"

Nan's heart went cold as she realized the complete truth of this. She was beginning to know fear. This was a new sort of creature before her, one with which she was acquainted only by instinct. She did not know what to do next, except that she saw surely that open opposition would only aggravate the situation.

"I must gain time!" she told herself, though to what end she could not have said.

Her pulses beat wildly, but she forced herself to a specious calmness.

"But Ben," she said as naturally as she could, "why did you do so foolish a thing as this? It might make all kinds of trouble. You can always see me at the house; you know that. Why did you get me out on this mad expedition? If we were to be seen here by anybody we would be deeply compromised."

The words reminded her of Mrs. Morrell; but out of sheer terror she resolutely thrust that idea from her mind. At this appeal Sansome suddenly became maudlin.

"You've treated me like a dog lately—a yellow dog!" he mourned. "What good did it do to go to your house and be treated like a yellow dog?"

Nan's faculties were beginning to rally after the first panic. Her heart was still thumping violently, but her eyes were bright, and her fighting courage was flowing back. For the first time his obvious condition registered on her brain.

"He's drunk!" she thought.

This discovery at first induced in her another, small panic. Then her courage boldly took it as a point of attack. The man was drunk and dangerous; very well, let us make him more drunk and less dangerous. That was a desperate enough expedient, but at least it was definite. She crossed deliberately to the other easy chair, and sat down.

"Well, let's sit down," she agreed. "No!" more decidedly, "you sit there, on the other side. It's more cozy," she continued, at just the right moment to get her effect on his instinct of good manners. "Now, I will have that sherry. No, don't bother; it is next my hand. You must drink with me. Let me pour it for you—with my own hands—aren't you flattered?"

She smiled across at him. This sudden reversion to an easy every-day plane had brought Sansome's first mood again to the surface. In this atmosphere of orderly tete-a-tete he was again the society man. Nan breathed freer. He murmured something inane and conventional about Hebe.

"Meaning you're a little tin god?" she chaffed.

He said something still more involved, to the effect that her presence would make a god out of the most unworthy mortal. It was all vapid, unreal, elaborate, artificial.

"If I can only keep him at this!" thought she desperately.

She had drunk her glass of sherry because she felt she needed it. Now she poured another, and without comment, refilled Sansome's whiskey glass.

"Here's to us!" she cried, lifting her glass.

Nan's plan of getting him so drunk that he would not interfere with her escape had the merit of simplicity, and also of endorsement by such excellent authority as melodrama and the novel. It had the defect of being entirely theoretical. Nan's innocence of the matter in hand had not taken into account the intermediate stages of drunkenness, nor did she realize the strength inherent in the association of ideas. As she leaned forward to fill the glasses, Sansome's eyes brightened. He had seen women pouring wine many times before. The picture before him reminded him of a dozen similar pictures taken from the gallery of his rather disreputable past. His elaborate complimentary mood vanished. He pledged her ardently, and deep in his eyes began to burn a secret covetous flame. Nan poured her, sherry under the table.

"This really is a cozy party!" she cried. "Will you have another with me?"

The third glass of neat whiskey whirled in Sansome's head. He was verging toward complete drunkenness, but in the meantime became amorous. His eyes turned, his lips fell apart. Nan tried in desperation to keep on a plane of light persiflage, to hold him to his chair and to the impersonal. Deep fear entered her. She urged more drink on him, hoping that he would be overpowered. It was like a desperate race between this man's passions and the deep oblivion that reached for them. Her mouth was dry, and her brain whirled. Only by the greatest effort could she prevent herself from flying to pieces. Sansome hardly appeared to hear her. He wagged his head at her, looking upon her with swimming, benevolent eyes. Suddenly, without warning, he sprang up, overturning with a crash the small table and the bottles and glasses.

"By God, you're the most beautiful woman I ever saw!" he cried. "Come here!"

He advanced on her, his eyes alight. She saw that the crisis had come, and threw aside all pretence.

"Keep away! Keep away!" she warned him through, gritted teeth; then, as he continued to stumble toward her, she struck at him viciously again and again with one of the small light chairs.

For a moment or so she actually managed to beat him off; but he lunged through the blows and seized her around the shoulders.

"Reg'lar little tiger cat!" he murmured with fond admiration.

His reeking breath was on her neck as he sought her mouth. She threw her head back and to one side, fighting desperately and silently, tearing at him with her hands, writhing her body, lowering her head as he forced her around, kicking at his shin. The man's strength was as horrible as it was unexpected. The efforts to which she was giving her every ounce did not appear to have the slightest effect on him, His handsome weak face continued to smile foolishly and fondly down on her.

"Reg'lar little tiger cat!" he repeated over and over.

The terrible realization dawned on her that he was too much for her. Her body suddenly went lax. She threw back her and screamed.

LXXIV

The plot which Morrell had first suggested idly and as sort of a joke, but which later he had entered into with growing gelief, was quite perfect in all details but one: he assumed that Keith had accompanied Durkee's expedition, and was sure that he had seen the young lawyer off. As a matter of fact, Keith had been recalled. A messenger had at the very last moment handed him an order sealed with the well-known open eye, and signed "33 Secretary." It commanded him to proceed with certain designated men to the arrest of certain others inscribed on the black list. This was a direct order, whereas the present expedition was wholly a voluntary affair. Keith had no alternative but to obey, though he did so reluctantly, for this search for arms had promised sport. Therefore, he stepped ashore at the last instant; a proceeding unobserved by Morrell, who was surveying the scene from a distance, and who turned away once the sails were hoisted.

The duty to which Keith had been assigned took some time. The men had to be searched out one by one, escorted to headquarters, and the usual formalities there accomplished. It was late in the evening before he was free to go home. He let himself in with his latchkey, and had just turned up the low-burning gas in the hall when the sound of hurrying feet brought him back to the door. He flung it open to confront Mrs. Sherwood and Krafft. They were both panting as though they had run some distance and Krafft's usually precise attire was dishevelled and awry, as though it had been hastily put on. "Nan!" gasped Mrs. Sherwood. "Is she here?"

Stewart Edward White

Keith, with instant decision, asking no questions, threw open the parlour door, glanced within, ran upstairs three steps at a time, but almost immediately returned after a hasty inspection of the upper story. His face had gone very pale, but he had himself in perfect control.

"Well?" he demanded crisply, looking from one to the other.

But Mrs. Sherwood did not stop to answer. With a stifled exclamation she darted from the house. Krafft looked after her, bewildered. Keith shook him savagely by the shoulder.

"Speak up, man! Quick! What is it?" demanded Keith. His voice was vibrant with suppressed excitement, but he held himself outwardly calm, and waited immobile until the end of Krafft's story. It was characteristic of him as of all strong men in a crisis that he made no move whatever until he was sure he had grasped the whole situation.

Krafft was just going to bed—he always retired early—when he was called to the door by Mex Ryan. Mex had never come to his house before. He was a shoulder striker and a thug; but he had one sure streak of loyalty in that nothing could ever induce him to go back on a pal. For various reasons he considered Krafft a pal. He was very much troubled.

"Look here, boss," he said to Krafft, "It just come to my mind a while ago: what was the name of that bloke you told me to keep off'n? The Cora trial man, I mean."

Krafft recalled the circumstance, and named Keith.

Mex slapped his head.

"That's right! It come to me afterward. Well, there's dirty work with his wife. That's where I see the name, on the outside of the note. I just give her a fake letter that says her husband is shot, and she's to go to him."

"How did he know what the letter said?" interjected Keith at this point.

"He'd read anything given him, of course. Mex knew the letter was false. I came up to find your house. I didn't know where you lived, so I stopped at John Sherwood's to inquire. Mrs. Sherwood was home alone. She came with me."

"Where did this letter say I was supposed to be?" asked Keith,

"Jake's Place."

"My God!" cried Keith, and leaped for the door. At the same instant Mrs. Sherwood's voice was heard from the darkness.

"Come here," she cried, "I have a rig."

They found her seated in a buggy. Both climbed in beside her. Keith took the reins, and lashed the horse with the light whip. The astonished animal leaped; the buggy jerked forward.

Then began a wild, careering, bumpy ride into the night. The road was fearful and all but invisible. The carriage swayed and swung dangerously. Keith drove, every faculty concentrated. No one spoke. The dim and ghostly half-guessed forms of things at night streamed past.

"Who sent that letter?" demanded Keith finally.

"Mex wouldn't tell me," replied Krafft.

"How long ago did he deliver it?"

"About an hour."

The horse plunged frantically under the lash as this reply reached Keith. The buggy was all but overturned. He pulled the frantic animal down to a slower pace, and with an obvious effort regained control of himself.

"Can't afford an accident!" he warned himself.

"Are you armed?" Mrs. Sherwood asked him suddenly.

"Yes—no, I left my gun at headquarters—that doesn't matter."

Mrs. Sherwood made no comment. The wind caught her hair and whipped it about. In the distance now twinkled the lights of Jake's Place. Keith took a firmer grip on the reins, and again applied the whip. They swept into the gravelled driveway on two wheels, righted themselves, and rounded to the veranda. Keith pulled up and leaped to the ground. Nobody was visible. From the veranda he turned on them.

"Here, you!" he commanded Mrs. Sherwood sharply, "I can't have you in this row! Stay here, outside. You take care of her," he told Krafft. "No, I mean it!"

On his words a scream burst from the lighted room. Keith sprang to the door, found it locked, and drew back. With a low mighty rush he thrust his shoulder against the panel near the lock. The wood splintered. He sprang forward into the room.

LXXV

After turning the key in the lock outside the parlour door Mrs. Morrell slipped along the dark veranda, passed through a narrow hall, and entered a small back sitting-room. Jake's Place especially abounded in sitting-rooms. This particular one was next the parlour, so that one listening intently could be more or less aware of what was going on in the larger room. Here Morrell was already seated, a bottle of beer next his hand. He raised his eyebrows on her entrance, and she nodded back reassuringly. She, too, sat down and helped herself to beer. Both smoked. For a long time neither said anything.

"Don't hear much in there," observed Mrs. Morrell finally, in a low guarded tone.

"Not a sound," agreed Morrell. "You don't suppose she—"

"No, I don't think so."

"Then I don't see what ails that fool, Sansome! It'd be just like him to jib."

"What does it matter?" observed Mrs. Morrell philosophically, "We don't care what is happening inside as long as those two doors stay locked until Teeny and Jimmy Ware get here."

As has been mentioned, Pop McFarlane was also of the party; but, characteristically, neither would have thought that fact worth mentioning.

"Just the same, as a matter of academic interest, I'd have expected her to make more of a row," said Morrell. "I'll wager for all her airs she runs the same gait as all the rest of you."

"Do you mean me?" demanded Mrs. Morrell, her eyes flashing dangerously.

"Moderate your voice, my dear," advised he. "My remark was wholly general of your charming sex."

From the parlour now they heard faintly the first sounds of struggle.

"That's more like," he said with satisfaction. "I hate to have my ideals shattered."

Wheels became audible.

"There's Teeny, now," he observed, arising. He sauntered down the hall and looked out. "Keith!" he whispered back over his shoulder. "Where in hell did he come from?" He continued to peer into the darkness. "There's two others. Well, at any rate, we have plenty of witnesses!" He turned to Mrs. Morrell. "You'd better make yourself scarce. You locked that door, you know!"

"Scarce!" she repeated, staring at him. "Where? How?"

He looked at her through narrowed lids.

"Get a horse of Jake," he said at last. "I'll meet you—oh, at the house. We'll arrange later."

He watched her rather opulent figure steal down the dim hallway. A cynical smile flashed under his moustache. He turned back to the drama before him. The buggy had disappeared; the veranda was apparently empty.

"Now I wonder who will shoot who?" speculated Morrell.

He stole to the first of the windows. The lower blinds were drawn, but the upper half of the window was clear. Morrell cautiously placed a stool nearby, and mounted it so he could see into the room. For several minutes he watched. Then his hand stole to his pocket. He produced a revolver.

Stewart Edward White

LXXVI

Blinded by the light, Keith stood for a barely appreciable moment in the wrecked doorway. Sansome, startled by the crash, relaxed his efforts. Nan thrust him from her so strongly that he staggered back. Keith's vision cleared. He appreciated the meaning of the tableau, uttered a choked growl, and advanced.

Immediately Sansome drew and presented his weapon. He was shocked far toward sobriety, but the residue of the whiskey fumes in combination with a sudden sick and guilty panic imbued him with a sort of desperation. Sansome was a bold and dashing villain only as long as things came his way. His amours had always been of the safe rather than the wildly adventurous sort. Sansome had no morals; but being found out produced effects so closely resembling those of conscience that they could not be distinguished. In the chaotic collapse of this heroic episode he managed to cling to but one thing. That was Morrell's often reiterated warning: "Don't let Keith get his hands on you!"

At the sight of his levelled weapon, Nan, who was nearest, uttered a stifled cry and made as though to throw herself on him.

"Stop!" commanded Keith, without looking toward her. But so quietly authoritative was his voice and manner that in spite of herself her impulse was checked. She remained rigid.

Keith advanced steadily on Sansome, his hands clenched at his side, his eye's fixed frowningly and contemptuously on those of the other man. The pistol barrel was held on his breast. Sansome fully intended to shoot, but found himself unable to pull the trigger. This is a condition every rifleman knows well by experience; he calls it being "frozen on the bull's eye," when, the alignment perfect, his rifle steady as a rock, he nevertheless cannot transmit just the little nerve power necessary to crook the forefinger. Three times Sansome sent the message to his trigger finger; three times the impulse died before it had compassed the distance between his brain and his hand. This was partly because his correlations had been weakened by the drink; partly because his fuddled mind was divided between fear, guilt, despair, and a rage at himself for having got into such a mess; but principally because he was hypnotically dominated by the other man's stronger personality.

So evident was this that a sudden feeling of confidence replaced in Nan the sick terror at the sight of the weapon. She seemed to know positively that here was no real peril. A wave of contempt for Sansome, even as a dangerous creature, mingled with a passionate admiration for the man who thus dominated him unarmed.

Sansome's nerve broke. He dropped his hand, looked to right and left frantically like a rat in a corner, uttered a very ratty squeak. Suddenly he hurled the loaded pistol blindly at Keith, and plunged bodily, with an immense crash of breaking glass, through the closed window. Keith, with a snarl of baffled rage, dashed forward.

The sight seemed to touch Nan's sense of humour. She laughed at the picture, caught her breath, gasped. Keith whirled and snatched her fiercely in his arms.

"Nan!" he cried in an agony, "are you all right? What did that beast—"

She clung to him, still choking, on the edge of hysterics. In a moment of illumination she realized that the intangible barrier these past years had so slowly built between them had gone crashing down before the assault of the old love triumphant.

"I'm all right, dear," she gasped; "really all right. And I never was so happy in my life!"

They clung together frantically, he patting her shoulder, her cheek against his own, murmuring broken, soothing little phrases. The time and the place did not exist for them.

A scuffle outside, which they had only vaguely sensed, and which had not at all penetrated to their understandings, came to an end. Mrs. Sherwood appeared in the doorway. Her dress was torn and dishevelled, a strand of her smooth hair had fallen across her forehead, an angry red mark showed on one cheek. But she was in high spirits. Her customary quiet poise had given place to a vibrant, birdlike, vital, quivering eagerness. To the two in the centre of the room, still clasped in each other's arms, came the same thought: that never, in spite of her ruffled plumes, in spite of the cheek already beginning to swell, had this extraordinary woman looked so beautiful! Then Keith realized that she was panting heavily, and was clinging to the doorway. He sprang to her assistance.

"What is it? Where is Krafft?" he asked.

She laughed a little, and permitted him to help her to an armchair into which she sank. She waved aside Keith's attempts to find a whole glass in the wreckage of the table.

"I'm all right," she said, "and isn't this a nice little party?"

"What has happened? Where is Krafft?" repeated Keith.

"I sent him to the stable for help. There didn't seem to be anybody about the place."

"But what happened to you? Did that brute Sansome—"

"Sansome? was that Sansome? the one who came through the window?" She dabbed at her cheek. "You might wet me a handkerchief or a towel or something," she suggested. "No, he didn't stop!" she laughed again. "Are you all right?" she asked anxiously of Nan.

"Yes. But tell us—"

"Well, children, I was waiting on the veranda, obeying orders like a good girl, when, in the dim light I saw a man mount a stool and look into the room. He was very much interested. I crept up quite close to him without his knowing it. I heard him mutter to himself something about a 'weak kneed fool.' Then he drew a revolver. He looked quite determined and heroic"—she giggled reminiscently—"so I kicked the stool out from under him! About that time there was a most terrific crash, and somebody came out through the window."

"But your cheek, your hair—"

"I tried to hold him, but he was too strong for me. He hit me in the face, wrenched himself free, and ran. That was all; except that he dropped the pistol, and I'm going to keep it as a trophy."

Keith was looking at her, deep in thought.

"I don't understand," he said slowly. "Who could it have been?"

Mrs. Sherwood shook her head.

"Somebody about to shoot a pistol; that's all I know. I couldn't see his face."

"Whoever it was, you saved one or both of us," said Keith, "there's no doubt in my mind of that. Let's see the pistol."

It proved to be one of the smaller Colt's models, about 31 calibre, cap and ball, silver plated, with polished rosewood handles, and heavily engraved with scrollwork. Turning it over, Keith finally discovered on the bottom of the butt frame two letters scratched rudely, apparently with the point of a knife. He took it closer to the light.

"I have it," said he. "Here are the letters C.M."

"Charles Morrell!" cried both women in a breath.

At this moment appeared Krafft, somewhat out of wind, followed by the surly and reluctant proprietor from whom the place took its name. Jake had been liberally paid to keep himself and his staff out of the way. Now finding that he was not wanted, he promptly disappeared.

"Let's get to the bottom of this thing," said Keith decisively. "If those are really meant for Morrell's initials, what was he doing here?"

"Mrs. Morrell came out with me," put in Nan.

"Jake told me there was to be a supper party later," said Krafft.

"It's clear enough," contributed Mrs. Sherwood. "The whole thing is a plot to murder or do worse. I've been through '50 and '51, and I know."

"I can't believe yet that Sansome—" said Keith doubtfully.

"Oh, Sansome is merely a tool, I don't doubt," replied Mrs. Sherwood.

"I can find out to-morrow from Mex Ryan who sent the note," said Krafft.

"Let's get out of this horrible place!" cried Nan with a convulsive shiver.

Again they had great difficulty in finding any one to get their rigs, but finally repeated calls brought the hostler and Jake himself. The latter made some growl about payment for the entertainment, but at this Keith turned on him with such concentrated fury that he muttered something and slouched away. It was agreed that Krafft should conduct Mrs. Sherwood. They clambered into the two buggies and drove away.

Stewart Edward White

LXXVII

The horse plodded slowly down the gravelled drive of the road house and turned into the main highway. It was very dark on earth, and very bright in the heavens. The afternoon fog had cleared away, dissipated in the warm air from the sand hills, for the day had been hot. Overhead flared thousands of stars, throwing the world small. Nan, shivering in reaction, nestled against her husband. He drew her close. She rested her cheek against his shoulder and sighed happily. Neither spoke.

At first Keith's whole being was filled with rage. His mind whirled with plans for revenge. On the morrow he would hunt down Morrell and Sansome. At the thought of what he would do to them, his teeth clamped and his muscles stiffened. Then he became wholly preoccupied with Nan's narrow escape. His quick mind visualized a hundred possibilities—suppose he had gone on Durkee's expedition? Suppose Mex Ryan had not happened to remember his name? Suppose Mrs. Sherwood and Krafft had not found him? Suppose they hadbeen an hour later? Suppose—He leaned over tenderly to draw the lap robe closer about her. She had stopped shivering and was nestling contentedly against him.

But gradually the storm in Keith's soul fell. The great and solemn night stood over against his vision, and at last he could not but look. The splendour of the magnificent skies, the dreamy peace of the velvet-black earth lying supine like a weary creature at rest—these two simple infinities of space and of promise took him to themselves. An eager glad chorus of frogs came from some invisible pool. The slithering sound of the sand dividing before the buggy wheels whispered. Every once in a while the plodding horse sighed deeply.

With the warm cozy feel of the woman, his woman, in the hollow of his arm, his spirit stilled and uplifted by the simple yet august and eternal things before him, Keith fell into inchoate rumination. The fever of activity in the city, the clash of men's interests, greeds, and passions, the tumult and striving, the sweat and dust of the arena fell to nothing about his feet. He cleared his vision of the small necessary unessentials, and stared forth wide-eyed at the big simplicities of life—truth as one sees it, loyalty to one's ideal, charity toward one's beaten enemy, a steadfast front toward one's unbeaten enemy, scorn of pettiness, to be unafraid. Unless the struggle is for and by these things, it is useless, meaningless. And one's possessions—Keith's left arm tightened convulsively. He had come near to losing the only possession worth while. At the pressure Nan stirred sleepily.

"Are we there, dear?" she inquired, raising her head.

Keith had reined in the horse, and was peering into the surrounding darkness. He laughed.

"No, we seem to be here," he replied, "And I'm blest if I know where 'here' is! I've been day-dreaming!"

"I believe I've been asleep," confessed Nan.

They both stared about them, but could discern nothing familiar in the dim outlines of the hills. Not a light flickered.

"Perhaps if you'd give the horse his head, he'd take us home. I've heard, they would," suggested Nan.

"He's had his head completely for the last two hours. That theory is exploded. We must have turned wrong after leaving Jake's Place."

"Well, we're on a road. It must go somewhere."

Keith, with some difficulty, managed to awaken the horse. It sighed and resumed its plodding.

"I'm afraid we're lost," confessed Keith.

"I don't much care," confessed Nan.

"He seems to be a perfectly safe horse," said he.

By way of answer to this she passed her arms gently about his neck and bent his lips to hers. The horse immediately stopped.

"Seems a fairly intelligent brute, too," observed Keith, after a few moments.

"Did you ever see so many stars?" said she.

The buggy moved slowly, on through the night. They did not talk. Explanations and narrative could wait until the morrow —a distant morrow only dimly foreseen, across this vast ocean of night. All sense of tune or direction left them; they were wandering irresponsibly, without thought of why, as children wander and get lost. After a long time they saw a silver gleam far ahead and below them.

"That must be the bay," said Keith. "If we turn to the right we ought to get back to town."

"I suppose so," said Nan.

A very long time later the horse stopped short with an air of finality, and refused absolutely to proceed. Keith descended to see what was the matter.

"The road seems to end here," he told her. "There's a steep descent just ahead."

"What now?"

"Nothing," he replied, climbing back into the buggy.

The horse slumbered profoundly. They wrapped the lap robe around themselves. For a tune they whispered little half-forgotten things to each other. The pauses grew longer and longer. With an effort she roused herself to press her lips again to his. They, too, slept. And as dawn slowly lighted the world, they must have presented a strange and bizarre silhouette atop the hill against the paling sky—the old sagging buggy, the horse with head down and ears adroop, the lovers clasped in each other's arms.

Silently all about them the new day was preparing its great spectacle. The stars were growing dim; the masses of eastern hills were becoming visible. A full rich life was swelling through the world, quietly, stealthily, as though under cover of darkness multitudes were stealing to their posts. Shortly, when the signal was given, the curtain would roll up, the fanfare of trumpets would resound—A meadow lark chirped low out of the blackness. And another, boldly, with full throat, uttered its liquid, joyous song. This was apparently the signal. The east turned gray. Mt. Tamalpais caught the first ghostly light. And ecstatically the birds and the insects and the flying and crawling and creeping things awakened, and each in his own voice and manner devoutly welcomed the brand-new day with its fresh, clean chances of life and its forgetfulness of old, disagreeable things. The meadow larks became hundreds, the song sparrows trilled, distant cocks crowed, and a dog barked exuberantly far away.

Keith stirred and looked about him. Objects were already becoming dimly visible. Suddenly something attracted his attention. He held his head sideways, listening. Faintly down the little land breeze came the sound of a bell. It was the Vigilante tocsin. Nan sat up, blinking and putting her hair back from her eyes. She laughed a little happily.

"Why, it's the dawn!" she cried, "We've been out all night!"

"The dawn," repeated Keith, his arm about her, but his ear attuned to the beat of the distant bell. "The gray dawn of better things."

LXXVIII

As the Keiths, on the way, drove across what is now Harbour View, they stopped to watch a bark standing out through the Golden Gate before the gentle morning land breeze. She made a pretty sight, for the new-risen sun whitened her sails. Aboard her was the arch-plotter, Morrell. Had they known of that fact, it is to be doubted whether they would have felt any great disappointment over his escape, or any deep animosity at all. The outcome of his efforts had been clarifying. The bark was bound for the Sandwich Islands. Morrell's dispositions for flight at a moment's notice had been made long since; in fact, since the first days of Vigilante activity. He lingered in the islands for some years, at first cutting quite a dash; then, as his money dwindled and his schemes failed, he degenerated slowly. His latter end was probably as a small copra trader in the South Seas; but that is unknown. Mrs. Morrell—if indeed she was the man's legal wife at all—thus frankly abandoned, put a bold front on the whole matter. She returned to her house. As the Keiths in no manner molested her, she took heart. With no resources other than heavily mortgaged real property, she found herself forced to do something for a living. In the course of events we see Mrs. Morrell keeping a flashy boarding-house, hanging precariously on the outer fringe of the lax society of the times, frowned upon by the respectable, but more or less sought by the fast men and young girls only too numerous among the idle of that day.

Ben Sansome went south. For twenty years he lived in Los Angeles, where he cut a figure, but from which he always cast longing eyes back upon San Francisco. He had a furtive lookout for arrivals from the north. One day, however, he came face to face with Keith. As the latter did not annihilate him on the spot, Sansome plucked up courage. He returned to San Francisco, There in time he attained a position dear to his heart; he became an "old beau," frequenting the teas and balls, appraising the debutantes, giving his opinion on vintage wines, leading a comfortable, idle, selfish, useless, graceful life. His only discomfort was his occasional encounters with the Keiths. Mrs. Keith never distinguished him from thin air unless others were present. Keith had always in his eye a gleam of contempt which, perhaps, Sansome acknowledged, was natural; but it was a contempt with a dash of amusement in it, and that galled. Still—Ben was satisfied. He gained the distinction of having discovered the epicurean value of sand- dabs.

The Sherwoods founded the family of that name.

Terry, arrested for the stabbing of Hopkins, was at first very humble, promising to resign his Supreme Court Judgeship. As time went on he became arrogant. The Committee of Vigilance was rather at a loss. If Hopkins died, they could do no less than hang Terry: and they realized fully that in executing a Justice of the Supreme Court they were entering deep waters. To the relief of everybody Hopkins fully recovered. After being held closely in custody, Terry was finally released, with a resolution that he be declared unfit for office. Once free, however, he revised his intention of resigning. His subsequent career proved as lawless and undisciplined as its earlier promise. Finally he was killed while in the act of attempting to assassinate Justice Stephen Field, an old, weak, helpless, and unarmed man. If Terry holds any significance in history, it is that of being the strongest factor in the complete wrecking of the Law and Order party!

For with the capture of the arsenals, and all their arms, open opposition to the Committee of Vigilance came to an end. The Executive Committee continued its work. Numberless malefactors and suspects were banished; two more men,

Hetherington and Brace, were solemnly hanged. On the 8th. Of August the cells were practically empty. It was determined to disband on the 21st.

That ceremony was signalized by a parade on the 18th. Four regiments of infantry, two squadrons of cavalry, a battalion of riflemen, a battalion of pistol men, and a battalion of police were in line. The entire city turned out to cheer.

As for the effects of this movement, the reader must be referred to the historians. It is sufficient to say that for years San Francisco enjoyed a model government and almost complete immunity from crime.

One evening about twilight two men stood in the gathering shadows of the Plaza. They were old friends, but had in times of stress stood on opposite sides. The elder man shook his head skeptically.

"That is all very well," said he, "but where are your Vigilantes now?"

The other raised his hand toward the great bell of the Monumental silhouetted against the afterglow in the sky.

"Toll that bell, sir, and you will see!" replied Coleman solemnly.

Stewart Edward White

Choose from Thousands of 1stWorldLibrary Classics By

A. M. Barnard	Booth Tarkington	Edward Everett Hale
Ada Leverson	Boyd Cable	Edward J. O'Biren
Adolphus William Ward	Bram Stoker	Edward S. Ellis
Aesop	C. Collodi	Edwin L. Arnold
Agatha Christie	C. E. Orr	Eleanor Atkins
Alexander Aaronsohn	C. M. Ingleby	Eleanor Hallowell Abbott
Alexander Kielland	Carolyn Wells	Eliot Gregory
Alexandre Dumas	Catherine Parr Traill	Elizabeth Gaskell
Alfred Gatty	Charles A. Eastman	Elizabeth McCracken
Alfred Ollivant	Charles Amory Beach	Elizabeth Von Arnim
Alice Duer Miller	Charles Dickens	Ellem Key
Alice Turner Curtis	Charles Dudley Warner	Emerson Hough
Alice Dunbar	Charles Farrar Browne	Emilie F. Carlen
Allen Chapman	Charles Ives	Emily Bronte
Alleyne Ireland	Charles Kingsley	Emily Dickinson
Ambrose Bierce	Charles Klein	Enid Bagnold
Amelia E. Barr	Charles Hanson Towne	Enilor Macartney Lane
Amory H. Bradford	Charles Lathrop Pack	Erasmus W. Jones
Andrew Lang	Charles Romyn Dake	Ernie Howard Pie
Andrew McFarland Davis	Charles Whibley	Ethel May Dell
Andy Adams	Charles Willing Beale	Ethel Turner
Angela Brazil	Charlotte M. Braeme	Ethel Watts Mumford
Anna Alice Chapin	Charlotte M. Yonge	Eugene Sue
Anna Sewell	Charlotte Perkins Stetson	Eugenie Foa
Annie Besant	Clair W. Hayes	Eugene Wood
Annie Hamilton Donnell	Clarence Day Jr.	Eustace Hale Ball
Annie Payson Call	Clarence E. Mulford	Evelyn Everett-green
Annie Roe Carr	Clemence Housman	Everard Cotes
Annonaymous	Confucius	F. H. Cheley
Anton Chekhov	Coningsby Dawson	F. J. Cross
Archibald Lee Fletcher	Cornelis DeWitt Wilcox	F. Marion Crawford
Arnold Bennett	Cyril Burleigh	Fannie E. Newberry
Arthur C. Benson	D. H. Lawrence	Federick Austin Ogg
Arthur Conan Doyle	Daniel Defoe	Ferdinand Ossendowski
Arthur M. Winfield	David Garnett	Fergus Hume
Arthur Ransome	Dinah Craik	Florence A. Kilpatrick
Arthur Schnitzler	Don Carlos Janes	Fremont B. Deering
Arthur Train	Donald Keyhoe	Francis Bacon
Atticus	Dorothy Kilner	Francis Darwin
B.H. Baden-Powell	Dougan Clark	Frances Hodgson Burnett
B. M. Bower	Douglas Fairbanks	Frances Parkinson Keyes
B. C. Chatterjee	E. Nesbit	Frank Gee Patchin
Baroness Emmuska Orczy	E. P. Roe	Frank Harris
Baroness Orczy	E. Phillips Oppenheim	Frank Jewett Mather
Basil King	E. S. Brooks	Frank L. Packard
Bayard Taylor	Earl Barnes	Frank V. Webster
Ben Macomber	Edgar Rice Burroughs	Frederic Stewart Isham
Bertha Muzzy Bower	Edith Van Dyne	Frederick Trevor Hill
Bjornstjerne Bjornson	Edith Wharton	Frederick Winslow Taylor

Friedrich Kerst
Friedrich Nietzsche
Fyodor Dostoyevsky
G.A. Henty
G.K. Chesterton
Gabrielle E. Jackson
Garrett P. Serviss
Gaston Leroux
George A. Warren
George Ade
Geroge Bernard Shaw
George Cary Eggleston
George Durston
George Ebers
George Eliot
George Gissing
George MacDonald
George Meredith
George Orwell
George Sylvester Viereck
George Tucker
George W. Cable
George Wharton James
Gertrude Atherton
Gordon Casserly
Grace E. King
Grace Gallatin
Grace Greenwood
Grant Allen
Guillermo A. Sherwell
Gulielma Zollinger
Gustav Flaubert
H. A. Cody
H. B. Irving
H.C. Bailey
H. G. Wells
H. H. Munro
H. Irving Hancock
H. R. Naylor
H. Rider Haggard
H. W. C. Davis
Haldeman Julius
Hall Caine
Hamilton Wright Mabie
Hans Christian Andersen
Harold Avery
Harold McGrath
Harriet Beecher Stowe
Harry Castlemon
Harry Coghill
Harry Houidini

Hayden Carruth
Helent Hunt Jackson
Helen Nicolay
Hendrik Conscience
Hendy David Thoreau
Henri Barbusse
Henrik Ibsen
Henry Adams
Henry Ford
Henry Frost
Henry James
Henry Jones Ford
Henry Seton Merriman
Henry W Longfellow
Herbert A. Giles
Herbert Carter
Herbert N. Casson
Herman Hesse
Hildegard G. Frey
Homer
Honore De Balzac
Horace B. Day
Horace Walpole
Horatio Alger Jr.
Howard Pyle
Howard R. Garis
Hugh Lofting
Hugh Walpole
Humphry Ward
Ian Maclaren
Inez Haynes Gillmore
Irving Bacheller
Isabel Cecilia Williams
Isabel Hornibrook
Israel Abrahams
Ivan Turgenev
J.G.Austin
J. Henri Fabre
J. M. Barrie
J. M. Walsh
J. Macdonald Oxley
J. R. Miller
J. S. Fletcher
J. S. Knowles
J. Storer Clouston
J. W. Duffield
Jack London
Jacob Abbott
James Allen
James Andrews
James Baldwin

James Branch Cabell
James DeMille
James Joyce
James Lane Allen
James Lane Allen
James Oliver Curwood
James Oppenheim
James Otis
James R. Driscoll
Jane Abbott
Jane Austen
Jane L. Stewart
Janet Aldridge
Jens Peter Jacobsen
Jerome K. Jerome
Jessie Graham Flower
John Buchan
John Burroughs
John Cournos
John F. Kennedy
John Gay
John Glasworthy
John Habberton
John Joy Bell
John Kendrick Bangs
John Milton
John Philip Sousa
John Taintor Foote
Jonas Lauritz Idemil Lie
Jonathan Swift
Joseph A. Altsheler
Joseph Carey
Joseph Conrad
Joseph E. Badger Jr
Joseph Hergesheimer
Joseph Jacobs
Jules Vernes
Julian Hawthrone
Julie A Lippmann
Justin Huntly McCarthy
Kakuzo Okakura
Karle Wilson Baker
Kate Chopin
Kenneth Grahame
Kenneth McGaffey
Kate Langley Bosher
Kate Langley Bosher
Katherine Cecil Thurston
Katherine Stokes
L. A. Abbot
L. T. Meade

L. Frank Baum
Latta Griswold
Laura Dent Crane
Laura Lee Hope
Laurence Housman
Lawrence Beasley
Leo Tolstoy
Leonid Andreyev
Lewis Carroll
Lewis Sperry Chafer
Lilian Bell
Lloyd Osbourne
Louis Hughes
Louis Joseph Vance
Louis Tracy
Louisa May Alcott
Lucy Fitch Perkins
Lucy Maud Montgomery
Luther Benson
Lydia Miller Middleton
Lyndon Orr
M. Corvus
M. H. Adams
Margaret E. Sangster
Margret Howth
Margaret Vandercook
Margaret W. Hungerford
Margret Penrose
Maria Edgeworth
Maria Thompson Daviess
Mariano Azuela
Marion Polk Angellotti
Mark Overton
Mark Twain
Mary Austin
Mary Catherine Crowley
Mary Cole
Mary Hastings Bradley
Mary Roberts Rinehart
Mary Rowlandson
M. Wollstonecraft Shelley
Maud Lindsay
Max Beerbohm
Myra Kelly
Nathaniel Hawthrone
Nicolo Machiavelli
O. F. Walton
Oscar Wilde

Owen Johnson
P.G. Wodehouse
Paul and Mabel Thorne
Paul G. Tomlinson
Paul Severing
Percy Brebner
Percy Keese Fitzhugh
Peter B. Kyne
Plato
Quincy Allen
R. Derby Holmes
R. L. Stevenson
R. S. Ball
Rabindranath Tagore
Rahul Alvares
Ralph Bonehill
Ralph Henry Barbour
Ralph Victor
Ralph Waldo Emmerson
Rene Descartes
Ray Cummings
Rex Beach
Rex E. Beach
Richard Harding Davis
Richard Jefferies
Richard Le Gallienne
Robert Barr
Robert Frost
Robert Gordon Anderson
Robert L. Drake
Robert Lansing
Robert Lynd
Robert Michael Ballantyne
Robert W. Chambers
Rosa Nouchette Carey
Rudyard Kipling
Saint Augustine
Samuel B. Allison
Samuel Hopkins Adams
Sarah Bernhardt
Sarah C. Hallowell
Selma Lagerlof
Sherwood Anderson
Sigmund Freud
Standish O'Grady
Stanley Weyman
Stella Benson
Stella M. Francis

Stephen Crane
Stewart Edward White
Stijn Streuvels
Swami Abhedananda
Swami Parmananda
T. S. Ackland
T. S. Arthur
The Princess Der Ling
Thomas A. Janvier
Thomas A Kempis
Thomas Anderton
Thomas Bailey Aldrich
Thomas Bulfinch
Thomas De Quincey
Thomas Dixon
Thomas H. Huxley
Thomas Hardy
Thomas More
Thornton W. Burgess
U. S. Grant
Upton Sinclair
Valentine Williams
Various Authors
Vaughan Kester
Victor Appleton
Victor G. Durham
Victoria Cross
Virginia Woolf
Wadsworth Camp
Walter Camp
Walter Scott
Washington Irving
Wilbur Lawton
Wilkie Collins
Willa Cather
Willard F. Baker
William Dean Howells
William le Queux
W. Makepeace Thackeray
William W. Walter
William Shakespeare
Winston Churchill
Yei Theodora Ozaki
Yogi Ramacharaka
Young E. Allison
Zane Grey

www.ingramcontent.com/pod-product-compliance
Lightning Source LLC
Chambersburg PA
CBHW020827030726
47496CB00001B/126